SURFACING

SISTER SEEKERS BOOK 4

BY
A.S. ETASKI

Published by Corpus Nexus Press
ISBN: 978-1-949552-07-2

etaski.com
patreon.com/etaski
goodreads.com/etaski
bookbub.com/authors/a-s-etaski
facebook.com/asetaski
twitter.com/asetaski

Cover Design by Eris Adderly
Book design by Guido Henkel

Dedicated to the courageous among us,

traveling unknown territory to meet our past and present

in the flux forming our future.

CHAPTER 1

MY FIRST DAY ON THE SURFACE SAW THE SKY COVERED IN A THICK layer of grey clouds. The rain had stopped and started again, heavy and loud. Eventually, the drops lessened. Then paused. I waited to confirm that it was finished.

Yes.

The outside had fallen quiet at last, while in the void left by the downpour, I heard first one creature's call—a peep and a whistle—and then another, rustling and chattering. Others soon joined, fluttering, scratching, and chirping. Elder Rausery had warned us the outside was never quiet in the way a Dark Elf might crave. We hadn't slept since reaching this precipice, this last shelter within the Deepearth. The Red Sisters hadn't retreated into familiar depths, but we also hadn't stood exposed to that vast sky.

That time was coming.

I sat closest to the cave's exit where the once-muted light lay in a confined spotlight, gathering strength and intensity. The bare stone and pebbles formed shadows of relief, and I flinched with each passing moment. Tears arose in my eyes no matter how often I blinked them away, and my head throbbed in regular pulses even after I'd accepted defeat and closed my lids. Still the brightness seeped through my eyelids, threatening to stab my sight should I open them again. The Sun wasn't fully risen and still masked by clouds, but it already hurt beyond endurance.

Rausery touched my shoulder, speaking in the common Trade tongue that Shyntre had begun teaching me. "It will get worse."

I smirked, blind with my other senses overloaded. "Yes, leader."

My Sisters were farther back in the darkness. No one had spoken until then, and that was about to change as well. Deliberately, my Elder's boots ground the stone as she turned, startling them.

"Gaelan. Jael. Sit here with Sirana. *S'tharl ghil.* Sit here."

The Red Sisters heard their names and responded to the order in our native tongue. I hoped they noticed the repetition in the Trade language as well. Neither Gaelan nor Jael had any exposure whatsoever to it, which could prove deadly if their Queen-given task involved dealing with Humans and Dwarves.

Jael's task does. I heard Her. 'You will find him and kill him, Aurenthietti.'

Who was she supposed to find?

Learning the most common Surface language was also crucial to my own magically compelled mission. The Valsharess, our visionary royal—highest Matron above all, who knew I was pregnant and thought my womb was quickened by the wizard She claimed as Her Son— had commanded me to return to Her with "stories."

Fucking stories.

Rumors about our Priestess from a century back going missing near a Ley Tower. Tales about half-bloods of Elven origin, no doubt the Sathoet Son who had been with her. Information about mages harnessing death magic, and devils "fouling the crossroads." There was also an assassination required, a tainted death mage I was to kill before I could return to Sivaraus.

Even then, my Queen wasn't done with me.

Next, I must atone for exposing our Sisterhood and our city to the Elder Mind and its conclave. I must answer for losing a Red Sister to the Ornilleth.

Reishel's face lingered behind my eyes. I'd watched, helpless, as she obeyed the fugitive mind-flayer, carrying the atrophied prisoner on her back. She had left me to my bloody fate with Kerse to sleepwalk toward her own.

I nearly puked where I sat; sweat broke out on my forehead, and I heard an impossibly high pitch in my ears. Tears drained faster down my cheeks as I sat next to the punishing daylight, enduring the pain. Fortunately, my Sisters couldn't tell if I made no sound; they couldn't open their eyes to see it.

I'm sorry, Reishel.

Elder Rausery suddenly, her rich voice filling the cave. "All is well. *Tenu.* Let us talk. *Ori'dossa telanth.*"

I held my breath at first, then sucked in deep through my nose. *Is she talking to me?*

"Allz well," Jael muttered in response. "Less talk."

Rausery chuckled. "Let *us* talk, Jael."

"Let *us* talk."

"Good. *Bwael.* Calm. *Honglath.*"

"Let us talk," Jael repeated with care.

Our Elder listened to the youngest Sister, then there was a pause. Rausery turned to me with a smirk in her tone. "Good. We will learn how much sunlight you virgins can take this first day."

Each of us were made to speak. Gaelan and I croaked past a tightness in our throats first, and the others noticed but it got better. We listened to the new words, the repetition and translations, over and over while our headaches grew from the pain behind our eyes. It pushed me to nausea once again, and my Sisters to disorientation.

"Hood up. *Kri'phor.* Breathe. *Naerden.*"

After we had obeyed and proved we wouldn't topple over, Rausery commanded us to stand at the opening of the cave, but only let us move out if we knew the Trade words for what we touched and smelled.

"Help each other." There was no translation into Davrin.

"Stone," I said, patting the solid wall so they could hear my glove slap against it.

"Stone," Jael and Gaelan repeated, each finding their grip to keep balance.

"Water," said our youngest, sniffing the air, then licking the wetness from the spongey growth off her fingers.

"Good," Rausery said again, coming up close behind us, subtly coaxing us farther out.

We resisted, pausing; my eyes were still closed and dripping tears. I kept my face pointed down, felt moving air lift my cloak as I leaned out from behind that shield of stone. "Wind."

"Breeze," Rausery suggested, again with no translation. "Wind is faster, longer."

"Yes, leader."

I was not familiar with the word for the spicy scent of trees. I did not dislike it, however, and took another whiff. Next, I detected the decomposition underneath it, of dead things breaking down, of mushrooms and molds overtaking them. It was a scent any from the Deepearth could recognize.

Someone touched my arm. I tensed, but Jael murmured, "Here are you."

"Here you are," Rausery corrected. "Repeat."

We were familiar with that command by now. She did.

"Good. Any of you to step out?"

"You see, leader?" Gaelan asked, the discomfort thick in her voice.

"Not yet. But, no need. I know this place."

She nodded. "Yes, leader."

I took a half-step, turning my ear toward something chirping, and Rausery accepted this as volunteering. She took firm hold of the braid at my nape and pushed me forward. My heart pounded as it seemed I had lost connection with anything familiar, that I had been set adrift.

The ground dropped at a steep decline, something I expected from the view last night, but it was still unnerving to take it blindly at this rate with no feedback. Sound did not bounce back to me or work the same with no ceiling over my head. I became disoriented, a stone slipping beneath my boot. I swallowed the panic, wincing at the way the stones continued to fall. They turned end-over-end, clacking against other rocks. So many thumps before they came to rest.

"Noisy," Rausery commented, yet kept pulling me forward at a rate I thought unwise.

Given no choice, I evened out once I used at least three points of contact and managed to keep pace with Rausery, despite the grip on my hair as she dragged me down that rockslide. My cloak snagged on things I couldn't see, and damp rocks and pebbles slipped and bounced away from my boots. We made an incredible amount of noise. I wondered why Rausery would tolerate it, until it struck me that we weren't the only ones making a racket.

"What cries?" I asked, eyes tightly closed.

"Birds," she answered aloud. "Good sign. Storm is passed."

"Birds cry in good weather?"

"Birds sing, not cry. And yes."

I supposed there was a difference. "Why?"

"Birdsong claims and protects nest place."

You're jesting...

"Birds screech loud in attacks," Rausery said as we skidded farther. "Birds fall silent before storm, quake, or hiding from a hunter. Including two-footed."

"Yes, leader," I said, feeling cool moisture pass through my gloves from how often I touched the stones. "Not hide from us."

"Too much noise, too visible. They are above us with good eyes. They know where we are."

The ground leveled off at last, though I stayed in a partial crouch as Rausery stopped us. She still had a hold on my braids and pulled me to a standing position, then pushed me toward something. I could sense an obstruction coming and put my hands out to prevent colliding with it face first. As soon as I touched it, Rausery let me go and stepped back. I felt something hard, rough, and round like stone but it was not. I smelled pungent life-scent coming from it, an individual source for what I had known was the fragrance of the wet forest as one.

"Tree," I said.

"Correct. *Pine* tree. Note the smell. It is unique. Open your eyes."

My Elder was generous in the time given to do so. My eyes continued to water, and I gritted my teeth against the strain. I could not hold out for long, but I saw a blurred layer of browned needles and flat, mulched leaves on a rocky outcrop partway down the mountain from our cave. Rausery wasn't visible, though I could sense her near. I glanced up the rockslide but didn't spot her; I couldn't see far before the light forced my eyes closed again.

Where did she go?

The stone did not envelop me to help recycle sound or heat, and the birds made it impossible to hear my Elder's breathing. All information I habitually used to locate unseen quarry was muffled and swept away by the endless, open air. I truly didn't know where she was, yet there was the certainty that she was close, watching me. She was waiting.

I must use my sight to find her; there was no other way.

Gathering my strength, I forced open my eyes again. Finally, I made out her shape crouched down a few trees from me. My sight was blurred, and my head pounded but I kept looking where I knew she was. Eventually I realized the grey light and foliage created dappled patterns beneath the forest canopy, similar to the mottled dye of her cloak and hood. The unevenness broke the lines of her form far better than my black cloak did. I stared a moment but then, feeling my tears thickening again, closed my eyes tight. If it was like this now, what would it be like when the clouds left and the Sun shone bare and gold in the sky?

I heard Rausery approach. "What did you see, Sirana?"

I was not sure of the word. "Hide in daylight."

"Close. Camouflage. This and being still is greater here than in the Deepearth. Surface creatures use this like Sathoet bending light, yet they need no magic. Camouflage."

I nodded my understanding. "Camouflage."

"Good. Later task is to mottle your cloak. Now, find the way back to the cave."

She left at a sprint. My ears told me which direction she had gone, and I felt the impulse to follow her. But... that wasn't the way I'd come down, was it? How could I be sure? The deep pulse of my city was long gone, and the gray light made no shadow to hold my direction. I could miss the cave and go too far up or down.

I can't even open my eyes.

I breathed out. I wasn't too far away. All I had to do was climb up the incline by feel. Rausery would remain quiet but Jael and Gaelan might move to lure me their way.

I made less noise climbing up, trying to separate the soft step of a Red Sister from the flap and chirp and whistle of the morning birds. Eventually I made it to the ledge and the cave mouth, and Rausery next dragged Gaelan down the mountain as soon as I staggered near Jael. The youngest Sister touched my face within my hood, startling me.

"Jael?"

She found my mouth with her lips the moment after that.

Oh...

I responded strongly, pressing in harder, surprised at my own hunger to touch her, to kiss back. I never stopped hearing the birds as we lingered in the contact and yet we calmed each other.

"Mmm, good," she murmured, a smile in her voice.

She had used the Surface tongue even when Rausery wasn't present to hear it. A good sign, I thought. *She wants to learn. Knows she needs to.*

"I taste," she said, and it sounded like she licked her lips.

"Tears," I replied. "Eyes hurt."

"Yes, as me. Will stop?"

I shrugged. "I know not."

Elder Rausery returned and answered, startling both of us from the suddenness of it. "It will always hurt. Twenty or thirty sunrises to accept pain and notice less. Unless you retreat for days, then it is months. But the pain never stops."

She took Jael into the forest next, and Gaelan eventually found her way to me as I scraped my boots for her occasionally. My Sister breathed hard having finished her climb back up, though it was not pure exhaustion. She was as disoriented as Jael and me.

"Oi," I said, a Trade word to get her attention, and reached out to find her shoulder before moving my hand closer to her neck and cheek. "Gaelan."

"Sirana?"

"Sisters?"

There was a pause. She didn't know the word.

"*Dalnanin,*" I risked in a whisper. "Sisters."

I felt her nod. "Sisters."

Leaning in, I kissed her as Jael had me. It helped her a little, but she pulled away first. She patted my arm in reassurance, struggling with the Trade words.

"Feel not...up."

Fair enough. That wouldn't flow unchallenged in the Cloister, I knew, but we were a far distance from that space and those rules. I returned the pat, and we waited together.

Through the morning, our Elder proved right as my entire head never stopped hurting. Before midday, we were exhausted from enduring the light even that long.

"Retreat into darkness," Rausery ordered, first in Trade and then in Davrin. "Sleep until sunset. At night, we will hunt for food. I will teach you."

My Sisters and I had no trouble falling into Reverie for the rest of the time the Sun traveled across the sky.

I didn't know if Rausery was aware that I was pregnant or not. She may have been informed by my Elder D'Shea, but if so, there was no change in her behavior toward me. I hadn't confessed to Jael or Gaelan; I kept them ignorant because I didn't want to distract them. Any impulse to give me quarter or extra care, most likely from Gaelan, would only make their own survival harder.

They must focus. We need to learn the words and the outside.

Besides, for brief marks—or rather, for a few hours that first day —I had forgotten my condition in the drive to keep up with my Elder. It was so new, the only sign of it was my own worry. I was surprised, maybe relieved, that my thoughts could be lured away from it.

Likewise, I'd forgotten my three guardian spiders until it was time to let them out of their pouch. That was one detail I hadn't kept secret, for the safety of the others. Elder Rausery, Jael, and Gaelan were aware, introduced, and somehow the creatures knew these Davrin were not threats to me. Today, the black spiders remained on guard above my head, above my Sisters' heads, as we lay down to rest.

The moment I slipped into an exhausted Reverie between Jael and Gaelan, my dreams churned through my memories, warping them, although perhaps not into a mirror much worse than the reality. For all the trouble I'd been, for all I'd cost my allies and my enemies alike, the least I could do was experience the alternative.

I clasped iron bars down in solitary confinement, but I kneeled on the inside reaching out. Auslan remained in his cage across the way; I could see him, but he was far beyond my reach. Between us stood the Valsharess and Wilsira, smirking with greed above us.

"The healer did well," the Conceiver boasted. "He saved my grandchild when he saved you. The Queen has blessed this new path for our people."

I'd taken Curgia's place, bred by a fully mature demon on an altar I tried desperately to forget. I couldn't. I carried a Sathoet's seed, and I was held in the Valsharess's dungeon to await the birthing. I waited in doomed dread, knowing ahead of time that the tainted baby was to be given to Wilsira, and I would be given to Auranka the Drider Mistress, if I still breathed afterward.

Shyntre was there after Auslan had been taken away by the Prime. The wizard was instructed to care for me through the pregnancy, through the bars. He would obey. He would make sure I ate, that I slept. That I did not try to harm myself.

He said to me, "I'm... sorry. Again. You should know I'm not angry at you. You're young. You didn't do any of this."

I lunged out of the terror just before I saw that horrifying birth. The bloody images felt like being struck repeatedly with a giant club carved with a message on the side: *Lucky pawn. Best regards, your Mistress Braqth.*

My breath loud in my ears, my heart racing in the dark, I stared at familiar Radiants of the ceiling. Bare, dry fingers reach over to brush the sweat on my brow. Gaelan was awake, lying on her back, head turned. I could see the outline of her hands and the calm energy about her.

She signed, ★Bad dreams?★

I signed an affirmative.

★Rituals, like before?★

I sighed softly and signed the same again. Gaelan turned on her side, facing me, and laid her head on her arm. She shifted closer, touched my face, and I watched the grace of her hand again.

★You are alive, Sirana. You are still with us.★

Yes, I was. She had found me in time. They all had; Jaunda, Gaelan, Jael... Shyntre. Unconsciously, my hand slid down to rest low on my abdomen. *Please, let the baby be full Davrin. Not tainted.*

★Thank you,★ I signed. After a pause, I added, ★Thank you for *both* times, Gaelan. I am glad to be alive.★

I heard my Sister's lips draw back from her teeth before I glanced over to confirm she was smiling.

★You're welcome,★ she signed. ★Return to Reverie, while you can.★

We each drew in a breath and let it out slowly, ready to do just that, though my mind drifted before I slept again. My Sister couldn't speak or sign who she was, but I knew where she had come from. This Red Sister had once been the merchant paid to salvage Jilrina's botched ritual from decades ago, where I lay dying in a shed.

She told me what it would take to free myself from my elder sister's binding. But I don't remember her saying it.

Gaelan was also the Mother of Natia, a young cait currently in the direct care of my Mother, Matron Rohenvi Thalluen. The merchant had courted a House Guard of ours, one for whom she held a genuine affection rarely admitted among the female Davrin.

She chose Treyl. Natia's sire. Gaelan still dreams about him, and her Daughter.

I knew this from the last mindlink I'd attempted down below, trying to discover why Gaelan seemed so broken over the Valsha-ress's decree to travel the Surface. I'd seen the separation from her lover in her memories, knew that he had died—that Jilrina had killed him—before Gaelan had been able to speak with him again. The regret was searing.

I *hadn't* stayed to witness Gaelan's separation from her child by Elder D'Shea. Even if I'd had the courage to watch, Gaelan wouldn't have allowed it.

Yet, I could still hear her weep.

The three of us received a kick in the ass as a wake-up call. Elder Rausery strode past us and spoke aloud.

"The Sun is set."

She tossed the words casually over her shoulder and kept walking; she didn't stop to wait. We scrambled to situate the couple of weapons removed for sleep, and I climbed up the stone to gather my spiders. They were quick and leaped onto my bracers, already moving toward their home pouch on their own, allowing me to hustle after Gaelan and Jael.

Passing through the cave's mouth this third time, we stood beneath a stunning, clear night sky. The Moons had not yet arisen, and I noted to my left a bare smudge of red-purple light faded behind the horizon. That way was West; the darkest part of the sky would be East. I noticed it seemed warmer after the Sun had set compared to just before the Sun had risen, even if the sky was just as dark.

Well, almost.

Starlight was far less harsh than a candle, spread as countless points above my head, some brighter, some faint or barely there. At first, feeling no pain, I was unsure if my eyes saw the Radiants of Dark Sight instead, but no, I was certain I saw it all in color. The stars provided the best kind of Surface light yet; the mountainous forest, which had been soaking wet the previous night was clear and in stark relief. The landscape was outlined not in colorless, shifting energy, but in nuanced blue shades and silvery shadows caressing every tree branch and stone.

I had never seen this before. Light without fire. Color without blinding flares, surges, or bursts. Just a constant, gentle trickle from above.

No. Not above. Shyntre said it was 'out.' Away, not up.

Those stars were simply too far out to be as punishing as the Sun was up close. Sitting in the wizard's library, I had tried to imagine a limitless cavern over my head once; I knew it was wrong *because* something remained over my head. To see this river of stars, to know the space between them was so vast, and somewhere out there was the Abyss, where Kerse had been trying to reach with his wings.

How can it be? How could he get from here to there? Or his sire from there to here through a summoning?

...Where did we come from to know how to do this?

Watching the sky, I could breathe through the choking memory before I pushed it away again. I was unable to grasp my response to it, like a silent song deep in my mind, deep in my chest that I knew was there. I wondered about the pale-skinned Elf that Jaunda had captured, tormented, then released. The trespasser who did not get far into the Deepearth.

Now we are the ones trespassing.

Rausery lifted her hand, caught our dumbstruck eyes, and signed in silence. ★The Moons will rise one after another and may be in the sky together. This will hurt your eyes but is easier to tolerate. You are not looking at the source but a reflection. The light of the Moons is still from the Sun.★

We nodded, and she continued.

★We start with basics. How to find water, plants known to be edible in this season, and we will try to track game. We will practice building shelters and getting to know what you may have at hand to burn if you need fire. We are at the end of winter. Spring will come soon, but this is the sparsest time for food, so ration what you've got. Come the warm seasons, there will be abundance, though your rations will be gone unless you make more.★

★Yes, Elder,★ we signed.

★You will learn how, in night and in day,★ she signed, staring hard at us. ★There shall be no 'night-only' activity. Before I leave you, we will practice combat in all lighting, dusk and dawn especially where it can get tricky for day creatures. Expect irregular rest. The weather and conditions will determine your training, and I will call it as I see it best.★

★Yes, Elder.★

★Let us begin.★

Our cloaks tripped us up more than anything else during our run the first night. Every snag on tree limb or bush broke the tough pace Rausery had set, made unwelcome noise, and earned proper excuses for the occasional signed or slapped humiliation at the hands of our demanding Elder.

I grew to enjoy how creative she was with some of her insults in Trade, even though my ears stung just as much as my Sisters'. It was as though the seven-century Davrin was rejuvenated to a much younger turn as she slipped through the Surface's night forest with astonishing silence and dexterity, held back only by her three bumbling students.

The physical bruises and sore muscles were the punishment for making noise. They also increased our fight responses and kept our blood high as well, easing the drastic variance in the temperature whenever the air moved.

"You think your back burns now, milk squirt, wait until I sit on your shoulders."

After an hour, I recalled that Rausery had said we would be finding food and water, learning our resources. Instead we were being run through an obstacle course with a distinct lack of stealth, smacked around, tearing our cloaks which we would have to repair later, and becoming hungrier and thirstier by the moment. All this while scaring away the night creatures I couldn't catch more than a glimpse before they disappeared. We weren't anywhere near catching a meal, and our main supplies were at the cave.

Jael and Gaelan were bewildered, too, and losing strength, but neither of them had said anything yet. They wanted to keep what little, thin air would stay in their lungs and their jaws free of hairline cracks.

None of this helped us; this was moving without looking. It was as though we had skipped training to a much later test of endurance without the basic experience to aid us. Granted, the Sisterhood was known for such treatment in the Deepearth, but that wasn't how Rausery had been handling our preparation before.

This makes no sense.

We had passed sign a bit back of a converging trail made by game in the area. By Rausery's own notes and under Shyntre's tutelage, I knew in theory that the convergence was possibly pointing at a source of surface water. I was thirsty, I would not waste what I had on me, and I was sure that Rausery was testing us.

We'll run all night until we just... stop.

I drifted to be last of the four, choosing a bend to turn and backtrack as quietly as I could, intending to find that branching game trail again. My energy flowed freely, and I thought reaching the water before Rausery might lessen any response to my insubordination. Perhaps.

Or perhaps I would call her on her Drider shit, so I believed that I fully deserved the consequence.

Left to my own pace, I could be much quieter. I gathered my cloak close to my body for simplicity and speed, coming to a punishingly steep hill we had tackled earlier straight-on. I tried this again at an angle, keeping my eye on one tree above me to judge progress, while star brighter than the others helped me maintain my orientation.

I breathed deep so as not to wheeze, enormous draws to get enough air yet it burned somehow. The scents were so lush here in the thick of the vegetation, even compared to standing on the mountain's layered outcropping. The stone was dry but not the soil, still dark and musty with moisture. The patches of grass were short due to the early season, but green.

Grass.

This soft plant layer of the forest fascinated me. It resembled extremely aggressive moss; it was everywhere that the taller trees and woody stalks did not poison it away or block its sunlight. And yet, it was not close to as long as Shyntre said it could grow each year. Given time, I would see it happen before my eyes.

I found our own trail with embarrassing ease, further insulted by how obvious it would be to other hunters which direction we'd gone. I had no trouble finding the convergence, and I followed that. The pressure of many feet before mine compressing the soil was the only reason I did not walk in mud after the rain, though grass strained at the edges to invade and no doubt would by "Summer."

The air never stopped; it swept past my ears and through my hair; my eyes watered easily as the wind stole too much moisture from them. I blinked a lot as my heart slowed and my breathing became regular. I listened to incessant noise from forest creatures, as in the daytime, though it seemed subdued. I followed the trail, climbing and descending two hills before I heard a familiar rushing sound.

That noise is the same whether underground or above it.

Fast-moving water was safer to drink than some sources. Stone and sediment had a knack for filtering odd tastes, while few parasites and other tiny creatures had the time or safety to infest the swift flow.

Dark shapes of trees kept the pool out of sight until I was nearly upon it; I smelled the refreshment and felt the vapor on my skin long before I emerged from the trees to get a good look. It was the loudest thing in the area, white and frothing as the rapids churned over large boulders.

Next, I noticed that the game trail led farther upstream, along its edge to a double-waterfall and, between them, a bedrock platform just wide enough to create a relatively calm pool. The waterfall higher up was a shorter drop than the lower one. Eagerly, I headed for that pool, opting to climb the rocky wall beside the lower falls rather than follow the trail bending back into the forest before it returned.

Once I had crested the second waterfall and stood at the edge of the pool, I took a turn around me for moving shadows or signs of life aside from trees. I heard nothing thanks to the water and again relied on my eyes.

A bit of light in my periphery drew my focus; the first Moon was rising, ready to shed light on the forest. It was not full, about half, although the wavering reflections on the pool surface reminded me much of the sickle shape of silverwork cradling the sapphire in the pendant around my neck.

Oh, Goddess... the Moon?

My hand covered where it had often been beneath my leathers. Is that what my wizard had based the pendant on? Something he had observed up here. I wondered, had he stood in this same spot, seeing what I saw now?

"*Arrgh*, fuck it," I muttered against a too-strong memory.

Looping my waterskin over my head, I set it on the stone. It was half-full of pure underground water, and I wanted to taste this source before I mixed it. Tugging off a glove, I scooped into the astonishingly frigid liquid with my bare hand and sipped. I almost moaned. It was crisp. Pure. Somehow, it was *better* than any that had ever passed my lips before.

What is the source? I racked my mind for Shyntre's tales, trying to remember. *Ah, yes.*

Snowmelt.

Frozen raindrops turned to crystalline flakes. Snow, white as a Davrin's hair, falling from the sky during winter, piling up, and waiting atop mountains until the days grew longer. It melted under the increasing light, only to rush down from the tops of mountains. The proof was before me with spring just starting.

"*Where does it go?*" *I asked in the library.*

"*Some of it flows to the Deepearth,*" *Shyntre said.* "*Eventually. But most on the Surface becomes vapor again beneath heat and Sun, which becomes clouds and then more rain...or snow. And the journey starts over again.*"

There was a grand majesty to that predictable, life-sustaining loop that held some order on the Surface. It rivaled the reforming heat and chaotic surge of lava from the deep earth. I wondered why the drops returned to the Surface rather than becoming lost among the stars. Was the pull of the world's core responsible for holding it as Air, just as it was somehow holding all of us to it? How did it first come here? I knew Braqth hadn't made it; nothing in our stories suggested that She had ever created the world.

Just took advantage of it.

We had no story of what did, or whether it formed on its own from the Void...

A twig snapped.

I gasped, spun. By sheer habit, I looked up first, but there was no ceiling and no trees above me; it was a wasted move. The sound echoed in a maddeningly unfamiliar pattern, and I was not sure where to look next. I was surrounded without an easy escape but also difficult to attack from any except one direction on the ground. I focused on that one direction, on the forest behind me as I'd sipped from the pool.

I didn't wait long. I spotted movement within new moonlight touching the trees; my attacker was an impatient one. I recognized her and smiled, drawing my fighting daggers: black, non-reflective, single-edge blades elegantly curved and the length my forearms.

Jael surged out of the brush without being snagged by it, her own daggers drawn. I welcomed her engagement with a wide, white grin which certainly stood out in the night. In contrast she frowned in concentration and fatigue, but I hoped soon to have her smiling as well.

Our weapons clashed, revealing our location to the others. I kept a wide stance on the slick stone as we circled, engaged, and broke apart again. Our sparring ground was not so different from our native home: water and stone. Strike, block, evade. Try to get behind—

Oh, no, you will not.

I tumbled to the edge of the waterfall's pool, dipped my blade, and flicked the cold snowmelt into Jael's face. She drew a startled breath, and my next surge disarmed her right hand, the dagger clattering a short distance away. I saw her lick her lips, collecting some of the droplets, and I saw pleasure in her eyes. Her body needed water. She knew it; so did I.

I yield, she signed and sheathed her left blade.

I nodded acceptance and sheathed both of mine as she lifted her other and secured that as well. We kneeled to drink our fill, and the cold water was even better sharing it with one of my Sisters, though our stomachs cramped from drinking too much, too quickly after a hard run. My teeth, throat, and tongue ached from the cold.

Where are Rausery and Gaelan? I signed.

Watching, probably.

And you attacked because…?

Because you are such a cunt sometimes.

She glared at me, though I knew the subtleties of her face well enough; she wasn't truly angry, only miffed at herself for not thinking of my idea first.

When you broke away, she continued, *Rausery set us to tracking you, but only to watch you and learn. Then she disappeared as well, but I found you.*

We heard a chuckle, and a chill swept me to see that something I'd taken for a boulder when I arrived was a crouching Davrin.

Rausery. Damn. How long were you watching me?

She could have pounced before I tasted the pool.

Our Elder dropped the two body-lengths down to our level, landing on both feet and bending her knees well, absorbing the impact with no apparent discomfort for the height or unevenness of the rock. At that same moment, Gaelan walked calmly out of the forest, following the game trail.

"Fill your skins, ladies," Rausery said aloud, her grin visible beneath the ever-rising Moon. "Keep it close to your body beneath your cloak."

I lifted a gloved finger.

"Yes?"

"Ladies?"

Rausery winked. "*C'intrin.* Pampered Noble Woman."

Jael and Gaelan made faces of distaste, and I grimaced. Another insult.

The three of us filled our skins, Gaelan drinking what she had left before refilling, and the Elder chuckled again.

"So you've wasted time finding this place," she continued as if she hadn't been herding us like nervous mountain goats for a solid hour before I'd begun tracking a water source, which had taken that long again. "Now. Take from your stores or forage something edible?"

A thought flicked to the second body growing inside mine, and the choice seemed plain enough to me. I reached on my belt for one of my travel bars; I would need food to forage for food, and I knew it. The wasted run was a mistake that would cost, but that was why I had the stores in the first place. I bit in.

My Sisters blinked at me as I chewed. Rausery cocked her head a bit.

"Tell us your thinking, Sirana," the Elder said, interestingly, in Davrin, not the Surface Trade language.

I swallowed and delayed my next bite, answering in the same. "It took too long to decide *not* to follow you, and it cost me too much. I have to use my stores, though I know better next time."

Gaelan and Jael both looked confused and a little stunned. Rausery was grinning, though in a fashion that implied I just might get that broken jaw.

"So, don't trust me or anything I say from now on?"

"I can and will, Elder," I replied. "But also, do what I need to do. Use your training but think for myself. You aren't going to be here long, so I should not rely on you even this first night."

To my relief, she nodded. "Glad one of you got it. If you're curious, Shyntre chose the same in under half an hour."

"Of course, he did," Jael muttered in resentment as all three of us flushed.

I said, "And he endured more harassment with Red Sisters, and he has not likely been under your direct leadership in battle."

Rausery smirked. "So you had more conditioning to overcome, is that it? Nice excuse, Blue Eyes."

I shrugged. "Excuses. Reasoning. Perception. Has it been so different for any Sisters before us, Elder?"

She didn't answer that; she moved as if to punch me in the stomach. My reaction shocked me as much as her action did. I hunched over and twisted, taking the blow to my right breast instead. I couldn't override that base instinct to protect my gut, and the best I could do to hide my condition was let my arm drop from my abdomen rather than leave it there as I staggered backward, watching her. My breast throbbed from the hard strike; stubbornly I kept both fisted hands at my sides. Rausery quirked a brow and shook her head.

"Sloppy," she said, switching to Surface Trade. Then she gestured for the three of us to follow her. "We walk and forage. If we pick up a trail, we stalk, but only until midnight. We return to the cave before Sunrise. Conserve, be silent." She offered a smile. "How does that sound, ladies?"

We signed affirmative, learning the Surface at night in word and in deed.

CHAPTER 2

RAUSERY BALANCED MOST OF HER ADVICE WITH HOW OFTEN WE took initiative or showed forethought: mending cloaks before the tears grew worse, considering an eventual substitute for the fiber-stalk bolts used in our one-handed crossbows, and pondering how to either collect rainwater at our cave site or find larger storage for what we could carry to build a reserve.

The largest disadvantage of our base was that the nearest water was a slough at the mountain's foot; good for washing but not to drink, and the rushing snowmelt I'd found was an hour away.

"A closer cave to water we could move?" I'd asked, speaking Trade when silent sign wasn't required.

She had shaken her head. "I've looked. Nowhere new eyes like yours can rest from the day." She smirked at me. "Speaking of, we stay out past Sunrise again when we get back. A first look at a clear, blue sky... Blue Eyes."

Gaelan, Jael, and I had exchanged apprehensive looks. We were tired already with more work ahead, and we knew how it would hurt.

Through the night, we hunted for food. Rausery focused on the smallest and most ubiquitous: ground and tree rodents, birds, rabbits, eggs, fish, grubs, insects, roots, mushrooms, greens. With warmth, she said, would come reptiles of both land and water and the fruits, pods, and nuts of numerous plants.

We would use almost anything we could find or catch, and I held no reservation calling on Callitro's ring to assure I caught something else before the night ended. The magic worked as it was supposed to, boosting my perception and timing, and was comfortingly familiar. With my crossbow, I hit a ground-digger large enough to share, and it dropped instantly.

"Kill good!" Jael had crowed with glee, and I grinned.

"Kill magic," Gaelan noted with one brow raised, and our Elder grunted.

"Sirana?" Rausery asked.

I tugged off my glove to show the ring which my Elder had seen fit to return to me after Kerse's attack. She nodded, recognizing it.

"Properties?"

"Aim sense is greater for one strike, *zotreth tangi*."

The Elder frowned as I'd switched to the Davrin measure of time, once per cycle. "Mm. How often up here?"

I blinked. "Um. Test and see?"

She nodded. "Do and report."

I signed acknowledgment and moved to dress the kill.

"Come," Rausery said. "We eat back at base."

I had the leisure to think about my young battlemage in the Wizard's Tower, but when some horny memories had me longing for sex yet too tired to suggest it, I considered the golden ring he had made for me instead.

Callitro had said that my strike could be by blade, fist, bolt, even a slung stone, and his spellcraft imbuing the ring would help me hit where I looked. This was confirmed; I'd practiced in Sivaraus before it all went down with Wilsira. I could use the spell utterly blind as well, but my attack would hit center mass: potentially good, not always ideal, better than nothing. The wizard had also said that the golden ring granted me one strike per cycle, as it had to draw magical strength again. I would need to see what that meant in relation to sunrise and sunset on the Surface.

At least it works.

The imbued gift had proven practical beyond measure already. I knew how it could be lifesaving for me, even being useless against Wilsira and Kerse in Sivaraus. It made me smile to think I couldn't have known what to ask for, but Callitro had chosen well, and my Sisters and I had our taste of an early-waking fur-bearer outside our cave. It was lean and stringy. It was edible.

"Maybe better cooked," Gaelan said.

"Be wary using fire," Rausery replied. "It sends strong signals in sight and smell."

We knew that already; the smell alone traveled far in the Deep-earth and led creatures right to you, even if the light was blocked by multiple bends. Magical light was smokeless and easier to control the brightness, but such gems weren't handed out to commoners like they were pebbles.

Between smoke and light, the sight signal on the Surface might reach farther. One had only to look up, the distance unimpeded while it dissipated.

Jael twisted a skinned rabbit joint with high concentration, preparing to gnaw but putting it off to say, "Talk more, leader. Who see or smell smoke?"

Rausery looked East as if gauging how long before Sunrise. She grunted. "Humans from villages or towns hunt deer and larger creatures. They hunt for many. They also grow food in gardens and fields, like us."

"Surface Dwarves?" I asked.

Our Elder nodded. "Use traps, like those underground. They do not chase prey as often or far as Humans will. Trade for them, instead."

"Too squat to chase," Jael snickered.

Rausery smirked. "True. But they are smart and make excellent tools. Also larger than the Tragar, very strong, from better food. Surface Dwarves are dangerous at short distance, novices. Poking one is poking a bear holding an axe."

We nodded, well able to imagine. As often as we disparaged Dwarves for their short legs, no Davrin I knew would walk up to one and give a shove to the chest.

"So, Dwarves familiar," I began. "What of Humans?"

We didn't have an equivalent in the Deepearth. My Sisters and I waited while Rausery pondered for longer than I thought she would. My Lead Jaunda had spoken of short-lived male Humans escorting the pale-skinned, blonde Elf in disguise, but the Red Sisters seemed thoroughly unthreatened by them in the retelling.

They were in our territory, though. They can't see in the dark.

Rausery exhaled through her nose and made no attempt to use the Trade tongue; she wanted to make certain we understood the nuances.

"Difficult to predict without watching a group, first. Even direct contact two decades ago may not help. They vary much and change quickly, even their words change. The Trade tongue I teach you now, you *will* have to adjust it. My advice, stay out of sight if possible, listen, observe as much as you can. Remain outside of settlements, do not steal there, this will be for the better. You borrow more trouble than you can handle alone if you draw the attention of many."

"Just hide?" Jael asked, frustrated. "That's it?"

"Unless you're sure of the language and identify a wise one, yes," Rausery repeated. "Human males are larger than the females, and these 'Men' are often the protectors of the 'Women.' It is likely men you would clash with. Unless educated otherwise, most won't see you as anything but a malicious demon. They can be dogged going after a threat in their territory. Being ignorant of us also makes them erratic in what they will do if they catch you."

"Are they ignorant because they change so fast?" I asked.

Rausery's deep umber red eyes slid to me and she pushed a raw muscle sliced from a squirrel's haunch between her lips. She chewed slowly, swallowing before she replied. "Partially. I've also seen some learn fast enough to overcome it."

My younger Sister demanded, "Why do they change so drastically?"

"They *age*, Jael, faster than any sentient race I've seen," our Elder replied, staring hard at her. "You must see them as they are to survive them. You are the youngest of us yet have already lived longer than most Humans *can*."

"What?!" she blurted.

Another exhale, a pinch to the bridge of her nose; Rausery attempted again to explain.

"This race is intelligent, and a small number of them are capable of magic. They have created the Trade tongue I teach, and they have built most of the living cities on the Surface by working with the Dwarves. They can act as a ranked collective or as independents. Most Humans do not live past half a century, and those that do depend on the young to sustain them. The young can be protective or dismissive of those elders, who are almost all younger than you."

Our mouths were sagging, and Rausery continued.

"They will be unpredictable *to you*, because you do not have the same understanding of time, and each group is different from another. The Dwarves are easier to understand by that view than Humans. You won't be able to judge a Human's age well, yet this matters greatly in that one's life view. You risk underestimating what one will choose to do when confronted with a threat to them and theirs."

Gaelan was silent, staring blankly at a spot on the ground; her tension felt general, but I could better read Jael's expression. None of us had attempted to speak of our missions and, like my pregnancy, I didn't know if Rausery had been briefed on what they were or not. Still, it was clear to me that Jael had to go to a settlement, probably a Human city, and find someone specific.

She must kill a man. A known protector, like us. Whether the Humans are ignorant or educated, she is a threat to them regardless.

It didn't bode well for the youngest Aurenthin, and the Valsharess had said my Sisters were "lost" to me.

As if they were already dead.

That was when I noticed the barest shift of a black sky to deepest indigo in the East. The first Moon had set and the smaller, second Moon hovered just above the Western horizon as a mere sliver.

"Sunrise," I muttered in Trade, and my Sisters followed my gaze and trepidation.

"Will we sit out long?" Gaelan asked Rausery.

"Long enough to know what sunburned eyes feel like. We'll get to the sunburned skin later."

The birds had begun singing before the colors began to change. It was a tense and wordless wait upon our remote outcropping as the Eastern horizon shifted in shade with alarming speed: indigo to the Queen's own royal purple, moving straight to a strange mix of purple, pink, and orange. The stars faded and disappeared before the relentless march of daylight and, high above the smear of strange, fiery shades, I could finally see blue.

There it was. Sky blue, though paler and did not yet seem to be as rich as my eye color. I believed Rausery that it would become so, though; she'd seen it on calm days closer to midday. It may be many days before I could stand the light long enough to do the same.

The Sun crested not as gold but as blood red, and the three of us had been looking right at it when it did. We averted our gazes. I blinked, seeing a moving blind spot in the shape of a partial disc, blocking the detail of my sight. It took a long time to fade; I wasn't sure if it had by the time my head began to pound. Still, I watched the full green of the evergreens and new grasses coming into view, saw that the bark covering each sentinel was brown. Like the old needles and mulched, dropped leaves and pods.

Gaelan whimpered.

"Keep them open, novice," Rausery growled. "It hasn't even gone to gold, yet."

And yet it was brighter than anything in existence.

The red tint changed to orange before too long, and I knew that the bright gold from dreams was next. My dreams? No, from Auslan's. From the Valsharess's punishing Visions. Both these strange Davrin knew this golden sunlight was real, somehow.

Jael keened a high sound of discomfort, and Rausery kicked her with the toe of her boot. She went silent. We all leaked constant tears long before the Sun finally turned brilliant gold, swelling full and two finger widths above the horizon. By then I suspected it was the same for my Sisters as it was for me: I was blind whether my eyes were opened or closed, and the pain wouldn't stop.

"Elder…" I whispered.

"You're not intended to see today. Tell me when something changes."

What was that supposed to mean?

We remained either seated or lying down for another hour in full daylight on the rocks. The birds' singing was incredibly loud. Blood pounded in my ears and behind my eyes, and it seemed I would get no peace and no relief. I could feel the heat of the Sun even this early, touching me or the black of my clothing. It warmed me and felt pleasant compared to the chill of night, but I knew it would be dangerous to stay exposed for long periods.

I blinked sightlessly once again, and it felt like glass dust lay beneath my eyelids. Frayed nerves scraped themselves raw against my own flesh. I cried out.

"Sirana?"

"Something…changed, Elder," I said, gritting my teeth.

"How so?"

"My eyes…"

"Tell me what you feel."

"Ground glass."

"That's it. They're burned. Go inside, bandage your eyes. Keep them closed."

When I staggered to my feet, I had no idea where I faced. Rausery's hands took firm hold of my shoulders and pointed me in a different direction than I'd been.

"This way. Straight ahead."

"Y-you can see…?"

"No, still can't. I know this place. No more stupid questions, get in the dark."

I obeyed, and in moments, my Sisters joined me, though the Elder remained outside for somewhat longer. As I felt blindly in my pack for something with which to wrap my eyes, I recognized that my spiders were anxious. They threw their little bodies against the inside of the pouch, softly tapping and thumping to tell me that they needed out.

Alright…

I loosened the drawstring, and the three crawled quickly over my arms, making little hops from spot to spot. Their agitation was intense and unfamiliar, but I wondered if they sensed my pain. If so, had my Elder Sorceress made them that way?

Or is it me? She said they might respond to the psionic commands.

"I'll be fine, fine," I whispered aloud, aware they had settled on my shoulders. I located a thin, dark scarf and bound it around my head to cover my eyes. "Suppose I should see how you little ones do in the light, too."

"A good idea," Rausery said behind me. "I doubt D'Shea created them for this world. They may die quickly, Sirana."

"Or they will hide and listen," I replied with a dry smile. "I have pouches and crevices, and I bet they can tell when the Sun is too hot."

"If you think so. They're your brood. Open your hand."

I did, and she placed a tiny jar into it.

"Smear it on your lids, pass it around, give it back," she instructed. "Then, don't take those blindfolds off."

"Healing potion?" Gaelan asked.

"No, it will take days for your eyes to heal so you can see at night without pain. This will stave off dry skin and keep your tears longer."

"Days? Wh—how will we hunt and get water?"

"We gathered extra, and you're ready for another test: navigating the night forest without sight of any kind. You should be able to do that by now, and if you can't, you deserve to collide with a tree. Meantime, get some sleep."

It took a while to ignore the pain long enough to drift into Reverie. Eventually, our belts off and again with my spiders keeping guard overhead, we managed it.

Putrid yellow eyes shifted toward gold, burning into me like the Sun, the only thing that mattered in the dark. My heart galloped in panic as I lay helpless inside the ritual markings. I could feel the Sathoet's arousal and ambition to escape deep inside my head, and my skin began to smoke and char on the outside. Looming above me, Kerse chanted the ritual. He suffered everything alongside me but wasn't afraid. I was his sacrifice, the blood price paid to his sires to be allowed to join them.

He *would* pay the price.

He wants his freedom too much to stop before fulfillment.

As Kerse opened my legs wider, leaning forward, someone was shaking me hard by the shoulders.

"Shh, shh, Sirana," Jael whispered in Davrin, patting my chest. "You're awake. Wake up. Come on, wake up."

I bit both my lips, silencing myself, strangling any whimper remaining in my throat. My cheeks were hot, and my blindfold was damp. My eyes still burned from the Sunrise. Two days in a row I'd woken another Sister, with dreams *worse* than what once irritated Qivni.

Web-eating dirt crawlers. This'll get me captured on the Surface. I must make it stop!

Jael held my cheek in her gloved hand, turned my face toward her though neither of us could see. She kissed me lightly, then whispered, "How long since you wiped down?"

I'd have taken much longer to understand her except that she slid her hand down my abdomen and rested her palm on my mound. Even then, I couldn't decide my first response. I'd just awoken from staring down a demonic, thorny cock aimed *right there*, terrified and about to relive it again—

Decide.

Reaching to cover her hand with mine, I pressed down. There! There was that first spark of familiar pleasure, as I moved our hands in a slow circle. I breathed out in relief, trying to relax.

Yes. Don't think. Don't repaint it.

"I wiped down at the waterfall," I whispered, "same as you."

She tugged at the hip ties of my leathers. "Figured. Gonna eat that filthy slit, anyway."

I sealed my lips a second time, withholding a laugh. I was grinning as my pants loosened from my hips, as my crotch tingled, anticipating her touch, her tongue. I reached for Jael's crotch as well, cupping and squeezing through her leathers as she propped a leg up, lying on her side. Gaelan wasn't far from us, but if she was awake, she couldn't see us and hadn't said anything.

I helped push my pants to my knees, lifting the soles of my boots toward the ceiling, while Jael slipped free of my groping fingers. She moved by feel to take my bare thighs in her hands, folding me in half, dipping her head down. The tip of her nose trailed lightly along my fur; her lips kissed mine once, then again. A lick, then a firmer one, tasting. So soft, and so nice. I moaned.

Holding still for her, I gradually realized that Jael explored with deliberation, with focus, tracing and making note of the terrain. She had seen me naked before this point, but maybe that didn't tell her what my cunt was like after Auslan had healed it.

Maybe she wanted to know before she left.

My eyes watered again, having as much to do with the burn as the reminder and memory of home. My Consort had returned to me something I wanted, and my wizard had helped me confirm everything still worked before this point, thankfully, because Jael sought reassurance and confidence from me. Like our first time in the Cloister, when she was confused and scared but trying not to show it.

I sighed, whispered, "Oh… yes…eat my sweaty slit…"

My hands covered hers upon my thighs, and she growled and feasted like a stubborn hunter at her largest meal in months. Soon, she added two bare fingers. My breath conveyed how it was work-ing for me, building, and by now, Gaelan *had* to be aware.

I heard no complaints.

Nothing distracted my Sister from her task, and for my part, I relaxed and let it come. My netherhole tightened in the cool, cave air as sensations arose, peaked, and left me drifting in the dark. She stroked me, sucked me, and I emptied my thoughts of all but this. Climax wanted to come, and by the cutting web, I wouldn't fight it.

I was healed. I was pregnant, but no one could tell, yet.

"Ngh!" I grunted, blood rushing in my ears as the familiar surge overtook me, as my sex clenched my Sister's thrusts, as my nub sang between her lips and against her pressing tongue. *"Oh!"*

Ten heartbeats before they began to slow. I still couldn't see but heard Jael gasp in surprise. Someone took my left boot and tossed it to one side; I rolled with it, and the youngest Sister flopped forward to rest on my upturned hip, clinging to me like a raft in the middle of a lake.

"E-Elder?" she said, the sound of leather shushing over thighs. Then she yelped and tensed.

"You have stamina to serve at one end, Jael," Rausery cooed, "you have the same to serve at the other."

Jael groaned in agreement as our Elder sank the Feldeu into her before settling into a hard and focused fuck. Both my young Sister's hands tightened on me, and she fell into the rhythm. I wished I could reach between her legs to make sure she peaked by the time Rausery got off, but—

Gaelan moved closer. She touched me, sightless, then touched Jael's quivering, bucking body. After a pause, our youngest sucked in a huge breath.

"Augh, yeah, fuck, yeah," she growled.

"That's right," Rausery grunted. "Push her over, Sister. Shove her off the cliff."

Gaelan did what I couldn't that moment, working with Rausery to bring Jael to a squealing rise and fall, her release well-earned. I touched the hair upon her head as Gaelan caressed Jael's down below; I imagined what we would do next, when it was my older Sister's turn.

Our Elder climaxed from using her Feldeu, and Jael stayed in place until Rausery was finished. Afterward, Gaelan just sighed and turned over, asking for nothing in exchange before going to sleep.

Our cycles took on a certain torturous, reliable pattern from that point: blind foraging, running, and fighting, followed by a cold night of hard hunting for meat and all edibles, only to endure another warm morning and usually burned our eyes again in hot afternoon—though not as bad as the first time. Then we'd start over again, given more tricks to ease the pain or lessen the damage.

Making a sun-blindness mask from flexible bark, for example.

"Extra good for snow blindness, too," Rausery had said. "Snow reflects sunlight the same as the surface of water. A pale-yellow soil or quartz rock is nothing compared to the shock of glittering snow."

The masks blocked the worst glare and protected our eyes against burning, though it played hard against my peripheral vision to the point I looked forward to the day that I did not need it. Even unable to see, I could not always hear as well as I had in the Deep-earth. It was more than birds and insects.

It was the wind.

Gusts whipping past our ears was their own sensory overload; it varied day to day and throughout each hour with no discernible pattern. I understood why the Surface creatures must be inured to constant noise. The roaring of air across our most sensitive sense—often worse the higher we climbed in those mountains, especially the crests and peaks—could make it where I lost *both* sight and sound.

I began to pay more attention than ever to smell and taste and touch. The "acclimation" I had thought would be just my sight turned out to be my entire body, with my mind learning to cope with so much detail, to discern new patterns within the morass.

After a long climb, we stood on a flat promontory of dark stone, overlooking our usual hunting valley. We had just stepped out of the shade of the trees, the Sun was straight overhead, and the sky was cloudless and deep blue. Although the air was cool in the early-green season, helping with our midday exercise, I'd already noticed each night passing seemed a little shorter; any day without a rain-storm, warmer.

Rausery stripped down first, removing everything, setting it all in one place. She always looked powerful in her uniform, red or grey-mottled, it didn't matter. With her standing nude, I thought how I'd rather not get into melee with her, given the choice.

"Everything off except the sun-masks," she said in Trade. "Don't touch your equipment. Sirana, let me check the seams on your spider pouch."

I obeyed, and although I held it up, closed and by its top, Rausery was the first to lay her fingers on it since D'Shea had given it to me. Satisfied, she grunted.

"Keep it knotted. No risks."

Ominous.

"Yes, leader."

Our Elder watched every move we made, all the pieces including our newly-mottled cloaks, and where they went. She nodded approval as I secured my tiny but vigilant guardians and removed Callitro's ring from my finger, tucking it in a pouch.

"Where is that Tragar stone?" she asked. "Did you bring it with you from underground?"

I froze, an unpleasant flush barreling through my gut and out to my limbs. Gaelan glanced at me, her expression one of concern. Jael knew about it but looked as though she hadn't given it any thought in a long time. To be fair, neither had I.

"Um. Yes, *Zhuantur.*"

"Show me."

I pulled it by its black cord from a separate pouch than where I'd stored the magic ring. The silver wasn't tarnished, so I knew it wasn't pure; it shone as bright in the daylight as the sapphire-colored gem.

"You haven't worn it at all?"

"It… has no purpose here, *Zhuantur*," I answered.

Jael said, "You test to drain magic-user, yes?"

"I doubt," I told her honestly. "Lessen spells, maybe, not mage. Know more of blue stone on Tragar weapons?"

I could still read her surprise with the sun-mask, and she looked to Rausery, who shrugged.

"Say what you will, but in Trade," she said. "Self-kept secrets don't matter anymore."

I raised one brow behind my mask. *Didn't they?*

Our youngest considered, but lifted a bare arm to study it, rubbing it as if she noticed the Sun's rays. We all stood naked at this point.

"Talk in shade?" Jael suggested.

Rausery grinned. It was playful, almost sinister. "No. Talk in Sun. Whatever words you want. Practice."

Uh-oh.

Gaelan said nothing but crossed her hands across her nipples.

"Blue stone in Tragar weapons," I prompted.

Jael exhaled, clawing for the first foreign words. "Spider... cleric?"

Rausery nodded. "Ours?"

Jael confirmed, and I got it. A Priestess of Braqth. *Spider cleric. Okay.*

"She and son disappear from a... fort. Many years ago."

"A tower," Rausery corrected, her head turning South. "But, yes, connected to a fortress."

My mouth went slack, incredulous. Shyntre had told me this story in the library, but Rausery had told Jael? Why? And what the fuck did this have to do with Tragar weapons and the blue stone in my palm?

"Cleric and son gone from tower," Jael reworded. "You search for them, leader."

Rausery motioned an affirmative, watching each of us.

"You find man at tower later. A dead mage."

"Death," Rausery corrected again, amused. "Death mage."

The Valsharess's eyes pierced my mind's eye; Her voice unfurled like a silken sheet. *"Mages of death and decay have encroached upon it... The crossroads are fouled by machinations of the Hells attempting to usurp them."*

I was stunned; I also felt sick.

Jael nodded. "Death mage know nothing of spider cleric and son. You believe after much test, no link. Old man claimed tower too late to attack Davrin. You trade with him to tempt low-born or Tragar back home. Lure *saphgar* weapons or find traders with contact to Surface."

Our Elder her eyes scanning our masked faces, our naked bodies. "Both unsuccessful. Davrin traders are unknown and did not trade with the death mage at the tower, yet he is closest to here."

Was he?

"And the Tragar still wouldn't trade their weapons. D'Shea leaped farther giving the *saphgar* stone to Phaelous after Sirana stole it from a miner."

I looked at the pendant Shyntre had made again, nauseated but bulling past it to think. At least I had a better name for it. *Tragar's sapphire.*

"Mind mages use *saphgar*, maybe," Jael said, looking at me, "but no mix with magic. You said."

I wet my mouth to speak. "Yes, I said. The stone gives magic disadvantage in time. Drains potions or gems in same box. Not, um, *now.*"

"Instant?" Rausery suggested.

"Yes. Not instant, not fast. Slow."

Gaelan twisted her mouth, clearly dubious. "So why carry on belt with potions? Then all be useless after long on Surface."

I clutched the necklace Shyntre had given me, that hard focus for so much recent agony and violation. Yet, leaving it behind had not crossed my mind.

Why?!

I felt both the impulse to pitch it off the side of the mountain as far as I could throw it, and the need to cling to it, associating it with the wizard who'd made it for me. I had no rational answer why I'd kept it on my belt instead of wearing it after mindlinking with Gaelan that final time.

I flushed with humiliation. *Well done to put me on the spot, merchant. You've felt it with me, even if you don't know why.*

"Pendant may be valuable for trade later," Rausery offered, although it didn't explain why I had brought it in the first place. She signed an order for me to put it away.

It seemed our word practice was over, for as I tucked the gem inside my leathers, Rausery pulled out her Feldeu and a tiny vial from her gear, donning the former. The ever-present wind swept her command from the mountainside, yet the potent spell was unimpeded, granting our Elder a hot and sensitive erection between her strong legs. Jael and Gaelan exchanged looks with me; we each had mixed reactions to the clear signal of more testing, of resistance and submission.

"Haven't we already passed this trial, Elder?" Gaelan said in Davrin.

"If you had, novice, you wouldn't assume you know what it is."

Rausery shook the vial, twisted off the seal, and quaffed the liquid, making a brief, bitter face which changed before our eyes. She grew taller, immensely broad of shoulder; the neck was fat with a prominent bump at the front. Her skin paled like it was bleached by a flash of lightning, sprouting uneven patches of dark hair all over.

A wild crotch bush overtook the black cock, hiding the base of it as the phallus itself changed from dark monochrome to blotchy purple and red. She also grew a wrinkled scrotum with long, individual hairs poking out. She had huge, wide feet; hair grew on the tops of those, too.

"What the fuck?" Jael began, wrinkling her nose as the solid illusion took hold.

Gaelan and I were speechless.

"If I had three of these," our Elder said our in native tongue, a disturbing bass leaking in so that it became less her voice with each passing word, "I'd play with you separately."

Play? I couldn't tell if she was serious or mimicking a role. I looked around the flat ledge, felt the rock becoming quite warm beneath the Sun. I touched my shoulder. *I think it's starting to burn. Fuck.*

The huge male figure wrapped one hand around his hard cock. "Easy to see what he wants, girls. Bargain's done, by the way. You've agreed to fuck a man. For whatever motive, for whatever outcome *except* to fight him. No fight, got it?"

Jael bristled; Gaelan was baffled, undecided.

"So, who's first?"

I tapped my chin. *No fight? For whatever reason...*

Maybe I shouldn't be curious what man-Rausery had in mind, but I was. I raised my hand, and my Elder laughed out loud, her deep voice booming in the wind. She strode up to me, landed a heavy palm on the back of my neck and massaged it, a lopsided grin on her bearded face.

"Kneel down, Blue Eyes. All fours. Take in the scenery, if you like, while I use your twat for a bit."

Crude, but familiar. Not unlike Jaunda, really, but Rausery had never seemed interested in blunt rutting the brief time I'd known her naked. She was too observant.

I got down, my hands gripping the gritty ledge, looking at scraggly trees and shrubs clinging to the steep decline, then up and out at the rest of the valley.

"That's good," she said, taking to a knee behind my ass, squeezing and spanking it a few times. "Spread your legs. Keep looking out."

I did, and I counted eleven different shades of green as I waited to be taken. All of it smudged as I had trouble seeing distances in this light, but I had never felt such a vastness at once, with my entire body, as when I kneeled naked on the edge of a high, flat rock.

The seeping heat of the Sun above coated my bare back like a blanket, and man-Rausery took tight hold of my hips, sliding her hot Feldeu along my crack. Without thinking, I moved my hips around, pleasuring myself and her, slickening her weapon just before she plunged it inside.

"*Auuugh*, yeah!" the deep voice groaned.

It was *very* convincing, almost someone else, although I didn't feel all the hair which my eyes had claimed should be there. Her muscled thighs were smooth, like Rausery. Still, my Elder churned my sex with enthusiasm and Feldeu, and soon it came clear that rutting man-Rausery was the *noisiest* experience I had ever had!

Even Kerse wasn't this b— I gasped at a searing memory; my cunt clenched down. Greedily, I listened to those ridiculous grunts behind me, letting them anchor me. *Here and now.*

"Graaaah, aaahhhh! Yyyeeeahh, uh-uh-uh! Fuuuuu—!"

To our right, Jael and Gaelan were snickering.

"Hey! Quiet!" man-Rausery barked, her deep tone wavering with mirth. "Tryin' a concentrate on some slip-tasty quim, here!"

"That *cannot* be real!" Gaelan exclaimed in disbelief.

"Black witch has watched man mate from the trees for centuries!" our Elder crowed. "Bouncey-smack, bouncey-*smack!*"

She popped my ass a good one, and I put my head down, chortling helplessly while she plowed my slit, slapping my buttocks with her broad, ruddy hand.

"Yeah, you laugh, girl! I'll pound you till your tits shake off!"

I did; I laughed, as loud as she was being, and she slammed so hard that my voice shook. It started to feel pretty good, too, though I doubted she'd let me cum. I did anyway, the moment after she finished squeezing her slimy girth into my netherhole and strummed my nub twice.

The man mounted on my ass bellowed, "Churlin gaw! Yer trying tah squeeze me dick off! *Gah!!*"

Jael and Gaelan were rolling, gasping in hysterics upon the stone.

That experience, for once, was fun as well as new. The aftermath, no surprise, was miserable. We were all sunburned; our skin had enriched the usual tone to a purple-black, as if the color of my aroused netherlips had been smeared all over my body. It was painful to the touch, heat rising as if sunlight itself leaked out of my pores. Clothing felt hot and scratchy, its weight nearly impossible to ignore.

Rausery also kept it a disturbing surprise until our skin started peeling in delicate, grey strips after a few days. My Sisters and I needed to groom each other for the places we couldn't reach, like rude animals.

At least that part was painless.

"It's not so bad," Rausery told us, pulling strands of her own skin from her shoulder. "We could have had blisters."

"What?!"

"Yeah. Burned as though we put our skin over a candle for too long. The Sun burns just like fire, it just takes longer to get there."

I could only imagine what it looked like after longer exposure than that required to gain blisters, but it reinforced both the power of the Sun and the warning against careless baring of our skin. Extreme exposure was possible on a good, calm day upon the Surface, just as it was in storms and cold, rain or snow.

Fucking weather.

CHAPTER 3

By the twenty-fifth day, our endurance had improved enough to move normally at midday wearing the masks and keeping our hoods up. Some rainy days gave our eyes much-needed relief. On the sunny days, though, I marveled at that vibrant sky-blue color while unpleasant heat pounded down on me from above. I was not used to sweating so easily and grew grateful for those ever-shifting breezes and winds in the spring chill.

My spiders eased into traveling with me during the day rather than staying in the cave. Although, as expected, they disliked the light so much they stayed in their pouch. They only came out at night, tolerant to moonlight, to sit at my nape beneath my hair or hunt for food. If I tried to force them into daylight, however, they would crawl deep into my glove or bracer and were impossible to extract without crushing them. I had to seek darkness and let them emerge on their own.

My little guardians would not obey at the expense of their own survivability; at least, not if there was no threat to me. A pity I wouldn't know how much risk they'd take on my behalf during the day until there *was* a threat. We could not practice before the fight.

A memory returned from down below, when these spiders were given to me.

"How do I direct them, Elder?"

"They respond to your aura already, and I think your mental gift is sufficient, though you may have to practice. Try a mental push. Simple commands, no more."

I frowned in thought, considering the saphgar pendant which was the focus of that "gift." After man-Rausery had rutted me to sunburn, when Gaelan had pointed out my foolishness keeping the magic-dimming gem on my belt, I had returned to wearing Shyntre's necklace around my neck to preserve the rest of my supplies containing any magic. It hadn't glowed once in all these days of training, and I hadn't mindlinked with anyone, whether intentional or not.

My "gift" was enough, she said. Try a mental push. *Mm-hm.*

I stared hard at the void-black arachnids in my palm, willing them to jump onto the cave wall without any physical signal, without my bringing my hand to it as they were accustomed. They could make the leap if they knew they should.

Jump to this wall, guardians. Jump. Jump and hold still.

They crawled casually over my hand, unresponsive to any imperative. They weren't "pushed," for certain, and I felt no change in my head. I grimaced, unsure what I was doing wrong but let it go easily when Jael poked her head in from outside.

"You come?" she asked.

"Always," I replied with a tease.

"Pfeh."

But she was smiling.

My Sisters and I had innumerable opportunities to see many of the creatures which lived in the forest, both day and night. If edible at all, there were none I would refuse to eat. When plants grew with the warming and lengthening of each day, our selection expanded at astonishing speed; the Deepearth would never produce this much food by existing. Elder Rausery had shared enough of her experience to convince me that I would not starve with this abundance, even on my own.

Although, that confidence wavered a little as I noticed a greater hunger that must be related to my pregnancy. It would come upon me suddenly, always before Jael and Gaelan, and my empty belly was difficult to ignore until I found something to chew. Until then, sharp cramps or a constant, dull ache sounded my priority like a drum.

If my Sisters or Elder noticed, they didn't point it out, as gathering food became our focus for several weeks. We were in competition with the birds and rodents for mushrooms, berries, nuts, and blossoms as the season arrived in full. I knew why we were grinding and pressing them into rations, not only making some for the three of us soon leaving the valley, but also gathering enough food for Rausery to make the return trip to Sivaraus.

None of us had spoken about our own mission; we *couldn't* speak about it if we wanted to. Rausery and Jael had stumbled upon some of mine in discussing the Priestess going missing at the tower, with the old death mage who had moved in but had nothing to do with it. Before I returned home, I was supposed to kill this Human for the Valsharess. I wondered, would I do it before or after I sought word of Davrin or half-bloods on the Surface? Did it matter?

This death mage is the closest inhabitant to this cave, Rausery said, but not trading with the Deepearth. So, who is? How far away are they?

Some Humans and at least *one* blonde Elf knew about this passageway and where it led. Surely, the pale one whom Jaunda had attacked but allowed to escape might know more, if I could find her. There must be a trail of rumors to follow out of this isolated wilderness, if I knew the language. I kept practicing my Common words, no matter how banal or unhelpful the observation, and Rausery tolerated it, even encouraged it.

Sometimes it sparked a story of her own.

"Last time I was up here," she said at the end of one day, "with my Sisters, almost thirty years past…"

We each fell silent, waiting.

"The death mage, Sarilis, received the help of ten Red Sisters to claim the Ley Tower."

"Shyntre was of the squad?" I asked, my easiest curiosity which also hid the magical discomfort as we nudged closer to the forbidden.

Rausery shook her head. "No. Just caits this time. Lucky, we had one mage, though she did not survive."

"Why 'lucky'?" Jael asked, looking confused.

Rausery smiled, although her humor was tentative. "Magic of the Ley Line crossing had gone bad. Sarilis knew of it, called it 'warp rot.' An unstable 'phenomenon' settled in an area, twisting the living into something worse than dead. Mad-eaters of flesh, with no will or mind to control their hunger, and their bite…"

We held our breath as she considered the word.

"Their bite spreads. A contagion of madness. The Human mage could not purify the Ley Tower alone, but with a Davrin mage, he did. The Red Sisters defended the two mages from mad-eaters long enough to cleanse the source of warp rot. But…" Any hint of a smile vanished from our Elder. "Our mage and one other, bitten. We could not discover how to stop their decline before they would go mad and attack us. We had to kill them, burn the bodies."

A subtle tremor had taken Gaelan's body; her eyes were wide and her ears open, but she said nothing. Both Rausery and I noticed, and nausea strengthened in my middle. I knew in an instant.

Oh, Goddess, she's our only mage sentenced by the Queen. Gaelan has been sent after warp rot, it must be…

"Hm," Rausery said, looking elsewhere and pondering with patience. "Sarilis claimed the tower and willingly traded with us, answered questions, told stories. He enjoys talking. I think… I sensed another watching. The death mage appeared alone without allies, except for us and those thralls he makes of corpses, yet I do not trust all he said."

"Wait," Jael interrupted with disgust. "Thralls from corpses?"

Gaelan darted the younger a look of annoyance, and our Elder chuckled.

"There were a lot of corpses after the warp rot had its way. A mage uses the magic best understood. He best knew death."

"What of 'another watching'?" I asked, backtracking. "What you did not trust that he said?"

Rausery grunted, readily coming back to that. "That he found this tower and its rot alone. I never believed that. But... I do not know who helped him."

I discovered that I could ask no more. Gaelan could not, either, as she remained quiet and distracted.

Jael could speak on it. "You say, he talk much. What about?"

Our Elder pondered longer than I expected. I began to suspect only then that there might be things Rausery *couldn't* say, either, regardless if she might want to.

"The men of power he served only to use them," she said at last. "Most would be dead now, though children may live. Sarilis followed death, so he followed men who led groups to kill other men."

"Corpses he need not make?" Jael asked with cocked eyebrow.

Rausery chuckled. "Exactly." She pondered. "He followed small groups, hiding his tastes through his young years. But he heard of big groups of fighters. Organized and ranked, serving like Red Sisters and Palace Guard. They recruit to replace those who die."

We nodded, following her thought, and it seemed this did not get too close to our missions. It was a relief.

She continued, "Two big groups may still be, even decades later. Augran and Manalar. Two cities, like Sivaraus. Far from here, but enough wealth and reach," Rausery stretched out her arm straight, grasping with her fingers, "for Sarilis to talk of them."

Jael stilled. She was rarely ever *that* still.

Rausery hit it, again. Jael's mission is in one of those two cities.

Far from here.

I swallowed. Our Elder pretended she didn't notice, and I began to believe that Rausery knew as much about the tasks our Queen wanted us to perform as I did, excepting my own.

"Which way is Augran and...?" I asked because I could.

"Manalar," Rausery repeated, watching Jael.

She stood up and wordlessly stalked into the cave. Gaelan and I stared after her with our mouths open, but our Elder wasn't surprised.

"Manalar is due East from here," Rausery murmured softly, then got up to follow our youngest, extending a finger as she walked past. "Stay."

Gaelan and I remained outside, listening but the early evening noises weren't much quieter than the day and drowned out whatever movement or voice might be in the cave. We looked at each other, meeting eyes for a handful of heartbeats; Gaelan looked away first. I felt no tingle in the back of my head, although...

I had attempted to connect again. A bit.

Maybe I should try harder. Elder D'Shea and I had gotten around a Priestess's compulsion to silence with a mindlink. Could I do the same for a Queen's? I wanted to know where they were going and why. Their missions seemed more dangerous than mine.

Mad-eaters and Human cities...

We were being split up when working together would see better success for the Queen's goals. Why was no mystery to me, for the Valsharess's voice filled my ears yet again.

"They are lost to you. They shall serve their Penance, but only you must return."

Our punishment mattered more than the missions themselves.

It took another fifteen days to be able to go out in daylight without the mask, although I always kept my hood up. By then, I spoke the Trade names for nearly everything I could see, and I could judge sound with accuracy. I swiftly perceived in my resources, the angles of ever-changing shadow, and obstacles of ground and plant.

During this time, Rausery talked about many things: the strangest or most dangerous weather she could think of, more of what lay outside these mountains, and about Dwarves and Humans. She didn't speak specifics unless it was direct experience for her, but she continued to dance around topics of death magic, the corrupted consciousness of warp rot, of other contagions, of Human cities in general, especially where there were likenesses to our own forces we could relate to.

Rulers, magical key holders, enforcers of law...

Despite the constant edging and illness from our overlapping compulsions, I listened for knowledge with a hunger as sharp as my belly's growing need for food. With rising confidence, my Sisters stalked the forest with me, absorbing our Elder's wisdom on both counts. Hearing about Rausery's explorations, I almost looked forward to seeing beyond this mountain and its valley where we'd been living well into the season of renewal.

My regret was that my Sisters and I would not see it together. I held a lingering hope that this training would be enough for each of us to return, and yet, in this quiet landscape devoid of urgent threats, I knew it to be a foolish one.

We haven't seen a true trial yet.

Once we did, we would be alone. This Surface world would be as unforgiving of mistakes as the Deepearth and the Abyss. I worried more for my Sisters than I did myself.

Gaelan was cautious and tended to follow a stronger will; she was unaccustomed to solitary assignments as far as I knew; she wasn't like our Lead Jaunda, or even myself in how D'Shea had begun to groom me. She also grieved for Natia when she thought I couldn't tell, but I learned the hunch of her shoulders as she turned to hide the pain from us. I worried the grief would make her slow.

And then, there's Jael.

She was so young. She had not had the opportunity to mature much beyond when I'd first met her in battle. I was only fifteen or twenty turns her senior, far less than those which separated Shyntre and Auslan, but I had been pressured to change from challenges beyond the Nobility, the Court, or the Sisterhood.

Pressure from Kain and Lana, from Kerse and his Mother Wilsira, from D'Shea's own compulsion driving her decisions on what to do with me.

And Reishel.

Even recently, I'd changed again from Shyntre's obstinate passion and Auslan's troubling dreams and too-gentle care. I was pregnant, and I'd avoided the Sanctuary sentence I'd dreaded only by order of my Queen because it seemed that...

She wants my child for Herself.

My eyes squeezed shut against the resurging memory. Her arms around me. Her gaze wandering over me, studying me. Her voice. Again.

"Our First Son. He has touched you. He has not exposed his Vis to a cait in centuries."

I made a face at the blank cave wall. Her aged hand slid over my stomach, covering my womb. She said, *"He has not sparked a new gift for Us in even longer. He has been spiteful."*

A new gift. No.

"Do not disappoint Us. We have infinite ways to punish you and all for whom you care... There is no place you can hide from Us, Sirana, and you will not reject what We've laid upon you."

"Shut up," I muttered. "You're wrong. You've got the wrong brother."

"Sirana?" my Elder asked.

A lump slammed into my throat. She'd overheard me.

I shook my head, standing up. "Nothing, Elder. Was back in Sivaraus. I'm ready to work."

She nodded and let it be. I brooded for most of that day, and even having noticed, no one asked me anything else.

My Queen's sentence was such that I would carry my first catching on this journey for as long as I could. I was neither ready to end it nor test my Queen's wrath trying. The unseen spark inside me was the largest pressure for survival yet; it loomed together with another choice, far from the ruler upon the royal throne.

The little vial D'Shea had given me.

Each time I thought about my active womb, there was my Elder's warning and the power she had given me. It was terrifying, the imminent threat clear. If things got bad, if I was trapped or enslaved…if my own lack of choices gave other races the intolerable advantage, if it handed them all power over not only my life and death but that of my unborn, what would I do?

Fuck.

If I couldn't make the choice at the right time, maybe I would go missing like the Priestess and her Sathoet. Too much sign they were captured, Shyntre had said in the library.

Rausery couldn't track them farther North when the snows came.

I believed neither Gaelan nor Jael knew about my condition, just as I didn't know precisely what they had to do or where they would go after our training was complete. Rausery probably knew a little bit of all of it. If she hadn't been briefed, which seemed possible, then seven centuries of observing and training recruits gave her keen instincts.

Our Elder added new details to the stories of past missions. She continued to paint a portrait of her previous journeys and let us imagine the Humans in ways that made us wary, baffled, and laugh out loud. All of it was subtle enough not to set off the Queen's Illness, which had gripped Jael that one day when she left the discussion.

"Testing the boundaries is expected," our Elder had said one day, a non sequitur barely connected to what we were learning. "But careful if an obsession threatens to grip you, especially when you feel sickness. In some states of mind, you forget to eat, drink, or rest. You only feel the obsession."

I thought that over. Jael *had* seemed to have lost her appetite for a while at the mention of Manalar, and she hadn't slept the next day in her anxiety. Rausery hadn't mentioned the Human city in her hearing again, and neither did I.

We have infinite ways to punish you and all for whom you care...

After a night of preparation, sixteen days past the spring equinox, Rausery checked over our stores and nodded. "Good. No work tomorrow. We rest."

We exchanged glances. I didn't see the point; none of us did.

"Yes, leader."

Given the peace, however, we lay in Reverie longer than usual, through the morning and deep into the afternoon. Even though unwelcome, skewed memories returned to plague and wake me again, I had disturbed neither Gaelan nor Jael with my whimpers or rustling. Was I getting quieter or did they sleep deeper today?

My Elder was already awake, lying against the tunnel wall with her arms folded, smirking at the three of us. She made eye contact and motioned me over. My spiders remained on their small ledge above where my Sister slept, although they crept out, forming a vague triangle and making certain I wasn't going far. Rausery looked up, watching them with amusement.

D'Shea did good work, she signed.

Yes. I glanced up, too. *I think she had other plans for them than this.*

For certain. They're yours, now. Use them to their fullest.

I signed affirmative.

Come outside with me, she ordered.

Tracers remained in my vision as I stood in sunlight wearing my mottled, grey-black cloak. "Tracers" were what Rausery called those spots and bending colors that impaired precise vision at long distances. It was part of the reason none of us bothered with making a bow. We'd have to get by with stalking and ambush, using our strengths in shadow, to listen, and to fight blind. We must be able to tolerate sunlight, but we would not be able to counter long shots or anyone with the eyes of a hawk. We would have to hide.

"Never leave your ass open," Rausery had said then. "Always stop with something at your back."

She tapped my shoulder, and I jumped. Smirking, she shook her head, motioning me to climb around a familiar bend where we wouldn't be seen if my Sisters stepped out. We took to deeper shadow out of direct afternoon light, and Rausery squared her shoulders, capturing my gaze with her presence.

"You haven't been reading minds," she stated bluntly in our native tongue. "Or we'd know more than we do. Why not?"

Heat swept my face. I looked to some new green leaves. "I can't find the thread."

"Have you tried?" She paused, adding, "Since reaching here. D'Shea told me you did in the throne room. That's how we got Wilsira to attack."

"Yes, I tried," I muttered.

"And gave up?"

I shrugged. "The saphgar isn't responding like it used to. That's how I used to make the leap. It's just a stone. No heat, no light."

"Does it need a mage casting to work?" she asked. "To give it charge, perhaps?"

"Maybe?" I thought. "A lot of mages were around when it worked. Mostly during…"

"During?"

"Um. Fucking, Elder."

Rausery's eyes narrowed in thought. "And Gaelan hasn't been interested. I've noticed."

I grimaced; Gaelan had been caught brooding as often as me. "I know why, Elder. I can't *make* her interested in lying with me."

"Okay, tell me what you know."

A subtle presence and movement caught my attention then, and I looked away. My three spiders were coming to find me; I couldn't help but smile. Rausery cleared her throat, cocking a white eyebrow.

"Um." I grasped for thought. "Sh-she wanted to see her Daughter before she left. She's been waiting for over a decade for D'Shea to grant it. That's been torn away, she's here, and she…has little hope."

"Yeah, I've noticed. Did she tell you all that?"

"Not with words," I muttered. "She can't. D'Shea set a compulsion on her not to tell that she had a Daughter at House Thalluen."

"You know about that, too, huh? How? Not D'Shea, herself."

"No. The last time Gaelan was open to me, we mindlinked."

"Which was?"

"After the Queen's sentence. The eve before we left for the Surface, you remember, she was weeping." I met her umber red eyes. "The link *hurt*. More than I can describe. I haven't tried again."

"Because it hurt."

"And because she's not willing. I promised."

Rausery's gaze pinned on me. "What if I'm willing? Will you try?"

My hand trembled; I stilled it. "You're not a mage, Elder. The stone changed with magic applied, you know that from Phaelous. I don't know if it would work."

My Elder exhaled in disappointment, watching as three black arachnids dropped from a branch above and into my hair. She suppressed a smile.

"Fine," she said. "Then, I guess there's nothing else to do. It's time for you three to go, and for me to return below."

My guardians rushed down to my shoulders, standing alert as I jolted in surprise. "What?"

"Spring is aging," she said with a serious expression. "I know Jael has far to travel, and she needs as many days of warmth and plenty as I can give. She can head out tonight, after the Sun goes down."

"W-wait—" I stammered, and she pinned me with her gaze.

"You want to try?"

57

I nodded. "Yes. I'm sorry, Elder, I didn't know why you were asking."

"You knew. You're afraid. I get why, but we can't wait on it anymore."

I stood there, at a loss. "Um. Sh-should we fuck, Elder?"

Rausery grinned with ease, gloved hands on her hips. "Later. Let me anticipate it a little, novice. Back to the cave."

The rest of that day, I focused hard on making bolts for my hand crossbow, on mixing up poison paste and more food—separately—and strengthening my belt and pouches with spare strands of darkened hide leftover from hunting. I applied a fresh coat of waterproofing solution on cloak and boots and gloves, mixed as Rausery had shown us using Surface reagents, knowing from recent experience that it would also help against elemental wear and control odor. I waited for my Sisters to wake, and they joined me in the work when they did.

I didn't see Rausery after her query. I figured she was watching to see whether I would say anything to Jael or Gaelan. I tried but got nowhere. There were certain things we just couldn't talk about, and Gaelan more than the rest of us. When the Sun set and it grew dark, and I still hadn't seen my Elder, however, I went to seek her out.

"Stay and rest," I suggested. "She mentioned she'd be doing the same."

"Why bother her, then?" Jael said.

I shrugged. "Just something she said."

Neither questioned me.

I did not find a trail or sign of passing, nor did I expect to; I found Rausery on a hunch. If I were her, comfortable in my element and released from all duties in Sivaraus, far from the immediate concerns of other Davrin plots yet soon to return, I would spend my remaining time watching the sky a little longer. I would also choose somewhere I could see the mouth of the cave and spot any figure moving to or from the tree line.

Keep an eye on the novices.

"Need something?" she asked in Common.

I jerked upright, having just finished climbing to the second ledge above our cave. She was there, reclined on a cradle of rock, lounging with her hands folded just above her belt. I took a seat on a second rock within easy talking distance. Rausery didn't comment; she stared out at the night's view, then up as a breeze passed over our ears in a low whoosh. I followed her gaze, temporarily entranced. The Moons hadn't risen yet, and the stars were radiant against the black sky.

She began, "It's lives or objects."

I blinked, tearing my eyes from the stars to her.

"There is something about this place," she murmured. "The Valsharess blocks and punishes curiosity. Any idea of expansion. She restrains us down there, yet She *knows* about lives and objects up here, and not all from me. I don't see how, but it is so." She shifted her gaze to me. "Or you wouldn't be here, and She wouldn't be Queen."

Rausery had my complete attention. She smiled a little seeing it, drew in a breath, and let it out. Then, she spoke in Davrin. "Question, novice. Straight up."

I nodded, waiting.

"Have you caught?"

I froze, the fear and vulnerability locking my voice inside my throat. However, no illness or dizziness came, no magical shackles with which I was too familiar. I *could* speak it, if I wished. She hadn't taken that freedom from me.

"Yes, Elder," I whispered and waited for her response.

The Elder General exhaled slowly; it held the disappointment I'd expected but no anger or derision. Just acceptance.

"The Consort that D'Shea dragged into the Cloister?" she asked.

I looked down, wordless.

"That explains it." Rausery lifted her chin to the sky, expression thoughtful as she scanned the stars. "Does the Queen know?"

"Yes, Elder."

Her brows shot upward, then she smirked. "Surprised you can answer that one. She let you go, knowing? Can't fucking believe it."

I pursed my lips tight, feeling many sources of discomfort that had nothing to do with my "secret" missions. Rausery would soon return to Sivaraus, and I wasn't forbidden from saying more.

Maybe she can use it. Or D'Shea, if they talk.

"I don't know why," I said. "But the Queen thinks Shyntre is the sire. Sh-She could see our auras 'blended' and knew we'd bedded each other."

Rausery blinked, pinning her gaze on me. "Yeah, I know that's what triggered all this, but I'm surprised you know She can see who's fucked Her 'Son.'"

"The Consort told me later in solitary," I said, my voice small. "He could see it, too. He explained it to me. And the Queen... suggested that Shyntre 'chose' me, and it mattered to Her that he did."

My Elder was dead silent for a long moment. Then she breathed out. "Fuck. Well, that's good information to know before I get back to the shit."

"Would you help D'Shea keep my Consort alive?" I blurted, and the General gave me an odd, judging look. I backtracked. "He's a powerful healer, Elder, you *saw* the results. I wouldn't be here if his magic wasn't on par with a Priestess. And he has dreams of the Surface, like the Valsharess does, he-he *showed* me!"

Rausery narrowed her eyes; I could see both fear and skepticism. I bit my tongue wondering if I'd lost her. If I'd said too much. Again, the General looked to the stars, frowning in concentration.

Finally, she said, "If that's so, then hiding him for long is going to be difficult. And it's going to get ugly when he's found."

My shoulders were hunched; I tried to relax them. "He is already reported dead. From the Purge."

Her mouth twisted. "Yeah, I know. Can't see how that's *not* going to fuck us at some point." She rubbed her eyes with her thumb and first finger. "Hm. But you can talk about this, so I'm going to add something. Just for you."

"What, Elder?"

Her tone was the gravest I'd heard from her. "Be wary of any death mage who becomes aware that you carry. It's the kind of stuff they deal with, whatever power or essence is released when a body dies. Unborn can die, they are no exception, and I don't know how tempting that might be to a short-lived Human looking at a pregnant Elf who can live *centuries*."

I was stunned, my fingers cold. Rausery paused, and I had nothing to say.

"Did D'Shea…*give* you anything?" she asked. "In case it's your freedom or your belly?"

I nodded earnestly, forcing my voice to work. "Sh-she did."

Rausery breathed. "Good."

"Wait. You *know* she has those vials?"

She huffed, a dry smirk stamping her mouth. "I encouraged her to make them after she came back from delivering Shyntre to the Priestesses. We have *that* experience in common."

My mouth sagged. "You have a…?"

"Had," Rausery corrected tersely, staring straight ahead. "Dead. Somewhere in the Sanctuary. Priestesses used her up."

I swallowed down a nausea having nothing to do with compulsions. In my mind, I saw the hidden altar in that deep pit where Wilsira and Kerse had taken me, where Auslan had claimed he was "made."

Priestesses stealing commoners to bear for them, and those matas never leave.

Rausery's Daughter might have been one of them, but I didn't know for sure. I didn't *want* to.

"Is that why you once told me you'd kick my ass if I got pregnant?" I murmured with forced levity.

My Elder smiled tightly, accepting the shift in topic. "If you were careless, before you finished basic training. Not much you could have done about catching, Sirana." A pause. "Kind of glad the Queen has it wrong about the sire and let you go up here, instead. I don't understand it but know Shyntre won't correct Her."

"What about Auslan?" I asked again. "Will you help D'Shea hide him?"

"She and I will talk about it."

A stern look told me this was all she would promise. I had to let it go.

We were quiet for a while, then I watched as my Elder removed her belt and set it next to her. A surprise flush entered my cheeks as I watched.

"Wanna give it a try?" she asked, her voice smooth and calming as she next tugged at her leather ties. "I could use a good fuck."

I reached for my belt, too. "Yes, Elder."

She gestured toward the East. "Sister Moons are rising full together. Been waiting for that. We've been here sixty days."

I looked at a pale set of bluish orbs just cresting the jagged horizon. Even moonlight hurt, but the recovery was faster than sunlight, and I grew accustomed to it eventually. I'd never seen both full Moons in the sky, however, and not traveling together. It was beautiful, and I liked thinking of them as "sisters."

My vision was hampered when I looked away, tracers following my gaze like in the day. I could hear, however, that my Elder had lowered her leathers and began touching herself. She did not yet ask anything of me. The wind shifted direction, and I caught a whiff of her scent. I blinked and patiently waited for my night vision to clear.

Eventually, I could make out Elder Rausery leaning back, pants around her knees and her legs bent, a bare hand between her muscular thighs and two strong fingers disappearing into her cunt. She sounded wet, and the slick noise made my gut clench. Her eyes were closed, but they opened periodically to look at the stars or the Sister Moons. Not at me. Given what we were just discussing, that was no surprise, but I couldn't help wondering what she thought about to help get in the mood.

Give it a try. Maybe I'll know what arouses her this fast.

I waited for the order to strip, or for her to reach for her Feldeu, but though she was aware of me, she didn't acknowledge me. I didn't think I could do better for her than she was doing for herself, so I stayed still.

Do nothing unless she asks.

I watched her industrious hands, the flexing of her thigh and ass muscle; I listened to her breath, drew in her scent in slow, deep draws, and slowly became aroused as well. The more I relaxed, the warmer my leathers felt by the time the Elder began her accelerated rise.

She dug strong fingers inside her cunt, stroking hard while mashing the heel of her hand against her mound. Her hips jerked with spikes of sensation alongside her breath. Where I'd felt chilled before on the side of the mountain, I felt overly warm beneath my cloak. I didn't blink unless the wind forced me to. Soon, Rausery climaxed with a deep, satisfied growl, admiring the stars as she drifted down.

I was trembling, thinking how few Sisters might have witnessed this from our General. Like the young buas at Court who had felt safe enough to stroke and spurt while I sat nearby, it was something like that here, I thought.

Rausery didn't command me, didn't ask anything. I *wanted* her to.

Fuuuck…

"Liked that, eh?" she murmured, her voice smoky and loaded with amusement.

"Um. Yes, Elder."

She nodded and relaxed in her afterglow, closing her thighs and wiping off her hand with a small cloth from her belt. It seemed she would prefer to lie there with her pants down. Meanwhile, I squirmed inside mine, waiting for the command.

She said we should give it a try. Said she could use a good fuck.

Maybe she wanted me to ask instead? Wanted to make me beg her? No, not *beg*. If that was how she got off, she wouldn't look like she was about to fall asleep. Maybe it was like my first night out? Maybe I shouldn't wait for her to direct me. Very soon, she wasn't going to be there to ask *or* obey. She'd been telling us that for weeks.

I removed my cloak and slowly stripped out of my armor, boots, and clothing, though I kept Shyntre's pendant and Callitro's ring on. Rausery had opened her eyes and was watching me. I saw the spark of interest as I revealed skin, and my nipples tightened to hard, aching points when the cool air hit them. I enjoyed the feel of my leathers sliding down my thighs while her eyes followed them, and another small part of me relished the way my bare feet were so tolerant of the stones and pebbles beneath them. I was strong. And healthy.

"Very nice," Rausery commented, her low voice barely louder than the breeze. "I can see the work you've done in the mountains, novice."

"Thank you, Elder."

I sighed, reaching to massage my netherlips, standing on that ledge high above the forest. I still ached. A fingertip tested my hole; I was almost ready. Rausery watched appreciatively, a tiny smile on her lips. Finally, I just said it.

"Wear your Feldeu for me, Elder. Please."

Umber red eyes lifted from my crotch to my face. "You sure?"

I allowed myself a smile. "Let me show you how I ride a cock."

Rausery's ears perked up hearing that in Davrin, and her dark face opened in a wide grin. "Mm. Let down your hair first and get ready to climb aboard."

I unthreaded my braid as Rausery retrieved her Feldeu from her belt. Finger-combing my hair to let it spread out across my naked back, I watched with rising eagerness as she set it between her open thighs, pushing in the bulb end and murmuring the command word.

My pendant was uncovered and hanging between my breasts, and I waited to see if something would happen. Despite the visible flare of magic as the phallus attached to my Elder's body, however, the saphgar stone didn't blind me with light. There was no warmth, not a glint beyond the natural reflection of moonlight.

Hm. Not a good sign.

Still, if Rausery thought about the ostensible reason for us to couple outside under the Sister Moons, I couldn't see it. She welcomed this, either way.

The better way to go. Don't think, just do it.

I crawled onto the flat stone between her ankles, kneeling there with my arms resting on her drawn-up knees. My eyes flicked to the new, jutting appendage then to her face, my tongue tracing my lips with a mischievous grin.

She chuckled, spreading her knees out from under me. "Fuck, yeah. Know you're good at that, go on."

My cheeks were certainly warmer, and I leaned down, parting my lips and catching the head of her Feldeu between my lips. I swirled my tongue around it, and my Elder groaned, stripping off her gloves and reaching to thread fingers in my loose hair. I expected her to tighten her grip and push my head down like Jaunda did, maybe thrust her hips up and actively fuck my mouth and throat.

Instead, the Elder General exhaled and relaxed under me, playing with my hair while I sucked her how I chose. She massaged my scalp and my ears, which felt good, and she squeezed my bare shoulders when I did something *really* right.

At one point, her rough hands slid down to cup my hanging tits, massaging them, and it felt like too much. When she pinched my nipples, I yelped around her staff, surprised and freezing in place before I either bit her or pushed her hands away.

"There we go," Rausery murmured, caressing gently, though my nipples were too sensitive for it to feel pleasant. She patted my hard abdomen. "Earliest sign there's a babe in there."

I lifted my mouth off to look at her without speaking. She shrugged, returning her fingers to my hair.

"Tits will hurt for a while, you should expect."

I hadn't known that, and Rausery could read it on my face. She shook her head with a wry smile.

"Alright, get up here if you're done sucking me."

My Elder's strong hands took hold of my waist as I lifted my body up to straddle her. She held me steady as I wiggled to get into position, my knees to the stone on either side of her. That was going to hurt, too, but physical discomfort was continuous in the wilderness. Rausery wouldn't be complaining about her shoulders and lower back, so I could hardly complain about my knees.

She reached up to touch Shyntre's sapphire between my breasts, leaving my tender breasts alone this time. "Make sure that doesn't knock me in the teeth, or I'll knock you in the head."

"Of course, Elder," I breathed.

She stroked my skin as I reached beneath us to settle the dark head of her cock against my wet folds. I squatted down, felt that favored tool slowly spreading me open, and I groaned. "Ohhh, Goddess…"

"Ah, yeah!" Rausery grunted in agreement, holding my hips long enough to thrust her own, penetrating deeper and making me gasp. Then, she touched my ribs and arms, covered my breasts again gently with calloused palms. It set off another crackle of sensations in my nipples that I wasn't sure was pain or pleasure.

"Ride me, novice. Show the Sister Moons how you like it."

Her voice was thrilling, and this was so fucking strange. Anyone back home to witness this would say the General had a weak fetish to play the submissive male, yet I felt to be in that role, even being on top and without the cock. Gladly, I gripped her shoulders for leverage, stroking her magic cock powerfully with my hungering cunt, setting myself in for a grunt-worthy fuck.

More than once, Rausery squeezed my buttocks, spread them, circling and dipping her finger teasingly in my asshole before pulling out. I squeaked, made noise every time though my effort never flagged, and the Elder Sister underneath laughed and groaned as my sex clenched harder around her. Eventually, she took firm hold of my bare hips and helped the pace and my knees at the same time.

Ah! So good!

That delicious tension was building fast.

"Elder...!" I groaned, helpless for a moment as I grabbed her rock-hard forearms; my fingers dug in as I bounced with abandon on her lap.

My sore tits jiggled before her gaze. She growled low and brusque, releasing me only to grip my arms and pull me down so we were pressed breast-to-breast. She held me tight, my knees splayed on the stone on either side of her. It kept me open as she took over the pace and thrust deep inside my cunt. She shocked me utterly by kissing me. It sent me soaring into orgasm.

"Mmm-*mmm!*" I cried, my wet sheath convulsing around a thrusting pole as she swallowed excessive noise.

The pleasure rushed through, I wallowed in it without pain or fear while her mouth pressed hard to mine. Hungry strokes of her tongue, then the tip running along the sensitive edges of my lips before giving them a full suck. I was just coming down when I heard my Elder arrive at the precipice right behind me.

I opened my eyes; I *wanted* to watch her come.

Rausery was looking straight overhead at the stars when she pounded out a quick succession of thrusts. Gritting her teeth, she growled in release, her eyes squeezing shut, and I grinned to witness her helpless throes. I stared without blinking, wanted it to go on for as long as it could.

Her eyes opened unexpectedly. Feverishly, she looked at me, and I saw a brilliant gold flicker deep within her expanding pupils. I stared into the depths, held that freefall, about to emerge into a strange space—

And barked in alarm as something exploded inside my head.

Goddess!!

I ripped my eyes away, buried my face in her neck. I moaned as the throbbing ache brought instant tears to wet my Elder's skin.

"Sirana, what—?"

"I can't…" I whispered, choking.

I focused on her scent, her living warmth while I shivered violently as a cold sweat broke out over my body. Rausery was aware. She clasped me tight until I calmed down, her hard cock remained deep in my slit.

"Shh. Breathe, novice. Easy."

We said nothing and, soon enough, noticed how the thin Surface air had dried my juices on my thighs and around her erection. It felt odd. We were also getting stiff, aware of the sore spots. My Elder withdrew her phallus, and I crawled off. Without talking, we each did what we needed to clean up, dress, and set ourselves to rights. Only once we looked like Davrin warriors again and my pendant was buried under my clothes did Rausery speak.

"So, what happened? You tried to mindlink with me?"

I grimaced. "No. Not tried. It…began to happen. It didn't finish."

Rausery frowned. "What do you mean?"

I swallowed, thinking how to explain it to a General when a Sorceress used a different language entirely. "A mindlink sort of… spills in, and I'm there, watching or hearing. Feeling. Usually a bit of me, but mostly whoever I spilled into."

She tilted her head. "Is the other aware you've 'spilled in'?"

"Not…always. It's been so, but I didn't control that. D'Shea wanted me to learn to do it without the other knowing."

Rausery smirked. "Of course, she did. Hm." She looked out at the Moons again, thinking. "So, you don't require a mage to start. That's good. Maybe you can use that, Sirana."

"It didn't *work*, Elder," I muttered, recoiling at the idea of falling unexpectedly into a Surface-dweller's mind.

She was about to say something but changed her mind. Instead, she suggested, "Maybe try again with Gaelan? See if her magic boosts anything."

"Elder," I whined.

"Please."

My frown crumbled to surprise. *Please?*

The General shrugged. "I can't order you to. I don't know what you do, exactly, and the Queen's missions take priority. But I can delay sending you three out another day, if you want another. If not, travel has to start at midnight."

Not fair!

I bit my cheek and didn't say it. I looked at mottled lichen on the stone, then up at the Sister Moons ascending toward their zenith.

One more day.

Or, I was alone at midnight.

"I'll try with Gaelan, Elder," I said.

That same night, Rausery helped in grounding me and my Sisters to imminent reality.

"Tomorrow," she said, looking at each of us in turn.

We nodded. She needn't explain. She also didn't tell us to keep working. We must prepare anyway, even on a "day off," but there was some time to relax.

Let's go for a wander, I suggested to Gaelan, thinking I had timed it right to be private, but Jael saw my gesture.

"Me, too," she said, coming to stand beside me.

Rathole.

Then Gaelan smiled at Jael, wordlessly inviting her, so I shrugged and went along with it. We picked a direction, moved off the deepest slant of the mountainside, and filtered quietly into the moon-dappled shadows of the trees. We were each doing well to be quiet and unobtrusive to the night-dwelling creatures. We showed off our skills, which had greatly improved compared to when we first arrived.

Bright night, Gaelan signed. *Brightest of all.*

Jael and I looked up, and my younger Sister blinked and grimaced when a shaft of silver light bludgeoned her in the face.

Might as well be day, she signed with a grumble, rubbing her watering eyes.

I smiled, not agreeing but seeing her point.

So, what next?

How would I convince Gaelan to try a mindlink, so we might get around the compulsion, as I did with D'Shea? Ask her to cooperate? Attempt to seduce her, convince her to have sex one more time before we were separated?

Reishel's blank face and empty eyes jumped into the fore of my mind, and I gasped aloud, stopping in place as doubt engulfed me.

What? Jael demanded, eyes darting around for the threat.

"Sirana?"

I blinked, looked to my older Sister when she spoke. I was at a loss. They watched me but didn't press. We had all been acting weird at times since hitting the Surface, distracted by the myriad unknown things inside our heads but remaining silent. There was so much we couldn't say, this behavior had become our usual.

I shook my head and signed, *Nothing.*

Oh, it was something, alright. D'Shea and I had had a conduit between us when we reached through her magical binds to share our knowledge.

Reishel.

Psionically vulnerable after going catatonic in the Ornilleth battle, more than the Sorceress had realized at the time. This was a Queen's compulsion I thought to get around, not just a potion Gaelan or I drank. Even the Elder Sorceress D'Shea couldn't find a way alone against a Priestess's spell, and I hadn't "spilled in" to her at all. I had only listened to her speak across a deep chasm, where she had been screaming for two centuries for someone near enough to hear her.

How long had that trance taken? Six marks? Half a cycle? I remembered how dazed Reishel had seemed afterward, and I knew what we'd left her open to while sitting there so long. What we'd left *all* of Sivaraus open to.

I can't do this alone. I can't even command guardian spiders created to obey me and jump onto a wall.

Rausery had been *willing*, and I barely saw a speck of light before it felt like someone had broken a metal staff over my head. I recognized and might never forget that moment on the Surface when I'd given up on knowing what Gaelan and Jael were supposed to accomplish, what their chances were. Rausery had given us hints with our own responses to her stories but I could not give her, or any of us, something more.

There's nothing left to wait on. Go to the death mage's tower. What else can you do, Sirana?

I reached out to take Gaelan's arm, to stop her. She turned, curious, and I cupped her face, kissing her, wanting her taste and scent one more time before she left. She let me, responded a little, but in her lackluster response wasn't the hunger for living, for seizing the moment, that I'd hoped for. She smiled and patted my hand, stepping back from me.

Damn it all to the Abyss.

Jael scoffed into the night; her arms folded. "Come on, Gaelan, you've pushed us away since we left, and I'm sick of mages getting away with being so moody. Sirana has a reason to cry at night, but you do while you're awake! She's glad to be alive and hasn't given up before she started. I sure as fuck won't."

I flinched at her beratement while anger darkened our Sister's face. *Oh, that's not going to help.*

"You little shit," Gaelan hissed.

"There's more to it, Jael," I said, my voice rough. "Back off."

"Then, what is it?" she demanded, looking between us. "*Tell* me something! Anything! We've been muzzled and egg-stepping for Moons!"

I glanced at Gaelan; her mouth was a thin, tight line. I said, "She can't tell you."

"But *you* can," Jael said, reading my face. "Come on, say something, Sirana, this silence is wearing on *all* of us. We can't give up!"

House Aurenthin must not keep many secrets.

I looked at Gaelan, whose eyes were filled with tears, and her throat on lock down. Her expression was crumpled, but I couldn't know what she wanted me to do, what she wanted me to say. D'Shea's secret about the potion makers who allowed Jilrina to silence me didn't matter up here, did it?

Why would it?

"I found out just before we left," I began, "that Gaelan helped me when she was a merchant, and I wasn't full grown."

Gaelan choked a bit, leaning against a tree, clutching her fists to her middle.

Shit. It was hurting her, but it wasn't like what struck Jael down before. Should I continue? Did she want me to speak for her? What should I say? I didn't want to describe how I'd been stabbed.

"She defied a First Daughter," I said, "telling me how killing Jilrina would release my compulsion against her. Because of her, I got free and eventually joined the Sisterhood."

The young Aurenthin brightened with admiration. "Wow, I didn't know. How daring, Gaelan! I didn't know you had it in you."

Our older Sister began to keen, sliding down the tree toward the ground. The response was inexplicable to Jael, who looked to me, pleading.

"Sh-she lost her Mother and siblings to the dungeon," I murmured, "and her baby was given to my Matron... as a servant."

Jael jerked like she was struck in the face. "She has a baby?!"

Gaelan surged up and bolted away from us, disappearing in the direction of the cave. I drew breath to shout after her but she not only vanished inside the first dense copse but had done so like a shadow.

She was *trying* to be quiet. Noticing made me hold myself in check.

Jael had both her hands over her mouth after her blurt. "What? What just happened?"

I wished we could say; either I could mindlink or she could use her tongue.

Or maybe just the latter.

"I know she wanted to see Natia before it was too late," I said. "And it's too late."

"Oh." The youngest Sister looked at me, folding her arms in discomfort. "Fuck farts."

An inappropriate smile threatened to rise, and I shook my head, rubbing my forehead to hide the moisture in my eyes.

"So, that's her name?" Jael asked. "Natia?"

I nodded. "I've seen her at my former House."

"You have? Does Gaelan know that?"

"Thanks to D'Shea, yes. Gaelan was there for my reports."

"*Ungh.*" Her arms folding tighter, my Sister looked where Gaelan had vanished. "But her cait's alive and has a place to eat and sleep. That's something. I'd *use* that as a reason to come back, not mope around."

I didn't reply, only stood there feeling stupid and helpless. I could see Jael's point but hadn't begun to understand Gaelan's.

I touched my stomach. *But I might get there with her, just like she did with me and a silencing potion.*

Despite the regular abuse heaped on the lowest House in Sivaraus, and despite Jael's extremely rough introduction to the Sisterhood, the young Aurenthin still said whatever she thought. She didn't know what it was like to carry a heavy secret for decades or be forced into silence. Not until this mission. Maybe part of her had cracked when she'd begged me to talk to her. To say something. Anything.

It hadn't helped Gaelan as much as I'd hoped.

"You mean to come back," I said to Jael.

"Yeah," she answered with supreme confidence. "What about you?"

"Yes. I will."

Jael smiled in relief. "Well, then. Um. Meet you here? We could go home together."

I smiled just to think of the ludicrous, impossible chances of that happening. "It's a deal."

It was telling that my youngest Sister just accepted that. No thoughts or plans followed on how to attain that goal. Instead, she watched me, her eyes turning warm and suggestive; I spotted the invitation.

"Kiss me like you did Gaelan," she said. "It looked nice."

And Jael wouldn't withdraw from it.

Mmm. Alright.

I took my younger Sister's face in my hands and kissed her firmly with that familiar affection, as I had Gaelan. Jael's arousal flared like daybreak, and she clutched me, grasping for more kisses. I kept going. Our belts came off quickly, mine delayed only by setting my spiders on watch in a tree above.

"Quick," she urged eagerly. "Quick."

I helped strip her leathers down her hips and legs, bunched at the tops of her boots. Kneeling fast, I went down on her first, my gloved hands gripping and smoothing her inner thighs. Jael kept her gasps and her shudders quiet and restrained as I probed and mouthed her like a delicacy, drawing my tongue slowly across her folds, inhaling deeply the fragrance within the tuft of her mons.

Jael gripped the bark as the urgency of my strokes escalated with the involuntary jerk of her hips. I dug my fingers in to where she would feel it and forced them in place. I used my forearms and elbows to splay her thighs wider for me.

With a peep escaping, her slit became wetter; her scent strengthened as the cait tried to hold still for me, trembling from the effort. I rewarded her by attacking her slit, lapping and sucking with aggression, thrusting my tongue inside her before flicking and swirling the tip around her nub. I could feel every muscle in her body straining as she ached to reach her peak.

"Sira—*ngh!*" she gasped before being swept up in ecstatic convulsions.

I kissed her netherlips gently as she came down, breathing deeply, heat radiating from her skin. I rose up to kiss her mouth again, and she eagerly shared the heady whiff and moisture on my lips.

"Now, you," she whispered.

We worked on lowering my own leathers, and Jael fervently returned the favor. She wouldn't give up, wouldn't stop until my sex was swollen, scalding, and drenched, smeared all over her cheeks and jaw. By the time she was finished with me, and as my knees trembled and my heart pounded in my ears and my chest, the tension melting away, I heard her chuckle.

"You taste different," she cooed. "Those new Surface berries, hm?"

"Mmm," I hummed. "Maybe."

Maybe not.

Later, when Jael and I returned to the cave, Rausery was standing to one side of the opening, her back to the stone, hood up with cloak draping down. Her powerful form was bathed in silvery light, her face withdrawn in deep shadow. She'd have scared the skin off anyone who didn't know who she was.

"Leader?" I asked.

We heard her slow exhale first.

Uh-oh.

"Gaelan requested permission to leave," she said. "I granted it."

It struck like a blow. "What?!"

"She's gone?" Jael said, regret tinging her voice.

Spinning around, I tried to determine which direction she'd gone, seeking any movement down off the mountain, and trace—

"Don't you dare, Sirana," my Elder growled. "I'll tie you to a fucking cliff."

I rounded on her. "She should have said farewell!"

"Yeah, I'm assuming things didn't go how you were hoping. You took your time getting here if it mattered that much. Saw her crying before, but never like that."

My lips sealed against the hard pain in my throat and the image that suggested. I'd thought I had until tomorrow to try again. I only had time for one of them, as it turned out.

"Jael goes at daybreak," Rausery announced quietly. "Sirana, you're staying here with me while they get a lead on you. You're not to track them, I know that much. Queen's order."

Jael glanced at me, betraying her nerves, wanting to speak. *Unable.*

She signed with a tremor to her hand, ★Yes, Elder. I'll get ready.★

"I'll help," I whispered in defeat.

My mind drifted often to Gaelan moving farther away beneath the Sister Moons. It was the same sky, and soon, it would be the same Sun. Even after another forty days of travel, she would still be under the same sky as I was. As Jael would be.

I wanted us to meet again beneath it; I wanted the Queen to be wrong in that "vision." I wanted Rausery's thorough training to be the balance-breaker, the Game-changer, but that depended on the Red Sister, on her will and her luck.

Willpower weakened with grief. Why couldn't Gaelan see that and do what Jael said? Why couldn't she use Natia living at House Thalluen to strengthen her determination to come back? I should have promised her I would help. I could have found a way to talk with my Mother.

I wasn't sure who grabbed who first when Jael and I had those final hours before daybreak, when we'd gone to rest deep in the tunnel. No matter who started it, our stripping was desperate. Jael bit my lip on purpose when we kissed; I grabbed her hair at the base of her neck and yanked, forcing her to look at me as I held her tightly.

"Fuck me," she hissed. "Do it."

Naked, we entwined our legs, our chests pressed together, and lips locked once we were on the ground. We struggled to find a rhythm, trying to show just how much we wanted there to be a next time. Finally, I let Jael lead—she needed it— and gasped as she ground my sex hard with her thigh. Soon I was moving with her.

There! Like that.

At last, we were in tandem.

"Yes," I whispered, pressing harder between her legs as I squeezed her buttocks in both hands.

I didn't care that the stone scraped my knees and knuckles and hips; it enhanced the youngest Sister's teeth on my earlobe, on my neck. Jael whimpered with primal pleasure, climaxing instants before I did. I held on as our heartbeats gradually returned to normal; my Sister didn't seem to want to move.

"Red Sisters don't leave each other to die," she breathed.

I didn't reply at first, but I remembered saying that before our sentences. We'd been outside Auslan's prison cell, when Jael and Shyntre had begun fighting. I hadn't realized she'd taken those words in like that, though it sounded as if she tested it on her tongue.

Without a doubt, Jael and I *would* disobey orders to find each other. We had done it before against the Tragar. That was why the compulsions were in place.

Was there a way out? Were we doomed forever to be silent of our missions, even if we saw each other again? How would we ever be this close again if that was the case? The looming specter of those who had been in such a trap for much longer, D'Shea and Shyntre especially, suggested the most likely answer to those questions.

"Meet me on the way back?" Jael asked again

She held me from behind, her mouth pressed to my shoulder.

"Yes."

Her voice quavered, and she trembled for a second. "Stay alive. I will, too."

"Deal," I whispered. I had more than one reason to work for it.

Jael breathed out, her hand running down my back, and we fell asleep like that, naked and wrapped up in a tunnel leading to the Deepearth. At daybreak, I would watch her leave the mountain for the last time with Rausery standing guard beside me.

It must be enough that we shared the same sky.

CHAPTER 4

"TELL ME ABOUT AUGRAN AND MANALAR, LEADER."

Rausery smirked. "Nice try, novice. Irrelevant to your mission."

I made a face. "It will be a long day, waiting to be released."

"I can keep you plenty busy."

"What about stories?" I amended. "Maybe not from Human?"

She frowned. "Dwarf?"

"Any others?"

My Elder considered that. "A lot of those in Human tongue, but impossible to tell how true."

"Like what?"

She shrugged. "Spirits, creatures of night and shadow, half-bloods, Dragons, summoned beings from the 'other' space. The Davrin know most of this is true in some sense, but the Humans may never see any of this before they die. What they do not see, they hear about, and then imagine they have seen it, and it is so."

I tilted my head in confusion. "What?"

"Inventions and dreams of truth," Rausery stated. "Greater stories they will believe in absence of proof. Humans are like bored children in some ways, even the elders. They are aware of greater knowledge held by the Dwarves and possibly others unfamiliar, like us, who live longer. Perhaps they are envious. They will believe grand tales quickly and only true in a tiny seed. Humans sing and repeat many tales, they are hungry for them. All change with each telling, so assume all claims are untrue unless you have proof."

I nodded. "How does this compare with Dwarves?"

"Haven't met many," she said frankly. "But they seem grounded. More of their tales are true, though far from all." She paused. "You can use this, Sirana, if you speak with these races. You have a better chance, with your eyes."

I squinted at her. "What do you mean, leader?"

"Some talked to me because I have brown in my eyes with the red. Shadows helped my eye color look familiar. You, Blue Eyes, have it even easier. Many Humans and Dwarves have the same color, it's familiar, and I know they don't see it as a threatening color. They may talk to you easier."

I got what she meant. Easier than Jael's fiery blaze or Gaelan's deep purplish-red.

"Learn what they wish to see and show them that mask. Don't be wholly truthful."

"What?" I smirked. "I should lie?"

"No, you are no good at that." She grinned at my expression. "But give away as little about your life and the Davrin as you can. Remain a mystery. If they see you as less than they imagined or something easily understood, even if understood wrong, they can turn on you in contempt and it is difficult to turn them back."

I frowned. "They... *want* me to be 'more' than them?"

Rausery nodded. "If you are 'forever young,' they expect this. You must deserve this longevity, somehow. If you present yourself as the same as them but live long for no reason, they will resent it. They want a reason the world lives. If they cannot discover one, they invent one, and the view is often small to match their lives."

She smiled ruefully. "I have made mistakes like this, Sirana, trying to open their view too large or too quick. It does not go well. Our fortune as Davrin is the Humans forget quickly, and most mistakes are forgotten in time and become another wispy tale. The Dwarves remember longer but spin fewer fancies from ether. Make sense?"

I needed time to contemplate it. Give little away, leave something to the imagination. I'd confessed a lot of truths lately, being unpracticed spinning lies with Red Sisters, but I remembered the Court. I observed and understood the theory. My first mask worn before those powerful females had been based on Jaunda before I knew her name.

Laugh more. It confuses them.

I wondered how that might work with Humans? Observe and learn the group, first; Rausery's training had hammered that into my mind over the weeks. I worked the rest of the day, listening to Rausery talk when she would. Small things which might prove useful; I soaked them all in. She'd managed to give me the direction for the Ley Tower more than once without triggering the sickness.

At night, however, Rausery wouldn't let me leave; I had to wait for daybreak. We passed part of it underground with sex. We wrestled, like in the Cloister, and I lost, yielding my netherhole to her when she pressed for it between my buttocks. She was rougher than when I'd been on top under the Sister Moons, reminding me how it could hurt and how to manage the dominant rut. Even with a raw pucker, my slit still drooled after she'd cum, and my Elder was satisfied enough to rub it for me afterward to my peak.

"Don't lose sight that you will need to kill or be killed," she said as we lay upon the stone, her muscled arm around me. "Sooner or later, it'll come that way. You've done it before."

"Yes, leader."

"Don't hesitate when there's no other way out. Don't linger, and don't get caught. You're as ready as I can make you, Red Sister." She met my gaze in the dark. "Our farewells in the morning, but I expect you to come back to Sivaraus. Got me?"

"Yes... Elder. I will."

I had the least distance to travel to reach my target than did my Sisters, though that did not mean that I would reach it the same day, or anywhere close. I hiked steadily the entire first day, stopping rarely but doing my best not to hurry, to conserve my strength and the food and water I could carry. I didn't want to miss an obvious warning sign, either; shadow and stillness were my best protections, and brooding on anything too long threatened distraction.

No excuse. Put it away for now.

I spent my night alone inside a large tree hollow, as there were no conveniently placed caves on my stroll. It kept the wind and the dew off me and that was good enough, if cramped and cold. I did not worry about sitting on the ground or being cornered because of my three spiders, who held their vigil on my bracers as I slowed my breathing and closed my eyes in that meditative state prior to Reverie.

I heard only one warning that brought me quickly awake. My small passengers were agitated, crawling and preparing to leap. Whatever had caused this was not in view yet, though I could hear the padded, plodding steps.

Soon a skinny, black bear walked in front of me, not much larger than I was and outside of my spider's jumping distance, fortunate for the bear. I stared at the hairy beast, studying the fascinating details as it swung its head my way, considering my presence with dull surprise. Then it kept moving, rustling and snapping its way through the forest. The spiders returned to a resting, if watchful, stance.

I considered hunting the bear—it was a large opportunity and Rausery had said not to pass anything up. I would be stupid to let it go, wouldn't I? Except that I did not need food and was weighed down already, having properly prepared. Say I killed it today without getting hurt, there was an extra day or two it would take to clean, butcher, and smoke it alone, which was hard work and only a day into my journey. What would I do with the hide, leave it?

Stretching it and treating it to prevent rot would take as long as drying the meat, and then I'd have to carry it…

Bah. The thing has not yet fattened up after hibernating through the Winter.

Mostly justification and impatience on my part, I knew, exactly what Rausery had warned about in passing up opportunities, but also practical. I did not need the kill. I even preferred the small creatures, just for their convenience of size.

I closed my eyes again before rising at daybreak. It may have been easier and more comfortable to time my travel with the Moons instead of the Sun, but I did not want to get complacent or lose what endurance I had built up to the harsher light. The weather would only become warmer for months yet, and it was better for the next season that I do not take the easiest way.

I used every bit of lore Rausery had taught me to find water, and I got used to being the only two-footed creature wearing boots in the mountains. I heard the cry of wolves far away—it astonished me how their calls to each other traveled such distances—and could not count the number of seed-seeking and insect-eating birds fluttering overhead, or tree rodents scampering from limb to trunk to limb.

The Surface was never still. Never quiet.

As often as the noise startled me, they also led me to hidden sources of new seeds, bits that Rausery had called 'plant meat' in the Trade tongue, to convey the good it did for mind and body. They led me to non-poisonous insects, both for me and for my spiders. It was quicker and much less work than hauling a slaughtered bear carcass would have been.

I grew delighted with the variety of mushrooms to collect early each dawn. This was an area of harvest in which I had practical knowledge from before. I could draw knowledge from the Deep-earth; there were many similarities, and even the toxic ones had their uses to me. If I held one up and inhaled gentle and slow through my mouth, then a distinct tingle along the roof of my mouth would separate the poisonous from the nonpoisonous. The likenesses were comforting, and I looked forward to testing some of the poisonous aspects of the unknown ones on a few creatures. Maybe there was something new I could bring back to cultivate.

By the fourth day, heavy clouds rolled in and remained. I had trouble knowing my direction by which side the Sun struck me. Even using general landmarks and memorizing the shape of some of the farther slopes, I had to climb several trees to get a higher view to make sure I stayed on track.

Sometimes, I had no choice but to take a deep, rock-strewn ravine, trail up or down, rather than scale the dangerous, sheer vertices on either side. This worked against my sense of direction as well, slowing me down. I was irritated that I could not sense the Ley Lines as well as Gaelan might have; it would have helped overcome the challenge of the clouds. Her face returned, her upset when I'd last seen her, and I paused on a hillside. I looked up and imagined which horizon she'd aimed for, then I pressed on toward mine.

I did not remember my dreams that night, but I woke to find my cheeks wet and chilled. As I wiped them with a gloved hand, I considered numbly that the only reasonable source for the moisture would have been tears. Had I made any noise in my rest? There was no Sister to say. If I had, I was lucky nothing came to investigate.

On the sixth day, I followed the crest of a mountain beside yet another valley; this one held a visible length of silvery, weaving water. By midmorning, I felt something maddening on the edge of my senses, like the high whine of those tiny, blood-sucking insects that caused itchy welts. This noise went much deeper, however, trilling at the base of my skull. *Inside* my skull.

Follow the Ley Lines, find the magic users.

Had I found the Ley Line? Creating new pathways to magic was not my talent, but I was still Davrin; I could use those mage's inventions. I understood how it felt when I did. If this was right, it may lead me straight to the tower.

Easier assumed than executed, as it turned out. I did better to keep direction with physical signs than trying to follow that subtle, buzzing pitch. I grasped for patience, didn't give up, balancing the physical and the metaphysical as I noted changes in the landscape. There were fewer pine trees, and newly budding deciduous trees and bushes. I was going down in elevation as well; the air I breathed did not seem as thin.

The underbrush was thicker amongst the thin, young trees, full of noisy obstacles and bright light. I preferred moving from copse to copse of the tall ones, whose wide branches covered the forest floor with deep shadow, blocking the Sunlight to the smaller plants. The shade was a relief to my eyes while it was possible to crisscross over the Ley Line by "feel."

My nose warned me of the next change, however. I paused downwind from an unusual richness of plants, flowers, and herbage. So far, these had not shown to grow together in the wild, and there were new fragrances I didn't know yet. A chill spread over my back.

Cultivation.

There was no obvious tower jutting out of a mountainside within sight, so I assumed the farmer wasn't also the death mage I sought. So, avoid this place entirely, or observe it for a time? What benefit might there be to approach?

I checked my waterskin, pursing my lips. The obvious answer was the safe drinking water. If there was a tended garden, there would be a well, a pond, or access to a stream or river. Would it be worth it? It depended on who lived here, and how many.

I stalked forward, taking my time and crouching in mottled shade where even the birds forgot I was there at times. More grasses grew here, in green, yellow, orange and red. I saw colors amongst the flowers, too, and there was a discernible pattern to the placement of the bushes. The design wasn't rigid like the Web Gardens of the Palace, and there were no curated walking paths, but there was a visual appeal and a balance that didn't appear in the natural state that I had studied for weeks.

The garden also had a well. I saw the raw, flat stones laid in a rough, circular form atop each other, defining its boundary so one would not fall in amongst the grass. I saw a bucket and rope, too.

Hmm.

This was the most dangerous source of water I'd found. Unfortunately, standing atop the last crest, I estimated that the silver, winding river was half a day's journey away *and* in the wrong direction from the Ley Line. Right here, on the other hand, I believed that I stood directly *on* it. The annoying treble was constant.

What were the chances that a non-magical sentient would build a well in the middle of the forest? *Might have to find out.*

I stepped laterally over a woody vine twining up a massive tree, and it moved. The thing crackled like an alarm as it wrapped and twisted tight around my ankle in a snare trap.

Shit!

Even as the vine whipped back and yanked me off my feet, I drew and held tight to one fighting dagger. Suspended upside down, I curled up and struck at an angle just above my foot, severing the vine, only to drop with a groan onto several knobby tree roots. I rolled on my side and loosened my spiders' pouch before I did anything else, and they scrambled out and took up position beneath my hair while I replaced my hood over my head.

I crawled to center myself away from any vines, watching the one that attacked me shrink back against the tree. I did not doubt that someone knew I was here.

Flee or fight?

Before I could decide, a body came into my periphery, and I dodged behind a tree. This one had a bow.

"Who is there?" a female voice cried in Trade, projecting well for the distance. "Show yourself!"

Rausery was right about the accents changing; I almost didn't understand her. What now? An arrow might be trained on me this moment should I try to bolt. I waited for any others to back her up, men especially, but heard no other feet running, saw no shadows slinking in to flank me.

Her voice shook when she called again. "Show yourself!"

I frowned, glancing at the vines; knowing what to look for, I saw how many there were. Traps all over.

Just one mage? Is it possible she is alone?

Not what Rausery had said to expect. If this was true, however, I might bargain. I was not burning for a fight.

I drew breath to speak. "I seek only water."

Quiet. I wasn't sure if she heard me, as I was not used to shouting in open space. She drew a breath.

"Only?" she asked, skeptical.

"Yes. Only. Will you bargain?"

She hesitated. "Not without a face or a name. Stand in the light."

Not with that bow ready and aimed.

Squinting against the brightness, I peeked around the tree. The tracers were bad at this distance while she stood in plain view in the greyish daylight; it blurred the details. I saw what I expected, though: a *very* pale face and a slender, feminine form taller than me. She wore daytime forest colors which blended in, and I believed that she knew how to use that bow. I had to remind myself that the golden hair did *not* mean she was old, but instead, that she was young.

I heard tension relax on her bow. The arrow tip was down, but she said nothing.

What's she doing?

From lifelong-habit, I checked the tree limbs above me, and it was good and bad that I did. A bird of prey was watching me with eerie intensity in its yellow gaze.

A falcon.

Our eyes met, and I could have sworn it glared at me. The bird emitted a piercing screech and launched out of the trees and into the garden, flying straight for the blonde figure. It landed on a stump near her and cried again in my direction.

What in the Abyss?

"Leave now, Dark One!" she cried, anger and fear making her voice hoarse as she lifted her long bow again. "No bargain! I will pierce your eye if you approach this home!"

Dark One? She thinks I'm a demon? Or a devil.

More immediate: how had she known? Did the bird *tell* her somehow? Change her mind about a bargain?

A mage that speaks with animals.

I hadn't heard of such a thing.

"I've no choice," the tall blonde whispered, near sobbing and far less confident. "You'll not go away, will you? You've returned to punish me again."

Um?

A crack sounded above me, and I looked to see another vine unbending from the trunk. It had thorns. Another undulated closer to the ground, coming to life like a snake as it lashed out in my direction, though fortunately falling short.

Talks with animals, and plants!

I shifted around my tree, moving to another, trying to avoid them both without exposing my back. A third vine trembled in front, and I saw I would soon be surrounded by ropes of long, wicked thorns.

She was forcing me out of hiding and doing a good job of it.

No choice. We are agreed, Surfacer.

Any smart fighter always incapacitated the mage first.

Vines darted for me, one snagging and tearing my cloak as I dropped my heavy pack and pulled out two web pellets in one hand, gripping one long dagger in the other. I closed my eyes, felt the tiny brush of my guardians' legs as they settled farther out of view, and sprinted out of the trees. I kept low and to the same side where the falcon was perched, but then an arrow struck the tree near my head—*Sucking web!!*—and I tore the ground sprinting in an erratic pattern.

Unlike my home tunnels, I had plenty of space to move, and as the flutter of wings came over my head again, I pitched the web pellet just ahead of where I judged the falcon to be. It flew into the pellet, bursting it and splattering the magical webbing. Angry shrieks pained my ears as it crashed into the ground, though the piteous squawking which followed proved it hadn't broken its neck.

"Pilla!" my target cried.

Another arrow sank into the dirt near my feet, and I forgot to breathe.

She dropped the bow as I closed in, drawing something else from her waist. I didn't think before disarming her, sending whatever it was spinning into the tall grass and sweeping her legs out from under her. She grunted as she landed.

"No!" she screamed from the ground as I pitched my second web pellet at her and immobilized her as well.

"Stay down!" I barked, panting.

She wailed, the pitch rising to a terrifying panic. I heard snaps and cracks, and then something flung earth into my face.

Fuck!

Suddenly, the roots in the ground thrust up, winding together to answer her call.

"*Li'shentinae!*"

I hesitated. *Was that Davrin?*

Something wrapped tight around my thigh, and it had a set of spikes that punctured my leathers, and then me. It burned! Another four such torture-ropes wrapped around each arm, my waist, and around my neck, pulling me to the ground as the spikes tore into my skin where armor didn't protect me. I hooked two fingers between one vine and my throat, freezing in terror as spikes pressed into my gut against the leather.

No!

I hadn't screamed that I was aware; I forced myself to breathe. My binds constricted, cutting off blood to my limbs, pushing the spikes deeper, trying to choke me, all at the same time.

"Stop!" I wheezed.

My guardians jumped out, skittering down the vines to the ground. My eyes squeezed shut, I heard the gold-haired mage yelp in pure surprise once, then twice in quick succession. All three had bitten her.

"You have no time!" I growled in Trade as one of the thorns pressed into the hollow of my throat, scraping my skin and seeking to silence me as my hand trembled fighting against it. "Release me! I give you cure!"

"You lie!" she screamed, sounding like fire had entered her veins.

"No time! You die! Bird die! Free me!"

A single moment passed before the constriction stopped, then the thorns were yanked out by the vines unwinding from my body, withdrawing into the soil. I couldn't know if this happened because she wanted to live or because she could no longer concentrate on her magic, but I heard her choking, struggling to breathe as she thrashed from seizure in the grass.

I scrambled clumsily to her web-covered body, sightlessly cutting the sticky ropes from her torso before dropping my dagger, exchanging it for a small, fiberstalk cylinder at my belt. A quick, sharp twist shed the casing from the pre-scored end, exposing the finest, glass needlepoint that a crafter could manage. The closed tip was clear, vial behind it filled with the antivenom for the guardian spiders.

I needed the largest muscle possible in which to inject it, so I flipped her over, blindly hooking frayed webbing in one hand, and put a knee on her back to hold her down. Her loose trousers had enough give to pull them down and expose her skin. My gloved hand confirmed one naked buttock, and the other pressed the needle to soft skin.

Quick.

I jammed the glass point into the muscle at the top of her ass, and her whole body jolted with pain, then I snapped the tip off inside to release the potent serum. Pressing the rubber stop-rod at one end with my thumb, I plunged the dose deep into her flesh before withdrawing. The needle was still in there, but the vial was empty.

I pulled her pants up and rolled her over again so her lungs wouldn't struggle to work against the ground. The blonde archer continued to breathe but it was labored, and her body was taken with small, shivering tremors.

Meanwhile, my spiders returned to me lethargically, retreating into their open pouch. Their calm suggested she and her vines were no threat anymore. Preparing myself, I opened my eyes and stood on my feet beneath the clouded sky. I blinked several times before I could see anything; it was all blur and aching. Once my sight at last cooperated, I was close enough to study her.

Her eyes were open and animal-like in their fear as they moved everywhere, unable to focus on me. They were bloodshot from effects of the venom, but her irises were vibrant green, the same color as leaves on the trees. I saw the three sets of fang-bites low on her neck, around her collar, the pale flesh streaked with red. All the rest of her pale skin was covered up in doeskin.

Then I saw her ears.

They weren't rounded, but long and pointed, like mine.

She wasn't Human. What was more—

Oh, goddess damn it. I know who you are.

Maybe. Unless there were several pale-skinned, blonde Elves up here, living in this spread of mountain valleys?

The squalling falcon fighting on the ground drew my attention as its mistress fought for every breath. With every stubborn attempt to flap its wings, "Pilla" strained and stretched webbing, though I didn't believe she would be free any time soon.

Looking back at the pale-skinned Elf, I saw that she had finally set her gaze on me. Tears dripped from her eyes, across her temple and into her hair as she watched me, watching her. Then, I realized I was bleeding. The thorns had given me deep puncture wounds. I counted twelve which hurt and wetted my black leathers to a concerning level.

Shit. I'm truly injured.

I reached for the first of the little brown pellets that Rausery had given me on Shyntre's behalf. I placed it beneath my tongue, agreeing with my Elder that it tasted like a mudball, and allowed the bitter thing to slowly dissolve while I retrieved my dagger from the ground. Not a week away from Rausery, and I'd already used one of two antivenoms, and had a dire need to prevent festering.

You're doing great, Sirana.

If these pellets did what Rausery claimed, then I was grateful to the stubborn wizard. Maybe I wouldn't have to use one of the few healing potions I had as well, if I could find some place to clean the thorn wounds in peace.

I eyed Pilla, the flopping, floundering falcon. Did the creature ever get tired? Or shut its beak? Worse, the clouds were thinning, the day grew brighter, and I was lightheaded and aching.

"We go to your dwelling," I said. "Out of Sun."

The blonde Elf shook her head, a good sign, I thought, though she trembled violently as she tried and failed to sit up. She was far too weak.

"N-no..." she gasped. "No, just k-kill me... if you intend to pleasure yourself in m-me...again."

I shifted my weight as the bleeding holes in my limbs throbbed and the falcon screeched. For certain, this was the same Elf my Lead had found in our tunnels.

"I must clean my wounds," I said, ignoring both the plea and the accusation.

"Y-you deserve worse, by His love," she whimpered. "You're evil, fallen..."

I arched a brow. *Evil? Whose 'love'?*

I'd heard this word only because Rausery and Shyntre had, but still I did not understand it. Doing harm counted for much of it, but then, that made every warrior evil. What was the point having a word, then? Add greed or some other excess, maybe, and I could see counting the Priestesses as "evil." But then, did the excess of violent sex taught by the Prime make the Sisterhood evil? What purpose was the word in either case, when "enemy" or "competitor" worked just as well?

"I asked bargain," I said, "for water."

"You l-lie," she repeated.

"You said this. I did not lie. I stopped the poison. You and your bird live."

"At your p-pleasure."

I didn't respond, as that was true enough. I could just take the water and leave her here, though at a price to my body.

The struggling falcon inside its webs finally drew my attention. Pilla diligently worked one wing, wearing the strands faster, so I stepped over to pick it up by the base of the tail for a distraction. It worked; the bird *really* hated that. I stretched out my arm, grateful the talons, beak, and one wing were stuck together to create a furious, swinging bird-ball.

Quite the determined guardian.

"Oh, G-God, please, don't h-hurt her!" the Elf whined, managing to roll herself over in a surge of panic.

I let her sweat a moment. Then, "We rest in your dwelling? Clean wounds in quiet? No fight."

She wept, "Y-yes. Don't h-hurt my baby."

Baby? You could have killed mine, mage.

I kept my mouth shut, nodding agreement as I set the sticky, protesting bundle of feathers down beside her, where the falcon finally calmed a little. Exhausted, the pale Elf's forehead drooped to the grass.

"Stay here. I get my pack. Then, I help you walk, and you show me safe place and safe water."

Pilla swatted at me with that one, freed wing, the falcon's tan-gold eyes communicating a baleful stare. This one would never give up. I felt the urge to smile, and so I did, winking at the forest Elf's noisy guard before I went to retrieve my pack behind the tree.

I could hear Rausery asking me what the shits I was doing.

I can't continue to Sarilis's Tower like this; I must tend the wounds first. And I can't kill her after Jaunda let her go. Not without need or provocation.

Wiser Rausery in my head had an easy counter: "Ah, but someone else might be at her dwelling, novice, and she's not saying, hoping for help when you get there."

Sour milk farts.

I avoided the obvious vine traps and returned with my possessions. Even being shorter and weighed down, I held the falcon again by her tail and helped the blonde archer to her feet, guiding her by my grip on one upper arm. All this time, all this noise and shouting, and no one had come to help her.

"Get water here?" I suggested, tossing my chin toward the rustic well, although I already had plenty to carry.

"S-Some at…my dwelling."

"You lie?"

The pale-skinned one dared to look insulted. "No."

We'll see.

She needed my help as we walked; she was unsteady on her feet, sweat poured down her face, and I could sense the weakness in her body as it struggled to recover from what the venom had done to her insides.

We walked slowly across the rich and colorful meadow, eventually made it to her dwelling on the other side. It was a shelter constructed of rock, soil, wood, and grasses up against a tree-covered hillside. Not only was it well-camouflaged but it also seemed quite sturdy, and it would be dim inside with its two windows covered by mats of tightly woven fibers. A fine place to get out of the light and weather while my skin knitted together.

Assuming no one else was in there.

The falcon's constant struggle made it so I couldn't have heard a Dwarf trip over a basket of tools before the mage pushed open the door. I needed to rely on the pale one's face; she looked ill and defeated, not a glimmer of a shrewd thought or cunning.

Upon entering the musty, blessedly dark dwelling, I passed a store of clean water; she had made a large, woven basket waterproofed with something dark and scentless. I allowed her to lie down on her thick mat only after checking it for hidden weapons —a good thing, as I found a flint dagger, figuring I had knocked another out of her hands during the fight, and it was in the grass somewhere.

"Mine," I said, then motioned to the bed. "Rest. Perhaps I dissolve webs so Pilla can guard you."

The blonde lost her strength in surprise, falling into the bedding as I set the bird down beside her.

I watched her. "Well?"

"Tell me wh-what you want," she said. "Do not lie."

Crouching like this hurt a lot; my muscles were torn and sore, stiffening up around the bloody punctures. I winced and shrugged, my patience thinning as I kept it simple.

"Water and rest. Quiet and dark. Maybe talk."

She looked pathetically sad. "You will interrogate me."

I tilted my head. "What is this?"

The pale Elf blurted a weak laugh of disbelief, and I frowned, waving my hand in dismissal and standing up. It was that moment I remembered the Trade word for a forced torture session to extract information from a reluctant source. Embarrassing to forget *that* one, as she could be right. I had questions, like, why was she here?

But not now. I have plenty to do first.

Leaving her bird sticky and bound, I drank my fill and scoured the place for surprises and useful items. I found a few tools, all un-refined in origin rather like the bow and flint knives: a staff, a well-balanced club, several ingeniously crafted pricker-balls that she should have had with her during our fight. I set them all outside, within my reach but not hers.

What remained inside were my own blades of forged metal, my hand crossbow and stout little bolts with their poisoned tips, all the powders, pellets, and other resources at my belt, not to mention Callitro's ring of true aim.

Clearly, the superior selection when I'm not surprised by magic vines.

There was a small hearth in which a fire could burn while the smoke was filtered outside through a screen which broke up a large, visible plume. I also found what might be her only metal possession: an iron boiling pot. I started a fire and set clean water to heat while mentally sorting my belongings for the tending and bandaging my body needed.

The pale Elf and falcon conserved their strength and stayed qui-et while I removed my cloak, gloves, bracers, and belt, setting them on the small worktable. Finally peeling my black leather armor from my torso, I got a good look and noted with satisfaction that there were no holes in it. The damage from the thorns were all in my cloak, clothing, and skin. All which needed to be mended.

Hot water ready, the archer emitted a soft moan of dread when I stripped off my shirt. I looked over at her in surprise, dipping a clean cloth to put on the back of my scored neck. I frowned and nearly said aloud that she need not worry, I didn't have a Feldeu. I withheld that, however, because of Rausery's advice not to volun-teer information which lessened my advantage.

Besides, if I did have a cock on my belt, I couldn't imagine mounting a pallid, sweating, spider-bitten hermit when she was barely breathing not two hours ago while getting pecked in the face by that bird for my trouble.

Pfeh. I'm truly driven mad with lust. Move over, Auslan, let me rape this long-legged twig on the table, instead!

The pale Elf mewled, and I turned abruptly toward her.

"What?" I barked irritably, topless, the damned pendant swinging between my sore tits. "Come, admire the damage, mage. You paid much for it."

The blonde swallowed her noise, withdrawing from my glare to turn her gaze to the ceiling. Pilla opened her beak and somehow hissed at me. I didn't know that falcons made that sound. Then I noticed the Elf's spine was twisted where she lay, favoring her left buttock.

The one with glass in it.

I frowned, considering how I would convince her it should come out and she had to let me do it, then shook my head. *Eh. Forget it.*

Methodically, I cleaned my many wounds instead, privately concerned if Shyntre's pellets *didn't* work as I'd been told. Puncture wounds were dangerous for lingering, putrefying rot, especially when one must travel. She chose her attack well, and I could see it escalating to this after Jaunda had both enjoyed and terrified her.

Letting the pale one go might not have been that much of a mercy. She didn't go far from where she'd been left.

I dabbed a topical oil from my pouch over each hole in my arms before bandaging them, then did the same for my neck, wrapping it like a scarf before I donned Shyntre's sapphire. I next removed my boots and leather pants, and the archer made a loud sound of denial.

"No!"

I stopped to frown at her, and her wide, green eyes stared at me. I straightened to inspect the thorn wounds around each leg and, incidentally, allowed her to see clearly my white-furred and female sex. She focused on my crotch, perplexed, and I nearly smiled.

What? You think we all have a swinging, black staff to stretch your pink hole?

I bit my cheek, again not spilling too much though left no doubt as to my shape. I did not speak while I tended my thigh wounds and repaired the holes in my shirt, pants, and cloak. It sank in that I would be extremely sore after my next Reverie. Depending on how things went with my captive, I might stay here another day or two.

I wonder if she knows about the tower.

It was a decent thought, though I doubted I would get any useful information sitting naked in front of her, so focused on getting myself put together again. I wanted everything righted to a point that Rausery would have been proud.

It helped my own confidence when I was ready to speak.

"Thirsty?" I asked.

The blonde Elf nodded; her face shiny with sweat. I dipped a wooden cup where she could see my every move and brought it to her. She carefully got up on an elbow to drink. Then I brought her another. Pilla squinted at me each time, stretching and pulling against the resilient magic webbing.

"Please, release Pilla," she asked, softly. "I will tell her not to attack you without provocation."

"And tell her to be quiet," I added. "Her shrieks hurt my ears. Enough noise, and I will find a way to silence her."

Her leaf-green eyes glistening. "Y-You said you could dissolve the webs?"

"Or they will wear off by next morning," I said, reconsidering how smart or stupid my offer had been. "What is your name?"

A deep pink color entered her cheeks. Was that a visible sign of strong emotion? She was at a disadvantage there.

She answered, "Tamuril lu'Marikoth."

Tamuril. The name sounded nice. Lu'Marikoth sounded like a family name, similar to Thalluenduv, the title held by my second sister, and the pale Elf had volunteered it.

"Are you second daughter?" I tested.

Her look of shock answered my question; she didn't have to speak. I smiled at the lucky guess and the familiarity, intrigued despite myself.

"Tamuril lu'Marikoth," I said. "I am Sirana."

She waited, then, as I expected: "Your family name?"

My gaze was steady. "I have none." Pointing to her falcon, I reminded her, "Tell her not to attack. I will free her to watch as you sleep."

I backed up a little, observing how she "spoke" to the animal. Mostly quiet, comforting whispers in her native tongue—sounding a little like mine, but I couldn't understand her—and light touches with her fingers while they met eyes. I didn't believe the falcon knew the Elvish tongue, but imagined the tone, touch, and a bit of magic aura worked toward what the mage wanted to convey.

I hoped it was accurate.

Pilla squashed her neck down, chest feathers puffing out, as she held still. I thought she might be pouting. She stayed quiet.

"There, she understands," Tamuril said, giving me a pleading look that made me uncomfortable.

Don't do that. Begging looks better on a bua.

"Very well," I said, standing and turning just so my cloak would obscure exactly which bottle I took, pouring a little of its contents into my gloved palm. Stoppering it and hooking it back, I took to one knee, trying not to tear my wounds further.

Tamuril watched unblinking as I "petted" her bird, rubbing scented oil over the sticky substance and making it not so anymore. I grabbed one of her rough-woven cloths because I didn't want to use mine for this, and stroked firmly in one direction, peeling most of it from the falcon's beak, feet, and feathers.

Pilla barely tolerated it; the instant she could hop up and flap noisily to a higher perch above her mistress, she did. She hunkered down for a long glare at me which I did not doubt she could maintain the entire time I was here, but at least she kept her beak shut.

99

"Acceptable?" I asked, and the pale mage offered a glance bordering on sarcasm. I kind of liked it.

"Yes," she said, despite the circumstances, "I... thank you."

She hadn't liked saying that, but her bird was free, and the next phase of this strange game began. My stomach growled loudly the moment I wondered where to go from here.

"Ah," I said, "you have food?"

"Take what you find," she murmured, uncaring, lying down upon her mats of grass. She was exhausted just from our efforts so far, and she still had glass shards in her backside.

I rummaged through the hut, finding plenty of crunchy seeds, roots, and toasted insects, likely from the previous season. The roots were raw, so I left those for later, but the seeds and bugs were cooked, and I had no trouble enjoying them as I stilled the complaints of my belly.

No red meat, I noted. *A pity.*

I craved some chewy meat and pulled out some of my own stores to satisfy it. I would have taken the pale one's instead, but if she hunted and killed for her stores, I found no sign of this today.

Yet, she has a bow and arrows. She knows how to use them.

This archer had nearly struck me, twice, in just two shots and under pressure. I figured she hadn't made a kill lately but practiced often so that she could if she had the opportunity and need.

Tamuril fell unconscious while I was eating and, as agreed, her falcon watched over her while I rested upright in her one, woodcraft chair next to the worktable. The forest Elf was good at making these; they were sturdy and somehow made without ties or nails. If the magical control I saw over vines was any indication, she had used magic to form the wood or grass in this hut, including many parts of the shelter itself.

The stone was raw, however. She hadn't magic-formed any of that like our wizards could down below, and the flint dagger I'd found was handmade and primitive. She owned but one piece of metal, and it wasn't a weapon but a cooking pot.

Magic with animals and plants.

What kind of mage was this? I didn't know an equivalent among the Davrin. Her kind must have a word for it. And if she did, what was the language that sounded a little like mine? Where were the others, and how far away? Was I in imminent danger but didn't know it yet?

These and other questions filled my head to the brim as my body rested in the dim hut. It was daylight outside, and I wasn't leaving before nightfall. I didn't know how long Tamuril would sleep, given my guardians had poisoned her near death in seconds, as they had Wilsira.

They sure worked well. *Too* well. I had already used one of only two antivenoms I had, as their first target was one that I hadn't wanted to kill, even not knowing the archer wasn't Human.

She shot at me, her vines injured and strangled me…so they did what they were made to do.

Without them, I might be dead, captured, or Tamuril could have injured me worse, our positions reversed.

Already. Not a week had passed on my own.

I opened my pouch to release my companions, my affection warming as they crawled into view on my thighs. I wished I could sense their moods better, guide them through those mental pushes that D'Shea had been certain I could do when she gave them to me. I could only judge their intent from their movements and subtle twitches, like any spider.

Pilla made ticking and churring noises in her throat, aware of the arachnid trio on my lap. Maybe she was warning them; I smiled at the thought. I wasn't experienced in reading the falcon, yet I felt I would be alright closing my eyes for a bit with my own guardians protecting me.

I woke with sound ringing my ears, and I surged to my feet with my guardians streaking up to the nape of my neck. A groan followed, I looked at the bed to realize it had been the blonde Elf's voice filling the hut. Tamuril was on her belly, one hand holding her ass and her face in perfect misery. Above her, Pilla was moving on her perch, agitated, opening and closing her wings as though she couldn't decide whether to fly or not. I exhaled the air I'd been holding.

"The shard must come out," I said.

She glared; her flushed face pressed to the mat. "Shard? What did you do?"

"Glass needle. Antidote forced into big muscle is faster than by mouth, and you could not swallow."

She blanched at being reminded. "You broke it off inside me?"

"The way it works. A trade for speed." I paused so she could absorb that. "I will pull the glass out. I have tools."

She huffed a strange laugh that sounded horrified. "No! Pilla will help."

I blinked, incredulous. "You jest! It is deep. She must tear you with beak and talon first, and those are dirty!"

She burst out, "I don't want you to touch me, Dark One!"

Ah.

Slowly, I reached into one of the smallest tool pouches and pulled out a precision pair of tiny, delicate, metal tongs. Useful for so many things. I held them up for her to see. "I can reach with less harm done."

Her jaw flexed, and her teeth remained gritted when she spoke. "In exchange for what?"

I hadn't thought about that, but if she was offering...

"We talk."

"About what?"

I weighed the risks. "Why you are here."

"I'll not say."

"I know the one who 'touched' you before," I said. "She spared you, after killing five Humans."

Tamuril clutched the pad beneath her, her eyes enormous. "She?"

I nodded. "My… sergeant."

Yes, that was the right word. Tamuril recognized it, repeated it. "Sergeant…"

Another nod. "And you are here alone after?"

She bit her lip, buried her eyes.

"If not answer why you are here," I continued, "what of why you trespass in tunnels below a few years ago?"

The pale Elf erupted into heaving sobs, taking me off guard. Her body was wracked more than Gaelan's had been leaving Natia behind in Sivaraus, although the blonde archer muffled her cries somewhat using her arm and mattress. Still, my mouth hung open watching fits so poorly controlled, especially as they grew louder.

This made no sense for a female. Was she acting this way on purpose to discourage me? If so, it was effective; she was swiftly overwhelming my ears in this small space with her wails and sobs.

I exhaled. "Enough! I will remove glass, no pay. No talk about sergeant. Just quiet, Tamuril!"

She barely changed pitch, and I thought she hadn't heard me. After a huge suck of air, however, the other Elf made effort to calm herself. I waited a little longer, meeting her red, wet gaze as she peeked above her arm.

She's acting like a dramatic child.

I frowned. "You have medicine at all? Make skin numb? Thwart festering?"

Tamuril swallowed, nodding. "Some."

"Where?"

Her green eyes flicked toward a rough wall with a small shelf. The only items on it were a few simple, wooden boxes. I went to retrieve them.

"Do not touch me," she repeated.

Fucking websucker…

"Your blood will poison," I said. "You wish to die this way?"

She shrugged. "I have no reason to live."

Moody little prick.

"Fine," I said, setting her box down, preparing for a bout of nausea. "Then before you die, speak of the death mage at the Ley Tower."

Tamuril jolted, alert. "Wh-what?"

"Sarilis, yes?"

Although I was prepared for the same, central upset that sometimes threatened me when I conversed with Rausery about the Ley Tower, that didn't come as I expected.

"Yes!" The pale Elf stared unblinking. "D-Do you go to stop him, Dark One?"

Alas, I discovered I *couldn't* answer that directly; my throat closed on the answer. So, I folded my arms, arching a brow and offering a sarcastic expression like hers a bit ago. Tamuril saw it and rephrased her words.

"He *must* be stopped, Sirana. I will talk."

No sickness. And, finally, something she wanted enough to use my name instead of "Dark One."

"Can you lead me there?"

She nodded. "It is not far."

"How far?"

"Two days."

Wisely, she didn't say which direction. I smirked. "Two days through mountains is hard travel. You need the shard out of your butt, the wound mended."

She grimaced and turned away, skin shifting a darker shade as blood rushed to her face. I was becoming fascinated by such a telltale sign of her fluctuating thoughts; she wouldn't ever stand a chance at Court with such expressive and surging color. Perhaps that is why she cried so loudly. If it can't be hidden, it might as well be used. It made me wonder about the buas among her kind, what they were like.

"You are right," she admitted. "I need your help to…remove the glass. But nothing more, or I will set Pilla to screaming all night!"

That was persuasive.

I grinned despite that she'd threatened me, or maybe because of it. "Agreed, Tamuril. Let us do it now."

There were many tense moments to prepare, as Pilla squawked her protests and I placed my spiders high on a jutting piece of slate with a crevice where a falcon couldn't reach them. Then, I retrieved the box of medicines and two bowls of hot water, a few cloths, and placed all of them on the worktable within reach.

From the box, I set out only the items she indicated I should use, and found inside a small, stout candle as well. I lit that so that I would be able to purify my own tools before digging into her. Last thing in the box, I pulled out a leather strap which already had teeth marks in it.

Huh.

"Best you lay across my thighs," I suggested.

"No, I will stand."

"Foolish. You will jerk and fall, and make it worse."

"Then I shall remain on my bed."

I shook my head. "Hurts thorn marks in my back and legs."

Oddly, she seemed shamed by that at first, though it didn't last. She refused again. "Besides, I will be lying on your wounds."

"Maybe one. This is better than crouching." I arranged myself in the chair by the table, all tools to hand. I removed my gloves, set them aside, and patted my lap. "Here. Lie here."

The blonde's tired, exotic eyes stared as if to pierce me, judging my words and action. She looked to Pilla as if for reassurance, trying to decide. The bird groused but took no action to prevent her mistress from rolling carefully onto all fours, preparing to stand. She nearly toppled over, dizziness sweeping over her with another cold sweat, and she had to crawl to me. It wasn't far.

I reached out to take her arm, helping her up to settle belly-down across my lap. It was almost amusing how clumsy we were getting the taller Elf into position, but instead of chuckling, I grimaced with the stress and pressure placed on my own injuries. Once there, I thought she might wish to undo her own leathers and pull them down for me, but between her weakness and passivity, she placed how and when in my hands.

Very well. I was kind of curious what she looked like underneath but, as with during my first time with a bua, I resolved not to make it obvious.

Reaching around in front, I tugged on the loose knot at her waist, spreading my sore thighs for access and balance. Once that was done, my bare fingers of both hands hooked the unflattering, doeskin trousers. I paused in surprise of how soft her skin was against my knuckles, but then I shook it off and tugged down, making certain the material avoided contact with the puncture wound in her left buttock.

Her anxiety heightened as she was exposed, however, and she turned her head toward me, biting her pink lip. I stared then hurriedly looked away.

I should *not* be aroused by that.

Focus.

I took my time bunching the unflattering material down, exposing her rear-end and thighs down to her knees.

"Not that low!" she squealed in protest, moving as if to stand.

I clamped an arm around her waist, pressed my free elbow into her spine. "Stay! I do not know how you may bleed, and a clear space to work is better."

She mewled an ineffective protest as I held her in place—her height meant nothing where my practice in body holds came in—and while she decided how soon to cooperate, I couldn't help admiring the shape and softness of her ass. Nor could I miss how stark the contrast was between the darkness of my hand and the whiteness of her skin in the low light of the fire.

Just as she was coming to accept the surgery's necessity once again, another color drew my eye, and I tilted my head somewhat for a better view.

Tamuril kept her thighs closed, exerting conscious effort to do so, but at this angle, I could see a hint of soft folds. Her sex was shaped like mine and, from what I could see, it was a dusky pink. The shade reminded me of the new spring blossoms on some of the trees. In that sense, this dark blush within a pale frame was welcoming the same way Rausery had said a flower's bright petals invited a bee closer to land and drink nectar.

Mmm.

I imagined Tamuril's nipples matched this color but wondered if she had mound fur that matched her golden hair. While that would imply advanced age in Davrin, it might not strike me as elderly against the pale flesh and lively blush of this Elf,

"W-well?" Tamuril stammered when I'd been still too long.

I blinked. *Whoops. The glass.*

Carefully, I placed the tips of my fingers around her wound near the top of her cheek. The shard had caused a hard, swelling knot and her flesh had closed on the glass needle. It would hurt even if I numbed the skin with her own potion; I doubted it would penetrate that far.

If Tamuril wouldn't be unconscious for this, I wished her bird might be. Pilla was clacking her beak and clenching and unclenching her taloned feet upon her perch, never taking her predator's eyes off me.

I asked, "Which bottle numbs your skin?"

Her voice was quiet. "The one with the blue cap."

"It goes muscle-deep?"

She paused. "Not deep, but below skin."

"Any healing potion for after?"

She thought about that, turning her head best she could toward the table. Blood had rushed to her face, and her cheeks were dark pink. "Powder. With the yellow leather. Lessens swelling."

I frowned. "Is that all?"

She didn't reply, and I figured she was hiding a stash she didn't want me to take. Wise.

I used what she had to cleanse and numb the wound, the candle to heat my smaller tools and burn off impurities, and finally began probing for the shard. Tamuril put the leather strap in her mouth to bite down; I listened to her breathing and soft groans while I kept my attention on my fingers and the injection site. She was doing well, better than I might have guessed, though she made more noise than a Davrin dared to down below when there was blood in the air.

When I found and got a firm hold on the shard, it was resistant to coming out, but I kept steady pressure on it. The needle was not barbed like some of our weapons and tools; if it had been, I would not be able to get it out without taking most of the flesh around it. Tamuril squirmed then forced herself to hold still, trembling in constant pain, and she whined as I slowly drew the shard out. She went slack immediately, gasping around the leather strap between her teeth.

I held the extraction up and studied it carefully. All that was missing was the tiniest tip. That miniscule amount of glass would have to be rejected by her own body as she healed—my tools were small, but not *that* small.

"Got it," I said. "Lucky, it came out whole."

"Thank God," she breathed, sounding worn and disoriented.

I almost asked her which one. "How do I fill the hole?"

"The pouch with three knots... one stained yellow. Mix powder with water into a paste and press in...as much as you can. Stops bleeding and swelling."

I did this and needed no further direction to clean the area, lay a pad over the treated wound and wrap it, even if it was awkward to put into place. I noticed the blonde's head was drooping low by the time I was finished, and Pilla threatened me with screeches and wing-blows as her mistress remained down in a light doze.

I frowned. *Damned bird.*

I might have satisfied my curiosity about the colors of the Elf's nipples had we been alone. As it was, I fidgeted some with the leathers, preparing to cover her up, but paused. On impulse, I parted her legs and took a better look while she remained bent over my lap.

I grinned to myself despite Pilla's admonishing squawks off to the side. I *did* see golden fur. Blonde curls crowned a flushed sex, gone from pink to almost red after the physical strain the forest Elf had suffered. She looked like an exotic flower. I inhaled.

Smells like one, too. No wonder Jaunda didn't share.

Abruptly, I could see myself nudging my tongue between those cheeks, and the imagined memory of a familiar black Feldeu parting her flaunted slit was cruelly vivid.

"Mmm," she moaned. "P-Pilla?"

Shit!

I snapped aware, pulling Tamuril's pants up over her haunches and careful not to disturb the wrapping. "Come, wound is clean and bandaged. Back to bed."

My own wounds and the difference in our height made this difficult as before, but soon Tamuril was back upon her mattress, lying on her side. I brought her water, considering it a good sign that she drank three cups this time.

"Hungry?" I asked.

She shook her head. "No."

The pale one soon returned to sleep. Looming above us was the falcon, and if she had been able to spit on me, she would have. I collected my own watchful guardians from the crevice and returned to my chair, breathing out. I was exhausted by this point.

The three magical spiders kept to the side of my arm and body away from Pilla as they rose toward my neck. I let them nestle in their usual place beneath my braid at the nape of my neck. The tiny little hooks on their legs held to the bandage there the same way normally they held to my skin.

"Thank you," I murmured in Davrin.

D'Shea's gifts would stay on watch as I gradually succumbed to the pull of Reverie; I trusted that they would. I'd grown attached to them in a way I hadn't expected as I took care of them, as they proved they would take care of me. They had been the deciding factor that won the fight between me and Tamuril.

Almost three turns ago, the Prime had ordered me removed from Lelinahdara's altar and set out in the wilderness to continue my trials. When I first woke to realize it, I had crushed a natural, clueless spider out of spite of Braqth. Now, I felt some regret. Not for cursing the Davrin goddess and gaining the attention of my Queen, but for killing a useful creature with no need, no plan, and no reason. Killing just for spite and frustration, or because it was small and easy, without serious consequence.

Was that how Wilsira had seen me, I wondered? Or how the Nobles at Court treated each other? It was certainly how Jilrina had viewed her littlest sister. Hadn't I always thought her, and those like her, wasteful and petty? Lacking self-control and a practical mind, their assumptions filled with hubris blinding them to the small things that would kill them.

Like a pincerworm.

When I returned to Sivaraus, would I be formed into the little spider guardian for the giant Queen against the Elder Mind? Or, if I was no longer useful without that spark of psionic talent, would I be crushed beneath Her hand? Probably. I didn't know, but at least I had my own choices while I was up on the Surface.

I could choose only deaths which were needed for me to survive, and I wasn't convinced the death of a pale cousin and a noisy bird would help me survive. It seemed a waste.

Like forbidding Red Sisters to help each other, in spite of our creed.

All of it, a waste.

CHAPTER 5

I AWOKE LONG AFTER SUNSET WITH MY STOMACH RUMBLING, the pains sharp and biting insistently at my middle. I used the pale Elf's stores which I'd prepared on the table to sate myself, further preserving my own rations. Thinking Tamuril might be hungry upon waking, I saved a small bag of her own food and stood up, intending to set it at the edge of the grass pallet. I gasped, filling my head with cursing as my back and limbs seemed set ablaze. Moving was *agony* after sitting so long in that chair!

Pilla chirped. It was an odd noise. A quiet laugh, perhaps.

Piss your throat, pest, I hand-signed, knowing she couldn't read it, and limped to place the food within the blonde's reach whenever she woke.

While I was there, I checked her pulse; her neck was moist with sweat. The falcon answered my sign with a grunt like an angry retort, but did nothing else; she blinked, watching me retreat from her mistress.

I sat down and, to my surprise, drifted toward Reverie again; there was no fighting it. Whether it was the fight, my wounds, or the demands of my changing womb, I accepted the call and fell asleep again in the Elf's wooden chair. The last sight I saw was a shaft of moonlight slipping through the blinds and touching the earthen floor.

I dreamed of an Elf.

Her skin was neither white pale nor ebony dark, but a warm, coppery brown. She rode upon a horse; it must be, as was described to me, although this one was vibrant. It had a white-blond mane decorated with turquoise beads, and its coat was a shining, sorrel red. The brilliant red hair of the Elf was tied up, woven with more of the same light blue stones.

The two charged across the red sand where all could see her, her fists balled tight in the light mane. There was no bridle or saddle, as the Elf seemed to guide the beast using other means. Her carrier fought the sand with nostrils wide, his single-toed hooves kicking up clouds of dust. The speed was incredible, even from this distance.

I stared, eventually becoming aware of the hard, smooth road beneath my boots; of a uniform and weapons which suggested a low-ranking enforcer or guard. The base color was a muted grey-brown, but there was piping in the Queen's royal purple as well as vibrant blue and gold.

"Hyah!" someone called to my right. *"Qivay!* You hungry?"

I turned my head to look at the merchant in his colorful, shaded stall. An older male Davrin stood behind a semi-permanent display of exotic foodstuffs. Smiling white teeth. Warm, garnet red eyes. He beckoned.

"Come closer. Have I not seen you around before? Have you tried Toushek's food?"

I couldn't speak; I could only stare. I was tempted, though. One foot lifted to step toward the stall, when someone loped up, panting on my left.

"I am sorry, I am late!"

I *knew* the voice.

My neck turned so fast, it was a surprise I didn't snap it. "Auslan?"

He smiled only a bit while he caught his breath. "For now."

Taking my hand, he drew me farther down the street, toward an alley between two yellow stone buildings.

"Come away, let us gain the shade."

Despite the reassuring shape of his mouth, his scarlet eyes were sorrowful, somehow much older than the rest of his face. He still had the golden streak from his right temple and flowing through his brilliant, white hair. He wore the familiar attire of a Consort; shirtless, with a pale silken wrap around his trim waist, reaching his middle thighs. His sandals accentuated the fine form of his feet, though these were decorated with polished stones of yellow, orange, and red such that I hadn't seen before.

When we left easy sight and stood in the shade between two buildings, I asked, "Where am I?"

He was apologetic. "I did not mean to disturb you."

I frowned as his gaze wandered restlessly, unable to be still.

"Curious," he muttered. "I had forgotten Toushek." Then Auslan met my eyes. "Where are you, Sirana?"

"On a Ley Line in the mountains," I said. "Resting."

"Ah."

My healer attempted a smile which I didn't buy; he had thought to say something but didn't. I saw the Elven horse rider again in my periphery and glanced out at the distant dunes and rocky canyons under the cloudless sky.

The red sands.

"Do you fear the Valsharess here?" I murmured.

"Always," he whispered.

He paused, scanning the sky and street like he was ready to run at the first big shadow. I became aware of a warm, dry breeze, unlike any I had felt before, and listened to the hush of grit being swept from hard stone. Auslan released my hand. We seemed lost, undecided what to do next.

I spoke quietly. "I have been gone from the city for almost ten spans. Does... does seeing you in Reverie mean D'Shea has kept you alive?"

Auslan turned from whatever he sought, confused. "D'Shea?"

I felt a chill. Was this my Consort? Was it an illusion wearing his skin?

It doesn't matter. I'm in Reverie.

Then I noticed something else out of place. A grey spot approaching. A storm cloud? It was too fuzzy to be sure, but it was the only mass that broke the clear line of where the sky met the land. I almost felt again the staggering grip of my Queen's hand on my hair.

"Look! Do you see this! Do you?"

"They may know we are here before long," said my Consort solemnly, following my gaze and calming down at last; only the hot wind tousled his long hair. "They reach out the same as we are, testing the boundary. Do not fear them, Sirana. They belong as we do."

"Who are they?" I asked.

"The youngest able to cross over."

I squinted. "What?"

Auslan smiled slowly and wider than before, though his eyes were still sad. "Find the crossroads, Sirana. I shall remain here."

Tamuril was awake when I arose from Reverie, something I didn't care for at all. She was upright, favoring her sore side, huddled on her nest with her back against the wall. She nibbled tiny amounts of her stores which I'd left for her. The Sun was up, Pilla was gone, and my spiders remained on guard at the nape of my neck. Outside, numerous birds sought their daily claim of territory with boisterous whistling and chirping.

Did I sleep so long? Did I make any noise?

When I tried to move, my breath hitched, and soreness assailed my entire body. The pale Elf was wary as I slowly stood up out of my chair and stretched gingerly. The holes in my skin would need cleaning and redressing again. I slipped another foul-tasting pellet beneath my tongue. Just in case.

"That necklace beneath your armor, what is it?" the blonde Elf asked.

I barely heard her over the morning noise. "Blue gem."

"I know that," she replied. "Is it a gift?"

I made a wry face. "Why ask?"

"Everything on you has a use," she murmured, green eyes sliding away. "Your ring is magic, and many things on your belt. That blue stone is not."

She can tell? Uh-oh.

"You would not carry useless weight on a long journey," she finished.

I grinned, partly because I didn't know if she was right or wrong. I shrugged. "The weight is slight."

Goddess, her face. I enjoyed her annoyance too much.

"Meaning you will not answer?"

"Meaning it is mine. What more do you need to know?"

She didn't reply, and I noticed how she had sweated through the night, her golden hair darkened and strands sticking around her temples and brow. I retrieved another cup of water so she wouldn't try to get it herself. Although she was surprised, Tamuril took it and drank. It gave her strength to ask me.

"Is the metal meant to be a newborn Moon, and the blue stone, the rest of the Moon in shadow?"

I was careful about looking down at a necklace I couldn't see, anyway. Instead, I fished for the cord to lift the pendant up to my face. I had once thought it to be a sickle or just some pretty design cradling the saphgar stone. It wasn't until my first night on the Surface beneath the Moons that I had wondered about Shyntre's inspiration for its design.

Was it so clear to this pale Elf what it was? Would it be so to anyone else?

"We see what we wish to see." I tucked the pendant out of sight.

Reluctantly, Tamuril let it go. "You said... perhaps two days to rest here? Then you will go to the fortress."

I began to nod then stopped. "Wait. Fortress? No, a tower."

The pale one blinked and then a giggle slipped out of her. She looked as surprised as I was by the sound; she blushed, again.

"The tower is attached to an underground fortress," she said. "There is much you can't see from the outside."

Of course, there was.

Sighing, I stirred up the fire and put some water on to heat; later, it would be divided between boiled roots and washing sticky wounds, faces, and crotches. We had some time.

"You say Sarilis must 'stop'," I prompted. "Talk of this."

"Tell me you intend to stop him."

I looked away in bodily discomfort. "I know not from what?"

"He lures men of magic there, using the Ley," she said. "To murder them and force their bodies to serve him after death!"

I agreed that was grotesque. About what Rausery had told me to expect from this death mage, as he had been doing it in his young years, too. "You know how many bodies serve?"

Tamuril was surprised by a practical question and took time to answer. She was counting in her head, implying she had spied on this tower before.

"Twelve," she said. "Outside. I know not how many he has inside. I have never looked in while he lives there."

I arched my brow. "But you know there is a 'fortress' there, and... you imply you have been inside *before* he lived here?"

Tamuril didn't try to lie. Her face changing to angry and miserable in a heartbeat. "I know you Dark Ones helped him win it when the intersection festered with warp rot. Why does only one of you come now? That is not enough to claim it from him. Are you a scout? Do others follow?"

"Is it the same with you?" I retorted. "You are a scout? Do others follow?"

I was struck by her reaction. That astonished grief was real, as were the returning tears.

No others. But for her falcon, she is alone. No one will come to help her.

Such as it was with me. I knew what I had done to be here. What about her?

"Why do you seek the Ley Tower?" she asked stubbornly.

"You must trade me same value," I replied irritably, checking the fire and the warming water, collecting some roots to peel and quarter with my shortest blade. "Why did you seek the underground with Humans?"

Dramatically, she put her hands to her head before lowering it toward her lap, keening softly, rocking slightly. I didn't know what it was supposed to mean.

We spoke no more until the water was hot and steaming. I poured part of it in another vessel for washing and left the rest, adding to it some uncooked roots from the stores. Again, I stripped down to clean, anoint, and rewrap my wounds; again, Tamuril watched me. This time she did not protest my stark nudity. As I studied my body, she spoke what I was thinking.

"You heal fast."

I glanced at her. Not usually *this* fast.

An untended puncture wound would be hot and puffy the next day; within a few days, it would leak pus and I would have a fever. A cleansed and tended one might do the same but to a lesser degree.

If the flesh didn't rot or the blood poison, in time the wound would close and scab over. Mine looked as though they had skipped the painful swelling and leaking stage and were scabbing over already. It would not take much to rip them open again if I was careless, but only one day and night of rest and I was this far along?

A different sort of healing potion. Shyntre is good at this.

He was good at a lot of things.

"Were you eating a fungus?" she asked, pointing at her tongue. "The little brown thing."

Well. I hadn't been secretive. "I don't know. I didn't make it."

"May I smell one?"

I chuckled at the mental image. "No. Why would you want to?"

She only hesitated a moment as green eyes shone wetly. "You may carry what I… was searching for, down below. To heal a… child's chest before he drowned in infection."

My smile lowered. It didn't take much to jump the rest of the way, that she didn't find it before being attacked and thrown out.

"He died?" I asked.

She nodded before collapsing into her pallet in another fit of sobs. Pilla arrived soon after she started, squeezing through the blind and gliding to her, fussing as only a hen like her could fuss. While the pale one cuddled her companion, I placed my palms on the table and took a steadying breath, contemplating my clean scabs and the fact that she had given me what I'd asked for. Though only a little, not a lot. I dressed while thinking it over.

Who was the child? Where? Why was he sick, and why would she care enough to venture so far down…again, alongside *Humans*?

Why is she alone? No other pale Elves, and not even any short-lived Humans.

"I am a scout," I said, loud and clear, waiting until her bawling had lessened and she tilted one pointed ear toward me. "Though, none follow close behind. I am to spy and return with knowledge."

Tamuril lifted her head as though it weighed a boulder. "And then?"

I shrugged. "Depends on the knowledge."

She remained propped on her elbows, Pilla nesting in front of her belly to sit, watch, and listen. The foreign Elf took a deep breath. "Are you... *forbidden* from killing Sarilis?"

"No, I am not forbidden that," I answered, surprising myself.

Green eyes blinked at me, considering, and she decided to believe me.

I checked on the cooking roots, piercing them to test doneness. "What stories do you know of the Ley Tower, Tamuril? How long is your memory of it?"

The pale blonde chewed her pink lip, reluctant to divulge what she knew. I exhaled, watching her wince as she shifted too close to her own stab wound.

"You may sniff one pellet," I offered. "You might place it under your tongue, to aid in your healing, if you tell me all you know of this fortress." I watched her face, adding, "These have high value to me, I do not offer lightly. And I would kill a thief trying to take them."

Tamuril swallowed. After further thought, she accepted the bargain at last. Not only did she ingest it to assure me that she wouldn't fall down a mountainside in delirium, but she confirmed what it was.

"It is not pure," she said, staring at the ground as all her concentration lay upon the bitter ball dissolving in her mouth. "But... within *is* the mushroom I sought to heal a Human child."

"Which one?"

She blinked and looked up. "*Jeneth'te.*"

I raised one side of my mouth at the similarity. "We call it *Genethsa*. And we've long known it is good for certain fevers and colored growths."

"This is more potent than the mushroom alone," the mage said with conviction. "If only you knew how they are made, Sirana, you could save many lives up here from too-early deaths."

I laughed at such a grand blanket of a statement. *Why would I want that?*

"We have some time," I said, glancing at the strength of the Sun outside the dim hut. "After two added days of rest, both of us will be ready for travel. Tell me your memory of the Ley Tower, Tamuril, before Sarilis. And then, you can show it to me."

Slowly, over the next two days hobbling in and around the hut, I pieced together the fact that Tamuril was older than me by at least two centuries. She didn't look it, in my opinion, nor did she much act like an elder that age. Volatile moments of tears and upset could come as quickly as in an infant, and I utterly failed to imagine her acting first to kill or torment another sentient.

"What sort of mage are you?" I asked.

"*Guded*," she answered in her native tongue.

I shook my head in the negative. "Have you a translation in Trade?"

Tamuril thought it over. "Druid, perhaps. I seek to understand balance in wilderness. The call of my magic lies within its foundation."

I smirked, noting the new word. "Wilderness, hm. Not fond of cities."

She shook her head. "No, not at all."

"You have been..." I sought the word. "Guardian for this wilderness for many years. Have you counted?"

Her golden eyebrows drew down in concern. "Not each one. Enough for... four generations of men?"

I made a face. "I do not know how long this is."

"Humans mature to breed in twenty years," she explained. "In shortest, eighty years for four generations. Sometimes longer if fathers wait longer to have children. I can be sure enough of one hundred years I have been Druid here."

She had been here since I had drawn my first breath. Sobering.

I leaned against the table, showing my skepticism as her description of counting Humans breeding sank in. "What of women? These bear the children, yes? The men help quicken them, but she decides when."

Tamuril blinked and seemed confused before looking away, visibly withdrawing. "Oh. Yes, the same count, men or women. Twenty years."

I frowned. Except they *weren't* the same.

"Easier to count generations through mothers," I pushed. "*Buas* flit around and may quicken another belly while she must wait years to birth a child. He is on the side, less important. *matas* do all the work, make each day choices. Children count for *her*, not him."

Tamuril's eyes were wide; her expression bordered on horror. "N-no, you… don't understand. Fathers know their children, too."

I shook my head. "Not always. Again, mother decides."

She gasped, shaking her head.

I stared. *You don't agree? How can you not?*

Her reaction was so foreign, I quickly turned away to get a grasp on my own. I was… surprised how abrupt, how insulting it felt for another female to imply counting *my* baby's birth as *Auslan's* accomplishment? It made no sense. Even my Consort would agree with me.

All he did was spurt in my channel while I was wounded. If I had taken D'Shea's vial before I left, his actions would mean nothing.

I breathed slow, in and out, moving on with the simpler truth. If this Davrin in my gut was ever to be born, it would be because of me. That birth wasn't assured, however. I had many, many choices to make before that time came.

"Never mind," I groused, flipping my hand and turning to face her. "You tell me, you have observed a century around this tower, and Sarilis is only there for twenty years. You do not want him here."

"C-correct," she said.

"Why have you not killed him with your bow? Or your thornvines?"

I witnessed yet *more* tears, but at least she kept them quiet as she looked around her hovel. "I am afraid. Coward if I fail. Coward if I succeed. I have never... slain a Human before."

I narrowed my eyes. "You meant to slay *me*."

She sniffed; her lower lip quivered. "I-I regret it. I... I did not *want* to kill you, Sirana, only scare you away. When you charged me instead, I lost myself. I am *not* a kinslayer. I am glad you stopped me."

I scowled at the table and that puzzling statement. Every cait, mata, and Matron I knew down below was a "kinslayer"—or would be, if pushed. That was expected, part of the fundamental will to live, and Tamuril was clearly the same as us, though she wanted to deny it. This might make sense if cautionary stories were told about the Dark Ones among her kind or, perhaps, she claims it solely by comparison to my Lead Jaunda's unapologetic joy in intimidating others.

We have no tales of warning about 'Pale Ones' in Sivaraus. As Rausery says, the Valsharess keeps us isolated. What we learn up here is kept locked in the libraries.

Yet I'd seen an Elf which was neither pale nor dark the other night; a brown-skinned horse rider surrounded by Davrin in the dream of the red sands. Where had that come from?

I shook my head. "Do not regret it, Tamuril. You wanted to live. I understand this, and I know your fear of my sergeant. My holding on to your attack is like seeking vengeance with a ground chit that bit me after grabbing its tail."

Tamuril lifted her chin, watching me as if my words did not fit my voice. Then the blonde nodded acceptance with surprisingly little insult to suggest she was no more than a rodent to me. She made a weak motion toward my spiders on my nape, eyes large and pitiful. "You could have let me die of their bite. It was no accident that I survived. You made great effort to save my life."

I smiled, letting her think I had greater control over my guardians than I did. "I did not start the fight, only sought to end it. I still need information, Druid."

Her cheeks remained blossom pink for a long time as we talked about the tower in the middle of nowhere. Her story went that it was built by Dwarves a long time before she entered this area, though *why* she came here, she stubbornly wouldn't say. Although in excellent condition, the mountain fortress was abruptly abandoned by those same builders.

"Possibly because the Ley Lines shifted," she said. "First one flowing west to east, and then another north to south, intersecting at the tower. It is a rare and unsettling change, invisible to most, yet few among the young races could tolerate such a place."

I was frowning. "But it would be of interest to mages of all kinds."

"Yes. Several have wandered in before being frightened away."

"By whom?" I smiled. "You?"

The Druid frowned and refused to answer. "Only Sarilis with aid from *your* kind succeeded in claiming it. He has been there two decades, and I fear his plans for the magic he can enhance, if he wishes."

I had nothing to say, although the Druid seemed to expect something. I gave her a questioning look.

"Impossible that it was *not* deliberate," she blurted, incredulous. "Your superiors put him there!"

Rausery hadn't been explicit whether her alliance with the death mage against the warp rot was the Valsharess's desire or not. I assumed so but perhaps the goal had been to cleanse the area at any cost, and my Elder let him stay because she didn't know the rareness of the site and thought to trade with him later.

My Elder had also said someone else had been watching them, and she didn't believe all Sarilis had claimed of how he found the place.

I shrugged. "I am not a mage. This is new to me."

"You *must* have been told something, 'scout,'" she said. "How would you know what knowledge to bring back?"

She had a point.

I sat in her chair, healing, eating up her food, dredging up anything I could say about the tower and what I sought. I prepared myself. "Some of our blood have gone missing."

Tamuril sat up straighter. "When?"

I refused that with a shake of my head. "Have you heard anything?"

"Not for a century."

"But you did hear?"

Her mouth dropped open. "You cannot only be thinking to search *now*."

My mouth twisted in amusement. "No. They're long lost. You know something from then?"

The pale Elf looked away. "I... saw a Dark One near the Ley Tower with a... beast guarding her. But I was afraid and I ran. They were gone when I dared come near again, I do not know where they went."

I nodded. "What of... the Hells? Or half-bloods."

It was reassuring for completing my mission, that I could mention these away from my Sisters. Even though my tongue couldn't begin to form the context in which I'd heard them.

Tamuril looked worried. "Do you search for devils?" She swallowed. "Who do you worship?"

Nobody I'm not drugged into worshipping.

The Druid could see my expression, and her eyes widened.

"No one," I said.

Abruptly, my heart began pounding in my chest.

"How can that be?" she asked. "Niraj needs our reverence."

Ugh. I rubbed my eyes. "Never heard of her."

"Niraj!" she repeated, showing her palms. "The great expanse you call home! The very land beneath your feet and the water you drink!"

The Druid sounded like a scolding Mother to an ungrateful Daughter. Somehow, it made me smile.

"Ah, I see. Your pardon, *Guded*, I have not heard that name before, but I am not *ungrateful* to be alive. I have fought for many chances to draw breath down below."

The following silence was awkward, and she turned it back to my question.

"The Hells," she said, tilting her head with narrowed eyes. "Why did you ask? You sound like you do not know what it is."

"Correct," I granted.

Tamuril blinked at me, astonished.

I huffed. "You *could* just inform me than judge my failed education, Druid."

Like Shyntre, Tamuril swiftly proved her learning was greater than mine in that respect.

"I've heard it told the Dark Elves worship the Spider Queen," she said. "Of the Abyss. The Void and its demons. Is this true?"

Fuck my shit. And I didn't know the first thing she worshipped, except something about "His love."

I opted to confirm. "Some of us do. Their power is greater for it."

"But not you?"

My lips twisted in her direction. "I hate clerics."

Tamuril jerked in alarm on her bed and swallowed. "Ah. A-and the Hells? You know nothing of devils?"

I shook my head.

"But you were sent by someone to listen for them at the Ley Tower?"

Goddess damn it. I shrugged. "Knowledge is power. Matrons are jealous of it."

She paused. "Were you sent by Clerics of the Abyss?"

Only the highest one. "And if I was?"

"Th-they are natural enemies," said the Druid. "The Abyss and the Hells. They fight over our attention, yearn for our magic and essence, with no care for us in the middle except for what we can give them, whether we are forced or tricked."

That sounded about right, for as long as I'd been alive. Yet, it was only her saying it that way which made me question a "wilderness mage" discussing worship and opposing ideals. That was the realm of a clerical, scholarly, or governance mind—all city-based stuff. Maybe she just listened to them at home before she left, wherever that was.

"Have you seen sign of these?" I asked again. "The Hells or any with 'Dark One' blood?"

Tamuril swallowed again. "No. I haven't."

"Not in a century of wandering these mountains?"

She shook her head. "Not since the first arrived and vanished."

I thought there was something she chose *not* to say, but her answer was true enough. I grunted, lacking the context to guess where we might go from here. By the end of the day, we had shelved divine and worldly discussions. There were smaller, practical concerns before us, and we could each move with care to contribute to them.

We focused on preparation and regaining our strength from our first meeting, so we could continue the next day.

Tamuril and I set out on foot toward the sunrise. The Druid was weaker than I was and so set the pace. Her long, slow stride was sustainable for her and comfortable for me. Pilla flew above us, keeping watch and scouting ahead, periodically coming to squawk at her Druid before flying off again. She never went far as I walked beside her mistress.

I could still feel the whine at the back of my head which told me we had not deviated far from the Ley Line, and every time the landscape forced us to go another direction, the Druid always took us unerringly to it. The first three times, I expected her to keep moving away in the wrong direction, but after the fourth, accepted that her intentions were truthful to take me there.

The blonde Elf looked down at me periodically as we hiked through the forest. I smiled back, tilting my chin up. I was aware of our difference in frames; the Surface had more food, no ceiling, and didn't require as much crawling, so of course the Elves would be taller. I said nothing, though, letting her choose the first word.

"It's strange," she said. "I remember your sergeant being so much larger than me. But that cannot be, looking at you."

I lifted a brow. "She is taller than me, but shorter than you. Broader than either of us, knows how to use her strength. She could toss a wolf, if needed."

By contrast, this Druid was reedy, even possessing her female curves. I had seen lounging Nobles at Court adopt such a shape, but Tamuril was quite active in the forest. It was a different kind of thin, all lean muscle and flexibility. She had endurance and reflex, if not raw power.

"Such aggression," she murmured. "And you insist your sergeant is female?"

I turned my head and smiled at a memory. "I've sucked her folds. They're real."

She flinched, although I wasn't sure if it was the crude image I'd suggested or the reveal that Jaunda wasn't born a bua with a large cock.

"How...? She had a..." stammered the blonde. "Wh-what did she...u-use on me?"

I weighed relieving her of that confusion and had to acknowledge I was halfway there already.

I shrugged. "Magic tool. Attaches to crotch for... different pleasure."

Tamuril's mouth hung open, her green eyes wide. "Y-Your kind *makes* those? To use for punishment and torture?"

"And bonding," I added. "Variety. No buas needed. We are sisters."

The Druid pulled away from me. "*Augh!* That's unnatural! You're all females *mounting* each other?! I-I can't imagine what else happens down there if that is encouraged!"

Insult scalded my core, and I barked, "Better for *you* that my sergeant chose *not* to take prisoners! You would not have to imagine, Druid, because it would be real *now*. The clerics are much worse than the sisters."

Her revulsion was raw and genuine, as was her terror at what I'd said. We stopped in our tracks, staring at a somewhat clearer vision of those who had shared a hovel to heal the last few days. I could hear both our heartbeats, then Tamuril stumbled to find a place to sit. Pilla darted right in from the branches to puff up, glaring at me in threat. Our progress toward the tower halted as the upheaval took time to pass, and Tamuril struggled with new sobbing.

I shouldn't have said anything. Nothing about nethers, folds, or Feldeus *or* Sisters. Perhaps I should have tried to pass Jaunda off as male, though the idea made me want to laugh. As Rausery said, if I can't have the lie, then I should keep the mystery. I did not know what else to say.

I took the moment to sit as well, and when the Druid glanced up, she seemed surprised to see me present.

"She might have taken me… below?" she squeaked. "Forever?"

"Sergeant was…" I searched for the word. "Berated by superiors for releasing you. She told me why she did. She does not regret."

Tamuril didn't blink until I spoke again. I licked my lips.

"Sergeant had choice after defeating you. She said you would wilt without plants, without Sun. I see she is right. She did not want the Spider Queen to have you. Like me, she is not loyal to spider clerics, but to sisters. She wanted to scare you away."

The pale one took that in slowly, reluctant to believe it at once and yet knew this was not the worst I could have told her.

"Your guardians," Tamuril murmured. "Are they not made by your clerics?"

I shook my head. "Made by elder mage, and sister."

She accepted that with a nod. "And… your pendant? It matches your eyes. Like it was made for you."

The Druid was trying to piece me together after I had shattered her illusion. For some reason, that necklace being a gift was a detail she wouldn't relinquish. What was the harm in granting that?

"Yes, it was. Made by a *bua* who works with gems. Frustrating male, but smart and tempting."

Tamuril smiled a little. "You earned it as a gift from him?"

I bit the inside of my cheek, but my dry smirk spread anyway. "In a game, yes."

"Game? Who won?"

"Good question," I chuckled, shrugging.

She blinked, and then she smiled as Pilla squawked the time of day to us. We agreed with the falcon by getting to our feet.

At night, we bedded down on opposite sides in a cave, and although I heard her suffering a dream as I came out of Reverie, I could also say she seemed stronger the next morning. Whatever way she viewed me was tolerable, and it was the same for me of her.

Rather far into the second day, I noticed the foliage changing again, seeming stunted and less robust, as if the soil was of poor quality. The evergreens were denser, their spice making me wonder if their berries might distill an interesting spirit. Leafy trees were here but scraggly, and the shrubs were woody and twisted, the grasses tougher, with less moss and mushrooms overall.

There were a few concentrated patches of toadstools that seemed odd to me, though. The soil was black and little else grew around it. I had barely raised my arm to point them out when Tamuril answered.

"Spoiled ground," she said. "The death mage's doing. Tomorrow we should see the tower."

"And after?" I asked. "Will you return to your hovel?"

"You expect me to leave?" She shook her head. "No. I will observe what you do."

I cocked an eyebrow. "And if you see something you don't approve?"

The Druid frowned. "I will observe what you do."

Hmph.

I was falling in deep, here. She was an Elf who had been in this area for a hundred years. She seemed alone in many ways, but she must have others she would tell about me. Otherwise, as not-a-kinslayer, what good would her observance be? Curious that she *did* consider us kin, even if "fallen" and terrifying.

"Who are the Humans you observe?" I asked, and her jolt of surprise gave her away.

"Wh-what?"

"A child was sick, so you trespassed to find a fungus to cure him. Who told you about *Genethsa*? I have not seen it up here. Which village sent men with you? Were they related to the boy? I heard reports you wore a disguise. They thought you were a woman, not an Elf."

I watched her face carefully. She was properly stunned, and worse at lying than I was.

"Oh, God," she murmured, a quivering hand hovered above her mouth.

"In exchange for my tale of my sisters and your insult to them," I insisted. "Speak! How do you know men to help you?"

Again, our progress toward the tower halted; I kept insisting. In time, I received an explanation.

"It is a mountain village where the boy once lived," she said. "One I have watched for generations. I care for their welfare. B-But the men your sisters killed were, thankfully, not of his village. They were mercenaries."

"Hired swords," I asked, knowing I sounded eager. "Where did you find them?"

"I didn't. My sister did. She prefers cities." Tamuril swallowed. "She also told me about *Genethsa* being in the tunnels, which she learned from someone else."

I tilted my head. "Someone who knows about the tunnel underground. That it is your nearest source in these mountains, if it even grows upon the Surface."

"It *does* grow here," Tamuril said, "but only in the warmest seasons. It was the wrong time."

"You asked a city-sister for help, and she gave you mercenaries," I surmised, smiling as part of this Druid at last felt familiar to me. "How often do you meet to share reports?"

The blonde glowered, tightening her lips.

I shrugged. "Which city does she prefer?"

Silence.

"Manalar?"

Tamuril recognized it, but the livid disbelief in her leaf-green eyes made me think it wasn't likely. I only had two current names to work with, and I eliminated one; the same one Jael is heading to. Not a friendly place for Elves.

I kept the other city back and dropped our discussion.

For now.

The land became greyer as it remained cloudy and I noted increasing bare rock and soil. Vegetation existed, and some of the trees were bigger than they had been three crests ago, though they were darker in color so as to appear black-trunked beneath the shade of their limbs. The area grew quieter. I heard fewer songbirds and saw almost none of the tree rodents to which I'd become accustomed.

Tamuril moved carefully, on alert, and I followed her lead as we stopped our chatter to keep focus on our surroundings. To my relief, Pilla ceased any screeching or fluttering, landing on the Druid's leather bracer before hopping onto an equally protected shoulder pad I'd been eyeballing. Now it made sense as part of her outfit.

Just past midday, we lay low to the ground to peek over one last rise, our hoods up to cover our bright hair, and I saw the Ley Tower at last. The same high-pitched whine seeped into my head constantly, and I could peg the source as the stone structure jutting out of the side of a mountain. The stout architecture appeared in excellent shape, at least from a distance, yet there was a sense of age to the thing. The natural and finished rock melded together in appearance, and it was easy to imagine a "fortress" hidden beneath the mountain as Tamuril claimed.

There was only one poorly maintained road leading to a high, wooden double-gate, a smaller courtyard fenced off by a high defense wall. While the mountains continued behind the Tower and rose up again, the road was far below, dead center of a wider valley that had once allowed agriculture and separate structures outside the gated courtyard.

"If Dwarves are squat up here but they built this," I muttered, "why is the gate so tall?"

Tamuril glanced at me. "Better for impressing or defending against the taller races?"

"How many of those taller races are there?"

"Well." A shrug. "Just Humans."

"And Elves?" I nudged. "You mentioned a sister."

The Druid swallowed. "No… no Elves visit here, except me."

"Where is your family, du'Marikoth? Your people and cities?"

She tensed, her tone like iron. "Far from here, Dark One."

"Heh."

I studied the gate and structure, deciding that it wasn't unusual, especially if there was no ceiling restricting their build. The Palace gates down below were similarly "larger than necessary." The top of the tower seemed, from here, to have a lookout which could potentially see over my head even where I was.

"Any closer," Tamuril said, "and walking dead sentries may sense you, and warn Sarilis somewhere inside."

Walking dead. I suppressed a shudder to imagine coming upon them unaware, scanning the valley for sign of such a thing. If they were here, they were hidden and not standing in the open.

"He uses animals to guard for him, as well as men," she added.

I made a face. *Keeps getting better and better.*

"So, bird sentries," I suggested, glancing at the falcon nestled beside her. "Like your Pilla?"

Her face saddened. "I have seen those, yes, and wolf or deer. They do not last long. The flesh and bone…deteriorate. He churns through animal corpses as he traps them. I am glad fewer creatures wander through here after two decades."

I smirked, finding a morbid humor in that. "Indeed, he should be less wasteful of his bodies and preserve them longer somehow. Respect their service, and he might not scare all candidates away."

Tamuril flicked an annoyed look at me, and I grinned. Then another thought struck.

"If you have observed them rotting quickly, then is it possible he has not mastered the Ley Lines as a source of magical enhancement?"

She considered that, seeming troubled. "I would not underestimate him on that basis, Sirana. He is cruel and greedy, and he draws the same to him in the men he murders."

If that was true, I wondered why Tamuril was concerned for Sarilis's habits, if she judged his victims so? Probably to do with not wanting the death mage to have unfettered access to a Ley Line intersection, even for a brief time. But Sarilis would die soon.

Wonder if he still talks a lot?

He had once, according to Rausery, who had said I had better chances of getting Surfacers to talk to me by virtue of a "normal" eye color up here. That seemed plausible just for how things had been going with Tamuril, despite her fear. Would she have talked much less if I'd had Jael's copper-red eyes? They would be distracting in a bad way, if Humans and Dwarves found red eyes to be threatening.

Why is that? I once found Lelinahdara's green eyes threatening.

Far less so in the Druid, of course.

"What now?" Tamuril asked. "You don't seem worried as you should be."

True, I was feeling oddly curious, a little excited though I'd been warned of the danger. Perhaps the months of isolated wilderness finally grew tiresome to me, being without my Sisters and finding a strange balance with an exotic, blonde Elf, whose baffling nature I had only scratched the surface.

"So," I said, "you said you plan to stay out here and observe what I do?"

Tamuril blinked. "What *will* you do, walk across the valley and up to the main gate to hail him?"

I smiled. "Would that work?"

She thought for an instant I might be serious then her nose scrunched, and she shook her head. I shifted my body backward, preparing to stand.

"Where are you going?"

135

"Have to water some plants," I said. "And I'm hungry. Going to take care of those while I think."

What now? It was a good question.

What would I do to approach an entrenched death mage in a tower?

What *could* I do?

We laid low with my spiders and watched the apparent emptiness of the area around the Tower for the rest of the day. The afternoon wore late into evening, and I took advantage of a sure shot to down a rabbit for a fresh meal.

"Wait," Tamuril said, approaching with Pilla on her shoulder. "Allow me…"

"To what?" I sounded annoyed as I removed the crossbow bolt. I wanted to skin and clean the meat and just eat it, since a cookfire wasn't an option with the tower in view.

"I will check it for corruption," said the Druid. "Regardless, we should thank the creature for its life and flesh."

The first sounded like a good idea; I hadn't considered that possibility. The second… I bit my cheek and refrained from commenting for the sake of staying healthy. I observed Tamuril perform a spell or ritual on her knees, her eyes closed, holding the rabbit's body in pale hands, gentle and reverent. It didn't look out of place for a mage though unfamiliar to me. Pilla was silent but watching with intense interest.

Don't you dare, bird.

I waited on my feet, arms crossed, and Tamuril nodded, her eyes briefly luminous in the dimming light.

"The meat is good," she said, "and I have thanked the rabbit for you."

I grinned at that, glancing at the falcon. "Want a leg for her, as payment?"

She looked as hopeful as her companion. "If... if you're offering?"

"Mages get something for using their skills where I am from," I said. "You want some?"

"Ah, no, thank you," she said. "Just Pilla, if you will share."

Her willingness to feed the same rabbit to the hungry falcon was proof the Druid was telling the truth. I followed through on the trade, chewing raw meat as I watched Tamuril feed it to Pilla in pieces from her hand. A bonding ritual, perhaps, as it wasn't strictly necessary.

"What sign or effect is there for corrupted flesh?" I asked.

"Illness, mostly," she said. "It may not be visible on the outside but is harmful when swallowed."

"Poison? Like eating spoiled meat?"

"Or infested with spores that rupture living flesh as well as dead."

Ew. I would have to be careful what I ate around here.

I was well-fed as I contemplated various approaches for reconnaissance that I might undertake at nightfall, discarding some, setting others aside as a contingency. Loitering outside the tower amid moving corpses seemed a waste of time if Sarilis was alone. Rausery's advice of observing a group before approaching didn't seem relevant here.

I wanted to get inside, and I leaned toward getting close enough to use a message pellet—which was walking up and hailing him, as the Druid taunted. I knew the death mage's name, though, so it might work; he might hear me. If I could put Rausery's name in his ear, he might see me willingly, invite me in. But, if that worked, if he was willing to talk, I also needed a way out. Those were two separate problems.

"What is the death mage's weakness?" I asked Tamuril.

The blonde tilted her head in thought, eyes drawn from where they'd been staring. "Were you told nothing before being sent here?"

"I never said that. I want your opinion. To compare."

She gave it some thought. "He is elderly, his body is weak. His advantage is having time to prepare defenses in his servants and traps, but other magic can easily disrupt them, and he would not be quick to raise more. A weapon can kill his body like any man."

"Your magic disrupts his servants?" I guessed, and she nodded.

I didn't have anything like that.

"If I could get us inside, would you make him vulnerable so I can get to him? Or help get us out if we fail?"

Raw fear clawed at her face. "No. I will not go inside."

"You want me to 'stop' him, do you not?" I reminded her.

Tears in her eyes.

"I owe you nothing. My body has been tortured enough by your kind. I will not risk a worse fate for you, though I wish you success."

Pilla punctuated that with a stubborn squawk of her own.

Silently, I sighed and returned to studying possible paths for approach. Barely a hour before full dark, something moved far below in the valley.

"Druid," I murmured. "Come here. Look."

She did. "Oh…"

There was a beast drawing a cart along the road down the valley, a dark spot just within my sight and still far from the Tower. The cart would reach the place just ahead of darkness, by my best estimate, and the area where the Druid claimed there were sentries in a third of that.

"*Is* Sarilis alone?" I thought to ask, the urgent feeling that I had to move coming upon me.

"I…I don't know," she admitted. "I have seen men come here but do not watch every day."

"Have you seen that cart and horse before?"

She paused, both her and her falcon focused on it. "I... believe so. Yes."

Good enough.

I started moving, taking the slope at an angle.

"Sirana!" Tamuril gasped, afraid to be too loud.

"Stay here and observe, Druid. It was your wish."

I had to leave her behind, stop thinking about her, as I edged down the mountain and into the valley as quickly and quietly as possible. If I was not to intercept the lone cart, then I would take a closer look. I kept every sense wide open, catching subtle whiffs of death and decay on the air but had yet to encounter any sentries. I loosened the ties on my spiders' pouch, just in case.

I reached the low foothills with about half the remaining daylight left. I smelled cold moisture in the taller grass before me, waterlogged soil, and the chirps of night insects. The road was on high ground, on the other side of this boggy slough. Testing it with my boot toe, I found it soft, enough to leave clear footprints if not sinking my boots. Not acceptable. I had to go around if I could.

I saw a ridge dotted with the dark-trunk trees farther down the valley, away from the cart and the Tower. It would do as a bridge, but I had to pace myself if I would catch up to the traveler without wheezing when I spoke. I used the trees and shadow and firm ground, silent, without hurry but wasting no time. When I was most of the way across and approaching the road, I heard the gallop of a four-legged animal heading my way.

Shit!

I dropped low in the brush, watching as a brown horse and its rider came into view, seeming to be catching up with the cart as well.

Two, now. Damn.

The rider was a man with a short beard, dressed similarly to Tamuril, with tough leathers and several tools of a woodsman, including a bow. I glimpsed a small ax and dagger as well. He was broad shouldered, muscular, and looked as tall as the pale Elf, but his mass was greater by far. His eyes were small, his nose big, and his ears round. His hair was darker than his beard, though both were brown and decently kept, though mussed. I caught his oily, pungent scent and that of his horse as he rode by without seeing me. Both were distinctive; I would recognize them in an instant. The overall image was almost exactly what I'd been told to expect, down to the dirty fingernails.

"Apprentice!" the man shouted ahead of him in Trade, though with an odd accent. "Hold up!"

His voice echoed off the valley walls, and I winced at the noise. At least this told me that the man felt safe in this valley; he had been invited and was not on attack.

I followed as it quickly grew dark. The cart had stopped eventually at the call; I heard the crunch of the wheels cease as hooves pounded and pawed at this wide, rough, and pitted dirt path they called a road. Voices murmured though I was too far away to hear. I paid close attention to the body language as I could read it.

The rider made one broad, open gesture with a muscular arm, leaving his torso exposed to the other as he made some comment to the man in the cart. The rider did not fear driver, and indeed, I could guess why. The robed and hooded figure sitting in the cart was hunched over, back bowed, and if there was eye contact, it was with the apprentice peering up from beneath eyebrows. Had he been sitting straight, I thought, the two would have been equal eye level.

The exchange was quick; the first acquiesced to the other man riding beside him, though the tension in his frame implied he was wary without saying so aloud. The rider did not acknowledge this, if he noticed.

There was a decent row of trees and shrubs in a ditch on the far side of the road from where I had approached. The ground was moist, but I found enough firm spots to move without sound; gradually, I caught up to them. Neither had noticed me yet, and when I was close enough to overhear their conversation while pacing them, I could not believe they sensed nothing. Any Davrin would know she was being watched.

"…figured you would catch up," the apprentice muttered in a low voice, just above the clop of hooves. I could not see his face within his hood, though part of his nose poked out far enough to imply he was Human as well.

"Fine thing that you nearly reach the tower before me, unless you mean to leave me to the sentries. I had to track you, apprentice."

"A fine test, Lord Briar. My master will be pleased."

The voice was low and masculine but not aged. I might wonder how close the two men were in years, as the rider appeared in his prime. At only about twenty-five years, Rausery had said.

"Lord Briar is my brother," the rider said with a twist to his face and a baring of his teeth that said he did not like his brother. "I am Mathias. Is your master hiring men or no?"

"Would my task have changed before I return to report?" the apprentice asked with dry curiosity.

"Don't try for a jest," Mathias growled.

"Not my intent."

"Just guide me through this accursed place."

"Of course, Master Mathias. Do stay close. The undead always hunger."

Good reminder.

I looked ahead. We could happen upon sentries at any time, and the man in the cart was confirmed to be the safe passage through them.

So, Sarilis has an apprentice? And the master is hiring.

Opportunity had landed, but only if I moved.

I puckered my lips and blew. The whistle startled them to look in my direction without a target in view, though Mathias did nock his bow. The driver stopped his cart before it had resumed any speed.

"Hold up, men!" I called, bouncing my voice off the trees. "I wish to bargain!"

The two peered into the dark shadows but hadn't fixed my position; Mathias's horse whickered and danced as if feeling its rider's tension.

"Who goes there?" the rider demanded. "Apprentice, was there to be another following?"

The apprentice didn't answer but secured his reins on a wooden stub to free his hands.

"I am seeking hire," I confirmed.

"A woman?" Mathias muttered, darting a narrow glance to the apprentice, who shrugged and did not deny it. Then, loudly, "Show yourself!"

"Stow your arrow and bow," I replied.

The driver of the cart looked at the rider and nodded agreement, which was both odd and interesting. It seemed he wanted to meet me.

Death mage apprentice. Be on alert.

I had my weapons of choice ready; they weren't so obvious as the bow that Mathias secured. Although the rider was unafraid of the apprentice and did not take orders from him, his curiosity added enough to wait. I approached from ahead of them, with the cart and drawing horse between me and the rider.

"Bargain," I said again, showing my black gloves empty.

My hood was drawn over my white hair and pointed ears, and with night falling, I doubted they could see the particulars of my race. I could read every twitch of Mathias's face from brow to lip. The apprentice wore something akin to a mage's robes, though made with muted, shabby material and a cruder cut than back home. He kept head and face obscured with his hood and cowl, his elbows upon his knees, and his large, pale hands in view with his fingers loosely entwined.

"Apprentice," I addressed him directly, "I heard Sarilis needs mercenaries."

"Walked all this way on rumor, did you?"

The young man remarked on this so quietly that I wasn't sure he had intended me to hear the words. The rider next to him didn't seem to pick it up even being closer, so I hesitated to respond. Meanwhile, Mathias appraised what he could see of me and shook his head, speaking much louder than necessary.

"Go home, young lady. I know not what Lord-father you ran away from, but this is not the place for a half-grown girl. Best leave. Terrible things may happen to you if you follow us up this valley."

I smiled at that, white teeth in a dark face, and stepped closer. I could see a glimpse of the apprentice's long, gaunt face, and by the widening of his dark eyes, the man just realized the color of my skin.

"I am no girl, Mathias. I seek audience with Sarilis. He has hired from my group before, he will know of it."

"Mm," the apprentice grunted, rubbing a pointed chin with what seemed abnormally long fingers. "What group?"

"The Red Sisters."

No lies to get inside, but I resolved to keep the mystery better this time.

Mathias blew air. "Never heard of them. Where are you from?"

I shrugged. "What place do you call home, Mathias Briar?"

He frowned at me. "I do not recognize your accent, woman."

"Nor I, yours, Master Briar."

"The why will be evident," the apprentice muttered, again so that Mathias did not seem to hear him beyond a mumble, which the rider ignored.

Aggravating to pretend the mage wasn't speaking. Why wouldn't he be louder?

I asked him, "Will you lead me through the tower gate, apprentice?"

"No!" Mathias insisted, as if I'd asked him. "You would be the only woman among rough men."

"Problem?"

The brown rider blinked in surprise then leaned toward me with his forearm braced on his saddle to look down at me. As if something about the words and pose was supposed to intimidate me.

"Ridiculous woman, why are you here? You know you will not be accepted as a fighter for hire, yet you may not be able to leave as you wish if others want something different from you. I'd *not* recommend it."

If *others* wanted. What did that mean? Mathias Briar claimed to be above it?

"You mean rutting?" I asked with a chuckle. "Watching fine fighters fail such a simple test might be the most amusement I've had in months."

The man's frown grew deeper.

"I think my master will wish to meet her," the apprentice said. "I will guide her if she cares to come."

I bent at the waist, keeping my eyes up, as Rausery had shown me. "My gratitude!"

Mathias shook his head and sighed. "I've given warning."

"Heard and understood, Master Briar." I offered another bow to the rider, falling back on my Court-learned charms, such as they were.

We resumed travel upon the rough road, Mathias and I on opposite sides of the horse-drawn cart. The Humans' vision in the dark must be poor indeed as neither tried to see my face. The apprentice, however, had made sneaky remarks to imply he may have some knowledge of Davrin from his master, if Sarilis had deigned to share any stories from two decades ago. Best to keep in mind that when Rausery was here, both these men may have been suckling their mother's breast.

In full night but the first Moon peeking over the mountain as the clouds at last began to clear, the daytime pain behind my eyes vanished. I gathered in the details of the men, the valley, and the approaching tower. The first walking dead sentries that I saw were a pair of raptors.

So... flying dead, too?

This was unconfirmed as they did not move from their perch, though they gazed with greyish-white eyes that should have been black. The raptors' featherless necks cricked audibly as they turned their equally naked heads in our direction. The apprentice took no notice of them, though their smell to me as we passed was that of rotting flesh and musty feathers; not pleasant in the least.

This was also the first time I had been able to feel a foreign sense of magic on the Surface, despite that I was not a mage. I sensed the second, larger set of sentries long before I saw them, and once I did, I learned what had been making those creeping, clacking noises.

Moving skeletons. Their jawbones striking their skulls.

Human, I thought, counting five. Death's grin and empty eye sockets, the bones weren't pale as if picked clean but held together with little pieces of meat and plenty of dirt clinging to them. It helped with the camouflage; Mathias and his horse were outright spooked catching sight of these puppets so long after I'd anticipated their shuffling approach. They brandished one short sword in each bony hand. From Tamuril's word, I would assume at least seven were in the sparse forest and field along the road leading to the gate.

Again, the apprentice paid the walking dead no mind, and the skeletons let us pass. Mathias and I were silent, looking to all sides before I looked ahead and saw how tall the gate really was. The woodsman was right; getting out again may be a problem if I couldn't work a deal with the death mage.

Rausery told you what to expect from him, Sirana. Use it.

Sarilis seemed both aware of our arrival and sure of his apprentice's identity, because two thralls lumbered to open the gate for us a fair distance before we had reached it. This would never happen in Sivaraus, but I had the feeling there was not usually much threat around this place, to leave the gate wide open as the cart continued at the same pace without urgency.

Crossing the threshold at last, I reflected there were gates in my city which felt the same except for the lack of a ceiling. Patches of stars showed overhead as moonlight strengthened outside, and there were low lights from torches or candles lit inside, seen through tiny windows near the ground floor.

This space between the guard wall and the main entrance was wide enough to hold fifty warriors and let them pass through the gate four abreast. The ground was bare, muddy, and smelly from feces and dropped flesh. The dung was relatively fresh; I could believe there were living men and horses here, somewhere.

I spotted the stable upon hearing no fewer than three riding beasts already there. They stomped their feet and blew air out of their noses, vocalizing and sounding agitated. Around this type of magic, with pieces of corpses strewn about, that wasn't a surprise.

No undead approached us, however; none were in sight as the apprentice climbed off the cart and reached for his horse's bridle. Drawing the mare farther in to a specific point, he blocked the wheels and began dropping the cart where it stood. The motions were sure and unhurried; this younger Human was familiar with the task.

Mathias and I waited for him. The bearded man tried once to peer farther inside my hood, but I turned, preferring to let the "hiring" mage see my true appearance first.

"Who are you, lady?" he asked. "You have the bearing of landed family."

Interesting that it translated between our races.

"And that is familiar to you," I commented. "Exiled noble, you?"

For the second time, he refused to confirm what I already knew. Instead he left to add his mount to the nearby stable. The apprentice finished with the cart and led his horse just after the mercenary. His mare proved the quietest of all.

The only one accustomed to the skin-crawling aura of this place.

The two men returned, and the woodsman tried again.

"You are being foolish," he said to me. "The gate is still open. You may leave."

I shook my head, calmer than I would be if Elder Rausery was saying the same thing. "Rude to leave before meeting our host. And, I wager the apprentice has a talisman on him to urge the walking dead to ignore him. I have no such bauble."

The younger mage of the tower at last lifted his chin enough for me to see his face. He was surprised by my insight, I could tell.

I looked at him. "Am I correct?"

I received a grunt-mutter that might have been an affirmative. Next to Mathias, Sarilis's apprentice was the uglier Human by a great degree. He had stringy, black hair falling forward from his hood, long and unkempt, not even tied back the way Mathias's brown waves were.

Briefly, I could study a long, scowling face with deep-set and dark eyes. A hooked nose hovered above a thin and tight mouth perpetually downturned. A pointed, hairless chin was flanked by pallid, sunken cheeks, and he possessed an enormous lump at the front of his throat. Mathias was almost the opposite with a warm skin tone, rounder face with robust facial hair, wide-set and balanced eyes, a modest nose, and fuller lips.

"You know something of magic?" the woodman asked me.

"I have worked with mages before. All Red Sisters do."

"Indeed," the apprentice all but whispered, giving me nothing more than that extra look at his appearance as he noted mine, before walking past me toward the main door. Again, he sounded disinterested. "Come along, the both of you."

"Made your bed, then, wench," Mathias sighed as we turned together.

I smiled at him. "In Trade, where does 'wench' lie? Less or more for 'woman'?"

The woodsman took me to be jesting, and he huffed a derisive sound. He refused to answer, looking instead to the apprentice, who opened the door and gestured with a bare, grimy hand. I let Mathias enter first, taking the time to inhale all the curious scents flowing from the dim inside. The apprentice waited until I was through the door.

Then he spoke.

"Consider wench the same as woman, but she is a common worker or servant, not nobility. A 'lady.' An imperfect insult, considering he acknowledged your breeding first."

I smiled slightly at the helpful comment, but Mathias frowned and shook his head, lifting his eyes to the ceiling as if he was familiar with his gods. We had stopped just inside with the door open.

"Word picker, I see," Mathias said, "reading insult where there is none."

"Words are not interchangeable, Master Briar," the mage remarked, "or language descends to gibberish and magic would be impossible."

Another huff. "Second-guessing every man's motive by a slip of the tongue explains why every mage I've met thinks his scribbles are worth a Dragon's hoard."

I showed teeth in a grin, listening to them. Such banter was nicely familiar, and the apprentice almost continued. I watched his chest expand and his shoulders twist our way slightly. Then he relinquished the matter, turning to look outside in the courtyard, and Mathias nodded, satisfied with his silence.

Damn. I'd wanted to hear what the mage intended to say. *Ask, maybe?*

I heard shuffling behind us and turned my head to see two undead thralls lifting packs from the cart and coming toward the apprentice at the entrance. Now that I was paying attention, one of the tall man's hands was tucked into a pocket on the far side, and he continued to mutter.

As the skeletal thralls clicked their way up the short steps with their burdens, Mathias and I were motioned forward by the death mage. We walked deeper in the entering hall, the apprentice between us and the upright corpses. Neither the woodsman nor I were at ease with having those things behind us.

Entering the stone tower, however, felt like stepping into the Deepearth, with its rough, sturdy stone blocks and narrow passageways encompassing me. My ears and all my senses heightened at once; without thought, I became oriented to the air movement and ambient noise, placed in well-familiar balance with the space around me. It would be difficult to sneak up on me in this place; but for the scent of death everywhere, this tower was the closest to home I'd been on the Surface.

There was a hearth fire up ahead, and soon we entered a larger gathering room, enough for twenty men, although only four occupied it. The hearth burned with a cauldron steaming over it, and my eyes teared up as I smelled a warm stew which set my mouth to watering. My stomach clenched once, painfully, and I sighed inwardly as I knew the pains would only get worse.

Not the time for this.

Standing just behind the apprentice and Mathias, I pulled out a pressed travel bar and tore off a piece, placing it in my mouth. As I chewed, I saw a large man, easily the largest in the room, sitting at the single, long table facing my direction. The dark-haired warrior possessed the whitest skin I'd seen yet and wore soot-stained metal armor and a bracer with spikes on his right arm. There was a somewhat smaller man, also pale with dark hair, sitting to his left. He was dressed in a dark green tunic overlaid with quality leather armor.

A wealthy man and his guardsman, perhaps? What use would that be to a mercenary hunt?

Also in the room, to my surprise, was a Dwarf. I looked twice because, at first, he sat facing away but turned to the new arrivals. He looked nothing like the Tragar. Unlike the bald heads of Kain's kind, this one had a full growth of overly wavy, reddish-yellow hair and an equally wild beard of a slightly darker color. He was pale skinned, but like Tamuril rather than the two men; a ruddy color was always ready to bloom beneath the skin's surface.

He's every bit as stocky and powerful as Elder Rausery described them to be.

Lastly, there was an elderly, grey-touched man in dark blue robes standing at the head of the heavy table.

You must be Sarilis.

His back was hunched as if he could not make it straight if he tried, and his hands were ancient, covered with visible veins and knobby in every joint. His face was marked by more wrinkles than I'd ever seen on any thin-lipped face, his nose seeming smooshed and flattened, brown spots marring his rough-looking, greasy skin. The old man made the attempt to smooth his thin, grey hair and tie it back. Oddly, he had no beard, and his red-rimmed, pale blue eyes possessed purplish bags beneath, as if he was in dire need of sleep. Yet, there was a potent sense of that foreign magic coming from him than the others.

I quickly swallowed my mouthful as Sarilis spoke.

"You're late, Gavin," he said in a reedy, grating voice. "Taken by bandits? If you lost any cargo I'll—"

The apprentice said nothing and moved to the side, revealing me in the hearth's light. He was obviously trying to distract his master, and it worked.

"Well, well." From his angle, Sarilis hadn't seen me in his tall apprentice's shadow. He grinned, his teeth yellow and twisted. "Two new additions to our party, not one?" He looked at the man first. "Mathias Briar?"

"Yes, sir," he answered. "I received your missive."

"Excellent. I take it you were pleased with the down payment?"

Mathias didn't look it. "That is why I am here."

"Welcome, welcome." Sarilis chuckled, then focused on me. His gaze had the crafty slant Rausery had described; in that instant, I believed everything she had said about him. "And you? Dare I hope? May I see your pretty face?"

He knows.

I breathed slow, embraced the techniques to keep my heart inaudible and my pulse from jumping in my neck. However, I could not help but feel the hard stare of every pair of eyes in the room, except the apprentice, Gavin, who had made himself inconspicuous along the wall at Mathias's introduction. It seemed he would serve himself some stew. I wished I could go with him.

I'd like some, too.

Setting my expression to cool confidence, I reached up to lift the hood, letting it fall onto my shoulders to expose my face, hair, and ears.

The response was abrupt and booming.

Mathias blurted a shout of alarm and scrambled away from me, drawing his long dagger. "What are you?!"

I closed the top of my spider pouch and held out my other hand with no weapon drawn. At the same time, the death mage shouted.

"Hold, Mathias!" Sarilis commanded, making an ugly face as the big warrior kicked back his chair and stood up to draw his sword. "You as well, Kurn!"

The fighter barked at him in a throaty, exotic language far from the roots of the Trade language, and the smaller man took his lead to stand but moved behind him, raising one bare hand while his other reached into a pouch, not quite to casting. The Dwarf rumbled a curse in his own guttural speech, rising to put his back to Gavin rather than me, standing before the death mage as if to guard him as he gripped an axe.

Another mage, and two fighters.

I glanced at the apprentice, who held his empty bowl in both hands and stood close to the fire. He watched with a passive face and shifting eyes, as if he debated grabbing his dinner and leaving the rising fracas.

Sarilis cackled aloud in a single, delighted burst, capturing the men's attention. He lifted a gnarled hand high, his skin beginning to glow ice blue. "Enough! She is my guest at my tower, as you all are. Sit down."

The others did not sit, but they stood down all the same, weapons and hands lowered. As soon as Sarilis focused on me again, I offered a formal bow with empty hands, a broad smile, and careful enunciation.

"My leader sends her regards, Sarilis."

The old death mage grinned so widely I could see a gap in his teeth on one side. "Well, well, well... a dark angel arrives at this perfect time. Welcome, Red Sister. I have such need for you."

CHAPTER 6

THE DEATH MAGE REFUSED TO EXPLAIN ANYTHING TO ANYONE until we had each collected our meal from the communal pot and brought it to the table. I'd observed the Dwarf across from me, eating away at what he'd taken, darting looks at me with blue eyes a like shade to mine. Becoming envious as steam rose from my bowl, I had followed suit.

"Mmm," I moaned, my lips pursed around the wooden spoon, and my host wheezed another chuckle watching me finish up.

"Enjoyed the stew, Sirana?"

Oh, yes.

It was the best warm meal I'd had since leaving Sivaraus, rich in animal fat with plenty of mushy root vegetables, the meat tender and melting in my mouth. I caused a ripple of muttering among the men when I helped myself to a second serving, the bowls already sized to feed Humans. Sarilis continued to grin at me from the head of the table; I sat down again on his right.

"I do love a beauty with appetite," he said. "I'll grant the stew is decent. My apprentice fixed it up before he left, kept cold in the box. I warmed it with a spell, easy enough."

I looked to where Gavin was deep into his second bowl as well, standing and leaning against the wall by the fire. He had not joined us at the heavy wooden table, had said nothing, and looked up only rarely. He was listening, though.

"Improved from aging," I said.

Sarilis's grin was enormous. "Indeed, exactly as I always say!"

Mathias made a sound like he thought that was funny.

Meanwhile, the big, white-skinned warrior—Kurn—stared at me from across the table without blinking. He wasn't the only one curious, of course, but the others I was sure had blinked by now.

In my own time, I met his eyes, my motions lingering on my first mouthful of stew from my second bowl. The dark-eyed gaze flicked around while I pulled the spoon from between my lips, chewed, and swallowed, as if trying to capture all that and embed it in memory. Eventually, Kurn locked on my eyes and held, as if daring me to blink first. I winked one eye and showed my teeth in a smile.

Finally, he blinked. The arising scowl, however, revealed a humorless and black mood opaquer than the apprentice.

Charming.

"What is this creature, Sarilis? Why have you need of her?"

He had as pronounced an accent as I did; next to Sarilis and Mathias, the man sounded to be from far away.

"On to business already, Kurn?" the elderly man said with a sigh.

The fire-bearded Dwarf, Rithal, squinted at me. "She's an Elf, I think."

My eyes slid his way. How could he know? I wondered only then if he might be psionic. My body flushed an ill warmth at the thought.

"An… Elf," repeated the other white man, Castis, in a tone suggesting he was digging with speed through his mental scrolls for a match.

Mathias didn't pretend he knew anything; he sat next to me, but not too close, focus in regular rotation between me, his bowl, and everyone else at the table. I took another bite of my meal but lifted my eyes to the Dwarf across the way with a mild, inviting curiosity. I couldn't tell how old he might be, how long his memory or that of his elders; I may not know unless he spoke of it, yet Rausery claimed that his race's stories were less fanciful than the Human ones. I was interested in what Rithal might know.

Sarilis turned his chin in the same direction, his creased, expressive mouth twitched with amusement. "Do tell, Rithal. I will confirm for Master Briar and our Ma'ab brothers, yes, she is an Elf. What else do you know?"

Useful that the death mage thought along the same lines as a Noble at a dinner party. The fact that he had requested the son of a "landed family" to come here hinted at an interesting link. At the question, however, a pair of bushy orange eyebrows drew down in stubborn and cautious defense. The Dwarf was not quick to jump into his people's tales.

"Come, come," Sarilis urged. "You revealed that you heard of the sharp-eared ones. You could have stayed silent, Rithal. I will add to what you say, of course, if you speak."

Persuasive.

Rithal's mustache and chin locks moved with his lips as he made a face and rumbled something in his native tongue. Then, "Once, there lived two intelligent races older than mah forefathers."

I could not help but think of Tamuril. *Two races, the Pales Ones and the Dark Ones.*

The old man smirked. "Indeed, and by which names do you call them?"

A cautious shadow passed across blue eyes. "Elf and Orc."

I held still, resisting a blink of surprise. *Elf and what?*

"Orcs?" Castis asked.

Rithal nudged his chin into his wild beard. "Elf. Dwarf. Orc. We were the three-point anchors spannin' every coast, present *long* 'fore the Humans arose tah explore and *conquer.*"

Kurn smirked in answer.

"Me an' mah kin have long told that the Elf and the Orc died out, unable tah breed an' compete with the new race. The Dwarves were the survivors tah stand wit' mankind and help rebuild the world after these others disappeared from th' lands."

Simultaneously, all looked at me as if to make sure I was here in the flesh.

I smiled, relaxing my shoulders. "It seems we did not 'die out,' Rithal."

"Clearly," Sarilis chortled wetly. "So *I* discovered decades ago."

"Aye," Rithal agreed, watching me. "But yewer rare as teats onna billy."

I hid my confusion, supping from my bowl but making a mental note to ask the apprentice about that. I thought it "loudly," waiting to see if the redbeard would volunteer a better definition for his words. He did not. Next, I checked on the younger death mage. *Yes, still there.*

"So, this small, black *kus* is not a demon?" Kurn asked, his massive, closed fist resting on the table.

To see a real one, you would know the difference, fighter.

I bit my cheek, letting another answer. It was Sarilis, again; the Dwarf had finished.

"Certainly not!" cried the old man. "Rather, she is of an enviably long-lived race with many secrets to tell, if you might withhold the disparaging insults for a single meal, Ma'ab."

"What?" Kurn asked, one black eyebrow rising in challenge. "*Kus?* It is accurate. Translation, 'baby-bringer'. My people revere the bearers of new life."

I saw Castis's subtle and admiring glance for his cohort's remark, so I didn't believe it as stated. Rausery had warned me, although it was ironic how true the lie was in this instance.

"Oh?" Mathias remarked. "Do those roving packs among your people 'revere' every healthy woman they can get their hands on, from any village in their path?"

Expressions darkened on both Ma'ab for an instant, but then Kurn smiled abruptly, ear-to-ear.

Fuuu... Put it away.

"The Hellhounds?" the bulky man volunteered, pride in his voice. "We are selected and trained to make more Ma'ab. It is our privilege and our reward, granted from the Divine Warrior."

"Bulls mounting heifers," Mathias said under his breath, and though Kurn narrowed eyes at him, it seemed he hadn't caught the words.

"Thought it was granted from someone higher," Rithal said, tapping the back of his spoon. "Ma'ab have a Matriarch, don't ye?"

Kurn looked annoyed but didn't deny it. Castis straightened in his chair, leaning forward and sweeping his eyes along the table.

"We'll not discuss our Gods," he stated firmly, darting a look to his ally as well. His accent was thick but the words clear. "We are getting distracted. What is a Red Sister, Sarilis? Again, why have you called her here?"

Subtle as a blacksmith's hammer.

The old man seemed happy to be asked and straightened up as much as his decrepit frame allowed. "Why, a Red Sister is a lady warrior, Castis. I daresay, any are a match for Kurn."

"Hakyad!" the big man barked in laughter, and I flinched as it stabbed into my ears. Kurn shook his head and picked up his mug to take a drink, spilling water at the corners of his mouth.

"Hmph," Sarilis frowned, annoyed. "What she lacks in size and brute force, Ma'ab, she surpasses in wit and speed. They are trained, as you were, to carry out any task, at any cost. We are fortunate that she has answered my summons."

"I don't want unknown like *this* in my *farkhid*," the Ma'ab growled.

"Your 'farkkid'?" Rithal asked with skepticism.

"A squad," Castis provided. "A team of men. Women do not belong. They are small and distracting."

"She is not a woman," Sarilis chortled. "And you *will* need her, small or not. You shall see when I reveal my plan. Timing is everything." He turned to me before any could response. "So, your leader sends her regards, you said. How nice. How does she fare, Sirana? It has been so long since she graced my humble dwelling. Does she still make five corpses for every one that another mercenary does?"

I smiled. "She fares like the eternal mountains and speaks well of your wit, Sarilis. She regrets not answering the summons herself."

Sarilis's pale blue eyes glinted in amusement, the corners crinkling in appreciation, and intrigue. Granting credit to his claims in front of the others pleased him much, and it sent a clear message that I was willing to play the game with him. I could expect a private discussion at a later point. His gaze all but promised it.

"Indeed. I hope you shall be as...accommodating. I know Red Sisters possess more than one *healthy* appetite. Ahh, to be twenty years younger again!"

I smirked, took another bite of stew; the men were too quiet, a few pairs of lips twitching in half-drawn smiles or sneers. There was no response I could give that would not seem like either a challenge to play harder or a promise. What had Rausery said? Best to ignore the words if there were no actions going with it.

"My elder sister led you against the cult before," I said. "Shall I do the same on this task? Of course, I am trained and capable."

Kurn thumped his gauntleted hand atop the table, jolting his empty bowl. "You will not! I am ranking *wargan*. We will not take orders from a black witch among dying Elfs. Not while the Ma'ab *thrive!*"

"I see." I turned to my host. "Hellhounds. A fighting force. What do they do besides breed in mud?"

Sarilis cackled in delight, bringing his fingertips together. "Usually sent ahead of the army, isn't that right, Kurn? Reconnaissance, looting, removing obstacles, infiltrating."

Smaller groups, then. Or just one.

"Even whispers of Hellhounds entering their land make our enemies quiver," said the Ma'ab mage, nodding to Kurn, who lifted his chin.

I noticed a scar on his jaw, then studied Castis. It was harder to tell, but he might be considered beautiful among his own, for certain compared to those other males here. There was a lighter balance to his bone structure, symmetry to his face, and his skin was smoother with fewer blemishes.

I shrugged. "As you like. You are trusted by your 'revered *kus*,' then, Kurn? Did she send you here?"

His flinch and jolt surprised me. He snarled, *"Manhat tenei almaradi!"*

Uh-oh.

Castis elbowed his big brother to gain his attention, though the tap to the armor barely made a noise. They exchanged a look, then the mage spoke again.

"Winds change, Red Sister," Castis said, "that is why we are all here. Once, that insult may have been true, but now we have a mission to further the balance of our race."

I smiled at the somewhat smaller man. "Interesting. What would you call balance?"

"The generals will cease being puppets," Kurn growled, "and take their rightful place determining the course of our history for the Gods."

I tilted my head. "Not 'contributing' to that course? Generals know little of trade or agriculture or crafting beyond weapons and temporary structures."

"We need not debate the particulars," Castis said with finality, another warning look directed at the Hellhound, who had to restrain himself.

I let it go though I could have pushed farther. The Hellhound would only keep his temper so long, and most of my meal needed to settle even as the rest in my bowl was tepid. I finished up my stew with the other guests knowing not much more about me than when I had stepped in. From glances to Rithal and Mathias, I wagered they weren't satisfied and were annoyed by the boasting but opted to bide their time. They would want to talk later. I need not do or say anything else to guarantee that.

"Care to give me a hint why I'm here, old man?" Mathias asked after a time.

"Tomorrow, Master Briar," our host answered cordially as if he'd been waiting for it. "No doubt you are all tired after your journeys here, and you will be leaving again soon enough. Tomorrow."

Leaving again. To go where?

I wondered if Tamuril would be watching for me if I did.

"I have plenty of rooms up inside the tower," Sarilis said as we stood awkwardly in the space between the large hearth and the larger table. "Each has a bolt, so you can keep wandering rats out."

He snickered as we exchanged glances. The only one missing was Gavin; he had already left.

"We take the ground floor as before," Kurn demanded. "We were here first. The rest of you climb."

Rithal tugged on a facial lock, glancing at me. Mathias did similar, without the tug. Again, I grinned. Apart from Sarilis, I was doing the most of that by far.

"High up is well," I said. "I shall enjoy the view. Be careful leaning out tonight, that I don't empty my chamber pot on your head."

Sarilis cackled, and Mathias's mouth twisted in amusement while Rithal grunted at good advice. Of course, Kurn and Castis narrowed their eyes at me, looking for challenge and insult in my answer.

So reflexive. How is it with you and your women?

With a full belly and a fuller day behind me, I would need some rest if I was going to discover what was happening here; the earlier, the better, and the fresher I'd be. I took the room my host suggested—fourth floor overlooking the valley—and left the others to pitch the rest.

Sarilis hadn't known I was coming; I figured my chances were good that the room was free of Davrin-specific dangers or traps. True, all these men here knew where I would be resting, but—

Gently, I cradled my guardians' pouch, and they responded, moving inside. *That is their risk if they try to break in.*

If they were this stupid, I would *not* use my last antivenom on anyone in this tower. Tamuril had been worth saving. These ignorant loudmouths were not, and they were too short-lived to be worth it, anyway.

I had already considered briefly killing Sarilis in his own room this night and running off with my Queen's compulsion fulfilled, but it both felt incomplete and seemed foolish. I'd been told time and again that Sarilis was crafty and paranoid, and I'd just stepped into his lair knowing nothing. His Court-like confidence playing the host was strange for one living mostly alone as a recluse, with only silent undead and a skulking apprentice for company.

I wouldn't have predicted it; I could make no assumptions. It could not be easy to unlock his door and stab him in his bed. I also wouldn't discover what his "plan" was, or why this group would need to leave soon.

The build of the tower did feel familiar and comforting, though it did not really match structures in Sivaraus. Pieces of stone fit well together as a puzzle but without the obvious magic-forming done to the rock in our own buildings. Each floor made good use of its space, with four or five strides to run across, and the ceilings, while a little low for Humans, were generous for Dwarves. The place was pure Dwarven masonry, through and through, but I could note the quality and…

Admire it?

I moved from the first landing into the second set of spiraling steps, shaking my head. Could Kain be lingering, still? All my Surface interactions so far felt as my first days at Court; I could only watch and observe. There was no added sense of mood or whispers of thoughts like I had once absorbed, there remained no warmth or light from the saphgar around my neck. That part was quiet.

Numb.

After the aborted effort with Rausery, after the lancing pain in my head and failing to reach Gaelan before she left, I was, in a way, glad to observe again through the senses with which I'd been born. Even if it meant I couldn't tell whether Rithal might have the same talent as Kain.

I will just have to watch him. He'll give it away sooner or later.

On the second floor, a candle burned behind a door a short way down the curved hall. Its light leaked out from underneath, glaring to my sensitive eyes, though subtle to most Surfacers. Deviating from a path uninvited was certain to draw attention in any Sivaraus dwelling with a resident mage, and I would wager this place was no different.

Standing there, I sensed what could be my first ward up here, and it drew my curiosity as it heightened my wariness. I had not confronted any ward since Kerse had forced me to break the one guarding the Ornilleth's prison.

The pain swept through me, as did the feeling of blood leaking from my cunt. My eyes teared up; my heart kicked into a sprint.

Calm. I breathed in, slow, touching the stone with one hand. *Still.*

I checked with one hand. My crotch was dry, normal. As far as I knew, I was still pregnant. I exhaled in a soft, steady blow, my hand covering my womb.

Okay. Don't panic. Now what?

I took one cautious step toward the light beneath the door. Strong wards could cause miscarriages, but as I got closer, I felt that this one was weak. Very simple, and it had been erected recently.

You are tired. You want sleep. Go to your room.

Just a suggestion.

Next, I heard someone shifting behind the closed door. I focused on the sounds, stepping closer to challenge the ward. Yes, I was tired in truth, but I *must* know that a novice mage couldn't prevent me from entering a room.

I allowed it to affect me, resisting the temptation to leave and continue to my room to sleep. My body and mind listened together, detecting its "song," seeing in my mind's eye the arcane runes which would unravel the protection.

I felt it break. And I stood at the door. The man inside cursed under his breath.

Success.

I grinned, and the deep voice of the apprentice passed through the door.

"What do you want?"

I blinked. I hadn't thought of a want yet.

"I have a question," I said. "Open your door, apprentice."

I'd think of something by the time I got inside.

There was a frustrated exhale of air, and I heard several metal bolts and chains being undone. Gavin opened the door just wide enough for his face, a practical piece of chain stopping it at that length. I looked up, and he peered down at me with small, black eyes above sunken cheeks and pronounced cheekbones. He was much taller than he made himself out to be around the others. Always slouching before, he must stand straighter to keep the door secure against me. He was frowning, of course, though without his hood covering his head, his dark hair looked both longer and more unkempt than I'd first thought.

He waited for me to speak. I wasn't being invited inside.

"What is 'teats onna billy'?" I asked.

His expression hardly changed, though I heard the touch of disbelief in his tone. "That's what you came to ask?"

"As good as any other, is it not?"

Gavin stared at me; I was not sure what he may have been thinking, but he answered the question, which was the telling part. "The Dwarf referenced a male goat. A billy."

I nodded. *A goat.*

His dark eyebrow quirked. "Teats are on the nanny. The female that has teats where the kid suckles milk."

"Kid," I repeated. "A baby goat."

"Good to know Elves understand animal husbandry."

"Animal what?"

Though I was serious that I didn't know the word, Gavin just stared, unmoving, and something about his expression made me grin. I felt the urge to laugh, and so I did. Quietly.

"Is that all?" he asked, when he could have slammed the door in my face.

"Have you a question for me, in trade?" I offered.

The apprentice blinked, then shrugged. "Perhaps. How old are you?"

I smiled a bit. "One hundred years."

He took a long moment to absorb this. "About one hundred, because you don't count, or—?"

I shook my head. "No, counted. One century."

The tall Human grunted softly. "Is there a point your kind cease counting?"

"When everyone around you is younger."

I found amusement in that compulsive curiosity as he peeled my words apart; he couldn't help himself. It was very familiar.

"How much time have you been here?" I asked.

"How many questions do you plan to trade?" he replied deadpan. "Shall I get a stool?"

My smile grew again. "It may help."

"Perhaps you should find your room."

"You are not curious enough to talk?"

He sighed, the first hint of exhaustion. "Not really. Four days on the road tends to sap my enthusiasm for conversation."

I had the oddest feeling that I would prefer Gavin's company to Sarilis. Dare I hope he was educated as his master in the history of this world, if not as practiced in his magic? I tried to peek behind him to see inside his quarters, for hints of how he spent his time, but I had to rise on my toes. In response, he eased the door to a bare slit, only one eye and a corner of his mouth visible as the chain slackened.

His tone was chilly. "Are we done?"

"For now," I granted. "Thank you for the stew, apprentice, I enjoyed it."

"I could tell."

He closed the door with a jangle of iron. I heard the other locks thrown on the other side.

I left then to continue up the stairs. I did not hear voices downstairs and figured they had sorted out their rooms. Fortunately, I crossed paths with none of them as I found mine: small, round, and a bit drafty with a ragged tapestry courageously attempting to block the air outside. I tested the two locks on the door before securing them and sighed at the relative quiet and darkness.

There was a chair next to a wobbly table that I'd sit in rather than use the stained cot on one side. This wasn't a bad option, as I'd been sleeping outdoors or in a cave for months. It wasn't quite as cozy as Tamuril's place, but I wouldn't complain. I gave the room a thorough search, found nothing, and did not sense anything beyond a louder whine which I had to work to block out or I'd never sleep.

My guard spiders were in place beneath my loose braid, I settled into the chair, spine straight and head balanced, and closed my eyes. I'd wake before the night was through and invite Sarilis's company, if he did not do so first.

Someone knocked quietly, and my spiders moved. I awoke with the sounds of shuffling and a soft grunt outside my locked door. Standing silently from my chair, I stepped forward, listening and smelling in the dark room. There was a hint of a scent, decay and death, which told me what to expect as I considered how to open the door.

I couldn't assume the messenger meant me no harm, so I slid back the metal bolt but left the chain lock in place; the same approach the apprentice had chosen when I had stood outside his room. The locks had also been recently constructed, and the height was not Dwarf height, so I thought it must be Gavin's doing, possibly at Sarilis's command. I was impressed that I could open the door a hand-width and keep it secure while requiring no key or magic. I thought the mechanism was ingenious.

Peeking out on the tower's landing, the creature standing there didn't move or blink, only stared down at me. My messenger had once been Human and male, the general appearance of a guard with dirty blond hair. The dead, unfocused eyes had once been blue but were bloodshot and eerily pale. It wore gloves, clothing, and moderately preserved leather armor plus a stout sword, naked and loosely knotted to his belt without a scabbard. One tug would release the knot.

Perhaps drawing and sheathing is too much for this thrall to handle.

I noted black stitches across its windpipe and blots on the pale, waxy neck and face, like the blood had stopped and settled in the flesh, the skin having lost a degree of resiliency as it sagged in places, especially beneath the eyes. I didn't want to see the thrall beneath the trappings of imitated life, as the aura around it was cold and sent a mild nausea through me.

If the raptors and skeletons and unloading servants were any comparison, this messenger was one of the better-looking and refined that Sarilis could have sent. Perhaps it was one of the newer undead, proof of recent magic performed on the corpse of a living man just passed away. Unsettlingly powerful for a mage to make this choice with a husk, as I thought about it, although I didn't know how it compared to the Priestesses of Braqth.

I understood its message as it bowed to me, its spine cracking, and gestured that I should follow, another soft moan leaking out of its altered throat. I shivered but closed the door to remove the chain. I left the room with all my possessions, walking behind the guard and trying not to inhale too deeply.

We soon returned to the ground floor of the tower with no others intercepting us, moving across the great hall and toward the kitchen, which was large enough for an entire garrison but not heavily used by the only two residents required to eat. The fire at the hearth was banked, and all the bowls from dinner needed washing.

There was a hall beyond the kitchen heading farther into the mountain, beyond the Tower's base. There were no windows and it was only sparingly lit. I would have preferred no light at all, but although Sarilis did not keep a bright and cheery home, he needed light by which to see. With the small doors on each side—Dwarf-sized and not used much by the dust collected at the bases—I guessed they had been the servants' quarters once upon a time.

The corpse guard placed its hand upon the larger door at the end of the hall, waiting before I felt a pulse of *something*. A strange magic feeling, an acknowledgement. Then it opened the door, revealing a staircase with dressed stone steps perfectly level. These were original to the rest of the fortress, but something much newer was the handrail bolted along the left side.

I hesitated to follow the corpse. Should I go down there, I did not have a way out other than how I came in, and I didn't know what I'd find besides—I took a sniff—more bodies.

"Hello?" Sarilis called from below. "Is that you, dark angel?"

Just call it out like a slum crier. Sheesh.

If I didn't answer quickly, who knew what he might do as I came down the stairs?

"It is," I said, following the thrall below with care.

167

"Marvelous, marvelous. Come!"

Slowly, the basement room revealed Sarilis's workshop, which had the traits of nearly every mage I'd ever known—scrolls, powders, vials, and books on every level surface—but the tools of his particular trade weren't typical for my wizards at home. I noted saws, blades, surgical tools, vices, shovels, pickaxes, and—

Is that dried sinew and tanned patches of skin hanging with the bouquets of herbs?

There were glass jars tucked in rows upon a large set of shelves far in the back. From where I stood, they looked to contain suspension fluids with various pieces of flesh and anatomy.

Spell components and... I glanced at the standing thrall. *Spare parts?*

These physical details could not explain the foreign and unsettling energy that abounded in this place. I sensed no wards, but there was more in here than a dawdling hobby. I observed Sarilis's body language as he had his back to me; he felt safe here.

"Ahhh, my enchanting visitor," he said, turning around on one of three stools he possessed. The old man grinned to show the gap in the yellow teeth on his left side again. "Care to close the door behind you, my lovely? There are many guests in this place tonight, and voices carry."

"Fond of your endearments, I see," I said with a small smile and calm air as I retreated up the steps to close the door, noticing that it did not physically lock. I looked about as I came down again and off the steps. "Very nice space, death mage. I've never seen the like."

"Why, thank you!" he said, clapping with an enthusiasm that belied his advanced age. He laughed. "I do admire my laboratory. Your...ahm, what was it you said, 'leader'...which I take to be my dear Rausery?"

I nodded.

"Yes, she first commented on the smell."

I grinned. Oh, there was the smell, alright. Old blood and mold, rust, iron, a pungent, irritating odor I couldn't identify but came from the jars of liquid preserving flesh.

Sarilis continued, "I understand your delicate ears and cute little noses have been bred to be so sensitive deep down below without your sight, hm?"

I didn't comment his choice of words beyond a shrug but noted them. Sarilis gestured for the guard to come fully off the stairs and toward him. He twirled his finger and the thrall turned in place as if to give the old man a view of every side.

"Mmm, no misunderstandings, I see."

That made me chuckle. "No extra holes, you mean?"

"Correct." He cackled in the back of his throat, lips closed, then rasped, "I take it Sir Cullen behaved himself?"

I smiled. "Stared, bowed, and led. I am not the jittery sort."

He stroked his scruffy, grayish jaw. "You have familiarity with my 'sort,' perhaps?"

"I know that which I need."

"Ah! Preparation. Excellent. Then you *were* sent here?"

"I was."

"Most curious timing. I must assume your leader has been watching somehow. What is her interest in all this?"

In all this? How tacitly vague. I knew he was fishing, but it was reassuring that he wasn't asking about a queen. He might not know She existed.

I shrugged. "I could not claim to know, but she sent me to learn from you."

He cocked one gray, bushy eyebrow. "Learn what, precisely?" His lips twisted into a mean, teasing smile. "I already have an apprentice, useless as he is and tempting as you may be in his place."

I huffed a laugh and shook my head once. "No, I am not sent to learn death magic. But you have news and plans of your own, just as before with Rausery. Even remote as you are, your knowledge of the conflicts is more recent than my leader's."

Were his baggy, icy eyes not so small, I would not think his narrowing them could change so much of his gaze. He looked like a hairy, blind, cave golem.

"The conflicts," he enunciated.

I bluffed. "Twenty years ago, the Ma'ab were not in this area. Now, two of them sit at your table discussing changing winds and armies to make men quiver. There is a war approaching from their homeland. How are you involved?"

Sarilis grinned again. "You did not come with specific plans for involvement as well, Sirana?"

"If you wish to believe."

"Mmm. Eight legs spinning webs," Sarilis murmured with a smirk, wiping a palm on the dark blue fabric of his robe, "but who knows where the other seven are, hm?"

I smiled. That was an accurate translation of a common saying back home. Rausery must have offered the analogy at some point. "Were you genuine in wanting my help with your task?"

"Oh, yes. You increase the chance of success. Were you here for something else, my dear? Now is your chance to say while my plans are in a bit of flux."

"Information," I said, "on several things."

"Name them," he replied in utter confidence. "We may bargain, and I expect nothing less."

"Do you know much about Manalar?" I said. "Or anyone at the table tonight?"

Sarilis could not appear to express further glee. "You arrived planning to go to the City of the Sun?"

"I am gathering information, first."

"Meaning you have other priorities?"

I smiled with my lips closed and waited.

"Well, my dear. I know a great deal about Manalar, but it is through word of mouth and the tales from my former lords. I have not been there in person, as it is a long way. This is, however, why I invited Mathias Briar and Rithal in particular." Sarilis observed me for a few moments before asking, "Care to offer something in return?"

"I have been sent to scout for warp rot," I lied, "such as was here once, and we helped you. Have you heard of any such infections nearby?"

Sarilis shook his head, disappointed. "No, and good riddance. That sickness resembles the hungry dead in ways, yet those writhing dead men are something I cannot control. I keep my borders well, as agreed with my dear Rausery."

I pushed out a memory of Gaelan and nodded. "What of Augran?"

"My, my, such interest over a vast expanse," he remarked. "How long are you intended to be on mission above, Red Sister?"

I had no idea, aware that I already grew hungry again. Clearly, the warp rot Gaelan might be seeking and the two major Human cities in which I might find Jael's purpose were nowhere close to this Ley Tower.

"How long are the Ma'ab, the Dwarf, and Master Briar to be on task for you with your 'plan'?"

"Patience," he chuckled, "I shall tell you in time, and I hope there may be overlap."

"There may be," I granted. "Kurn mentioned demons. I know many Humans claim to have seen them without knowing what they see. Are there stories of black demons like me to which *you* would grant some weight of truth?"

His face creased with grotesque amusement. "You ask a hermit about the things common folk jump at in the dark?"

"You weren't always a hermit," I said. "You are too experienced entertaining guests. You had 'lords' you have followed around in your young days. Even old stories are worthwhile to old races."

"Mmmm," he hummed in satisfaction. "You seek another of your kind. Delightful. An exile, perhaps? Are you not sure if he is in Manalar or Augran?"

He?

I stopped myself from correcting the old man. "I listen for stories of warp rot and those who may be able to stop it, as my leader did for you. As old of stories as there may be."

Sarilis thought about it. "I may have some to trade, Sirana. A hint of truth to them, as you say, even if they are not recent."

"Which city?"

"Both." Sarilis cackled. "Each are *ancient* cities for us, dear Sister, with hundreds of years of 'stories' and many bouts of forgetfulness and periodic burning of libraries."

Burning libraries?

I forced a bored smile, noticing the smells of his lab giving me a headache. "Yes, so Rausery said. There is something you heard about my kind in both ancient cities which seems true?"

Sarilis scratched his chin with a sly smirk. "The killings are true enough, unexplained, blamed on a 'demon' of shadows assassinating men of power at their peak. Strewing chaos, shifting the balance. Such events haunt Manalar in particular. The Bishops of Musanlo claim this is why they are 'united against the darkness.'"

Bishops. I blinked slowly, tilting my head with interest but controlling my hunger. *Assassinations at Manalar at peak times, such as it might be for Jael?*

Sarilis enjoyed my clear interest and continued voluntarily. "Indeed, Rausery and I discussed this, how much it sounded like what a Red Sister might do if she was hiding out within the population. You don't mind if I sit again, do you? These old bones."

I watched as Sarilis leaned up against a blood-stained operating table and braced his palms, hopping his rear onto the edge with a grunt. His swinging feet appeared to have two sets of socks covered by a pair of soft-soled house shoes. He noticed my looking at them and shrugged.

"Poorly circulating blood. Anyways, a Dark Elf could easily live two and three hundred years to continue such tales among the rodents. I admit I found it fascinating to first consider such a practical explanation for what I had taken as a collective popular delusion. But… there were too many consistent details which we had *both* heard for Rausery to be wholly wrong."

"Which were?"

I saw the gap in his smile again. "You haven't lost a Sister upon the 'surface' for three hundred years, have you?"

I shook my head with confidence. "No. Only the mage at this tower within the last century."

"Ah. The mage fallen to the warp rot, or the one Rausery prodded me about? The cleric?"

"The cleric," I granted, glad he knew about both as I had guessed.

"Ah. Quite a mystery, that. I am glad to have been deemed innocent."

I let a pause pass after that. "You assumed I sought a male shadow, when you had discussed a possible Red Sister with Rausery."

"The tales *all* whisper of a male," he snickered. "At times massive and strong, others tiny and quick as the wind. Whether this is truth or illusion, neither me nor your leader know. It is only what the people gossip about."

I understood. "What of the Ma'ab men?"

He narrowed his eyes again. "You know little of them, I noted. A pity. Care to give a little *more*, my dark angel? I have been generous thus far, and you do not seem to have a focused purpose."

Damn it.

"Or I explore *all* the web before deciding where to ambush my prey," I quipped, nonchalant.

Sarilis pictured that. The old man chortled, bracing against his work bench with his palm perilously close to a black-stained cleaver, and he pushed to stand. He came toward me on soft-wrapped feet. This whole time, he had allowed me to stand near the stairs, not asking me to sit, not suggesting I move farther into the room.

Now, he came around his several tables adorned with restraints and closed the distance. I remained where I stood, checking around me that I wasn't too close to things that could fall on me or be flung at me, that there was nothing below me. The guard Cullen stood dead silent as ever, though too close for comfort.

"My dear Sirana," he said in his reedy voice, softer since he didn't have to project across the lab. "Such time we waste, dancing like this."

I could count the liver spots and smell his unpleasant breath. He watched me for a few moments, and when I said nothing, he stated, "You are a young Elf, aren't you? Younger than Rausery, for certain."

I lifted my chin. "Older than you, Sarilis."

He grinned. "In total sunsets, I grant you. You've not felt your mortality the way I have, however. Different from surviving battle, different from recovering from a mortal wound. You would *feel* your body breaking down, changing how it creates and shifts its energy, never in your direct control but as if under the sun each time it passes. You would wonder how bad it will get upon waking, every moment you feel a new ache or see a new bump in your skin. When you cannot lift the same box from even ten years earlier. You, Elf, do *not* know this. You are young."

I cocked an eyebrow. "Do you have a point, death mage?"

"Yes. Rausery did not feel it so acutely, but she *knew*. She had a few gold strands in her hair. Were those indicative of her age, Sirana? How long had she lived when I met her?"

The old man stared without blinking, his aura growing cold, and a shiver ran up my spine. I maintained my poise, but only just.

"What is your guess?" I asked.

"I have none. Please answer, dark angel, if we shall bargain at all."

I tried not to breathe in his scent too deeply. "Over seven centuries."

He was genuinely intrigued. "Astonishing. And… how long can your race live? Your lifespan."

I realized that I didn't know. We usually died of conflict, poison, or sacrifice. No one I knew ever thought about death coming in such a way, to wither like a shrinking, brittle mushroom exposed to direct sunlight. Not even the Queen.

"Have none of you died only once your heart failed beating?" he asked with a harsher tone. "I know you bleed and die."

"We *are* usually killed," I told him. "I do not know our 'lifespan.'"

Sarilis's eyes seemed bright with moisture. "Hm. Who is the eldest of you?"

"Um…the Mother? I do not know her age, or her true name."

He exhaled in surprise. "Fascinating. Then do tell me, young one, what do you want most in being here? Is there anything you need?"

Hot, dry wind and the sound of rushing sand returned, but I glanced at a set of death-touched tools to remain inside the Ley Tower.

I want to know where my Sisters went. I need to know what is happening among Human cities. Is this what the Valsharess meant about stories? I… I need… to kill this dying, old man, and return home…

My stomach growled like a wild beast, and Sarilis looked down, surprised. I laughed at his expression.

"Well!" I said. "I think I want more of that stew after we discuss your plan."

He smiled as easily, that eager cackle already familiar. "I like your whimsy, and your distraction. Rausery was never this ravenous, but then, I have lost appetite as I age, as well. Keep your secrets, but know that we share a strong mutual interest, you and I."

I maintained a smile. "Do we?"

"Oh, yes. The men gathered tonight?" He looked gleeful. "They head to Manalar, for one reason or another. You are correct about a war coming, and it being spearheaded by the 'thriving' Ma'ab. If all goes well, Manalar the *city* will be no more. The Bishops will be expunged, and the magic they hoard will be released for others to use. And, there *is* a library there containing many stories of their history thus far. But it will be burned, like so many others. Such is the way of war."

I didn't dare blink or show surprise. "You are allied to help the Ma'ab destroy Manalar?"

"Unofficially." Sarilis winked at me. "Of course, the Ma'ab Matriarch and her 'Divine General' *would* wish to take it over after purging all the Sun People. The library might be spared, if the right officers get to it fast enough, but the magic itself would be harnessed by the Northern Empire. Not helpful for those of us who understand the song of the Ley."

And what if Jael is there during all this? She may never make it out.

The death mage went quiet, watching me.

"You don't want the Ma'ab to claim what the Bishops lose," I guessed. "You have a plan to interfere with both sides?"

Delight showed in every wrinkle. "A joy that your wit can keep up, Red Sister. Perhaps… *we* have a plan to interfere. I know Rausery would have helped me with this. It is a true cleansing. A benefit to those like your Mother, with natural affinity to the Ley Line to find these places and protect them."

"These places?" I showed my confusion. "Is this tower somehow like Manalar?"

He almost squealed in joy, clapping dry palms once. "Yes! But my home is new! The heart of Manalar is one of the oldest, one of the greatest! And you *were* sent to me, Red Sister, the moment I decided what I would do to make certain neither Bishop nor Ma'ab 'God' controlled that heart. And there are many legs at work in your 'web,' is there not, Sirana? Tell me, does this not follow the threads? Are we allies once again in a common cause?"

Certainly until such a time as I could figure out what in the Abyss was really going on.

I nodded. "They *do* follow, Sarilis. We are allies."

CHAPTER 7

THE OLD MAGE ASSURED ME DETAILS WOULD BE FORTHCOMING when the others awoke from their sleep and the tangible plans began. He suggested I follow his lead in the discussion.

"I am assured that *any* century-old apprentice of Rausery's knows enough tactics and subterfuge to test the others."

I acquiesced, and Sir Cullen was given to lead me upstairs to get something to eat.

"I will not return to sleep," I said. "May I look around?"

This didn't tickle him as he eyed me. "Hm."

"I would prefer to know the layout should the Ma'ab become excessively hostile," I added with a smile.

"Ah, good point. I suppose you may, as long as your escort remains nearby." He saw my grimace and added, *"Also* for your protection, my dear, so my other shades do not draw close or get too curious about a beating heart."

I accepted.

"Try commanding him, Sirana. Simple things." Sarilis had an oily smile. "He will obey."

I licked my lips, looked to the standing corpse. "Climb the stairs. Go first."

Sir Cullen turned and led me out, and I heard Sarilis snickering as I followed. Nothing jumped the walking corpse in the servants' hall and, as I topped the steps myself, he turned his head to look at me.

His face so pale and wooden, icy eyes empty, the stitches in his throat straining as he held his pose in creepy stillness. There was no heartbeat, no lungs drawing breath, though there was the occasional gurgle and groan of gas trapped somewhere inside, as he was far from the skeletal state of those thralls I'd seen outside.

"Move on," I said. "Back to the great hearth room."

Cullen obeyed. I figured the thrall was not only protector but to observe all that I did, and since he couldn't talk, I must assume Sarilis could scry through those dead eyes at any point. This did not matter to me as I intended to avoid actions which might disallow my sitting in on a briefing of the mission to Manalar. I would appear to support Sarilis's plan regardless, at least until the finish.

By then, I will have chosen my path, yet I wasn't certain what it would be. Would I truly consider traveling with them on the spoken promise to help fulfill something so dangerous in between two battling armies? While leaving my true target here, safe and breathing? Would I choose the long chance of finding Jael alive over completing my own mission and returning to my Queen to face the mind flayers?

How was this "choice" possible? I thought I knew how. *The stories of our blood. I must follow them.*

The three-century killings in Augran and Manalar which seemed to share the same dark origin, according to Sarilis, and gave unity to the Bishops of Manalar. The likeness to the conduct of a Red Sister, something Rausery knew about and had discussed with this old, learned man.

A male, possibly. Massive and strong, or tiny and quick.

Surely, the "demon" wore many forms to prompt both of those claims.

Or, it is pure Human fancy.

This may not be linked to the Davrin through any mouth *except* Rausery's but that seemed to be enough, because hearing this story offered a familiar urge to go seek its truth. The desire fulfilled something, some part of the Valsharess's spell that She placed on me. It took priority over Sarilis's death, and that was freeing enough to make the choice.

I could go after Jael, if I dared. Once decided, there was no turning back.

We reentered the great room with the evening's fire banked in the hearth and a nearly empty cauldron of stew hooked above the coals. The embers glowed low, preventing me from seeing Radiants in full black, but my eyes were sensitive enough to navigate the obstacles and see the outlines of every shape.

Sir Cullen stopped by the door. I wondered at what the death mage had suggested, of the walking dead becoming "curious" about a beating heart. It implied the ears worked in a sense, but what of the eyes? Human, and in this little light, they should be worthless. Was that why he didn't follow me, or was it something else?

I shook off the thought and checked around each chair where Rithal, Mathias, Castis, and Kurn had sat, to see if they had dropped anything. They had not, although that wasn't disappointing, just a fact.

Kneeling by the last chair, I heard three different and loud resting patterns out the main entrance and into the hall to the tower. One was a rattling inhale and series of snorts of such decibel that I *never* heard underground. It occurred to me that anyone who snored like that wouldn't live long in the Deepearth.

Three on the ground floor. So who moved up a floor?

My guess was Mathias, as he had seemed warier of the Ma'ab than Rithal. Crouching in the quiet dark, the previous dinner's memories brightened in my mind's eye. I realized that I had yet to see master and apprentice speak directly to each other, except for that first comment about Gavin being late and a threat of punishment if he lost any supplies to bandits.

The younger leaned against the wall the entire time, through two bowls of stew, and Sarilis never acknowledged him.

Gavin was also much taller than he had appeared hunched in his horse-driven cart. He probably towered over the old man standing face-to-face. Perhaps that was why he had stayed away, so as not to disrupt Sarilis's sense of commanding the room?

If he gives such deference.

I hadn't seen enough between the two death mages to say, yet by judging my own interaction with Gavin, I didn't think so. He had been direct about his tiredness and his impatience at my coming to his door to the point of rudeness. He cared not for offending those of a higher class, even to his own detriment. The apprentice also seemed oddly indifferent to my appearance and why I was here. When I'd lowered my hood to reveal my face, his reaction had been so muted compared to the rest that I could not remember whether he had *had* one.

"Follow the Ley Lines," Shyntre had told me, "find the powerful magic users on the Surface."

Maybe Sarilis had not so much a trusted servant as a suspicious competitor.

Why did you come here, apprentice? When, and from where?

A glow from the staircase appeared. I lifted my hood to cover my white hair, low stepping into the deepest shadow of a large wooden cabinet against the wall. I watched as the subject of my thoughts entered the room with a candle lit in its holder. With a tired sigh, Gavin set the light down on a smaller table in the corner and moved toward the hearth to remove the cauldron. A few roaches scattered from inside the pot as he did so.

"What are you doing here, Cullen?" the apprentice grumbled, barely looking at the thrall as he added tinder and smaller pieces of wood from the metal cache on his right, stirring the embers to liven the fire once again. "You're blocking the kitchen. The lab is farther down."

Cullen had no response whatsoever.

The flare from a strengthening fire pained my eyes before they could adjust but, from the sound, Gavin moved through a familiar waking routine. He had begun his chores for the day, as a servant would, prior to his superiors rising from their rest. He appeared to have done this for some time, accepting the labor, as I detected no external signs of rebellion.

I weighed letting him know I was here, trying to engage him, but decided against it. Cullen was "watching." I could hardly probe how Gavin really felt about his master, and something told me the skulking apprentice might be cranky and uncooperative if surprised and interrupted from his usual pattern.

I also wanted food; I was surprised my belly had not already given me away. In truth, I hoped part of Gavin's chores in the darkness before the dawn was to prepare a meal for the "guests." His stew had been tasty.

Remaining hidden, I allowed Gavin to work unhindered; he never looked for long behind him and seemed not to sense anything unusual. Eventually he lugged the cauldron toward the kitchen, pushing Cullen out of the way with an annoyed curse, and soon after I heard clattering and the sound of water being poured.

Cleaning the old stew and roaches out before starting again.

I was about to leave my spot and spy on the apprentice in the kitchen when I heard much heavier rustling and steps coming from down the tower hall. I froze in place, and soon, someone had opened a door and was coming toward the great room as well. The breathing patterns of the other two continued unabated, including the snorer. How could they sleep through that? I thought they must be deaf.

Listening longer, however, I supposed the man awake had not been obnoxious in his movement; it had only seemed loud to me. It must be the Hellhound. No other had his height and size, the length of stride and mass to make his boots sound like those of a lumbering giant.

Great. His cheery demeanor is better than Gavin pre-dawn.

I waited patiently, wanting to observe the warrior before he realized he was being watched. It would be telling how long that took, but I must expect a bad reaction if he discovered me, and when or if I revealed myself. No domineering, self-sought leader liked being surprised, even if he wasn't female.

Kurn stopped at the threshold and looked around, his face lit by the duller red glow of the hearth fire. He was scowling, as expected, and I thought he was taking the moment to let his own eyes adjust before entering the room. First, he chose the same task I had done: he checked the table and chairs where the group had been sitting the evening prior.

Interesting.

However, he failed to notice Cullen until he crept closer to the thrall, who then turned his head, his pale, dead face mostly in shadows.

"Uj'nat!" he hissed, drawing his sword with a loud, metallic *shing!* as he shifted backward, gripping it with both hands.

The big man was quick for one his size, but I wasn't impressed that he did not see the standing dead man in his first sweep of the room. Still, it confirmed that Kurn couldn't see in the dark.

"Uj'nat," the Hellhound snarled again, his stance that of a barking canine threatening an intruder. Then his upper mind regained control, and he slowly straightened, muttering something in his native tongue and sheathing his weapon.

I kept watching as Kurn moved to one of the tapestry-covered windows, lifting the edge of the heavy thing to look outside. I saw only starlight seep in, and Kurn fast gave up peering into blackness, taking a slow turn about the room. Unfortunately, if he stayed close to the walls as he was doing, he would come upon me as he approached the hearth. The shadows weren't that deep; it was due to only his lack of sensitivity that he hadn't seen me already.

Worse, I would be cornered as he got close; the cabinet to one side, the wall to another, Kurn in the open area, and the table and a chair constricting my own space. If the Hellhound decided to block me with his size, he had the reach and might succeed in a seize or tackle. He'd be dead from stab wounds and spider bites before he could do much.

Let's avoid that outcome a little longer, shall we?

I waited until something on the tapestry caught his attention and moved low to the head of the table. I eased my body onto the table in one fluid motion, only my cloak whispering, and stayed in a crouch with my hood up, the hearth fire at my back. Resting elbows on my thighs, I dipped one hand into a pouch then folded both gloved hands before me, concealing my last web pellet, just in case.

The Hellhound had turned toward the cabinet and my former hiding place, eyeballing it as if he considered looking inside, but then saw me out of his periphery.

"*Kus umma!*" he blurted, reaching for something as I tensed to spring away, my spiders twirling excitedly on the back of my neck.

"Stop!" I barked. "Or you will purge your guts before you see your arm miss!"

He paused to hear my voice, recognized it and eased down, scowling. "*Garbuua.* You jump through shadows, now, *Elf?*"

He still didn't believe what I was. I showed my teeth in the firelight. "If taking the stairs is too difficult. Pleasant morn to you, Hellhound."

Kurn snorted and shook his head. "Foolish to startle me. You may have been pierced."

I didn't reply, for I heard a soft step from toward the kitchen and focused my ear that way. A slow breath and another shoe scuff against stone; I figured Gavin was peeking in on us. The Hellhound seemed unaware of our audience.

"What know you of demons?" I asked. "You mentioned them first upon seeing me."

"I know plenty," he said brusquely. "My Gods have long harnessed their power at will to aid the Ma'ab in battle."

I tried not to laugh. "How long have the Ma'ab Gods commanded the eternal void? The last I witnessed, the blood of the horde is never simple or obedient as common soldiers."

Kurn wavered in uncertainty, as if he did not know all the words I'd used. Then, "Have you seen demons, black *kus?*"

"Up close," I answered, assured. "I can distinguish them for you."

He watched me suspiciously, leaning to see farther inside my hood. I decided to oblige him and lowered it again. Even after a whole meal of staring, Kurn continued to gorge himself on my appearance.

"Do you like what you see?" I asked, holding his gaze.

His nose twitched in a sneer. "Glamor. Your real form is not so comely, though your demonic coloring is the same."

Is the same?

Was that a mistake in his Trade speech?

I tilted my head. I had to be frank. "Have you heard stories of beastly versions of me, Kurn? Male, with a white mane down his back? Yellow eyes?"

His jaw tightened. His lips pursed stubbornly on his answer.

I stared. Suck Braqth's spinnerets, he *knew!* He knew something about the missing Priestess and her Son! I couldn't believe it to stumble upon it so soon. Did the Valsharess *know* this Ma'ab would be here? I swallowed, my face like stone as my head felt too light. I had no choice; I *must* go on the mission with the four men. The Ma'ab knew of the Davrin in some way, though he didn't understand how.

The Northern Empire, Sarilis said. How far away is that? It wasn't on Shyntre's map.

I wanted to prod him about his homeland this moment, but I already knew he could be explosive in his temper. My stomach was also gnawing on itself. I squashed the impulse.

What is the hurry in questioning him if I have no choice but to follow?

Slowly, I stood up on the table, temporarily taller than him; he straightened in response. "Excuse me, Hellhound. I will check on our breakfast."

I hopped off the table, landed quietly enough for my pride, and strode with purpose toward Cullen and the hall leading to the kitchen. Slipping my unused web pellet in its pouch, I heard Gavin ahead of me, sneaking back to his post. A good thing, as I was feeling sick and I didn't know if it was just my pregnancy or my unwitting discovery. Food would help sort it out.

I snapped my fingers and made a gesture for Cullen to move ahead of me. "To the kitchen. Go."

Of course, the reanimated man obeyed not my will but as commanded by his master, yet I liked that Kurn could watch me do it. His face was amusing.

Better than seeming like I'm in retreat.

Which I was. I needed to think, and Kurn made that difficult.

The kitchen entrance had a swinging door that I thought suspiciously well-oiled. As I entered with Cullen holding it for me, Gavin focused on his tasks. The young death mage wore thick, woolen robes that covered all of his lanky frame except his head and hands. He hadn't washed his hair in a while as it hung flat from his skull in dark, glossy strands, though it did occur to me that I did not know the rate of build for something like that in Humans. Perhaps this happened in four days rather than a month?

The tension in his shoulders combined with the fact that he did not look up spoke clearly that he knew I was there.

"Pleasant morn, Gavin."

He grunted an acknowledgement before turning his head. The apprentice blinked his black eyes once and considered Cullen behind me as I came down the three Dwarf-sized steps into the wide work area.

"Your escort, I take it," he said.

"Your master is gracious."

Gavin snorted, his mouth twisting. "Explains why he was standing there when I came in."

"You are an early riser."

He scowled. "More mouths to feed, more work for me. I imagine you'd prefer I not have animates like Cullen help me prepare the bread. You might find a fingernail inside."

I smiled, my low mood lifting quite quickly. Why did this strike me as funny? It was plausible, if ludicrous, to paint the walking dead standing at the worktable, kneading bread. Something about his delivery and that straight expression on his face made it so.

"I'm sure it would add spice," I quipped, "rather like the roaches."

Gavin quirked a black eyebrow at me with a glance at his recently scoured pot. "A comment on the housekeeping?"

I shrugged, adopting a touch of his attitude from the night before. "Not really. I understand they are quite edible, tasty when roasted."

The tall, gaunt man stared at me for quite some time. It eventually occurred to me that he might be wondering if I was jesting, the same as I'd wondered if he was.

"All this talk of food," I said. "I am hungry, apprentice. Is there anything I might have before the others finally wake? Even roasted roaches, I will eat them."

He looked to believe me. "How long have you been awake?"

"Several hours. Humans sleep a long time compared to Elves."

Gavin turned that over; he found it interesting. Then, with a soft sigh, he turned and rummaged in a few built-in cabinets, the squawking hinges not nearly as oiled as the door had been. He found and grabbed a lidded, clay jar, placing it on the counter midway between us.

"Take it with you. I have work to do."

I lifted the greyish jar and opened the lid to sniff gently. A collection of dried berries and strips of preserved meat, with a pleasant mix of herb and spice that was new to me. It made my mouth water.

"Thank you, apprentice. I'll take my leave."

I met and held his eyes, the only thing I could do to communicate that I hadn't lost interest in him. Gavin glanced at Cullen without so much as a facial tic as he waited for me to leave.

"To the great room, Cullen. Go first."

After the thrall shuffled before me through the swinging door to the larger room, I paused long enough to wink at the apprentice. I chuckled when his whole brow drew down in confusion.

Kurn wasn't there when I reentered, but a pause and a listen told me he was in the hallway, talking low with someone. Castis. I picked the chair that gave me a straight hearing path into the hall, sat down with Cullen staring dully at me, and broke into the jar of preserves. I chewed slowly as I focused on listening to the voices bouncing off the stone.

They spoke in their native tongue, and it was too far and low to hear every word clearly even if I understood them. From the tones alone, I could guess the subject: the black *kus* and how to journey with her, if necessary.

I wonder the same in return, boys. The same.

My stomach stopped complaining with Gavin's jar of preserves, and the food agreed with me. My ears picked up early rustling from Rithal and, eventually up the stairs, Mathias, so instead of roaming around with Cullen in tow, I remained comfortable where I was, lying back with boots propped on the dining table.

It remained pleasantly dark inside the Necromancer's Tower, but I detected a gradual line of light around the tapestries, knowing the clouds had taken their leave of this part of the sky. Gavin had come in briefly only to put out breakfast, and I dropped my boots to the floor to watch him center three dense loaves of what resembled my favorite mushroom dark-bread, alongside three pitchers of water, bowls and spoons, and a larger dish of shredded greens tossed with oil. My mouth hung open as the scents tantalized me.

"Um—"

"Don't touch," he said.

I grinned. "Surely, if I'm eating it when they come in, they will know you didn't tamper with it."

Gavin narrowed his eyes at me and then rolled them and shrugged. "As you like."

The apprentice left before the others appeared, and I dove at the warm bread, breaking the crust and ripping off a large piece while it steamed inside. I moaned again taking my first bite, the scent of toasted seed filling my nose, but this time Sarilis wasn't here to comment. It wasn't mushroom dark-bread, but it was fresh and glorious all the same.

The men reconvened at once in the great room; Kurn and Castis first, followed by Rithal, then Mathias. They all noticed Cullen by the doorway to the kitchen and Sarilis's lab, considered him a moment, then eyed me sitting at the table with my jaws working energetically on the morning meal.

I swallowed, my smile stuck on my lips. "Lose something?"

The Ma'ab brothers didn't answer but came to sit at the table anyway, Kurn quickly breaking one loaf in half and handing one to Castis. Castis broke that in half and handed it to Mathias. Rithal took one loaf for himself. None of them touched the one I had broken, so I broke it again and placed the rest on the plate at the head of the table, for whenever Sarilis arrived.

Mathias cleared his throat and said, "Red Sister?"

I looked at him as the others began chowing down.

"Please pass the greens."

I smiled and leaned forward to place the bowl closer to him. He stared at my face for a moment, and I said, "It's safe as Gavin made it. I haven't sampled it yet."

The bearded man considered as he served himself. "You eat greens?"

"When I must. I am still learning what is edible."

The three others stopped chewing their bread to look at me.

"What?" I asked.

"You've never seen edible greens?" Castis asked.

Fuck me sideways.

Only Sarilis knew I lived underground, and he hadn't told them. I tried Jaunda's bold smirk. "Not until answering this call."

Without another word, I took the bowl and served myself some of those plants, using the fork to stuff in a nice, large bite. It wasn't as good as the bread, but the tangy coating on the leaves helped.

"Where do you come from that there are no greens to eat, 'Elf'?" Kurn murmured in a low threat, glancing at Rithal as if blaming him for being wrong.

The fire-beard caught it and frowned. "Lots o' homes built underground, ya bullock. I'd have thought any Ma'ab fool nosing around Taiding woulda run afoul that fact th' *hard* way."

My expression brightened as the Hellhound's darkened. I should be wary that Rithal got it just right, but his spine was in the right place. Mathias half-smiled and seemed mostly satisfied with that explanation.

"Where is Taiding?" I asked, figuring that aloof, mysterious silence was beyond me at this point, especially if Rithal was plucking up thoughts.

The blue-eyed, red-cheeked male blinked and considered the question. "Dunno yer point of reference, Elf."

"Yes, I would like to hear that answer first," Castis said with a smile as oily as the greens.

I shrugged coolly, taking the safest answer. "Reference Manalar."

Rithal nodded, a muscle in his eyelid twitching. "Three weeks ride northeast, as the crow flies. Halfway up the Great Lake's eastern shore."

"Ah," I bluffed, nodding as if I had the first vaguery where that was.

There's a Great Lake, now? Which direction?

Rithal didn't react to this.

Kurn, however, was watching me as he growled in the stout one's direction. "Dwarven trade town sits in direct path between the Empire and Augran."

Now Rithal smiled, the corners of his eyes crinkling. "Bit more than a 'town,' Hellhound. Y'all go 'round us into th' Steppes, fer good reason."

"A strong alliance between Taiding and Augran," Castis commented. "Blocking trade routes on both water and shore."

Rithal shrugged. "Surprised? Yer people made it necessary. Just self-defense."

"Are you from Taiding, Rithal?" Mathias asked curiously.

The redhead shook his beard, his eyes on portioning his bread. "Nah. The river-mounds southwest of Manalar."

"That's a long way from the Great Lake."

"News travels fast on lake an' river." The Dwarf paused and glanced at his hand; he'd squeezed part of his bread into a fist. Realizing it, he stuffed it in his mouth and chewed while talking. "Or... used to. Witch Hunners ran us out some decades back." He swallowed the lump and took a gulp of water to wash it down. "Bishops wanted control o' the river crossing. They went about it gettin' it like the deluded murderers they are."

I could hear his teeth grind, cracking a rogue seed. While I was fully lost in the talk of the landscapes and settlements, the tensions mentioned between factions and connecting those in this tiny group had hooked my ears. The gruff males had almost forgotten about me in their discussion, despite my handing leaves in a bowl to Mathias had started this conversation. I let it be so I could soak it all in.

Bishops and Witch Hunners? Augran and Taiding blocking the Empire. A river crossing connecting with the Great Lake.

I thought of my youngest Sister attempting to approach all that and more, alone.

I must go with them, whatever they intend to do to 'cleanse' the heart of Manalar. Listen to these stories.

Castis broke into my thoughts. "So, where *are* you from, Red Sister? What do you call yourself?"

"They call themselves Davrin, gentleman," Sarilis said as he stepped carefully out of his own hallway with the help of Cullen and a bone staff made of at least three femurs fused together. "Sirana is a Davrin Elf of the Deepearth."

"The what?" Mathias asked, while Rithal's eyes widened at me.

"Just what it sounds like," the death mage chortled. "Far, far below our feet. Vast, dark tunnels and caverns, much beyond a few dead-ends and caves like up here."

The old mage looked over our expressions and bowed to me. "I hope you don't mind, my dear, I thought it best to get this silly miscommunication out of the way. Unlike you, I do not have a lot of time left."

"For certain," I said vaguely, wondering how much else he knew and would reveal.

"Let your host get a little bread into his belly, and I shall explain." Sarilis finally arrived to take his chair at the head of the table, grunting as he fell into it with a pop or two of his bones. "Ahhh, I love that you waited for me, my dark angel."

The old man broke off a piece of bread for himself and offered me the rest, which I took with a smile. Mathias buried his expression in his mug of water while Rithal chewed busily.

"If she is from below, she is no angel," Castis observed.

"Do you have any real idea what *is* below, my young lord?" Sarilis asked. "Living cheek and jowl next to creatures that would make you piss your robes, yet her long-lived people are clever and vicious enough to hold their own city where none of you can go."

"Oh, can't we?" Kurn asked skeptically.

I grinned to imagine that, and Sarilis glanced at me, his own mirth spreading wide and yellow across his face.

"Well, it's not advisable for those frightened of tight places and things touching them in the dark. The Red Sister before you can see both with light and without, in darkness black as pitch, while the rest of you would bumble around in a single dim room, tripping by candlelight." A cackle. "As you gathered last night, she was sent by her leaders to assist me. She has come to the surface world to aid us in our quest. Like it or not, she *shall* be going with you."

"Could they not have sent a man from among them?" Castis asked.

The death mage could not stop sniggering for a good long time, enough for it to spread to me. I bit my lip, shoulders shaking to imagine sending Auslan or Micraen, or even Callitro, in my place. The only one who might make a good impression at this table was Shyntre, but he'd no doubt have started a mages' battle with Castis already.

"What is so funny?" Kurn demanded.

Sarilis waved an invitation to me to explain. How generous.

"The male Davrin are somewhat smaller than the female," I said. "They are meeker, as well. We take care of them, the mothers and grandmothers."

Seeing their faces, Sarilis whooped aloud, slapping his palm on the wood, and I chuckled along.

"There! Do you grasp it, Hellhound? You see the 'man' they sent to us! It will be easier if you treat her as such. She will be a great asset to your *farkhid*."

"She will not!" Kurn barked without pause. "She's tiny!"

"Of course, compared to a brute who must eat a nest of eggs a day—"

"He means she is sized like *our* women," Castis clarified. "We keep women out of the fighting. We protect them if they are in danger."

"And I'll say again, she's no woman you need to protect," the old man retorted with grey brows waggling. "If it helps, imagine you are both lovely she-Elves who can't see in the dark, and you will get along swimmingly."

Rithal covered his bushy face with one broad hand and grumbled something in Dwarvish. Mathias was swiveling his head between the death mage and Ma'ab with huge, brown eyes, his skin flushed like he wanted to laugh but dared not.

"I take it there's no negotiatin'," said the redbeard.

Sarilis shifted his yellow teeth in display. "Correct, Master Dwarf. You want the power to end the Witch Hunters of Manalar, I will give it to you, but on the condition that our Red Sister comes with you as your cohort. Surely this isn't difficult, for you have at least *heard* of Elves."

Rithal's eyelid twitched again. "Aye, an' I'm sure she won't distract the zealots at all."

Mathias blew out his breath at this. "Hm. Rithal's makes a point, Sarilis. One glimpse at her, and the Witch Hunters won't let it go."

Hunters, of course. Not Hunners. Now it made sense.

"Tut, tut," Sarilis tapped his fingers. "We'll get to that. How is everyone doing with their meal?" His pale eyes scanned the table. "Hmm, where's the rest of it? Gavin? *Gavin!*"

I would have wagered my left boot that the apprentice had been listening since the first word. In barely a moment, he entered carrying a wide, steaming platter of well-seasoned hash, placing it down and retreating toward the fire to listen and watch. I assumed he had already eaten when he made no move to serve himself. I moved fast, however, taking two bowls, placing some of the hash in each and setting one by Sarilis while digging into the other.

Flavor flooded my tongue. *Oh Goddess, better than the four-day stew...*

The old mage chuckled and bowed his head. "Thank you, my dear. Yes, I agree, let us eat first."

The food disappeared quickly but I got my fill, and that was all I cared about. I recalled I had half of the preserve jar left down by my feet and intended to keep it. Gavin wasn't acknowledged after he served the food, which I thought odd, though I kept him in my sideview. Perhaps the others did, too, except Sarilis, who was comfortable with his back to him.

"So, if we are taking the black Elf in our group," Mathias asked, "what may we expect of her?"

"I shall let Sirana speak on this when we get to it," our host said as he rubbed a black stone on his wrist, and Sir Cullen approached with the scroll caddy which had been on his back this whole time. "Each of you will do the same. But let us start at the beginning."

We pushed all the dishes to the end of the table and watched as Sarilis opened the stiff leather caddy and removed one scroll to unroll it before us. I leaned forward.

Not just a scroll. A map.

I couldn't read the script but recognized symbols close to those Shyntre had used for many Surface landmarks. A large river on the West side, hills in between, and mountains building to a large town or city. There were roads noted and other small settlements.

Sarilis stated, "You traveled far, Kurn and Castis, searching for a 'master of the dead' not allied with your people. And you heard of me through Rithal."

The Ma'ab agreed but the mage spoke, which was probably for the best.

"Our Gods are life and death for the Ma'ab, they choose both for us. But our mission is secret even to the rest of the army. It took most of a year to find you, a venerable man of death power, to listen to our cause."

Kurn added dryly, "Your home could not be farther from the Seat of Ennikar."

Sarilis chuckled. "Mages of my ilk do not choose our homes, but rather the home chooses us. But, do go on, for the sake of my other guests."

Castis nodded, glancing at me but looking to Mathias Briar. "We met Rithal Hobgaer in Augran. He did not know we were Ma'ab at first but appreciated our plan and knew where to find who we sought, if we were willing to travel beyond where any Ma'ab had been."

I frowned a little, both wondering if Rithal had really been fooled—he gave no sign one way or the other—and pondering how Kurn could recognize a Sathoet if these mountains were so far out of Ma'ab reach. Perhaps other demons sought by the Ma'ab resembled our half-bloods? Or was Castis mistaken? I listened.

"We have been waiting here for the time it took the apprentice to retrieve Master Briar." The white-faced mage looked at me. "And her."

Gavin huffed in amusement, and Sarilis heard it. Twisting around in his chair, he asked, "Something to add to that, boy?"

Dark eyes in a long, pale face glanced at Mathias. Gavin decided to tell the truth, since another man knew it anyway.

"I did not retrieve her. She appeared on the mountain road close to here, claiming to have 'heard' my master was hiring."

Sarilis turned to me with an enormous grin. "Well, now. That wasn't possible under mundane methods, as I hand-picked the skin hunter for this mission."

Skin hunter?

Mathias hardly acted like he had earned such a title.

I spread a confident smile across the table. "I have said I was sent. My superiors received your call, Sarilis. They are interested in this outcome."

"Marvelous," said the elder death mage, pleased with my reaffirmation. He faced fully those at the table, placing his gnarled, veiny hands on the wood. "Then we are each here as either strategic enemies of the Bishops of Manalar, or we wish great harm to their 'conversion' enforcers. Am I correct?"

Mathias smiled with easy agreement, while Rithal's expression blackened with potent hatred I may have only felt like a mouthful of poison. Kurn and Castis affirmed with their body language, and I quickly opted to be in the "strategic enemy" camp, should anyone ask. I could lay the reasoning at my leaders' feet and need not explain details.

"Excellent." Sarilis focused on the Dwarf. "And, you have heard of unusual activity among the Templars as far away as Augran?"

"Aye," Rithal grumped. "They have a new Captain, an outsider that don't always see eye-to-eye with the Bishops."

Sarilis glanced at the rest of us, his eyes bright. "You grasp the significance of this?"

"Of what? The Captain?" Kurn asked, less in his habitual dismissal as he handed our host the opening we all wanted.

"More. The Templars are the martial guardians of Manalar," Sarilis said, pointing to the defense wall of the city on his map, helping me to realize what I was looking at. "They do not roam the country roads as the Witch Hunters do, looking for heretics. They are kept close and under the direct control of the Bishops, in charge of the garrisons. And yet!" The old man raised his pointer finger high. "Rithal hears frequently of a new leader *not* groomed by the Bishops in the City of the Sun, rising in the ranks in a short time and disrupting the old order. The masses are unsettled, and some want this change."

Sarilis paused, leaning back from his map. "There is a split between the city's powers as there has not been for my lifetime. The Manalar soldiers have a different pole star to look to in a crisis and may question their clerics in the sway of this younger, persuasive soldier among them." He spread his palms out above the drawing and chuckled. "When complacent magistrates lose the full strength of their fighting men to their cause, the winds of change indeed begin to blow. I even think the Ma'ab Gods have heard of this and see a fruitful opportunity."

"Does the Captain have a name?" Mathias asked, scratching his beard but seeming intrigued.

Rithal grunted an affirmative. "Captain Willven Isboern."

"Isboern?" The Nobleman showed white, straight teeth. "*That* is a strange name among the Manalari. Sounds like a Western mountain man." He cocked one brown eyebrow. "Does anyone know where he came from?"

"Not that I heard," the Dwarf answered. "Stories been circulatin' about five years. Some are callin' him a Godblood. He heals with a touch o' his hand, his prayers to Musanlo get answered, the holy light shines about 'im, that sort o' thing."

Kurn scoffed, exchanging a nose wrinkle with his Ma'ab brother.

Mathias laughed. "Ohhh, the Bishops *can't* like that!"

"Indeed," Sarilis cackled, tickled that his briefing was going so well. "Now, the stage is set, we know the Ma'ab intend to lay siege to Manalar this summer. We have little time to get into place for the greatest advantage." He turned to me. "Red Sister. Tell us what your hidden mothers have commanded."

Clever, conniving opportunist.

I reworded what the death mage had been discussing in his lab last night without looking at the Dwarf. "There is a magical heart in Manalar, the focus from which the Bishops receive their mages' power. My mothers wish to see it taken from their hands."

"Yesss," Sarilis agreed with zeal. "Pierce and bleed the heart of their magic, lose the garrisons to their new paladin, and the Bishops *and* the Witch Hunters will collapse in the breeze of the first Ma'ab siege!"

The entire city will fall to the Ma'ab 'gods.'

Kurn and Castis smiled in pride and pleasure, knowing this as well. Mathias seemed untroubled, like he had no personal stake, and I wasn't sure what the man would get out of this. Rithal looked at the table, eyes hardening with determination, his expression introspective with no apparent suspicion toward me. Perhaps he wasn't pleased with the broader damage to "end" the Witch Hunters but that hadn't stopped him from leading the Ma'ab to the Ley Tower

Whether he was psionic or not, I felt a kinship there as my personal determination coalesce inside. I couldn't control the wider results and felt no need to, but I could discover more about the

Ma'ab and the Sathoet, and I might have the smallest chance to find Jael, even if I could not find Gaelan, and I would take it.

What else will I do up here before going back to face the Valsharess?

It was, indeed, as my mothers had commanded.

I learned next where this "heart" we were supposed to bleed was located.

"The Temple is built around a sacred pool of water," Sarilis said, "closed off to the masses, guarded to remain clean and pure. This is both good and bad, as no one else can abscond with the source of power at Manalar but you must go there and get inside to complete your mission."

Now I began to doubt the old man's sense of realism. Even had I not arrived, this motley group of Ma'ab and Dwarf would not be allowed into a temple. I had but to think of the same attempting to get into the central worship altar inside the Sanctuary.

However, as my gaze drifted to Mathias, I finally had an idea why he was "hand-picked" for this task. He might be the only one who appeared enough like the other men of Manalar to sneak in.

But then, he will be alone.

"Does Mathias Briar speak the local language?" I asked.

Sarilis leered. "You are sprinting ahead. He does."

"I would not sound exactly as one of them," the man added.

"Near enough, and you can be trusted to escort our Red Sister in disguise."

What?

"What?" Kurn echoed my thought.

Sarilis lifted his chin. "Lone women are not allowed in the Temple, if at all. They must have a man to escort them. I will make a potion to alter her appearance, and Mathias will grease the wheels."

"Why not make disguises for all?" the Hellhound asked sourly.

"Mathias blends in without effort, people forget him. It is his talent. Davrin are accustomed to silence and stalking in darkness.

Sirana's patience will seem inhuman, I promise you." The death mage chuckled. "I think a Ma'ab your size would topple over the first urn you brushed against, potion or not. You will need their help at the Temple."

"Aye," Rithal agreed without debate.

Castis wasn't at all amused by the description like I was but did his best to convince Kurn in their native tongue. Reluctantly, the biggest man allowed this to pass without further protest.

I asked, "How will we break the Bishop's hold on this 'sacred pool'?"

The death mage rubbed his wrinkled hands together. "I will make you a vial, perhaps two. You need only toss one of them into the water. It will corrupt their protections and release the caged heart of the Ley."

In the corner of my vision, Gavin moved. It took my every effort not to twist my head to look at him.

"Would that not cause magical backlash?" I asked.

"Indeed, that is the intent!" Sarilis grinned. "The disruption will be unstoppable for the sun worshippers. The Ma'ab will be just outside, their death mages waiting to take advantage of the opening I shall give them."

"Yes!" Kurn blurted, sounding eager. "We will give them warning. They will be ready to use the magic once it is turned."

I swallowed my other concerns rather than question Sarilis in front of them. I wondered, however, how it was possible to get out of the Temple if the flux caused by the vial was as disruptive as it needed to be to overcome a Priesthood.

Perhaps I wouldn't go inside. If I found Jael prior to that coming siege, I would grab her, and we'd run off. Leave the Humans to their war.

She could help me to kill Sarilis on our way back.

I glanced at Rithal. Still no outward reaction to my thoughts. The redbeard focused on the plan, maintaining that blended expression of determined discomfort as the discussion to corrupt the

Bishops' pool continued, and on our making it from here to Man-alar's Temple to begin with. Although Mathias and I would be most useful once there and the two Ma'ab brothers would rejoin their people in time for the siege, it seemed we would all depend on Rithal's knowledge of the land in between to make the journey.

As plans wound down for a break, I had a better sense overall for this small group of insurgents planning something big. Although I had risked my real motives at the fore of my thoughts several times, neither the Dwarf nor any others seemed to notice. I was nearly convinced not Rithal, Castis, nor Sarilis were accustomed to scraping others for unwary thoughts. They were not anything like the Priestesses or Elder D'Shea.

Perhaps it is only so common down below.

That would make all this easier.

CHAPTER 8

"Now I know what we need," Sarilis told me, "I shall be working in my lab, possibly well into the evening. I trust you all can entertain yourselves without death or maiming?"

"Horses need tendin'," Rithal said.

On that, they all agreed; the men and the Dwarf would take their horses from the stables for exercise. No one invited me, and I had no pretense to offer assistance when Gavin did not suggest the same for his own cart-drawing mare. Instead, he gathered the dirty dishes and disappeared into the kitchen before we'd stood up. I did not give a reason but said I would be in my room in the tower. They seemed to believe me.

I waited on the stairs, listening both to the sounds of horses and their riders drifting out of the courtyard outside and the clean-up in the kitchen by the apprentice. Before too long, Gavin crossed the great room again, and I expected to meet him on the stairs. Instead, his footsteps shifted away from me, down a smaller, alternate staircase. By what I knew of the layout thus far, it did not retreat into the fortress but may lead to a rear exit of the tower itself.

Where are you going, apprentice?

I followed him into the utilitarian area without running into another Cullen and spotted that backdoor just as he closed it. Approaching, I felt the fading ward which he had not taken the time to replace. I took the handle, tested it and the hinges for excessive noise before opening it a crack. Hood drawn down, I peeked out before stepping into the early afternoon.

Pain lanced through my head and my eyes watered as I found shade, though it did not take long to be able to see. The constant practice with Rausery still paid, even if I preferred to slip back into the lovely dimness of the stone tower.

I stood in a little garden tucked in a rear pocket behind the tower, just being touched with direct sunlight. It was surrounded by a stone wall and had no evidence of death magic like some of the forest outside. It was fully alive, the new green firmly taken, planned and designed with vegetables, herbs, and decorative shrubbery.

I would be stupid not to see it was tended daily, and I did not think the decrepit master or the corpses like Cullen would be the ones maintaining it. Food must come from somewhere, and most of what I'd eaten thus far were plants that must have been grown here. It was meticulously kept and healthy; significant if Gavin was doing it alone and without magic like Tamuril's.

Sarilis seemed comfortable as a counselor to governors, but the apprentice must have a servant's background. *You've practiced this for many years.*

I crouched in my shade, aware my cover was not heavy, admiring the garden as it only took moments for Gavin to reappear. He squatted and pulled out tiny, select growth by their roots and tossing them in a heap of dead plants. He had a trowel on his belt and a few other tools nearby but worked with his bare, long-fingered hands. Every so often, he unfurled his lanky frame and turned around, searching the entire garden. He expected he was being watched.

You're correct, apprentice.

I plucked up a small stone and gave it a toss to bounce along the ground and make noise. He looked in my direction, and I shifted my weight with intention between the stone and brush. He saw my shape and grunted.

"There you are." He returned to his gardening. "Come to trade more questions?"

I smiled. "Are you rested?"

"Never fully. I am accustomed to fatigue."

I watched him collect a large cup of water from a rain trough and carefully pour it at the roots of certain plants, making no splashes. His fingers checked the leaves and buds like he examined their health. It was oddly fascinating.

"How long have you been apprentice at this tower?" I asked, accepting the invitation to revive our first conversation, and this time he answered.

"Five years."

Not long at all. No wonder Tamuril hadn't realized Sarilis wasn't alone.

"And how many years since birth?"

He glanced up at me like the phrasing was off, though I struggled to recall how he had asked me the same question. "I am twenty-six."

I grimaced as the memory returned: Natia atop the stairs at my Mother's House. Gaelan's Daughter was the same age as this man.

"Is that unpleasant to hear?" Gavin asked like he did not care either way.

"No. I still grow accustomed to Human age."

He smirked a little, his features pronounced for the effort. "How does an Elf at this age appear?"

I leveled my hand near my hip. "About this tall. Under-grown. Still a child needing protection."

Gavin measured that with his dark eyes, lips tight for a moment. He nodded once. "That size is often about six years old."

Only six?

"You grow fast."

He didn't remark on my observation, which I'd known in theory but hadn't spoken with a man to confirm it until now.

I asked, "You are of breeding age at twenty-six, yes?"

He stopped gardening and faced me with an expression I couldn't read but I thought he looked repelled. "Why do you ask?"

I rephrased the question. "Humans can breed at what age?"

He grunted, nodding his understanding. "Fifteen, perhaps."

"Perhaps?"

"I understand it varies, and I haven't observed this directly."

"Why not? Where are you from?"

He blatantly ignored that and returned to pulling out unwanted plants from his garden, leaving me to think how this apprentice or another like him could have, in theory, been making babies with females for a decade already. How long was the growth in the womb? Not two turns, I would bet, as it was for us. For me.

No wonder their race spread over the lands, if it happened as Rithal described. But it wasn't the Humans mounting each other that drove us underground, was it?

I couldn't believe that. The one thing holding the Human numbers in check would be women's wombs, and abruptly something made some sense to me. If the males were larger than the females up here, and they claimed to "protect" those wombs as they waited for the opportunity to quicken them, maybe the men fight over them as we did over the best sires down below.

Only the methods of the fight might be different.

I turned my ear toward the wall built off the tower. Multiple horses tromped the ground, and some low voices called intelligibly. Then I made out the Dwarf warning one to stay closer. "Hm. I presume Rithal has the talisman to dissuade the sentries?"

Gavin looked in the vague direction where I tilted my head. "What prompted this?"

I blinked at his expression. "You can't hear them?"

Dark brows twitched upward. "Mm. Davrin hearing seems far keener than the average man."

"And in meeting one, you seem less unsettled than the others. Did Sarilis teach you about us?"

Gavin's arms were folded. "I've found he's not much of a teacher."

"He calls you apprentice. You *are* a mage."

His nostril curled. "Glorified manservant."

Yes, that matched what I'd observed so far.

"Why do you keep following me?" he asked, reaching for a long-handled tool to gently rake at soil that probably didn't need it.

I watched him work. Why, indeed? Rausery warned me against seeming mundane and explainable, and the others had done all the work for me so far in maintaining my mystery. As she suggested, I need not volunteer anything. Yet, that approach did not work with Gavin; he refused to accept it. Instead, he used the same tactic with me, young as he was, and I admitted wanting to know more.

"I seek a teacher. I agree Sarilis is a poor one. Far too much..." I floundered for a word, waving my hand and moving like I dodged swordplay.

"Fencing?" he suggested.

"What's that?"

Gavin grunted; no smile, but he might have been amused. "A game of skill for wealthy men, dancing with swords without being true soldiers in mortal combat. Sometimes used for one who must play a conversation as a competition, fencing with words instead of swords."

I grinned and pointed a gloved finger at him. "Yes, this! Sarilis is word fencing. Habit of misdirecting and gaining advantage with information."

"And you don't?"

Fair point.

I shrugged. "When I must be, but I can do otherwise. In a mage, I prefer your speech. While I am here, I want to trade with a teacher, not a fencer. You proved you *will* trade, Gavin."

The homely man pondered this for some time, trading his rake for a spade to keep his hands busy. I shifted with the Sun to wait in the shade, patient for his response and relying on Rausery's promise that Humans knew they didn't have time to waste.

"Are you from this plane?" he asked.

I perked up at this proof of a scholar. "Yes. I have no blood that is from 'out'."

I pointed up at the sky as I said this, and Gavin's mouth opened in surprise. He stopped working the soil to level his eyes at me, incredulous. "You understand this concept instantly, but not animal husbandry?"

"That is just Trade language," I returned. "Davrin breed animals for uses, too. I understand."

Gavin nodded. "Very well."

"Where are you from that *you* understand and ask this question?"

He hesitated.

"Is it such as Sarilis claimed," I probed, "that the mage did not choose the home, but the home chose the mage?"

"You suggest I am a mage of his 'ilk'?" he replied dryly.

"Again, you are not unsettled by me. You know of outer places, and you trade knowledge. You came here with purpose, yes?"

He stared at me, a chill coming over his demeanor. I spotted resentment which did not seem aimed at me yet it overcame his curiosity. He turned away to tend his garden.

"You *want* to know," I pointed out. "Do not lie that you know your mind. Trade with me. Teach me of this place, your words, the stories up here."

An audible breath passed in and out of his nose as he kept his head down. "I will think on it."

Maddening. What was there to think about? What consequence made him pause?

"You will not have a better opportunity to add to your book."

"My…book," he repeated.

"Every mage teacher has one," I claimed. "Or do you not know a script?"

Irritably, he said, "I can write."

"Same script as Sarilis?" I nudged. "Did you find his book from when he encountered my leader two decades ago?"

Dark eyes flicked at me. "Very well. Yes. I read it. You were not a complete shock to me as you were to the others."

Finally.

"But enough," he said, moving farther away. "Let me think."

The death mage sounded a bit like Shyntre there. *Hmph.* Some headstrong traits were the same in any male mage, either Human or Davrin.

I frowned where I stood, arms crossed, thinking how else I would pass the time until Sarilis emerged from his lab. I picked up further distant sounds of hooves and low voices, and wondered what the Ma'ab, the Dwarf, and Mathias were discussing; how much of it involved me?

Then, a familiar screech sounded high above my head. The Sun was too intense to look up and see the falcon, and that would draw unneeded attention anyway. I waited, and when Pilla cried again, eventually coming into sight closer to the valley floor like she was hunting, the signal could not be clearer.

Hmm, until evening, he said.

I had the time, if I hurried.

"Is there a way around the sentries?" I asked. "Or have you a talisman I may borrow?"

Gavin paused. "You want to leave the valley?"

"For a time. I will return by dusk."

His face skewed with skepticism. "You must report somewhere?"

I grinned. "I must think on things."

His eyes narrowed at the riposte. "The old man will know."

"Hm. Does he *know* you read his book? Or did he show it willingly?"

I enjoyed his blink of authentic surprise.

"Parry and touch," he grumbled. After some contemplation, he answered my question. "If you carry a talisman, you won't be bothered but he will be aware of your passage. He can see through their eyes."

Good to know.

"Are there blind spots where I do not need a talisman?"

"Yes, but not helpful for you if you can't sense where they are and have not watched their patterns before now."

"Indeed, as you have. Will you guide me?"

"I have work to do."

"Ask a price. Though no tool on me, I can spare nothing."

He bent down to rip up a weed, his face partly covered by stringy hair; he muttered something. I was certain it wasn't Trade, Dwarvish, *or* Ma'ab.

Then, straightening, he said, "The others will notice we are gone. And how will you return unless I stay out as long as you? It will bring trouble from all of them."

Reasonable. Though, all here brought trouble regardless.

"Let me borrow your talisman for coming back," I suggested. "I care less being seen then. Just lead me out and return here to do your work."

Gavin considered, and I waited.

"What is your most dangerous weapon?" he asked. "If you feared for your life or freedom."

Good price. "First, a question."

He sighed. "Of course."

"To your knowledge, do any here scrape thoughts? Could they glean this from you in an unwary moment?"

The look on his face was reassuring; it was a new thought he pondered, with no lingering paranoia as it was with me.

"I have never known anyone capable of that. Surely not Sarilis."

"Not the Dwarf?"

He pounced on that. "Why him more than the others?"

My mouth twisted. "The Dwarves of the Deepearth can scrape thoughts if you cannot defend against them. Some, not all. I wondered if there were stories for the same of Surface Dwarves?"

Gavin looked intrigued. "Not… to my knowledge. Not a whisper of any such talent for Dwarves, but bear in mind, I have not lived among them."

That must be good enough. Delicately, I plucked open my pouch, checked again that I was in the moving shade and we were unobserved in the garden. Gavin watched as I coaxed my three guardians onto my palm where they spread out over my glove. I held them up, and they cringed from the light, crawling toward my cloak.

"Spiders?" he asked, wary of coming forward for a closer view.

"My most dangerous weapon. Created by an elder Davrin mage. They obey me. Their sole purpose is to guard me. They bite with poison."

He grunted. "Any antidote?"

I shook my head, reaffirmed my thoughts that I would *not* use my last cure on anyone here. "No. Painful death. No stopping it."

The apprentice looked cautious. "Duly noted."

He replaced his tools into a tiny shed. I watched with interest while coaxing my small ones into their dark pouch.

"You will lead me out?" I asked.

He answered with a nod. "And best we hurry."

Delighted, I unhooked my skin, moving toward his trough. "I will fill my skin."

Gavin repressed a sigh as he waited, fiddling with something in his pocket as he peered above the wall.

Once I was ready, he urged me, "Stay close."

At first, I worked on memorizing the path we took to use again, but Gavin muttered that I shouldn't bother.

"The pattern the undead walk is predetermined, but the cycle is long. Chances are much greater the blind spots you need on the way back will have changed. The talisman must be enough, and I recommend *not* retracing your steps exactly."

Well, damn. Good to know neither mage was stupid or lazy.

I poked him. "So, you *are* competing for this Ley intersection, are you not?"

Gavin glowered at me, and I smiled.

"I know this 'song' draws those most sensitive to magic," I said. "It drew me."

"Perhaps," he admitted. "But I am not ready to challenge him."

I knew it.

Despite further probing, however, that was the end of the discussion. Gavin didn't speak again until we had woven through brush and ravine, copse and ditches before climbing partway up a mountain.

"We've crossed the extent of his reach," Gavin said, sweating as I was from the exertion under the lowering Sun, though he smelled in need of a wash. "I will leave you here."

He reached into his pocket to offer me a tiny bird skull etched with intricate markings, holding it by the tips of his fingers. I took it, glad for my glove as it felt... cold. It sent a shiver down my back.

"Try not to crush it," he said, turning to gauge his way before leaving alone, a state to which he was no doubt accustomed.

Maybe preferred.

I was familiar relying on myself through childhood, yet after just a few turns in the Sisterhood, I missed some of them. There were two about whom I kept thinking, and my chest tightened as began climbing the mountain.

Ridiculous, but I looked forward to seeing Tamuril after the mere night and morning apart, surrounded by both baffling and hostile males. The Druid wouldn't have left; she would be there waiting. She had sent her bird where I could see it, or perhaps Pilla had been watching for me to exit the stone structure, and I finally had.

I'd revealed my spiders to the apprentice to get out here undetected. If this did not suggest I wasn't always content working alone, then I lied to myself.

I moved up and along the most climbable, angled path, keeping an eye and ear out for the screechy, spotted falcon. Pilla reappeared before long, refraining from her sharp call; she curved around to show me the direction. I followed.

Tamuril's earth-colored cloak and doeskin clothes did a good job camouflaging her; I scented her first when the breeze shifted just right and moved in her direction until I spotted her crouched outline. Green eyes in a pale, Elven face appeared as she looked up at her companion taking to a branch; whatever the animal communicated without words reassured her I had come alone.

"You got out," she said in hushed tones as she stood up again. Now that I could compare, the lithe Pale One was about as tall as Mathias but shorter than Kurn and Castis.

I nodded. "I did."

Her eyes were worried. "There are a lot of them. What is happening? Why were you inside all night, and four ride their horses about in the morning?"

I figured "a lot" in this context was relative to Sarilis being alone. I shrugged. "Sarilis remembered when last the Davrin were up here. He invited me to stay on reputation of my elder."

"Why?" she demanded. "What is he planning?"

"What would you do if you knew?" I challenged.

Her lips closed, and she was silent. I caught myself staring at the pink color and tiny trembling as she seemed lost for an answer.

"It would… depend on what the harm might be," she murmured.

"Oo," I cooed, grinning despite myself. "You *might* act on it? And if the 'harm' was far from here, would you let it be?"

Blonde eyebrows drew down into a plainly sad expression. "Probably."

"I agree that would be better. If you have been in these mountains for a century, you should think with care to follow their trouble."

Tamuril worked to calm herself, glancing up as Pilla hopped to a lower branch above our heads with fierce, tawny eyes fixed on me. I was becoming accustomed to it.

"So, sell-swords?" she asked. "How far away will they travel? And what care does Sarilis have that they do?"

I considered how much to say and who else she might tell. "The Humans are close to another war, as I hear it. One group called the Ma'ab having their eyes set on Manalar."

"Again?!" she blurted. "Now?"

I blinked and stared as her face pinkened. "Um. By the summer. And, what do you mean 'again'? When was the last one?"

"Not two centuries ago!" she said, exasperated.

"How do you know that?" The answer struck me, and I lifted a finger. "Ah, wait, your city sister. Yes, she would know. And anything I say, you will tell her."

Tamuril looked angry at my deduction, which only made me smile in response. I wasn't finished.

"If the Ma'ab are soon to lay siege on Manalar, is our other pale Elf in danger? Do you need to warn her?"

"No," she replied imperiously. "She takes care of herself. And she is not in Manalar, in any case."

"Augran, then."

She flinched, and I grinned wider. *Finally, getting answers!*

"By the Goddess, Pale One, you are like an open scroll. I also just learned how rare sightings of Elves are, light or dark. How does your sister live in a city of Humans large enough to block the Ma'ab on the Great Lake? In disguise? As a demon shadow that others whisper about?"

Tamuril's mouth sagged open, her blush in full bloom. Oh, I wanted to learn more!

"E-Enough," she said, taking a step back and away from the tree behind her. "The war isn't what Sarilis plans. It shall happen regardless. Why does the death mage at this tower care to hire men after somehow hearing of it?"

I rubbed my chin, not daring to blink as I watched her face. "Well, it has something to do with a sacred pool that is inside the Temple."

She knew this place existed. I continued.

"Sarilis wants to make certain its magic is 'freed' from the Bishops of the Sun, but also that the Ma'ab 'gods' don't get it. He says it is like his Ley tower, but older and more powerful, and must be released for 'all' to use."

The pink drained away as she looked ill.

"What does this mean?" I asked her. "I'm not a mage, and I just learned about the Ley Lines. I don't understand them."

"H-Has he said how he will d-do this?" she asked me, such dread in her voice.

I offered her more. "He said he would make a vial to toss into the pool. That it would corrupt the Bishops protections and, I suppose, somehow make it inhospitable to the Ma'ab claiming it."

Tears formed quickly; one slid down her cheek. "Oh, S-Sir-ana... Th-that can't happen. You must stop them."

"How do you suggest I do that?" I asked sardonically. "Shall I kill them all because you can't? Let my spiders bite them in their sleep?"

I was discomforted by the fallen look on her face; she took my words harsher than needed.

She stammered, "I-I'm sorry, you are right. No, that is not what I mean."

Apology so easily? I kept my mouth closed, lest I say something else that struck the tender blonde like a club.

"Why now, I wonder?" she murmured more to herself than to me.

I shrugged. "The Humans were talking about a 'split' between the city's powers, the Bishops and the Templars. Prompted by an outsider man, the Templars' new 'Captain' Isboern, who sounds to me like a mage as well as a fighter, perhaps a healer." I paused with a frown. "Or a good illusionist."

Tamuril was still, eyes huge and limpid. "Wh-What did they say about him?"

"Just that he stirs up opportunity for those who want to see the Bishops and their Witch Hunters lose control of the Temple pool. His growing renown are why the Ma'ab prepare to lay siege."

The Druid quivered where she stood in the forest mulch. She turned her eyes to the East, as if she could see the city of which we spoke through the forest.

"What will you do?" she whispered, clearly afraid of the answer, as was I when the first touch of nausea entered my middle.

I shrugged. "I must go with them."

Her head jerked my way, eyes pinned on me. "Not to *help* them?"

I wrinkled my nose, forcing an even breath. "No. One of them knows something about our cleric going missing. I must discover what."

She was incredulous. "He knows her from a century ago?"

"Of course not," I forced a chuckle. "He wasn't born yet. He's heard about the cleric in a different way, however. He knows about the 'beast' you saw, and he's Ma'ab. From the far North and East, yes? I find that strange he knows yet Sarilis doesn't. Still, either the cleric or the beast could still be alive."

Tamuril twisted the hem of her shirt as she struggled with her next action or word. "Would you... come with me, instead?"

I shook my head in confusion. "What?"

"Come with me to Manalar," she repeated, pleading. "Don't go with the Ma'ab. Don't help them. Let us warn the innocents. The Templars, they will protect the pool if they know. They can know what the men look like who would corrupt it, you could tell them."

This thought hadn't crossed my mind, but now I turned it over for a second look. I didn't like what I saw. There were so many problems. Why would they believe me? How would I not be given to Witch Hunters? Why would I want to risk that for Humans fighting each other? Maybe I would prefer to see the Ley pool stripped from a greedy Priesthood's hands.

Well, I thought. *There is one reason. Jael.*

"You know the way?" I asked. "The language? You know how to get inside?"

Tamuril grimaced. "No... b–but my sister has friends."

Like the ineffective men who escorted you underground into Jaunda's trap? I bit my cheek rather than say that, but she could tell I wasn't impressed with the offer.

"Why would you need to get inside the Temple," she asked, "if you aren't with the group that would poison the heart of the Manalari?"

Why, indeed?

You will find and kill him, Aurenthietti.

One of my eyes winked involuntarily as the Queen's voice filled my head and the nausea grew a little worse. Who? Who is Jael supposed to kill in that city? Was he in the Temple, or the garrison? Was he a Bishop, a Witch Hunter, a Templar? None of them, but someone else? I had no greater way to find out with the Druid than I did going on Sarilis's quest, yet my illness grew worse the more I considered leaving the Ley Tower this moment.

I turned to look behind me at the dark tower in the aging afternoon, blinking against the painful light in my eyes. What was I leaving back there? Kurn, the Hellhound who barked at me for being small and distracting, and whatever story he'd heard about a Sathoet. Rithal the Dwarf, who knew about Elves and Orcs, who loathed the Witch Hunters enough to help the Ma'ab meet a hermit death mage.

I would be ignoring Gavin, the apprentice, whose reticence was like digging stones out of the soil to find useful tidbits to trade. And, of course, Sarilis would be left alive, and I'd dismiss his zealous desire to interfere in a war that should have nothing to do with him. What did he care who controlled the Temple pool's magic? What would he do with it if neither side wanted it?

"Sirana?" Tamuril dared to reach out and pluck at my dark cloak. "Come. Come with me. Let us talk as we travel away from here. I have others you may speak with. They know more than me. About the Ma'ab and Manalar. Perhaps they know about your cleric, too. Anything you want to know."

A good excuse. *Yes. Yes, they might know.*

This and the look on the Druid's face, to imagine the corruption happening, made me weigh Jael's mission with my own. It was less direct than Sarilis and the Ma'ab, but could they be blended?

Perhaps...

Without speaking, I motioned for Tamuril to follow and began walking to the East. Facing away from the tower and the Sun behind, the trees cast long, scraggly lines of shadows around us.

"Yes," the Druid breathed in relief. "Let us go."

I couldn't reply, abruptly sick but forcing another step.

"Who are your contacts?" I asked, trying to ignore the rush in my ears. "Give me a name, a g—."

I choked to a halt, my eyes staring at nothing.

No.

"Sirana?"

No!

A terrifying stasis gripped hold of me, brutal and insane, like claws sinking into my back and across my throat, tearing upward, leaving marks to dive like shadows into my mind. Shredding. Pulling.

"Augh!"

Listen to all stories and rumors of half-bloods of Elven origin. If you find any, bring them to Us.

Find the crossroads, Sirana. I shall remain here.

Stop. Stop!

The heartbeat took eternity, and I discovered myself on all fours, retching onto a bare patch of dirt. My entire body ached from such stress that I feared I would expel my unborn in an instant. I clutched my gut as if to keep my womb from wringing itself out like a towel. *No, no, please, not yet...*

"Sirana!"

Get away!

"Sirana, what's wrong? Please, speak, you look so ill!"

I scooted backward, blinking until the wash of blackness sweeping my vision eventually receded. Tamuril kneeled in front of me. She hadn't gotten too close, hadn't touched me, hearing my spiders flatly throwing themselves against the inside of my pouch. I could hear them in another way, too. They cried like a chime, like tiny straws of crystal clinking together. I caught a breath much needed, inhaled again, shifted again, this time with the explicit thought to return to the tower.

I'll return. I will.

Woefully, I felt better.

Tears blurred my eyes as a familiar, useless rage returned to beat my wits senseless against the compulsion, trying to find a way out. Furiously, I blinked them away, refusing to let them fall. Tamuril saw my expression and scrambled backward as well, putting her palm out between us as Pilla dove to land on the ground beside her with a piercing screech.

Damned bird, shut up!

"Don't hurt me," the blonde Elf pleaded. "I didn't touch you."

Just as well.

"Don't *want* to hurt you, Druid," I rasped through clenched teeth. "But I can't go with you to Manalar. I must go with the Ma'ab."

The pale Elf stared at me. "Why?"

"It's my mission. I must complete it."

I tried to sound convincing while shifting away from my own vomit. Carefully, I regained my feet. It took time to come upright as my head still swam, and by then Tamuril was standing as well.

"Just don't follow me," I added. "Otherwise, do what you will."

She blinked, looking up as Pilla took to the branches again. "What I will?"

"Warn your contacts about the pool. I won't stop you."

I could hear her heart racing as she shook her head; my head pounded in a similar tattoo. She wasn't going to leave the forest. The desire to give up and return to her hovel crawled plainly across her face. I preferred that spirit she'd shown a bit ago, when she thought she had a purpose.

I want you to go.

"There's another of me," I said, expecting to black out again to confess, surprised that I remained on my feet. "A Davrin sent ahead to Manalar. I mean to catch up to her. She was sent to Manalar to kill another. She won't have a choice but to try."

Tamuril gasped. "Who?

"I don't know. Male. Someone in a dream. He could be a Dwarf or Bishop or a Templar, or that new Captain with his prayers answered by his god?"

"No!" she said, hushed, hand hovering above her mouth. "No, not him!"

I nearly lost my balance. Catching myself against a trunk, I squinted at her. "Not him? Why? You can't kn—"

I swallowed the rest, seeing her face. Mathias had said that the name sounded like a Western mountain man. Compared to where the conflict would meet, we were in the West and in the mountains.

"You *do* know him," I gasped. "Captain Willven Isboern? The holy light shines about him?"

"Oh, God!" she cried, spinning around and sprinting away at full speed.

I stood dumbfounded before shouting, "Tamuril!"

Sprinting after her, I thought only to catch her, drag her back, and we would talk. Like in her hut. Neither of us made much noise through the trees, but she had the longer stride and it was starting to show. I pushed harder. I would discover the whole story; how she knew him, why he left for so far away, why she would care to go there now—

Sound broke the air around me, like enormous boulders clapping together yet neither crumbled, and an underlying rumble drifted like a voice from the clouds. It echoed like a word understood in the nerves but unknown upon the ears. I staggered and fell to my knees, clutching my head against the agony, my spiders stunned as we all waited for the roar to fade. By the time it did, and I could open my eyes, Tamuril was long gone, and I was shaking with intractable fear.

Fuck Braqth's cunt through a drawstring, what was that?!

I searched around me, my hands quivering as I strained to catch the slightest movement. Even the birds had fled the sound; it was dead quiet, and I was alone on the mountain. Alone, except for a lingering tremor of an unnamable threat, pushing me insistently toward the Ley Tower.

Go back. Before something worse happens out here.

Climbing to my feet, I double-checked that I had Gavin's bird skull talisman and it was unbroken. Confirming, I ran in the direction of the valley, facing the setting Sun just as I began to descend. It would be dusk by the time I reached the bottom, and this peak transition from day to night was already messing with my vision.

I was tired and hungry, too, my arms and legs trembling with fatigue as I braced myself without cease against slipping, against tumbling head over feet all the way to the foothills. I paused once when I felt alarmingly light-headed, cradling my spider pouch both to feel them move inside and to strengthen my resolve.

If I fall and they're trapped, they won't survive…

I opened the drawstrings and let them out to climb into my hair. At least if I lost my balance, they would have the opportunity to jump. Whether they did or not, I must wait and see if the need arose. I'd rather it didn't.

The dizziness was from hunger, I realized. I'd left the jar of preserves on the stairs to wait for and then follow Gavin. My mouth promptly went dry as I distractedly chewed a trail ration, trying to still my stomach which seemed caught, bewildered, in between famine and malady. At least I had water to sip.

Fretting for my head, my belly, my guardians, and the Druid having run off, it was a *long* way down the mountain.

When I reached the lowlands which were leveler, I sped up too soon and stumbled into a clearing containing a strolling skeleton. I stopped in my tracks; my throat clamped shut on a shriek.

Mother goddess fucking shit.

Death mages really were grotesque, though I'd tried to ignore the thought. Now, I couldn't as I watched how it moved. It was haunting.

Changing corpses into puppets.

Setting aside the shivers, I wondered if this was any worse than what the Abyssal Priestesses and Queen did with our living babies and their matas? Rausery had said it of her own Daughter. *Used up by the Priestesses.*

I exhaled as the skeleton wandered by me, uninterested, and I checked the bird skull again. Still whole. I continued, pushed by hunger, and opted for a direct route across the clearing which surrounded the stone wall and gate leading to the courtyard.

There was no cover unless I traveled farther to the South, and I didn't have the patience for the convoluted path that Gavin had led me out of the garden, staying mostly in the shade of the trees. Now, it grew dark and the lack of shade wouldn't be a problem.

Taking a long drink, I jogged across the valley. Although my abused ears picked up on the galloping of hooves, it took too long to filter through the rest of my befuddled senses. By the time I looked down the field and recognized the big man atop a massive, black horse, I had exactly two choices: try to outrun the beast to the gate or stand my ground and do…

Something.

My spiders scuttled around on my neck, agitated as I was, and I reached up to clutch two and stuff them in the pouch before grabbing and returning the third as well. My heart slammed in my chest as I cinched it closed. I *couldn't* kill this rider. Not quick or slow. The Queen's Geas had forced me back here on account of him.

"*Iiindhar,* black witch!" cried the Hellhound. "You are late!"

Fffuck, I don't need this.

There was no reaching the gate before the horse caught me, so I drew a big pinch of sleep powder between my gloved fingers and waited for him. I didn't know if the powder would work on both creatures or even one, but it was either this or draw a weapon I did not intend to use.

"Slow up, Hellhound!" I shouted, putting my hand forward in warning.

He laughed. "I give you ride, *amra'at!*"

Would he? What was he doing? Kurn wasn't slowing; he and his mount maintained their speed. I waited, judging the moment to leap out of the way if he intended to trample me. My choices were limited after that, being caught in the open. Escaping a mount such as this on foot was a fool's effort.

The black mount was nearly upon me, and I darted to one side. It was timed well enough, but the beast's training included a lightning response. The large steed spun as if curling around a pole in the ground, hooves scraping the ground, kicking up dust, the horse bellowing loud enough to vibrate my ears as it charged again.

I hadn't known a horse could be so combative, but its size and the power of its kick or its bite was all too real and threatening right then. In the chaos of its movement and sound, I lost my sense of space, and my next dodge was not successful. The Ma'ab's reach was long, and he hooked his bulky arm around my ribs, hauling me up into the saddle while I writhed. The next moment, I was facing him, sitting on his thighs with my legs dangling off to one side.

"Got you!" he said in his thick growl.

He pinned both my arms with only one of his; I couldn't raise the sleep powder to blow it in his face, most of which had fallen out of my fingers when I was plucked up off the ground.

Kurn demanded, "Where did you go, witch?"

His breath smelled like old onions, and his sweat contained a choking musk.

"Where did *you* go, hound?" I snapped.

He kicked his horse, and we lurched ahead toward the gate. He gathered me farther onto his thighs, holding me so tightly, I couldn't move, could barely breathe. My spiders were on the other side of my belt alongside my hand crossbow. I should have drawn that, or maybe my last web pellet.

"Cease your game," he snarled. "We have looked for hours, *am-ra'at*. What have you done? Who have you told?"

I couldn't answer even if I would have. The horse's canter rolled powerfully, and I heard the beast blowing air through its nostrils above the thud of its feet, catching the distinct animal scent which was somehow better than the rider's.

The Ma'ab and I locked eyes, once again daring the other to blink first. I was fully aware of the erection which plumped up beneath my ass cheek, rubbed diligently by the motion. He shifted his hips against me, his mouth leering as the impulse to fuck his capture crossed his face.

It was not a surprise.

Regardless. *I do not need this.*

I stared hard, leaning closer toward his face, and he did the same in response to my challenge. We were almost nose-to-nose, and he inhaled my scent, briefly focused on it. I stuck out my tongue and lunged up, licking his eye socket as hard and sloppy as possible. Kurn snapped his head back in alarm, his muscled arm loosening just enough for me to wrench my left hand free. I leveled it in front of my lips and puffed the remaining sleep powder straight up his flared nostrils. There was no blowback thanks to the movement of the mount, but I held my breath all the same.

"Kus umma!" he barked, rubbing the grit in his eyes as the horse took us through the gateway and into the muddy, manure-dotted courtyard.

"What in Shank's Kitch is going on?" Rithal shouted from the main door, tromping down the steps.

"Let me off this beast!" I demanded.

I struggled so that the Ma'ab couldn't clear his eyes and nose, hold on to me, and control his nervous, prancing mount all at once. Kurn acquiesced my release in poor form, giving me a hard shove off the saddle. I managed to land on my feet far enough away that the horse couldn't bite, though it snapped its teeth my way. I would have preferred not spinning my arms to avoid falling on my face, but I managed well enough.

When I spun around, Kurn rubbed at his nose as if the itch was maddening, muttering angrily while his mount sidestepped around in the dirt. Without another wasted instant, I sprinted for the stairs and the Dwarf standing there, choosing it as a safe place to catch my breath. My stomach growled; for a moment, I'd forgotten I was hungry.

"Ma almushkidneh, Kurn?" Castis said, exiting and nearly colliding with me and Rithal, who raised a broad hand.

"Oi!" said the Dwarf.

"Iya! Oh!" The mage stopped, glaring at me but spoke to Kurn. "You have found her."

"Mmm, *niam,*" said the other Ma'ab, fighting the powder's effects. "Sneaking around. She came out of the mountains."

"Ah." Castis seemed more concerned with his brother than with me. "Um, are you well?"

Kurn growled unintelligibly at him, and I hid my smirk. *Best dismount before you fall.*

The Hellhound managed this, staggering briefly but gripping the reins and saddle. "Castis… *Ahtaj lijul'si."*

The mage came down the stairs with clear intent to assist, narrowing a glance at me as he passed. I frowned back to witness that the Hellhound remained upright. Although Kurn was affected by the powder, he remained awake. It would have been enough for any sentient down below except an Ornilleth, so I must think the amount had been too little to put him down over him having that kind of willpower.

Worse, the Ma'ab had clasped hold of me, feeling my reality and keeping me under control with the help of his giant animal. He became aroused, and my non-lethal attack had failed to neutralize him the first time. I knew this only invited challenges for as long as I let him live.

Not good.

Despite these concerns, my middle ached so sharply it reclaim my attention demanding for food. I also needed more water to relieve the dry ache beneath my tongue and in my throat. Unable to think past these basic needs, I slipped by the Dwarf and went inside.

"Elf?" Rithal called after me.

I ignored him, aiming for the stairs and where I hoped I'd find the little jar of food from early this morning.

It was gone. *Damn.*

I turned around, hoping to slip down and around the bend. However, the redbeard blocked my path with his wide body.

"What do you want, Dwarf?" I groused.

His bushy brows drew down. "What did you do to him?"

"I didn't poison him. He is *lucky*."

Determined, I slipped by him, pushing at him, but the glancing blow against his hard shoulder gave me a bounce while the squat didn't budge. Rithal wasn't stupid enough to grab my arm, at least, and I sprinted through the main foyer, hearing Kurn and Castis talking in Ma'ab outside with confused hooves stamping. I cut through the great room toward the kitchen.

"Oh, there you are," Mathias said, lounging near the hearth with boots propped on another chair.

I lifted an empty hand in greeting. "Hello, skin hunter."

And left again to enter the kitchen.

Gavin was cooking, and I went straight to the water barrel to dip a cup or three, which was easier than fumbling with my skin's stopper. The apprentice paused in his work, watching as I drank my fill, listening as my stomach gurgled loudly around the fluid I'd just taken.

Without a word, he retrieved a familiar grey jar from the same cabinet he'd searched that morning and placed it at the end of his worktable. I snatched it, sniffed for anything that might have changed, and sat down on a crate, pulling off my grey-dusted glove before digging in. The apprentice watched every motion and grunted, going back to work.

While my jaw worked furiously at the preserves, I waited for part of my mind to catch up to me. What just happened with Tamuril? She tried to get me to come with her, yet my compulsion had come upon me in full force when I'd tried to walk away from the Ley Tower, and she had witnessed it.

It was nothing like the bit of sickness and sense of warning I'd been feeling thus far; this magical geas had been fully debilitating. Lethally so, if I had been in different company. I was lucky, but I might have made things worse, for it returned to me how impulsively I'd betrayed Jael's existence to the Druid.

To someone who admitted she had contacts in cities. In Augran.

Why?! Why did I do that?

Though horrified with myself, I knew why. I was angry with the Valsharess, what She'd done, where I was trapped… and scared. I felt as I had before; beneath my sister, clutched in Kerse's grip and pressed against the Ornilleth's prison. Taken by sensations I couldn't control, my body no longer my own. Helpless. If I couldn't control myself, I had pushed Tamuril to go without me by suggesting a threat from my Sister that might not be real.

Fuck.

What would the Druid do on account of me? Was she leaving her century-old home, going to Manalar to warn her sister? Would she be captured by the Witch Hunters before she made it? Was that moment Tamuril had run away from me the last I would ever see of her?

And… what was that thing in the forest?

The sound which stopped me. The rumbling voice. Was this part of the Queen's spell, too? Or had Sarilis set a trap that far out? Why would he?

Was someone else there? Something I couldn't see?

Gavin's voice broke into my whirling thoughts. "Did you find what you sought?"

I looked down at my empty food jar, giving it a little shake just to be sure. Sighing, I turned my eyes his way.

"I don't know what I sought," I admitted. "How could I have found it?"

He blinked his dark eyes, slow and with little expression. Gradually, it occurred to me that this ugly but hard-working young man had Kurn and Castis's same coloring, the dark hair and eyes and the white skin. His frame was nothing like the Ma'ab, although he was tall like them.

The apprentice answered cryptically. "One might hope that we know it when we see it."

Expecting interruption at any time, I watched the man prepare a large meal for six men and one pregnant Davrin. I thought this, hoping nothing had happened on that mountain to change my condition. I must check for color later but felt mostly sweat in my crotch, and my appetite was as strong as ever. That must be a good sign.

I frowned to consider this further, as I seemed fated to travel with these would-be saboteurs. Perhaps the men would begin to wonder why I demanded more food. Had they enough experience to recognize the signs, or were they different enough from Human women? I didn't know; my knowledge was sorely lacking as I didn't know all the signs and stages among my own kind. I hadn't ever expected to be pregnant after what Jilrina had done, then was terrified to catch by accident after becoming a Red Sister.

So, why did I want to remain so? My fingers tightened on the empty jar. *Why not just let it go? Drink the vial D'Shea gave me to bleed it out. Then it isn't a worry. I can focus on the real threats, and neither the Ma'ab nor the Valshuress control me this way. It may be necessary. It may be inevitable.*

In the dark of my mind, the sweet taste of Auslan's mouth returned; his soft kisses blended with the warm hum of his healer's song. His exhaustion was evident in the taste of his sweat; the power he'd gifted to heal me had manifested in the blond streak in his pure white hair.

Hadn't *I* been the one to pull him on top of me? Had I not commanded him to find comfort and relief between my thighs? Hadn't I rolled him and climbed on top the second time, our mutual keening and ecstatic release proof that I was alive?

I'd wanted it so much. It had been so real, and so *unreal*.

And then Shyntre...

Locked in his room in the Wizard's Tower, both of us fearing the Valsharess and the consequences. He'd been reluctant but, at last, willing. We'd coupled thrice in his bed, each time urgent, his aura boiling, entwined with me in a heat I recalled with no other bua.

Yes. He said it many times. Yes, yes.

My wizard had been *excited* that I'd caught, because I'd claimed that *particular* Consort, his "brother." I recalled how the tense, ever-angry wizard had relaxed after spurting his seed in my cunt; I remembered how he had slept next to me with his palm resting on my belly, his hand spreading over my womb, as if it was our baby. Mine and my two buas.

Ta'suil…

It was *my* baby, not Hers.

If I could think this, then what reason were ignorant, sneering threats like Kurn's enough for any Red Sister to abandon what was hers?

Keep going. *I'll find a way.*

I shot to my feet, shaking my head to clear of too-vivid memory, but dropped the jar. It chipped as it bounced and rolled. Gavin paused again, disapproving that I'd damaged his vessel.

I asked him, "Do you… have a task I can do to help prepare dinner?"

The young man arched a brow at me. He hadn't been waiting for any such offer.

"Plenty of them," he said, prepared to test my base skill. "If you truly wish to work."

CHAPTER 9

MY SECOND EVENING MEAL AT THE LEY TOWER HAD A MOOD much different from the first. Sarilis wasn't cackling his delight, for one. When he'd emerged from his basement, I could see he was aching and tired, his eyes bloodshot and a bandage still bleeding through on his forearm.

The death mage took his host's seat with a belabored sigh, his mouth pursed with ill humor as he looked around the table at us. He noticed Kurn's itchy, reddened eyes and the Ma'ab's withering looks my way, Castis's distraction and suspicion on account of this, and Rithal and Mathias sitting quietly.

"So," Sarilis rasped, "what have all of *you* been up to while I've been making our keys to success? Practice being a team, eh?"

The telltale corner of his mouth twitched.

"Nearly," Mathias volunteered, jabbing his utensil at his food the same as I was. "We left the Davrin here. Probably should have taken her with us."

"She did not have a horse," Castis said practically.

"She's gonna hafta ride with one of us," Rithal said. "Might as well talk now. She can't run alongside us all the way to Manalar."

I braced my chin in my palm and smiled at him. "Are you asking my preference, Master Dwarf, or is there another Red Sister you speak about in this room?"

The redbeard looked twice at me, blinking blue eyes, and his cheeks flushed a little like Tamuril's. "Apologies."

"Don't apologize," Kurn growled. "She knows exactly of who we speak. Kowtowing to remarks like this adds burden and distraction."

"Cuz you insist to make it so," Rithal retorted, his eyebrows shifting with his mood, moving like a fuzzy, leaf-chomping insect I'd observed in the early spring.

"You may ride with me, Sirana," Mathias offered.

"Aye," said the Dwarf, nodding to the Nobleman. "Or I'll volunteer, if yeh like. We can take turns."

"Thank you," I accepted at the same moment Kurn made a chuffing noise and leveled a look of dark amusement my way.

"Yes, dark Elf. We can *all* take turns. It's good for building a team spirit."

"That's enough, Kurn," Sarilis said.

Unfortunately the old man's voice broke in an amusing manner, and the Ma'ab just shrugged it off.

"What?" he said with mock ignorance while Castis sucked on his teeth trying not to smile. "She must mount and ride one of us at all times."

I would *absolutely* have rather gone with Tamuril.

"Cute," the old death mage remarked, eyeing the fighter like he wondered how many spare parts he was good for.

Sadly, when the Ma'ab mage couldn't stop his encouraging snigger, Kurn continued, addressing everyone except me. "I remind you all that this underground race is unfamiliar with the surface world."

And you Surfacers would fall into your first crevice down below.

"She will depend on us to teach her basic things."

Rausery's taken care of that.

"She has never ridden a horse until before this dinner, and I noticed she needed tutoring in the kitchen to be *modestly* useful there."

I opened my mouth to disagree but then closed it. Arguing these specifics would only volunteer information to be picked apart and reveal what annoyed me most. Anyone with an older sister knew that.

Instead, I smiled serenely at Sarilis. "To hear him tell it, I left my nursery just thirty years ago."

That stilled them, both in confusion and abrupt recollection of the "long-lived race" that I was.

Kurn looked at me and continued as if I hadn't interrupted. "I am unconvinced she has as much to offer us in return *before* we reach Manalar, so if she's coming along to tire our horses and eat our food, it is better if she does as we say. We need make no apology for telling her what is necessary to survive the wilds."

I stared, truly bemused how he expected that to work. I chuckled with a sad shake of my head and looked to Rithal and Mathias. To my surprise, they looked away, and neither protested this angle. The skin hunter shot me a subtle glance that said, *I warned you.* I could feel the change in the room. I was still the outsider, but with less value, caution, or curiosity attached as that caution went to the Hellhound.

I frowned. What happened this afternoon while the four were out riding together? What did the Ma'ab tell them? More importantly, was there anything I could do to capture the interest or the fear of at least the Dwarf and the bearded man?

Kurn was grinning, causing his chair to creak as he shifted in his seat. He adjusted his trousers before placing his bulky, metal-armored arm atop the table and leaning toward our host. "I *do* want to make clear, Sarilis, I've changed my mind about the Davrin and accept your generous offer. She shall have a use on our journey. I will make sure she can contribute. And we will make certain your vial lands in the Temple pool."

Sarilis seemed too worn down from his efforts to give much of a toss about this beyond rolling his eyes at the Ma'ab and muttering, *"Fool,"* under his breath before speaking louder. "For what this cost me, you had better, Hellhound. And the Red Sister shall make sure you do."

Maybe.

Kurn and Castis looked at me impertinently, and I smiled, holding the Hound's gaze, almost wishing I could push my thoughts into his head while I felt the anger slowly burn in my gut. It was too late to expect the Ma'ab to fear me unless I did something drastic to one of them; a torture I had witnessed at the Palace or among the Sisterhood but had not yet been called to perform. I hadn't expected Rithal and Mathias to give ground to the big man so easily, but it seemed I wasn't worth the added conflict.

Why must he act like this? Why turn the others against me before they had opportunity to know their own minds of my value when he found mine so low?

I knew why. *He's like the Prime, expects to be obeyed without question. Such 'leaders' don't want subordinates to know their own minds because they might prove greater than his.*

I had yet to see such a one admit fault in their way. I could choose to act upon him in ways that made the Matrons of Sivaraus fear the Red Sisters. With Jaunda in charge, Human men had their assholes stretched wide for pleasure before dying by a cut throat or poison dart.

Kurn's *people* knew something I needed to know, true, but once he spilled what it was, he was no use to me anymore. He didn't know why I stayed my hand when he and his horse bore down on me. Fool, indeed, but I dare not underestimate him for his blunt mind the way he dismissed me for my small size.

I wish I had a Feldeu.

After dinner, we went over the particulars of the plan again; details were decided, and contingencies discussed.

"So, we make our own ways after," Mathias said. "Break and spread out."

"*We* won't be coming back here," Castis said. "We shall rejoin our forces. You all do as you wish."

I caught Kurn watching me without blinking as his cohort said that. He smirked to be noticed.

Meanwhile, the Nobleman shifted to speak with our host. "Have you any messages for after the Midway?"

Sarilis exhaled, rubbing his eyes tiredly before giving it some thought. "Is he still alive?"

Mathias shrugged. "As far as I know."

"He is," Rithal confirmed, nodding to the Ma'ab. "We passed through the inn on th' way here. Lookin' good fer his age."

Kurn's mouth stretched wide open. "He has a Ma'ab daughter, grown."

"Hmph," Sarilis twisted his mouth. "Does he, now?"

"*Iya.* We did not know we had an ally this far West. He is why we chanced to come all this way on Rithal's word."

"Who are you speaking of?" I asked the Dwarf.

"Innkeeper at Troshin Bend, halfway tah Manalar," he answered, broad hands folded in front of him. "Well off. Been there fifty years, keeps the peace and the trade in the area."

"An... innkeeper?"

"Governor," Sarilis corrected with a slight sneer. "Unofficial."

"Hospitable to all sorts," Mathias chuckled with a wink at me. "Anyone passing through from Fortnight to Ahj'Zayr or crossing the Midway out to the Peninsulas is better off moving through Troshin Bend first. All the resupply you need and best news from the four paths one can take."

"He's a sorcerer, of course," Sarilis said, tapping his fingers and smiling at me. "No one maintains neutral ground atop a pile of wealth and resources for fifty years without magic."

Castis nodded firmly. "And exactly what Ma'ab mages need to see."

"*Iya,*" Kurn agreed.

Sarilis chortled. "Well, good luck getting him to join your cause as well. He will host Witch Hunters and Dwarves while begetting on a Ma'ab woman, somehow, so it's truly 'all kinds.' But most importantly, anything *else* you might need to make your way into the Temple, try to think of it prior to reaching his inn."

I was sitting back, head propped on my arm and realizing this talk, while useful, was also oddly familiar. This was how the commoners and Nobles alike talk of a well-standing Matron, down to the detail that they didn't speak this sorcerer's name. I decided not to ask in a group who had only boasted what they coveted and no drawback to balance it. Insisting on his name just invited more of the same, and if we stopped there, then I would hear the name eventually.

"You have the vials ready?" Castis asked Sarilis, who yawned in a long, creasing stretch of his jaw before he could answer.

"Yes, yes. I will show all of you tomorrow. I have yet to rest properly after the work required, and I want to enjoy the reveal."

"When are we leaving?" Kurn growled with impatience. "We have already been here two weeks waiting on Mathias Briar and working out the plan."

"You may leave tomorrow, if you wish," the old man said irritably. "Gavin brought the supplies to get you started."

"Done!"

"We thank you for your sponsorship, master of death," Castis added, bumping Kurn under the table. "We did indeed hear correctly what you may do for us, and we are anxious not to miss this opportunity."

Sarilis cackled, sounding a little closer to how I'd first met him. "Indeed, nor do I want you to miss it. I shall show you my master-works after a night's sleep, and the gate is open the moment you have need."

Soon after, with no other intelligence to add in favor of sleep, we stood from the table and parted ways—awkwardly so, since most of us slept in the tower rather than the fort—but Kurn had more on his mind than harrying me, so I took the opportunity for some quiet and rest. Even slipping into Reverie after my hectic day on the mountain, I would be awake and rested before the men.

But will Sarilis want to speak again? Is there anything else he wants to say, given I've been here not two days before we're to leave again.

Alone in my drafty room for a while, I carefully checked each piece of my equipment after being snatched up and pawed atop a horse. My hand crossbow's aiming nub was off, but a bit of time with the practice shaft put it right. I kept it on the same side as my spider pouch to remind me which side needed the most protection in a controlled fall or being grabbed in such a way. If I hadn't turned to shield both by long habit, just before Kurn's arm hooked me like a fish out of the stream, I would have been face-down bent over on the saddle instead of facing him. That had been his intent, I was sure.

That cannot happen again.

But how to handle this? The dark horse was trained to work with its rider, and the reflexes of the animal in a wide-open space were well beyond those of our riding lizards down below. The op-portunity I'd offered the Ma'ab was my first mistake, when I could have stuck to the trees, though I'd been shaken and distracted by too many things to see the danger until it was upon me.

I could see Jaunda shaking her head. *Excuses don't help when you're broken or worse, novice.*

No, nothing would excuse my mistakes, but it was worthwhile retelling what happened so I could be aware and act differently. Avoiding open spaces and horses wasn't practical, however. Not only was this entire Surface world "open space" compared to where

I'd been born, but from what the men said, the Midway was nothing but flat grassland without tree cover. No caves or mountains to hide within or hunt, terribly exposed, and to spend too much time there was more difficult than the mountains in which I'd been trained. Horses were necessary to cross it in as short a time as we could; the beasts were made for it.

My spiders free to hunt for any morsel they could find, I drifted off for a brief time in my locked room. I awoke again in my chair, not remembering if I had dreamed and not certain what had prompted my eyes to open. No one was at my door, no servant living or dead, no team member.

I shifted and sucked in air. *Ohh. That's why.*

My body was stiff and extremely sore. It took an embarrassing moment to get to my feet and limber up, but at least I could tell it would pass. Carefully, I peeked behind the tapestry and out the window, letting the cool air and marvelous scents roll over my face. Absently, I rubbed the silent saphgar pendant around my neck and under my armor, thinking about Shyntre and the Moons. Judging by the positions of the familiar glowing spheres, there was a lot of night left.

So. I am awake, and Sarilis didn't summon me.

If there was nothing more he wanted from my strangely timed appearance, what did I want? What of Gavin in the shrinking time I had to learn anything he knew which Rithal or Mathias might not know? The apprentice might be asleep, but he arose earlier than the elder man to work. What should I do until then?

My thoughts drifted to the much-boasted vials made by the death mage I had yet to see, and the reason I wore my magic-draining blue stone above my belt. Sarilis had mentioned wanting me to carry his "masterwork," but I wasn't sure I wanted to nor that it was good for its potency if it took us another month of riding to cross the lands to Manalar.

Jael has been traveling on foot for only ten days. Perhaps we will overtake her?

Then again, I could see her stealing a horse at the first opportunity and learning to ride from sheer hard-headedness. If her Queen's geas drove her as strongly as it had me when I thought to abandon my path, there was no telling what she might do.

As for me, sitting in a room until it was time to leave wasn't what any Red Sister would do whether one was to return to kill a man or not. I had everything on me when I left the room, prepared for dead eyes following my path.

The spiral stairs were unlit and dark as the Deepearth; all the windows to the outside were behind the doors of each room per level. Standing a moment, I heard nothing that suggested I head down immediately. Instead, I went up, reading the Radiants as easily as I had from my earliest memories. Beginning on the fourth floor, I was already halfway up; there were four added floors before I reached an obstacle blocking the way to the top—the only floor with the door in the ceiling and stone stairs leading to it along the wall.

That would be the vaulted loft seen from the outside.

The obstacle wasn't a body but an object; a plate of red-tinged silver affixed to the wall at the base of the stairs. It was marked in unfamiliar runes and pulsed a magical warning which kept me from approaching for a closer look.

Did Sarilis make that?

It stood apart from everything I'd seen in his lab. It did not appear linked to death magic, but arcane; like something a mage would create back home. Or a Priestess.

The crossroads are fouled by machinations of the Hells attempting to usurp them.

What had Tamuril said about demons and devils? They are natural enemies, the Abyss and the Hells. They fought over our attention, yearned for our magic and essence. I had assumed Tamuril spoke of Elves, but I wondered if Human mages were targets as well.

I knew why I should fear the power of the Abyss. The Spider Queen rewarded the Valsharess and Priestesses at the use and torment of the rest of us, yet I also knew how the servants of the Void could turn around to bite even one as powerful as Wilsira. The Spider Queen was at odds with Her Queen and Priestesses in the same breath and bloodletting as the goddess was empowering them. Not everyone in Sivaraus believed that about Braqth, but I had for decades. Nothing else made any sense to me, if sense were to be had at all.

What of the Hells? How were they different? What were the methods they used to get what they sought?

Pointless speculation, standing here alone.

I studied the plate from afar but did not stare too long at any one rune. I wasn't trying to read them or unravel a ward. For certain, I did not want to trigger some trap I didn't understand. Like the marked door leading to the Sathoet chamber in the top floor of the Sanctuary, did the object not only keep intruders out but also keep something else in?

Is it sentient, whatever is up there? If so, is it ally or enemy to the elder death mage in the basement?

It was telling that there weren't any servants guarding this place; Sarilis didn't need to spare them here. Perhaps Gavin had further insight, and the warning creep along my skin was too much to challenge with curiosity when this wasn't the core of my mission. I should know better after the Ornilleth's prison.

I descended the stairs with no apparent harm done, passing my room and heading to Gavin's door one floor down. The ward I'd first felt was in place, but it wasn't any stronger than before. This wasn't effective against Sarilis, was it? Maybe it wasn't his usual habit, only here because of guests in the Ley Tower. Or this was a difference with Human mages; they didn't learn stronger wards because they didn't need to defend against them.

I listened and heard the apprentice even through the magical distraction; his muttering in low tones seemed distressed. Was someone else in the room? Was one of the others harassing him, coercing him to reset his own ward with them inside? I crept closer, pushing, confirming it wasn't any stronger. I could choose my moment.

I turned one ear to the door.

"Nom.. ilu profini s-sanctov... shini...!"

I frowned as he continued, sounding disoriented. I wasn't sure if he was awake or talking in his sleep.

"Patertuis nome cogrevit..."

What language was this? How many tongues did the Humans use? I had understood it varied based on city and area but didn't understand why it was this way. Why maintain these other tongues if they knew they must have a "common" language among them to travel and trade as often as it sounded like they did?

Gavin barked once in pain, startling me, and I jumped. Then he quieted, his murmurs sounding as if he'd turned over and smothered his face in cloth. I heard no one else in the room but had broken the ward without intention. I had been about to act, to go inside uninvited, and discover how he was being injured and by whom.

I waited. The apprentice didn't curse and open the door when I broke his ward a second time. *But surely, he chained the door as before.*

Carefully, I tested this, bracing one shoulder against the stone doorframe and both gloved hands on the handle. I pushed gently, and a crack appeared. He hadn't set the iron bar locks. How could that be? I scanned the gap for the chain I'd seen before; this was missing, too.

I opened the door a little wider, inhaling the scents which flowed out from the closed space. Human sweat, burning oil, a mixture of herbs, old blood, and decay. Like Sarilis's lab but lacking the sourness of preserved meat in jars and poorly kept tools. If there were metals or acrid fluids in the room at all, the cleanliness was much better.

I paused, already knowing the younger man would not welcome my snooping around his private space. No wizard did. But I was leaving in the morning, what did it matter?

You must come back here, Sirana. That's what matters.

Ultimately, I could not walk away. I peeked inside, prepared to close the door should anything dangerous hurl toward me. The apprentice's long form lay in a cot identical to mine along the far wall, one well-wrapped foot hanging off the edge as the cot was too short for him. He was covered fully in clothing with an additional blanket on top, facing the wall and away from me. He was asleep.

Scanning the room, I saw it was cleaner and neater than Sarilis's basement. Too clean. Against the wall, a new shelf with a few dark, wooden boxes, and in the center of the room, a table and chair showing scrape marks on the stone floor not a month old. I spied sign of some dabbling with plants and animals; there were pressed or desiccated leaves and flowers, and pieces of carcasses and bones from no creature more advanced than burrowers and birds. These weren't strewn about as if dismembered for visceral pleasure or hunger but carefully dissected with tools and, in some cases, mounted on pieces of wood with small nails.

I narrowed my eyes, ever curious. Despite the signs of hobbies, this was not a room lived in for five years. I wagered this wasn't where he kept his secrets. Instead, if Gavin had moved his quarters not long ago, it might be when Rithal and the Ma'ab first arrived, before the apprentice left by horse-drawn cart to retrieve Mathias Briar.

Lastly, only because I looked for it, I spotted new stains which could be ink drops. He had done some writing here, but his materials were not out in the open.

All this caution, apprentice, and you forgot to lock the door?

Abruptly, Gavin turned onto his back, creaking and rocking his cot with his weight. I withdrew behind the door without losing sight of him, confirming his eyes weren't open. He talked in his sleep again, but it was yet another language, different from the first or any muttered at the tower thus far. I turned my ear to listen carefully.

"Uussh trenvissril…" He flinched like someone had stabbed him in the gut and he didn't yet feel the full pain. *"Veshkren lewensbluen othkrissss…"*

It sounded a *little* like the Ma'ab, less like Trade or Dwarvish. Sibilant and hoarse at once; if one lost their voice and spoke this tongue in a whisper, it would creep and crawl as writhing ice down my spine. My heart picked up as my mind seized on the possibility that it was a form of Abyssal.

I noticed that my fingers had become cold holding the metal door handle even wearing gloves. When I looked up again, from my stiff hand to the man in the cot, I saw… *something* above him. Dark, barely an outline blending in with the Radiants. It moved. Whether an eyeless head or a probing worm, it turned toward me. Twisting.

And smiling.

"Rasyic!" I cursed as I recoiled, skin prickling like a horde of ants, and I closed the door harder than intended.

It woke him up.

"Who… who's there?"

I cringed, my heart throbbing in my ears. He must know his ward was broken even if he believed he locked the door.

"It is I, apprentice," I admitted, strangling my voice to sound calm and amused. "Your ward failed again."

In truth, I waited for a scream of terror as soon as the dark thing above decided to grin down at him instead of me. I listened to muddled shuffling, the cot protesting, and Gavin muttering in annoyance rather than abject fright. I could tell that he had lit a candle to see, as yellow light seeped beneath the door at my feet. Then he approached me, pausing on the other side as if he noticed all the locks undone, and opened it to look out again without the chain preventing me from bursting in if I wished.

I did not wish.

Blinking uncomfortably against the flame flickering on its wick, I expected to see the creature coming up behind him. I looked above his head; he stared down at me, bewildered and vexed.

"Well?" he asked, his voice croaking. "Did you break it again for fun?"

No shadow appeared, and I didn't want to appear so jumpy. I smiled instead and damn the web if the mundane answer felt like the right one. "No. I heard you cry out in your sleep. I wondered if one of the others had entered. The door wasn't locked, but I see you are alone."

Deeply shadowed eyes squinted at me, and I *still* waited for the shadow-thing to appear the moment I claimed that he was alone. Nothing happened, however, other than a long-suffering sigh from the apprentice of the Ley Tower.

"I may as well get to work," he said, coming out, fully clothed in his worn, drab robes and boots. "I won't be sleeping anymore tonight."

I gave him room, watching as he used a metal key to set a locking bolt from the outside. I joined him confidently on the stairs.

"How many tongues do you speak?" I asked.

"Why do you ask?" He sounded wary.

"Three?" I guessed.

The ugly man frowned.

"More? Or less?"

"Shh," he hushed, "unless you want to wake the Ma'ab and the others."

Amusing to hear when his footfalls were heavier than mine.

No doubt, we were heading for the great room and the kitchen; Gavin would be in the latter until after sunrise if we reached it. I lifted a hand to touch his shoulder, to slow him. He jerked away, tensing up so much it set me on edge, yet he would not also meet my eyes; he continued downward.

Alright, don't touch.

Whether his reason was just me or everyone, it was too soon to know. How to stop him, though? Should I tell him about the shadow? No, then I'd have to admit I opened his door and looked inside. I hurried to slip beside him.

"What is *veshkrin lewensbluen*?" I asked, no doubt garbling the dialect.

He stopped dead on the wide, Dwarven stairs.

"I heard you," I said. "It was the last thing you said before you woke."

"You mean before you broke my ward."

Near enough.

I shrugged. "I noticed you didn't unlock all those bolts and chains like before."

Gavin said nothing to that. The next moment he seemed dizzy and wavered on his feet, reaching out to place his pale, long-fingered hand on the wall. I wanted to prod for information while he was distracted, his will weakened—it was an old habit—but I waited, unblinking.

"I often have... troubling dreams when I sleep," he said, eyeing me with suspicion. "Does your kind dream?"

"Yes," I answered, immediately thinking of Auslan and the Valsharess. "Some dreams are important."

"Like what?"

"Not what," I corrected. "It is who. Some Davrin can see a moment yet-to-be in dreams, though they are rare-born. Sometimes they...share those dreams with others also asleep."

Gavin's homely face altered a crease at a time. "Have any shared with you?"

I showed a touch of my own discomfort. "Why I am at this tower."

I'd have left with Tamuril already if I hadn't felt like I was about to die if I did; that was the truth.

The death mage wasn't sure whether to believe me, but I got what I wanted. He motioned for me to follow him and, at the bottom of the stairs, turned from the path that would have led to the great room and kitchen. We also eschewed the cramped, dark stairs leading to the garden. Instead, he guided me by candlelight to a third, wider staircase going up and deeper into the mountain fort.

"Answer me one question, word-man," I whispered, comfortable that it wouldn't carry with the dark underground around me. "How many languages do you speak? Or what is a *lewensbluen?*"

Gavin turned his head as though he was about to hush me again, using the excuse of others hearing. I raised one eyebrow in mimic of him earlier, daring him to do it. It was a point in his favor that he realized I was quieter speaking in the dark than he'd ever be.

"Three," he said, his low whisper bouncing off the walls. "And a smattering from a handful of others."

"You speak Trade," I prompted. "What is your native tongue, the first one?"

He did *not* want to answer that.

"Does Sarilis know? I could ask him."

What a *delightful* expression; it made me grin.

The apprentice grunted, resentful as he answered, "Manalari."

What?

Now *I* stopped in my tracks, staring. "Your...*first* tongue is the same as where we are going?"

"Kindly don't mention that to the Ma'ab," he suggested, continuing along a hall I sensed was also a shallow grade ramp.

"You are from Manalar?"

"No. An area outside it."

"But you know about the Bishops and Witch Hunters."

He grunted. "Unfortunately. One reason I am this far West."

"You've been listening to the plans at the table."

"Indeed, I am curious how you will do this, though I have nothing to add."

"Oh, don't you?" I squinted as we turned left at a perpendicular hallway. "You seemed alarmed when Sarilis spoke of throwing his vial into the Temple pool."

Gavin grunted. "You spoke correctly, it will create backlash. Any mage can deduce this."

"Castis said nothing."

"He is blinded by hubris. You would do well to not be in the Temple at all if the pool is corrupted."

"Why?"

"Because not even Sarilis can predict the results of an explosion."

I frowned, pondering the necessity of leaving with this party versus being able to bug out before the "mission" was complete. Sadly, there were too many days and too much distance to imagine.

Gavin's candle continued to smoke and dance as he brought us to another locked door. Nothing about it set it apart from the others we'd passed, and there was no ward on this one. He used a second key to open it and motioned me inside.

I stepped forward but paused when I inhaled the thick scent. *That* smelled like a five-year domicile for a Human; one who was used to being alone.

"Problem?" he asked dryly.

"Uh, no."

I stepped inside, and he followed, closing and locking the door while setting the candle on a small, dusty table near the door. The single flame disrupted what I would have seen in pure blackness, but I saw what I expected to see: a proper bed and long-term care tools; shelves packed full of scrolls, books, and oddities; a chest of drawers for clothing; a cluttered and stained writing desk; a blood-stained work table with short shelves beside it, and lastly, hidden tools carefully wrapped in cloth upon it. It looked much like Callitro and Shyntre's dormitories, just with a different discipline in mind.

A good thing, I decided, that Gavin already knew of my spiders and that I wouldn't be an easy target. Slowly, the death mage exhaled as if pondering how he'd come to be here.

"We passed several small sentries on our way here," he told me. "We'll know soon if Sarilis is awake and watching for this. He cannot hear through them, so our words spoken are safe, and there is a chance he slept through it or the creature itself is decayed enough as to be useless."

I stared at him. "Um...? Will they inform him when he is awake?"

Gavin quirked an eyebrow. "They haven't any intelligence or memory. He uses them mostly to make me think he is always watching me, but I have been here long enough to know the parts of his bluff."

"Why does he tolerate you, if he means not to teach? If he wants you to believe he is always spying on you?"

The younger Human shrugged. "He enjoys having a servant. I am not the first such 'apprentice' he has had. You've seen some of them already, outside."

I blinked slowly. "The skeletons?"

One corner of his mouth tightened in cynical response.

"You do not fear he will add you to them?"

"My advantage is he feels his age but pretends it isn't so. The winters are especially hard. Currently, he needs me."

I smirked. "This is not unlike where I come from, a noble waiting for her Matron to grow old so she may take her place."

"Reassuring that we can understand each other that way."

I could not tell if he jested or not. In the following silence, we each noted that nothing scraped at the door to interrupt us or tell us the master was coming.

"The other tongue I heard sounded like Ma'ab," I asked while I could. "Is it? Do you speak both the languages about to go to war?"

Gavin frowned, looking resentful that I wouldn't let it go. "No. That was… the dead tongue. I use it in my magic."

I was confused. "Dead tongue? No one speaks it anymore?"

His face changed at this, from glowering to a skewed and unsettling amusement. "No one living."

My skin creeped again at the look on his face; he was comfortable and confident in his own room.

"I may assume there are no death mages among Davrin?" he asked.

I wet my lips. "No. None who uses dead bodies this way."

He rolled his eyes. "It is somewhat more than finding further service in a corpse. My affinity has to do with what happens to the living essence in transition as the body dies. But if you have never seen it before, do not doubt that I am accustomed to the disgust and fear this inspires." He paused, squinting at me in study. "Indeed, you are oddly curious and tolerant thus far. Not a typical response. Men have beaten and tried to murder me for my practice."

I smirked. "If you are Manalari, and they are enemies with the Ma'ab that host death mages. This makes sense, does it not?"

He shrugged, not fooled by my attempt to shift the focus.

"Why haven't you joined the Ma'ab?" I asked.

"They are no less brutal than the Bishops and Witch Hunters," he said with a sneer. "Their class system is as rigid and hostile to outsiders as Manalar. In either place, I am filth. I prefer to live on my own, so that I *may* live."

I drew an odd parallel to House Aurenthin in Sivaraus. I imagined Jael saying something like this if she had a choice between being the low rat in two different cities, regardless if one was more tolerant of her using her favorite weapons.

"I see." I smiled. "Then, as you asked, I won't mention your mother language to the Ma'ab."

"Thank you," he said sardonically before something else came to him. "Will you not also ask why I chose death magic, if it only causes me difficulties around other men?"

I blinked in surprise. "I presumed that you *didn't* choose, apprentice. You were born as you are and learned of the path as you grew. Your magic revealed itself to you, yes?"

Gavin stared unblinking, his irises like black wells in his pallid face. "Is this… understood among the Davrin as a whole?"

"Of course. We know mages are born, and they cannot choose their preference. They practice what comes to them."

"Such as?"

I stared at that intense expression. Goddess, he was curious.

"Sorcery, divine ritual, healing." I paused to consider. "Potion or tool making. Rune magic. Elements or constructions, using stone, fire, or water. Or…a link with plants or animals."

"Visions?" he asked. "You mentioned being here because of dreams."

I bit my lip. "Rare. But, yes."

"All this is normal for you. There is only no death magic among you."

I nodded.

"Fascinating," he murmured, looking at a random point on the floor. "I wonder why. You *can* die, I know that much."

A smile tugged at my mouth at how familiar it felt to stand here. This ugly Human was a scholar down to his bones; we could be standing in the Wizard's Tower and not be out of place. Truly a pity that this would be my only time to learn from him before I left.

But I will return.

I listened outside the door for a moment then offered quietly, "Would you like to kill Sarilis when I return?"

"What?" he asked, disbelieving.

"You know his weaknesses. I shall need help to return below. I *cannot* go home with him breathing."

Gavin's mouth nearly sagged but, self-consciously, he closed it. "You were sent by a dreamer from the Deepearth to assassinate him?"

Near enough.

"Why go to Manalar at all? Why not just kill him and go home?"

"I must go to Manalar. I cannot say why."

Reluctantly, he accepted this.

"I may help," he said with caution. "If the Ley Tower would be my new residence afterward. Or do you want it for your kind?"

I shook my head. "No. Claiming this place is no part of my mission. I must return to the Deepearth."

Gavin watched my face for some time, again required to decide if I was being truthful. Ultimately, this did not matter to me, but I wondered if there was some unseen hand behind him, as there was me. I noticed he did not describe the Tower as his, but it being a new residence.

Being.

It was an odd word choice, yet I could believe it was deliberate. The first opinion Gavin had shared was that words were not inter-changeable. Most I knew would have said the Tower was "mine," that it belonged to them. Perhaps Gavin expected it to belong to something else. Like the Hells, for example.

"What is in the top floor of the tower?" I asked next.

He leaned back, on alert. "First, tell me what you observed."

"*First,*" I countered, "tell me if you had any hand constructing it."

He wavered, and ultimately my stare won.

"No," he stated, "I did not have any hand in it."

"Who did?"

"I don't know."

"Sarilis?"

Gavin shrugged.

"He's allied with someone," I told him. "My leader said she felt she was being watched here twenty years ago."

The apprentice lifted his shoulders again. "I've not observed any meetings. If he is, the link is well hidden."

"I recognize Abyssal signs," I confessed. "But not the runes on the plate blocking the stairs to the loft."

"Ah," Gavin said. "You went up there. I am amazed you came back down."

"Do you know them?" I asked, refusing to be distracted.

"No. By process of elimination, they are not Abyssal nor are they aligned with the death sigils Sarilis and I use. The script is not Davrin, Dwarven, Ma'ab, or Manalari."

Damn it. Nothing I didn't already know.

"My... dreamer suggested the Hells."

Gavin's brows lifted. "Infernal? Hm. As likely as anything else, I suppose."

I wanted to ask him how many "planes" he knew about but couldn't waste time on nonessentials before he was required to return to the kitchen, or we were discovered. I listened again for anything out in the hall. Nothing. "Devils, then?"

"They sound unfamiliar to you."

"Are they so familiar to you, twenty-six-year man?"

He stared at me then grunted. "Fair point. You know more than I do. I have not ventured there again since soon after I arrived. My nightmares were warning enough, and whatever is there has not made itself known."

Hasn't it? I wondered about that vague, dark shape while he'd been sleeping. "Has Sarilis mentioned it to you?"

"The old goat enjoys bragging yet hasn't offered more than he said. Did your leader find it in place when she was here?"

"She never said."

"Pity. Perhaps you can ask."

Hah.

"All I can offer," Gavin continued, "is his claim that it was here when he arrived, and that it might have something to do with why the Dwarves built then abandoned this post."

I stood there frowning in thought. I was stuck and unsatisfied; the apprentice sensed it and exhaled, looking at his door.

"I should prepare for the morning. If you would leave first, I will be down shortly."

Hesitant to leave as Gavin waved me out, I found myself scouring what imagery I could remember from those dreams in the dry, red sand. Something niggled at me. The Queen had claimed I would see signs in my dreams, but for what purpose? Had I missed something crucial already?

Auslan smiled at me. "Do not fear them, Sirana. They belong as we do."

"Who are they?" I asked.

"The youngest able to cross over."

I'd seen the same thing in both dreams, I realized: when the Valsharess had hold of me and later in Tamuril's hut, when I saw Auslan. I glanced suspiciously at this young Human who muttered Manalari and a "dead tongue" in his sleep and spoke of warnings in his dreams.

Visions, he called them.

"May I tell you something from my shared Elven dream?" I asked, close to the door and just before Gavin was about to pull it open.

The man looked uncomfortable and impatient. "What?"

"A grey smudge on an otherwise clear day," I said. "Upon the horizon between a land of red sand and enormous blue sky."

I heard it. His heart beat louder.

"Disappointingly mundane," he said, opening the door. "Please, leave. I presume you don't need the candle."

Again, his tone made me smile. I left willingly, because I recognized a mage pretending like he didn't care about what I'd just said.

He cared very much.

Rithal was awake and had beaten Gavin to building up a large fire in the hearth. I saw the light and smelled the smoke long before I entered to see he was the only one in the great room. With thick boot heels up on the table and the back of his chair facing me, he drew smoke on some dried herb packed into a tube as he contemplated the tapestries upon the wall and covering the large, shuttered windows. I didn't think he heard me enter, so I looked where he focused his gaze.

The tapestries were worn but had been here as long as Sarilis had. They'd been brought from somewhere, as their scenes depicted what looked like ominous groves of Human sacrifice and punishment. I imagined Sarilis had been drawn to the various separation of body parts in these darker works, while another intent may have been to worry a convocation, like in the main altar room in the Sanctuary.

"Thought you'd be here first," the Dwarf said with a rumbling puff escaping his beard and nostrils.

I smiled. "But I am not here first."

He grunted acceptance of the point, sucking on the smoking tube. I reflected that I had only seen this rarely, when burning a hallucinogen was the only way to make it effective on a target or sacrifice. As I watched the exhalation climb toward the blackened ceiling, I supposed it was just as well that we didn't fill the Great Cavern with our own fragrant puffs down below.

I took the handful of steps to enter the room proper, in case Gavin or Kurn was close behind me. Rithal turned his head and glanced at me out of the corner of his eye as I approached. He twitched, and I opened my gloved hands and stepped to a place where he could see me better.

"So," he began, "ya really gotta come along?"

I smiled and nodded; the Dwarf shook his head in response.

"This ain't gonna be fun," he said somberly. "What if the Hellhound hurts you?"

I cocked one brow. "What if I hurt the Hellhound?"

Rithal shrugged. "Haven't seen whatcha can do. Sarilis talks the Red Sisters up an' you enjoy the praise, but ya haven't done anything. That's why Kurn's got it on for ya. He wants to see. He'll test ya. What his kind're trained to do."

I smiled and, despite the strong impulse to scoff, offered nothing in return.

"You are not wholly comfortable with what will happen once you lead us to Manalar," I said. "I watched you during planning. You wish there was another way."

His blue eyes hardened, as did his mouth. "Ain't no way but this the Bishops and their dogs will believe. They earned it, an' I been lookin' for a way. Any way."

I thought about that. "Am I right in my guess that the Bishops and their 'dogs' did far more than take away your river crossing and your home?"

Rithal looked back at the fire, puffing and answering with a tight-lipped, "Yup."

The redhead exhaled smoke; it tickled my throat and I didn't like that, but at least it had a decent odor.

"Another thing ya have no idea whatcher gettin' into," he continued, "if we cross paths with 'em. Believe it or not, I'd rather no one get their hands on ya, Elf. They're all too ignorant in these times. Better you hide in the shadows. They wouldn't have any idea what they were lookin' at, anyway."

I frowned, deciding to take a seat across from him. He met my eyes without concern, and I felt not a tickle of psionic connection.

"How old are you?" I asked. "And where did you hear your oldest stories?"

Rithal grunted, giving a shrug. "Almost two hundred."

Fuck. He's twice my age?

I nodded sagely, like I'd expected it. "And your stories?"

He shook his head, then. "Not where I was born. I'm a simple Hill Dwarf. Found 'em in my wandering after the Hunters burned everything." He paused. "Around Taiding and Augran. Some older Halls there, they remember and pass down their tales."

"The same cities that control trade around the Great Lake and are obstacles between the Ma'ab and Manalar."

"Glad you been listening." Rithal's eyes drifted over me, a thought crossed his face, and he huffed a breath as he shook his head. "Not sure any of 'em will believe me if I told 'em I met one o' yah, though."

One of me?

"Does my coloring not discomfort you?" I asked. "Are there others like me among Dwarves? Dark skin, white hair?"

Rithal grimaced. "Nah. Most look like me, maybe a bit darker or lighter in hair or skin, but…nothing like you."

"Yet I'm not a demon to you, as Kurn thinks."

A shrug. "Skin turns pretty dark in the Desert, an' hair turns white with age. I see it on Humans aplenty. The dark tones seem a natural response to strong sunlight and hot lands without much forest or water. Some tales tell about dark-skinned Elves in the Desert along with the Sorcerer Kings. Long time past."

Sorcerer Kings?

"Desert?" I prompted. "What does a Desert look like? You said hot, not much water?"

Rithal grunted. "And sand dunes."

"What color?"

"I dunno, red, maybe. Or orange. Never been there, just bard song about the dunes moving like waves in the wind. And the sandstorms that flay yer skin."

Pleasant thought.

I sat back, briefly lost in the feeling of the Queen's Hand again: *Look! Do you see this?* What I'd seen, from Rithal's description, was a Desert, but through the eyes of the Valsharess.

"How far is the Desert from here?" I asked

Rithal blinked, a surprised laugh slipping out. "Hah! Ah… um, apologies. Whoof, it's about as far from here as you can get and still be on land."

I noted it but put it out of my mind as Gavin scraped the stone with his feet just prior to slinking into the great room. I smiled and straightened up.

"Excellent!" I said. "I've grown hungry waiting, Gavin."

"Indeed, quite an appetite on one with two working arms," remarked the homely man on his way by, avoiding our eyes and slipping down the servants' way.

I chuckled, and Rithal's bushy eyebrows were skewed as he looked after him then at me.

"What?" I asked.

"Er." Another shrug. "Must admit, Elf, if it's true the women are in charge down below, I woulda put coin down that a man talking to you like that would rile yah up."

"I'm not Kurn," I said with a pert grin, pushing against the table to stand. "I judge the better mind and watch this instead. It's what *my* kind is trained to do."

Rithal considered that, looking after Gavin. "Better mind? Yer kiddin'."

I tilted my head with a smirk. "I am… what about baby goats?"

Another blink, and the stern redbeard finally allowed a full chuckle to take him over. "Alright, never mind. In that case, Elf—"

"Sirana, Rithal. We will be traveling the same trek for many days."

"Sirana. 'Kay. In that case, take yer better mind while ya've got 'im but don't forget to watch where the bull is in the field. I'm warnin' yah."

I made a sign for an affirmative and excused myself to the kitchen, where Gavin was working quicker than I'd seen before.

"Do you hurry?" I asked with amusement.

"I'm late," he said with his head in a cupboard.

"I noticed. It took you some time to come downstairs."

He shushed me. "Kurn was on the stairs, and you know he's listened in before."

I shrugged, annoyed despite it all. *Always about the Hellhound. Thought they were smarter.*

Gavin handed out a corked, clay bottle. "Here, give this to the old man."

I took it. "What is it?"

"A tonic he likes."

"Where is he?"

The apprentice sounded exasperated. "In his lab. I assure you, he's there."

"All night?"

The tall, gaunt man motioned sharply for me to go away and then turned to prepare to cook, resolutely ignoring me. I glared at his hunching back then the bottle.

Very well.

I walked calmly down the hallway to the dead-end and Cullen staring in my general direction. The standing corpse moved to open the door again but looked a bit worse than when I'd first seen him. Blotchier. A bone in his wrist popped.

Standing at the top of the stairs, I called, "Sarilis! It is Sirana."

"I know, beauty! You bloom like a flower this morning."

"You can tell it's morning?" I jested, listening to him rummaging around.

"No, but it seems about that time. Are the others in the great room?"

"Just Rithal. Gavin gave me a bottle for you. A tonic."

"Ah! Marvelous, delightful. Care to check it for poison, my dear?"

I glanced at the thing in my hand. "Already done."

The elder was huffing as he came to the bottom of the stairs, a wooden box hooked in one arm. His gnarled, free hand grabbed the railing, smearing it with something dark. I watched him struggle up the next step, shaking. He was much weaker than the first night we'd met.

"Do you need assistance?" I asked.

Another stair.

"*Erngh!* It is not... normally the case that I have so many guests! Otherwise, I have meals brought to me."

And he hadn't come upstairs since last night; I confirmed by the smell wafting up. "Is your bed down there, then?"

He chuckled, taking two more stairs. "Are you flirting, Sirana?"

Ew.

"Possibly." I put a playful smile in my voice. "You are a bit young at seventy, but why should it be held against you?"

Sarilis stopped where he was, clung to the rail, and laughed loudly. He tilted his head such that I wondered if he would topple backward. I'd let him if he did, although I wasn't sure what volatile thing was in that box. *Maybe...*

But no, the old man came closer, stopping again to squint up at me.

"Ah," he panted. "Excellent. I need what you've got, my dear. Stay there."

I glanced awkwardly at Cullen and waited until it was time at last to move and let the death mage out of the stairwell. I offered the bottle, which he took and struggled next with the cork.

"Damn it all," he growled.

"I will open it," I offered, reaching.

Sarilis twirled away then flinched as he regretted the sudden movement. "Ow. No, ah... No, dear, I've got it."

Eventually, he did, and he sniffed then guzzled the tonic inside, clear fluid running out the corners of his wrinkled mouth to show droplets on his dark blue robes. He expelled a long sigh, corking the bottle and pushing it out toward me; I took it.

"Much better," said the old man, and indeed he sounded refreshed. "I hope breakfast is ready. I am famished and feel gaunt as one of my servants!"

"Don't you always?" I quipped.

Sarilis showed the gap in his teeth again. "Part of my devastatingly arresting visage, wouldn't you agree, my lady?"

I couldn't help it; I laughed. From the look on Kurn's face as we entered the great room, he had heard me.

In a short amount of time, Gavin managed to place on the table a cold meal of some sort of nut-and-vegetable mash in one enormous bowl, another filled with softened and shredded jerky mixed with seasoned oil and some kind of crumbly, cultured milk solids. Next to this was a mound of hardened flatbread that he could not have made himself just now but likely brought back in his cart. We each had a bowl and spoon as before.

It was exotic enough to cause suspicion, as if the men at the table had never seen it before. My stomach growled, however, and I started with spreading a healthy portion of the mash on the hard bread and topping it with the meat and cheese to take a bite.

Oh... delicious.

I could sense the nutrition in it, too. My thoughts flicked to the child inside me, imagining a portion of the food somehow passing from me to her. Rithal watched me, grunted, and helped himself;

he was soon followed by the rest. Sarilis watched us eat for a while, seeming disappointed and surprising me by acknowledging his apprentice at the fireplace.

"Hmph, not a hot and proper meal before you go, boy?" the death mage growled crankily. "You *know* I hate this castrated monk food you ate growing up. Like spreading dung on a tile."

Everyone stilled, including Gavin, and Castis found his words first.

"What did you say, Sarilis?"

"Hm?" Grey, wiry eyebrows lifted. "What?"

"About a hot meal before...?"

"Oh. Yes. I decided it would be best if you took someone who knows all the local rituals and scripture. He can read and write it, if necessary, and his tongue is native Manalari."

"What?!" Kurn roared, hurting my ears as I tried to work my jaw.

The tower's master burst out laughing at the Hellhound; Kurn's face reddened. Mathias, who had been quiet up, stood partway up as he spoke, hands light on the table.

"You aren't serious, Sarilis," he said. "You called me to speak Manalari for the group."

"I changed my mind, Master Briar," said the old man, glowering at Gavin, who resembled a rabbit trapped by wolves. "No insult to you, skin hunter, the group has great need for your skills. Let Gavin lift this one from you. He grew up in one of their monasteries."

"He did?" Rithal asked, peering at the tall, silent man like he couldn't see it.

"Yes, and his understanding of the nuances of our mutual enemy surpasses anyone here."

"You mention this now?" Castis asked.

"Don't trick us, I don't believe you," Kurn rumbled. "He has Ma'ab eyes. He is a *maknuut*, we saw it when we arrived."

Sarilis chuckled, pleased as he tapped his fingertips on the table, nodding his head. "Indeed, the boy can be quite blasphemous of his former religion. It seems one of your Ma'ab brothers planted a seed far to the South of your usual *haunts*." He cackled like he'd spoken a jest. "After his mother dropped him, they squirreled him away, trying to beat the Ma'ab out of him!"

Gavin managed to speak, but the words were not loud. "I am not leaving—"

"You are!" Sarilis snarled, his mood shifting like a storm. "You're relieved of your apprenticeship. You'd best pack all you'll take. *If* you return here without the pool being soiled, you'll join Cullen, there. *If* you return without the Red Sister in tow, I shall be very disappointed."

What the fuck was happening?

I stared as the old man took a bite of the "castrated monk" food as if it didn't bother him anymore. Sarilis wasn't looking at Gavin behind him, but the rest of us were. I watched the younger mage's eyes turn from mostly black to *entirely* black.

The air in the room chilled abruptly.

Fucking goddess...

Kurn sprang up and attacked him, first punching his gut and then his jaw before I was on my feet. Gavin fell to the floor, and the Hellhound put a boot on his back. He barked a command, "*Abac hidana, maknuut!*"

"The boy didn't grow up Ma'ab, Kurn," Sarilis said lightly without looking around. He took another spoonful of the mash, his hand shaking. "He can't understand your words yet, though I expect he'll get the hang of it."

Castis had turned in his chair, and Kurn watched me as I stood up. The Hellhound focused on my hands, ready to do something unpleasant to the scholar under him if I drew something.

I need the mage alive.

"Did you really study the scripture as one of them, *maknnut?*" the Ma'ab mage asked, sounding curious and unconcerned.

Kurn compressed Gavin's ribs until the former monk answered, "*Yes*, but—"

"Hmm, that could be useful to our leaders."

I narrowed my eyes as the Hellhound smiled agreement. *I found him first.*

"He can cook and has a horse, as well," I said. "I will ride with him. Let him up, Kurn. Gavin must pack to come with us."

The Hellhound glared at me and glanced at Castis, who nodded his head.

"Let him up," said the Ma'ab noble.

I was surprised I didn't hear a rib pop for punctuation as the big warrior removed his boot. Gavin rolled and scrambled to his feet, one arm pressing to his middle. Sarilis was nibbling away on hard bread.

"I suggest someone other than the Red Sister escort him to his *real* quarters on the second level," the old man said, tossing his head in a general direction.

Damn. Had he seen everything? Did he know?

Kurn made for Gavin, lifting his hand as if to grab his collar, but the reach was just a bit too far and the lanky man dodged out of the way. The bulky Ma'ab snarled something at him, and I made eye contact with Rithal, flicking my eyes toward the two men with clear urgency.

Please!

The Dwarf's shoulders slumped.

"I'll go," Rithal boomed from that barrel chest, calling everyone's attention as he stood up stomped away from the table. "Come on, Gavin. Let's get yer things."

"Excellent!" Sarilis said with glee, reaching down to lift the box he'd brought with him from his lab. "Now! Who shall carry my masterpieces all the way to Manalar's pool?"

Castis and I volunteered.

"Do be careful, apprentice," Sarilis said, standing in flat-soled slip-ons out in the soft dirt courtyard, watching us prepare the mounts. "I look forward to your return."

Gavin grunted and kept his face hidden within his hood as he mounted the same horse which had been pulling the cart two nights ago. I vaguely wondered what Sarilis was to do for supplies or travel should he need it; he could barely climb up the stairs just over an hour ago.

He's acting so strange.

Perhaps he had lost what bit of sanity remained in making his vial, and he would be dead of starvation when I returned. As for the brown mare, she was much taller than I'd realized. How to climb up behind Gavin without a stirrup such as he'd used?

I'll need a running start...

The apprentice solved the problem another way, guiding the beast over next to the fence.

Ah. Of course.

The Hellhound smirked at us as he sat astride the long-maned, black stallion he'd used to run me down before. The trappings of the horse's black leather and silver decorations screamed wealth. Castis possessed a beautiful reddish mare with similar quality tack, and I recognized Mathias's brown gelding from before. Rithal rode a stout, shaggy, grey beast that seemed like a mountain goat at first glance, although it did not have cloven hooves and, on second look, was a shorter horse appropriate for its rider.

I could not help but sit against the apprentice to get my legs ahead of the laden saddlebags; my crotch was squashed into the small of his back and my thighs lined up with his. I could tell he hated it.

I'm not pleased, either, scholar.

It would be difficult to reach anything on my belt, as I must lean to separate my chest from his spine. He was so much taller than me that I couldn't see in front of us, only to the sides.

"Be sure to send Gavin out front until you pass the last sentries," Sarilis said. "Otherwise they will home in on you."

This keeps getting better.

"Hold still," I said, planting my hands upon Gavin's bony shoulders.

"What are you doing?" he asked, his tension overflowing from the whole situation.

I folded my legs up until my heels got to the saddlebags then stood up quickly before any could react. I spent another moment balancing on the mare's rump before I turned in place and eased myself down, shoving my back and bottom up against the apprentice and setting my legs right. I grinned at the staring men. *Now* I could watch the rest behind us and reach most of my tools.

Sarilis laughed loudest, although I also heard Rithal and Mathias chuckle. Then Kurn guffawed.

"Want to show us that again, witch?" said the Hellhound.

I bowed and held up my pointer finger. "One performance per day, little man."

Gavin kicked his horse forward into a jolting trot before Kurn could respond, apparently of the opinion that the sooner we left and got another horse somewhere, the better. I sensed I would soon agree with him. This was *not* comfortable, but I could watch the others ride and learn from them, study how they worked with their mounts. Even Kurn might have his uses besides a story or two about demons.

As we navigated the old road away from the Ley Tower, it settled upon me that we were leaving as planned, and I could not deny the excitement in my middle. I had a real chance to find one of my Sisters as I sought out those involved in this giant game on the Surface.

In most games, someone claimed to win. I would be satisfied not to return to the Deepearth alone.

CHAPTER 10

MY FIRST JAUNTING HORSE RIDE BY MY OWN WILL WAS WHILE facing the wrong way, my palms planted on the animal's broad ass.

I noticed the unfamiliar pull of muscle at my inner thighs and wondered how quickly they might tire or get sore trying to squeeze around a creature much rounder than any lizard I'd guided below. I would adapt, but it wouldn't help any lingering sense of mystery if the Dark Elf couldn't walk straighter than a bow-legged waddle the first time she climbed off a mount.

This will be fun.

Gavin led us out of the narrow mountain valley as promised, with the walking dead peering out at us from the shade of the trees but coming no closer. Kurn made it a point to hold my gaze for an unnatural stretch, both ignoring the sentries and trusting his stallion not to stumble without his constant guidance. I smiled after a while, showing my teeth. Briefly, his face hardened but then creeped sideways into a leering smirk, like he imagined me in a vulnerable state. I knew the face well enough, be it Davrin or Ma'ab.

So much fun.

Castis, Rithal, and Mathias noticed this exchange, of course, and none looked surprised, though the brown-haired nobleman looked elsewhere as if to ignore it. I thought the Ma'ab mage was considering what he'd say to Kurn the next time they were alone, and Rithal had a displeased frown stuck on his bushy face.

Almost two hundred years old was the Dwarf. If Kurn knew that, would it change the balance of our group? Or did he know already? At the same time, Rithal told me directly that they hadn't seen me "do anything" and for this, Kurn wouldn't stop testing the boundary.

This wasn't a foreign concept to me; I would act when needed. Beyond the curse of needing to know what *he* knew about Sathoet, I hadn't much considered the potential consequences of killing the big man in this group. I didn't know enough about the rules of where I was, or those around me, to anticipate the response; not as I had when I'd killed my elder sisters at House Thalluen. I wondered who Kurn might have killed in his past, and why, given he was so distrusting of females.

"Mathias Briar," I said with blatant interest, rocking with the haunches and clopping hooves of Gavin's mount.

The man snapped his attention to me, guiding his gelding such that he plainly had ridden his entire adult life to get where he was going next. "Hm? What?"

"Why did Sarilis call you a 'skin hunter'? What skills does this offer?"

He glanced at the Ma'ab and Dwarf with a smile that reminded me of Court, pleasing and calming without being truthful. "I hunt bounties. On wanted men, mostly, when there is a good enough price on his head."

I did not quite understand the link to our mission, and Mathias anticipated this. He added, "If the bounty is paid with proof of their death, then that explains the name, Elf."

"Ah," I said. "To bring only a piece that identifies them and is not something they can live without."

Mathias grinned. "Exactly."

"Why not 'head hunter'?"

His grin dropped and he shrugged. "Just got that nickname. It stuck."

Unhelpful.

"Are we hunting bounties on the way? Or do your man-tracking skills reach beyond a head?"

"*Yadahata,*" Kurn muttered to Castis, who smirked.

I ignored them in favor of Mathias, who returned to smiling.

"My skill is knowing where to find news among my contacts," he agreed, "and I'm good at detecting when there's trouble coming our way."

"Aye," Rithal agreed. "An' he's our 'face' if we need negotiatin' with a town or people who don't deal with Dwarves. Not a good idea tah send the Ma'ab in for Mathias's job."

"Nor a Davrin," Castis remarked, as if it needed to be said.

Again ignoring the two, I showed my delight to Mathias. "Excellent. You are valuable, Master Briar. We are lucky you joined us."

"Thank you, lady," he said with a chuckle.

It was good that the skin hunter knew his worth, and I liked that Kurn glanced at him in irritated confusion at his choice to address me. It seemed that one day of intimidation wasn't enough to sway a man permanently against me. Rithal had claimed this wouldn't be fun. I might disagree, although this would be interesting regardless.

"Speaking value," Castis said, lifting his chin to point his gaze above my head at the man hunched over on his mare. "Gavin, let us hear your Manalari speech. I want Mathias to evaluate it."

The former apprentice had been tensed already yet his back heightened to a slight tremor, taut as Tamuril's bowstring against my spine. He didn't look around; his was the only expression I couldn't see.

"*Maknuut!*" Kurn barked. "Answer him."

Gavin muttered in response, "*Eri animvis tua fornicatis suos princi-grisat.*"

"What?" asked the other mage, glancing at Mathias, who shrugged that he hadn't heard, either. "Speak up. Again."

He stubbornly refused, and Kurn looked like he wanted to trounce the lanky half-blood again. I turned my head toward the death mage as his mare stepped carefully along the rutted, overgrown road leading down the valley.

Poking his thigh, I whispered, *"Another question in payment,"* glancing to confirm the others strained to hear.

After a few silent moments, Gavin turned his head to the side so that we could see his sharp profile. He raised his deeper voice. *"Lakitus es'puer lingukaet crescera iot."*

Mathias understood. "He's spoken the language since he was a boy, and yes, that's the dialect I've heard. Sounds natural."

"He's clearly fluent," Rithal growled, leading his short horse around a lump of rock in the road. "Now can we focus on covering ground?"

Kurn grunted his glowering satisfaction, and Castis motioned formally. The pace not only picked up, but by the time we were winding our way down to a connecting valley away from the Tower, the Ma'ab had taken the lead and Mathias had gone with them, eventually to leave and scout ahead. Rithal lingered near Gavin and me, although when the path became difficult and we needed to ride single file, he was in front. There was no one behind us now, so the moment it was level enough to turn around, I nudged the man's thigh again with my finger.

"Slow a moment, Gavin," I said over my shoulder. "I will turn around."

"Uncomfortable, is it?"

"Not bad, but I will have no purchase if you kick the beast into run."

The mare resisted in allowing the other horses to move forward without her but came to a stop at last, and I used one hand on Gavin's shoulder and another on the horse's rear end to come to a crouch and turn once again. It was not as easy as the first time.

"I do hope you don't wriggle this much as a rule," he said.

"I will move as needed," I answered. "Best become accustomed. I would rather ride with you than the others."

"Wonderful."

Loosely, I wrapped my arms around his torso, and I felt him tense. I paused as well, feeling something firm. He was wearing a form of protection beneath that tattered, grey robe.

Good thinking.

"Hm. Come, Gavin, catch us up."

He kicked his mare's sides with his heels, and we moved forward at a bouncy trot. I could barely see over Gavin's shoulder if I straightened stretched up, especially since he wasn't slouching as much. It annoyed me that I couldn't see ahead of us.

Grrr. Why are male Humans so tall?

Of course, reminded of the bounty surrounding me and the unlimited sky above us, I was curious to see a female Human to compare. Kurn had said the Ma'ab women were smaller, but was that only them or all breeds? Mathias had also treated me like a woman before he realized I wasn't. Going along on this trek, I would learn.

After we diverged from the meager cart trail passing for a road, we turned South rather than continuing North toward the nearest town, supposedly following Mathias's sign.

I wondered for all that first day why we rode horses in the mountains at all, given how often we needed to take the long way around a trench versus the direct route. I experienced the jarring ascents as the horses heaved their heavy bodies up a steep slope; I discovered what a test of nerves it was to lean back as Gavin said and let the beast pick her way down again, with regular slips of single-toed hooves that made me cringe. I was certain I could make much better time on my own two feet.

"Why do you all ride these creatures?" I asked.

Gavin paused as if he did not understand. "What else would we ride?"

"In these mountains?" I asked with some incredulity. "I've seen no wild ones in my time up here. I climb faster with my own limbs taking shorter paths."

It was a new thought for him. "They will be extremely useful when we reach the hills and flats, and we can let them run."

Yes, so that was mentioned.

"Is that where a horse is found wild?" I asked. "Not dense forest and slopes. Those are for lighter, cloven-foot creatures. Deer or goat."

"Now you mention it, yes. But I know of no tamed riding goats or deer for mountain travel. Perhaps you should try it."

I barely caught the tone of his voice; he was jesting in that deadpan way. I smirked. "But not you."

"I am far too tall. My feet would drag on the ground. You are the right size."

I chuckled to imagine that. "I am certain they wander the forest aching to serve in such a way."

Gavin was quiet as if he wasn't sure how to take that then shrugged lightly. He seemed in a slightly better mood; I knew I was. We would see how long it lasted.

With Mathias subtly nudging, Kurn found easier hollows and flatter areas following streams in which to ride, the mountains rising on either side of us. The water flowing downstream would lead us out of the mountain range. I could smell the water, the grass, and the stone together, breathing deeper the scent of this lower land. The air was so complex compared to the underground and changed often.

The pace was constant with brief stops for food and water, stretching and passing waste. My first slide off the docile, brown mare was quite tentative for how much my inner thighs complained; my feet tingled after landing on the ground, somehow unused to standing after dangling for so long.

"Need a lift down next time, Sirana?" Kurn offered with a smirk, holding the reins of his whickering, black animal.

"I have it," I said.

"Not yet, you do not."

I tilted my ear up, glancing at him. "Were you often required to serve your small women in such a way?"

Just as the big man's expression showed irritation, Castis subtly tapped Kurn's shoulder, and the Hellhound turned away while they shared private words. Rithal and Mathias looked at one another, and the Dwarf shook his head slowly before looking at me. Both of them thought it was better that I not come along.

A lead on or knowledge of the Sathoet or his Mother, Redbeard. That's all I need, and I can slip out at any time.

Probably taking the apprentice and one of Sarilis's vials with me.

While riding, I would prod Gavin for informative conversation while we remained at the rear of the line, but if he was too reticent, I let him be. He hadn't asked me for his payment yet, as few of our exchanges ventured toward the underground. He seemed to have much on his mind.

Meanwhile, I thought on how the Sun was stronger and the days much warmer than it had been when I'd first arrived on the Surface. I used my hood constantly and tolerated the dull ache behind my eyes that remained even after months. When I noticed my own eager anticipation of the shaded parts beneath the trees, grimacing when we left the shadow, I accepted being too warm in direct Sun.

How bad will it become on the flats with no trees?

Elder Rausery had suggested ways of keeping cool in our mottled black and grey uniforms. Traveling at night was one option as Summer encroached, but I wasn't traveling alone. The horses were not night creatures and could stumble and break a leg, assuming they would obey riders also not adapted to such travel.

They would get lost.

Wearing less was another option, letting the moving air touch the sweat on my skin, but the Sun also burned it, and the risk of losing my tools was higher every time it was off my body. I must bathe, too; I couldn't sleep in my armor continuously, even if it was made lighter than what Gavin and Mathias wore, flexible and far quieter than the heavier metal pieces that Rithal and Kurn either wore or had strapped to their saddle.

Cannot travel at night. Cannot strip down without cost.

A drop of sweat trickled down my temple, an unpleasant odor was coming from Gavin's armpits as well as the sweating horse, and I sighed. I had not had the time to think this through, yet I must adapt to rising heat and Sunlight. I could only travel in the day, and somehow maintain cleanliness while in the company of Human men who stared at me fully clothed.

This ain't gonna be fun, Rithal said again in my mind.

At least Gavin's mare allowed me to conserve energy and eat less; especially good as I had no time to forage. I would at night, at least, not needing as much time at rest. My one advantage was the window of opportunity between my Reverie and their sleep. I had more time in a day to use, and I must use it for foraging and bathing every chance I had.

I'll be sleeping up in a tree, unless I find a den or something.

Smirking with a bud of a plan, I rode with Gavin and the Sun lowering in the sky behind us.

"Who takes first watch?" Kurn asked.

We looked at each other in the evening shade of the trees, and he scowled.

"There are six of us, there will be six watches."

"Six," Mathias spoke up quickly.

"First," Castis volunteered.

Kurn grunted. "I'll take second. Rithal, do fifth."

The Dwarf raised a hairy, red eyebrow but nodded. The Hellhound looked at me and Gavin.

"You two can decide between yourselves third and fourth."

"Fourth," I said.

Kurn narrowed his eyes suspiciously, and I smiled.

"Mathias can make the fire and boil the water, then," Gavin grumbled as he unstrapped the bedroll from the front of his saddle.

The bounty hunter shrugged. "Of course. Nothing new."

"I assume we follow one of the Moons to judge our watch?" I asked.

The Hellhound sneered a little. "Of course. Then wake the other. And do I need to say to make clear, that if any theft, poisoning, or other threat occurs, I will punish you and cull you from this group."

He was looking mostly at me, but also Gavin.

I smiled. "This applies to you as well, Kurn, yes?"

He chuffed. "My mission is greater to me than causing strife."

"Don't lie, Hellhound, your existence *is* to cause strife."

The white warrior turned on me in a threatening pose, and Castis and Mathias backed up as Kurn stepped closer to me. Much closer. I could smell his stallion and the sweaty leather and the distinct, oily scent of male Human. He looked down at me, using his height to any advantage. I didn't budge.

The man's dark eyes and his teeth flashed in the low light. "I had planned to perform this mission with just four. You and the *maknuut* are unknowns and unproven. One misstep, and we will do without you."

I kept my focus on my periphery—on Kurn's hands, if his stance changed or if those around us moved—rather than stare directly at him. I alternated between looking at a small brown dot on his forehead and his nose with nostrils flared.

"You keep using that word," I said. "Mok-noo-uht. What does it mean?"

Castis huffed at my pronunciation but answered. "A Ma'ab mage from the *hayi'qara* caste."

"The what?" Mathias asked, narrowing his eyes.

"The lowest," Castis added, lifting his chin. "He is mixed blood."

"I am not Ma'ab," Gavin said, "and not of your 'caste.'"

A simple statement made while the apprentice was unpacking, which Castis shrugged off and Kurn ignored while facing me. His eyes narrowed and my hand drifted toward a dagger handle.

"Eh, eh, you can back up, Kurn," Rithal said as he straightened, pointing with his spade he'd been using to dig a pit for a fire. "Were I her, I wouldn't promise nothin' while breathin' the same air as you."

The broad fighter turned to the Dwarf and waved his hand dismissively. *"Ayi,* I *will* have an answer before we break."

The distraction allowed me to move a pace slanted from the Ma'ab. When he turned around, having to crane his neck, I offered a Court smile, nearly certain Kurn recognized something like it. His nostril twitched.

I answered. "No theft, poison, or threat from me, Hellhound. My mission is greater than causing strife, agreed? We can share our knowledge of demons, instead."

Kurn's expression iced over, and he was silent beyond that familiar sneer.

That's a negative. I took that moment to bow and disengage. "Enjoy your night, men. I shall return for my watch."

"Where are you going?" the Ma'ab demanded.

"Red Sister thing. See you at dawn. Come, Gavin."

The apprentice had just finished seeing to his horse, removing most of the tackle and allowing her to graze. He glanced at me, considered his options, and decided to follow.

"There's work to be done!" Kurn barked.

"Let 'em be," I heard Rithal say. "We been doin' fine, just the three of us, and we have Mathias."

"Yes, you do," the nobleman said, pleased to help.

I might have stayed to listen, but the brush and twigs crunched behind me as I entered the thick with Gavin catching up. Saying nothing, we walked a small distance until he noticed I was foraging. To my satisfaction, he began doing the same, and I watched him for any plants, roots, or mushrooms I did not already know about.

Having a handful of potential food in hand, I asked, "How far did we travel today?"

The stooping mage lifted his head, glancing at me, before a long-fingered hand grasped the bundled stems at their base and ripped a whole, pale tuber from the dark soil. I was using a dagger to dig around it. He was stronger than he looked.

"Twelve leagues, perhaps," he said.

Here we go.

"How far is a league?"

Gavin scrunched his face. "Your superior didn't tell you? We've used this measurement for centuries."

"She did. I want to hear your answer."

He sighed, straightening up to brush dirt off his root before tucking it into a satchel. He looked around for the next. "About how far a man can walk in an hour."

"Not very precise."

"Are underground tunnels measured in exact grids?"

I grinned. "Is that your question?"

"No," he growled.

At least he remembered.

"What of women?" I asked. "They can walk as fast?"

"I don't know. Sometimes."

"How can you not know?"

Gavin glared at me. "You do not know what a monk is."

I shook my head without argument, and he brushed off his hands, thinking. He managed to be quite succinct. "A cloister of men seeking spiritual purity. Monks are not allowed wives or children."

I blinked in surprise. "A cloister of men?"

"This makes sense?"

"Well…" I considered. "I am from a… cloister for warriors?"

"Barracks," Gavin defined, nodding. "Yes, that makes sense. Is it similar, in that your smaller males and children are not allowed to live there?"

"Is *that* your question?"

The mage looked exasperated. "Yes."

"It is similar. Sisters only. We are not allowed *zilbuas dara'ludal.*"

He turned his ear toward me. "Not allowed what?"

I cleared my throat, consciously resisting my hand drifting toward my middle. "Male companions and children."

Gavin had an odd look on his face. "Male companions. Husbands?"

I shrug. "Husbandry, yes. Breeding animals."

He went still. "Well. Not *incorrect*, I suppose. Hm."

I smiled at his expression. "But 'husband' is different from 'husbandry'? How, apprentice?"

He was discomforted. "Not important. Another time."

Now I sighed. "Indeed. We spoke of leagues and how far a man can walk in a day. I would like to understand this better."

"Yes, very well," he began, once again in comfortable territory. "If one traveled for eight hours for most of the day on foot, that walk is eight leagues. The horses gained us half again that, even in rough terrain, and we are not exhausted by a long march."

It *was* a better way to travel this gigantic world above. I couldn't wait for darkness in the trees again, though. "And about how far to Troshin Bend, and this inn of crossing trade routes?"

Gavin shook his head. "I did not go through there. I don't know."

"But you came this way once before from Manalar."

"Over seven years, and only from the area, not the city." He drew a small dagger from his belt to carefully work a stubborn root. "It was not a straight line."

"Where—"

"No," he refused.

I let it go; Mathias or Rithal could answer the league question easily. "Will you sleep tonight out here with me, or at camp?"

He hesitated, tucking a few last plants and bulbs in his satchel. "I left my bedroll there. And my cooking gear."

Oh, the cooking. I instantly regretted what I was about to say as I glanced at my raw fare. "Very good. May I ask later what you observe the others? Tell me what they speak of me before I come for watch."

He eyed me. "You *can* listen for yourself unobserved. You are quiet enough."

"I prefer privacy."

"For what?"

"Red Sister thing."

Gavin's dark eyes narrowed like the Ma'ab's. "So you said."

"So, it is. I will return to relieve you of watch."

Eventually, Gavin agreed and left with some edibles to cook, and I searched for a suitable place to eat and rest. I would have time to forage further and check my traps in the pre-dawn dark after my watch and as they continued to sleep; I had just enough time.

And perhaps enough time for that other Red Sister thing.

I took effort to cover my tracks and found a small hollow beneath some jutting rock that seemed previously used by animals. The scent was not so strong that I thought one would imminently return, but if they did, my spiders would be ready. There was only one way in or out, but it was easily defended; it would block the wind and dew as well.

A good place for the first night back in the wild.

I crawled in, removed my pack and belt but kept them near, and let my spiders out to hunt for food around the rocks. I sighed and got comfortable enough, so my thoughts touched on taking down my leathers and rubbing my sex. I hadn't had a chance like this to myself in weeks.

Before I so much as tugged on a tie at my hip, I drifted into that meditative state right before Reverie, when I'd see how dreams wanted to speak, if they did at all.

It seemed She had been waiting for me since Tamuril's hovel.

Her hair was pure white, kept in a single braid down to her waist. Her dress was a deep purple and lightweight, easily flowing in a hot, dry breeze; the sandals on her feet were gold and lovely. She kept her back to me, long fingernails delicately resting on a scroll unrolled upon the table.

"Why do you ask?" she said.

I blinked. *What did I ask?*

"He is fine," she continued, her voice smooth and young. "He is safe, you needn't worry."

Looking down, I saw that I wore a red uniform. Familiar, but different. There was sand beneath my boots in the canvas tent.

"Where is he?" I asked again. "I would like to talk with him."

"No. You should not. He is in denial."

Denial of what?

"If you and I are both here," I said, "who watches him now?"

The Davrin stood silent but regal. Her presence filled the tent, warning any to tread lightly.

After a pause, she exhaled. "He is safe. Who have you found to aid you?"

"No one strong enough," I informed her.

"Keep searching."

She never turned around, so I never saw the color of her eyes.

The tent around me blurred, disappeared, and I strode along that same desert street where I had first seen the brown-skinned Elf riding a horse without saddle or bridle. I was searching for someone.

"Ahh, greetings, Captain!"

I stopped to look at the merchant beneath the multi-colored shades of his stall. *Captain?*

"A long time since you've been through here." The Davrin's smile was truly arresting, his ruby-red eyes rich and sparkling. "Do you search for me?"

I let the name return with the face. *Toushek.*

Auslan remembered him, he'd said, after having forgotten.

"Come closer." Toushek beckoned. "Let me see you clearly."

I had been here before. The feeling was there.

"I'll stay here," I said. "Thank you."

"Suit yourself." The Davrin moved a few beautiful objects on his wares table, letting the light catch them just right. "What can I offer you today? You seem to be searching for something specific, yet you will only know it when you see it."

I frowned at the wares. "Didn't you serve food before?"

He shrugged. "One must adapt to the market."

Toushek reached out and selected a statue, setting it out before the others. "Have you seen one of these, yet?"

It looked like a blind crayfish from down below if it had been flattened. Eight legs, its body segmented in an external skeleton. It had pinchers like a crayfish, but also a tail that curved up to hover above its back, the bulb at the end coming to a fine point. It was semi-translucent and the color of tree sap in direct Sun, almost topaz.

"No," I answered honestly. "What is it?"

"A venomous, eight-legged hunter."

I considered my dark, glossy guardians. He smiled wider.

"Sound familiar, does it? Yet, *this* one is made for sunlight."

I stared at the statue then lifted my eyes only to see the merchant wink.

"Word of advice, my child," he crooned. "Beware the Scorpion's sting. It can come upon anyone, anywhere, at any time."

I stepped away, sensing the dim shade of the alley through which Auslan had once taken me. I turned and moved for that cover I knew would cool me down and give me space to think.

Think, before I tried to touch that Scorpion.

I wondered where Auslan was in this city, if I could find him. Or if I would see him again. I wandered in my dream for some time, never finding him.

A familiar voice returned. *He is fine. He is safe.*

If I picked a moment that surprised me most when I awoke, it was rediscovering as I crawled out of my den that I had muscles in my legs I'd been unaware of for decades. It even distracted from my empty belly.

Oh, Goddess. Horses… So wide…

Walking felt like tight, leather straps had replaced all parts of my inner thighs, and at first, I looked like Cullen trying to walk like a puppet. I spent an unaccustomed amount of time stretching before I ate anything. I hoped I would adjust to this new mount quickly.

I took my time returning to camp, enjoying the sight and smells. I could see much better at night, and the temperature was like comfortable Deepearth quarters, not warm at all. I tried not to think about how soon it would grow much hotter when the Sun rose, how just keeping my eyes open was taxing.

All so the horses won't break their legs and my travel companions won't get lost in the dark. Bah.

Well, if our destination was as far as they said, and if the mounts would indeed speed our journey and conserve my energy, it would be worth it.

I sneaked up on the camp, walking the perimeter and seeking wards, traps, or alarms. How much they might trust the apprentice's watch, and how well they could detect someone like me if necessary? I sensed three short-range wards from Gavin on three sides, but he also left the spot close to the horses open. I wondered about that. Did the beasts hate being so close to magical energy? Would they serve as their own alarm on that side?

There was another ward set by Castis, closer to him and Kurn. The two were asleep near Mathias and closest to the banked coals of the firepit. Rithal was farther away, on his back and unmoving but for the rise and fall of his chest.

The three in possession of armor were all without it at this moment, and it was interesting to see them shrink—either only a bit, as with Mathias and his stiff leather pieces, or a notable amount as with Kurn and Rithal. They wore clothing, but it made me reflect that my armor was made differently and did not increase my width or breadth much at all. They could tell my true shape without my cloak, while theirs was masked even without one. They all made noise all the time regardless of dress but, without the armor, some might have the ability to be quieter.

I considered breaking Gavin's ward again as I had before but questioned whether it was worth the energy or risk. If I walked next to the horses...well, Kurn's stallion was separated from the rest and tied to a branch three trees over, being aggressive. The gelding and mares might not mind me so much, but I could see the beast trumpeting an alarm just stepping close to the others.

Time to see. It's my watch, anyway.

I made just enough noise for two of horses to swivel their ears in my direction; the dark stallion raised his head and whickered low, not able to see me clearly but nostrils flaring wide to catch my scent. I murmured a few, low words I'd overhead the others say, and while Kurn's mount pranced his hooves in the dirt, the rest shifted their weight and looked about.

Gavin lifted his head to look in my direction as the mounts shuffled and burred, but he couldn't see me yet. That changed as I stepped beneath his mare's head, electing not to walk behind. I'd been warned they had a mighty kick if startled. He straightened, focused tightly on me. I stopped. There was no real firelight, I wore my cloak with hood, and I stood leaping strides away.

Is his night vision that good or is he certain of my size?

I wouldn't have been, were I in his place.

He said nothing as I approached and sat down beside him, resting my back against the log they'd dragged over for the purpose. We watched each other for a few moments, and I smiled.

"Guessing it was me?" I whispered. "What if you were wrong?"

Gavin shook his head. "I knew. I could make out your aura by the horses."

I frowned. "That easy?"

He shrugged. "I know what to look for, and you do not hide that you are magic-born."

At first, that made no sense to me. Gaelan and D'Shea could see auras, but they had only described other mages. *I* wasn't a mage, but this Human was saying he could see something like a mage's aura in me? That was concerning. What had Castis and Sarilis already seen? Not only that, but Rausery hadn't mentioned this. Another vulnerability for my Sisters on their own, especially Gaelan!

"And you hide that you are magic-born?" I asked, pretending I wasn't so surprised.

The death mage nodded. "I must. Some Witch Hunters can see auras as I can. Most mages surviving without the protection of someone with power know how to suppress it. Else they be either captive or dead."

They know how? I hadn't known that was possible. But then, many things are possible when it's necessary.

Gavin broke my line of questioning with, "You did not break the ward again."

"No. Having it will help you sleep better, yes?"

"I doubt that was your prime concern."

I chuckled softly, quieted as Mathias shifted in his sleep, and waited for the night sounds to return to the foreground before speaking further.

"How do you 'suppress' your aura?" I asked.

Gavin's dark eyes blinked at me in the night.

I added, "Surely you do not want me as a beacon to Witch Hunters? No one spoke of this, and I've never needed to hide this underground."

He considered, nodding as he at first agreed but then shook his head. "Save this for the road. Too complex to explain now."

"I will hold you to that." I resettled. "What about this eve? Anything notable, and is there food left?"

He gave me an odd look but shook his head. "They ate it all."

Damn it. Pigs.

Gavin eyed my expression. "It wasn't much, I prepared some rabbit and a bird they caught, and the vegetables. No large event. Some questions where you were, I told them I did not know but you would return on your own."

I smiled. "Hm. Anything else?"

He dismissed that. "Nothing that wasn't posturing or lewd remarks from the Hound."

To be expected.

I knew how quiet and observant Gavin was; I could put value in what he saw or heard and what he chose to share. He was also smart enough to hold something back if he wanted or fail to see value in remarks made above his "caste," but it would take some time to see those voids. I could only work with what he gave. It would be important to offer something useful in return, so doubt of my motives would not cloud his judgment. If ever balance was important with an ally, it would be on this journey with this Human mage.

"May I ask you a question?" I began, unable to keep the smile from my face.

Gavin said nothing but raised a brow in response after checking that the others were asleep.

"What did you say the first time in Manalari? The one Mathias *didn't* hear."

The ugly mage scowled. "It does not translate well."

"I imagine it was an insult. Try."

He shook his head. "Just profanity. Without the context, it has no meaning."

"I enjoy the profane. Would you like to hear a Davrin curse in exchange?"

He grew agitated in a familiar way; of a male concerned that something he'd said would reach the wrong ears. "Red Sister. Let it be."

Learning his limits, I sighed. "Very well."

A pause. "If nothing else, then do sleep, monk. I am here to watch you."

Gavin made a face quite eloquent without words, a skeptical brow and a wry twist of his broad mouth. Nonetheless, he gradually bedded down on Rithal's side of the fire and tried to return to the sleep that had been interrupted by third watch.

I waited some time in silence, patient, as the horses settled and the breathing of all five males made their regular patterns. Then, I shifted my location to be just close enough to Castis so I could prod at the boundary of his ward and discover its nature.

Hm. Simple repelling.

No illness or gripping fear, anger or temptation to strike with total loss of caution, neither to cause a distraction or loss of memory. Between Castis and Gavin's wards, I was rather surprised how uncomplicated they were compared to those in Sivaraus which I had confronted almost every cycle in some form.

And yet Gavin could still see my aura.

I wouldn't attempt to break the Ma'ab mage's ward this night, though I suspected that I could quickly, if the need somehow outweighed the risk of a miscarriage. With this kind of ward, that risk was lower than most Noble Houses, yet there was no reason to be reckless tonight.

My stomach cramped in hunger before my watch was finished. I nibbled on the last which I had collected prior to lying down in the unused den and waited out the Moons' nightly travels across the sky. It became a little colder, and eventually it was time to wake up Rithal.

I approached carefully. His eyes opened before I touched him, and he looked over to his left since I wasn't so foolish as to hover right above him. He grunted acknowledgement and sat up, his fuzzy, red beard and wild hair seeming to blaze beneath the Moonlight. Although I considered staying and chatting with this Dwarf, I hadn't checked my traps. The need for fresh sustenance to preserve my stores was more important.

"I will return at sunrise," I murmured, and left by way of the horses again.

The Dwarf watched me with suspicion until I disappeared into the forest. He said nothing.

The first several days of travel by horse were draining in ways I preferred not to make apparent. While I adjusted, my pattern of keeping with Gavin during the day and going off on my own at night continued. Kurn showed his annoyance openly, and I knew it kept the other three on edge. Not ideal, but it preserved some mystery.

On the practical side of the coin, I had little trouble staying cleaner than the men and fed well without taking their supplies.

Rithal and Mathias both noticed I was self-sufficient; they remarked on it. Additionally, less of my spare energy was wasted on bickering or contests of will—another thing Rithal commented on during the fourth night.

"Thought fer sure you were gonna play pranks on the Ma'ab at night," he had said.

"Why think that?" I asked.

"Old legends suggested the dark-skinned Elves were mean-spirited ones. Especially to the unwary and disrespectful. Big on revenge for a slight."

I'd smiled. "Not all of us. Sounds more like Kurn."

The Dwarf had exhaled, "Yeah…"

Rithal had received no other insight. Although such tactics weren't beyond me, I usually waited until I was harried first. I thought the Hellhound had meaner spirits to burn than me, although he wouldn't have matched my late sisters, Jilrina and Kaltra.

Our pace remained consistent for over a week, with the warmer weather broken only by a few small rainstorms, and Kurn's patience was further extended by a visible pattern on which he could rely. Gavin was able to stay in the camp most nights and give me a few insights on what was said when I wasn't present.

"They seem to think you spend all your time bathing and touching yourself," he remarked one day as I sat behind him on his mare, "for how light your scent is."

"You all could spend more time on the first," I replied, having already noticed I didn't produce a potent musk as they did. "I can hardly tell your scents apart from the horses at this point." Gavin had huffed, and I continued, "But enough on that. Describe it again how one suppresses a magic aura."

We traveled, descending toward the flatlands, and Kurn watched me always, crouching like the mountain cat I'd once observed take a fawn that wandered too far from its mother. I preferred this over the Hellhound learning more of my training, my weapons, or how my mind worked by frequent interaction. I could respond to an attack out of darkness, and I already had his poor impulse control on my side. I had less defense if he learned to turn my own against me while having studied the weapons and pouches on my belt.

The Hellhound also hadn't been responsive to sharing information about demons, yet, after that first mention. Kurn had walled it up, and if Castis was interested, the bigger man kept him from asking me about it.

Mathias was a little more curious.

"So, demons are real," he asked, managing to sidle up to me one evening out of sight of the disapproving Ma'ab.

"Without doubt," I told him. "As real as me."

The nobleman had a charming smile. "Not comforting, but better than deluding one's self. I should be careful signing any future contract, hm?"

I showed my confusion. "Contracts?"

He lifted brown eyebrows. "You know, the bargains for your soul you signed in your own blood?"

"That doesn't sound right," I said. "The demons I've seen were never that formal. Opportunists and ambusher, difficult to control in a summoning. Like too-intelligent beasts."

Mathias was frowning in confusion as well, and it struck me when I spotted Gavin out of the corner of my eye.

"Oh," I said. "You speak of devils?"

"Erm, they aren't the same?"

I grinned. "Not what I've heard. They are from two different places. The Hells and the Abyss both exist, though I am familiar with the Void."

"*Not* comforting," he said again with a smirk, his heart beating a bit faster.

About then, Kurn called for the skin hunter, and Mathias excused himself, keeping his interests private from the nosy strongman. For the better, I was sure.

One pattern I had missed for the first two weeks was Kurn's ritual sword practice at dawn, before he knew if I had returned or not. I had arrived earlier than before, possessing an abundance of edibles and having eaten my fill, with time to spare before the others got up.

Kurn wore only his trousers and boots, and a dark red pendant hung around his neck. I peered closer, touching where my blue saphgar lay beneath the leather.

Possessions we both keep well-hidden.

Was his simple jewelry or something else? Something of which to be aware.

His lack of dress also offered me a good look at the bulk beneath his daily hide and metal. He possessed scars which were bluish in color, his skin tone quite milky compared to Mathias's warmer tan and Rithal's ruddy complexion.

Castis and Gavin are both that pallid, though.

I watched him from shadows, some distance away from the camp, as he moved with his heavy, two-handed sword in deliberate guards, arcs, swings, and rolls. They were practiced tactics, difficult to engage directly because of his reach and the power behind the swings. One true strike, and someone my size would lose a limb. His strength afforded him greater speed than such a heavy weapon should allow, though I wondered how long he could maintain such a fight.

All my tools allowed me to keep moving, to continue a careful aim when attacking; it was expected during an Ornilleth battle. Overbearing a mass of bulky thralls with sword swings was not a smart tactic for any Davrin fighter, whether cait or bua.

Plus, then we'd be in the way of the mages.

Yet watching this morning suggested that Kurn would try this to win a battle *and* to display himself at the same time. If there were a lot of him doing the same thing, I could see it working against other men of similar size if morale suffered on account. These fighters could be tempted to see who lasted longer on his feet.

I sighed, rubbing my chin as I tried to understand.

Prior to the Sisterhood, I'd known a handful of male Davrin with reputations as gifted fighters among my Matron's House Guard; fast and focused, loyal and not lazy, they were favored by my Mother enough to remember some of their names.

Gaelan's chosen sire, Treyl, was among them.

If a bua fighter could keep up with the caits, I thought those buas were often better than those trained at Court because they didn't waste energy being fancy, just fast and effective.

Kurn is trying to be both.

So, what was the weakness? What suffered first, endurance, precision, or patience? I'd rather not be in the middle of a conflict before I found out but, given how well he paced himself in his exercise, that might be the only way to know. No way I would get near him in a challenge, however. He might have to swallow the fact that I found no hesitation running to find a better position.

But, then what?

I couldn't send my spiders to him. though they would defend me, compulsion or not. The thought of using Callitro's ring to shoot him through the eye with my hand crossbow made me sick, and every other weapon that wasn't a blade and might neutralize him required me to get close to him to be effective.

Like the failed sleep powder.

I turned it over a few times, but no defense to an attack like this seemed a sure thing. Especially if I didn't know what that ruby was for.

Just don't get trapped in a tight space.

"*Kus umma,*" the Hellhound rumbled, breathing heavily as he stopped his practice.

My mouth twisted. That insult again. Had he been imagining fighting me this whole time? Ridiculous, if so. He had less of a plan engaging me than I did him!

Kurn ran a hand through his shorter, black hair, wiping the sweat off his forehead. He scowled as he stepped to his belt hanging with his shirt on the nearest tree branch, sheathing his blade in its scabbard. He breathed in deeply and deliberately, his nostrils curling, before he let it out again. He did this a few more times, then reached for the leather ties at the front of his trousers.

Now I noticed the erection. *Hmm. Alright, why not?*

Always something new to learn. We'd see how accurate Rausery's shape-changing potion had been.

The Hellhound listened about him, looked for observers, to convince himself he was alone. He missed me and turned to brace himself against the tree trunk, one hand reaching for his prick. I didn't have the best view; he was turned three-quarters away, although I glimpsed that his staff was in proportion to his size.

I made out thicker genital hair than I was used to in males—the balls especially so, but also the wiry sprout of pitch-black crowning his penis and spreading onto his thighs. He freed his scrotum as well as his member and barely caressed it before he began stroking with efficiency and surprising speed.

No luxuriating, I see. Alas. Sometimes, one just didn't have the time.

Kurn grimaced and closed his eyes, his expression all wolfish aggression as he leaned on his left arm, his hand throttling his jutting cock. I sensed I had little time to study it. One thing Rausery had absolutely gotten right was the plump, purple-red head of his member rolled over by a flushed foreskin that moved with his hand. My buas always had foreskins to play with, but they weren't quite this thick or long; they tended to become quite subtle when they were excited like this.

Soon, redness beneath Kurn's skin began creeping up his neck and into his face, as it had during his sword practice. A few individual muscles flexed in his back as I watched.

"*Katha anath shubis,*" he growled low, spittle touching his lip and chin.

By tone, I guessed he had said something extremely lewd in his own tongue. I smiled. Some things seemed universal.

The breeze shifted, and I caught a whiff of the heated musk coming from him. I tried to convince myself that observing the brute in a vulnerable moment explained why I was aroused, but it was not that simple.

The aggressive growls and urgent strokes brought memories of my Lead Jaunda and several other Sisters, especially in the sluicers after the Ornilleth battle. The sounds also reminded me of Shyntre in the library in his greatest resistance, blatantly fighting me for control. My surge of excitement was real, remembering how the wizard had eventually submitted, and yet fought with such ferocity that I hit my head under the table after we were finished.

I felt a yearning for home, and I ached between my legs for this kind of rough play, but I didn't want to play with Kurn.

"Teez shar-...sharmuta...kus!" he groaned, closing his eyes tight and lifting his chin.

His spine straightened and his hips moved forward as he held still; his mouth open. The first spurt of white semen marked the tree trunk in a long line, and a second soon followed. He resumed stroking with smaller bursts, further coating the tree, intent on squeezing every drop of pleasure and spunk from his well-jerked rod.

My heart raced and a stark heat flushed my body; I swallowed, as my mouth was dry, and I forced myself to stop rubbing my sex as Kurn again looked around, listening. I held my breath as he gingerly tucked in his tender parts and secured his trousers, finally donning his belt and shirt. The red stone around his neck caught my eye again just before it was hidden from view.

Eventually, he lifted his heavy sword and strode away toward the camp. I'd intended to leave and try to make it there ahead of him but hesitated. My heart thudding in my ears, I looked at the tree stained with fresh cum. I felt inexplicably anxious, like time was running out.

I pulled out one of my limited, grey cloths, using a dagger to cut off a small piece, before tucking the rest of the cloth away. In silence, I approached the spot where Kurn had been masturbating. Nothing in the forest disturbed me as I wiped up semen onto the patch and rubbed the cloth together, spreading it thin and blowing on it so it would dry. I would add it to my tools.

Then I touched my crotch through my leathers, murmuring a pleasant, inarticulate sound as my sex tingled. My nose detected a potent scent as I braced against the same tree, in a similar stance as Kurn. The damp cloth in one hand, I rubbed my sex hard enough with the other through my leathers to climax quickly.

It was abrupt and strong, surging hot through my gut; my knees weakened as I leaned against the tree. I made no sound except a quiet gasp as I came down, and I didn't move while I listened for a sentient audience. I trusted my ears much farther than Human ones and believed I was alone.

Only as I walked to camp did the oddness of this strike me. I had felt strange, the need urgent, my actions thoughtless. *Why* had I smeared a cloth with Kurn's seed and kept it like a trophy?

I remembered what Wilsira and Kerse could do with such a thing. Those last moments in the Priestess's quarters rolled over me. I was bound, finally under their control after unending cycles inside the Sanctuary. I stopped in my tracks, nauseated. I dared not go any farther down that dark path.

Don't. Throw it away.

My head felt light, my mind uncooperative. I smelled blood and deep rock. All I saw was the Deepearth; the trees and the scents had disappeared. I lay in the presence of Drider guts. Kerse had killed one of Braqth's Blessed. Then something intangible tugged hard at my head and in my chest, like hooks. Someone gripped me, and I heard a scream.

Then I heard quite a few.

The screams were mine.

When I became aware again, I was on my knees, my body curled small and tight in the brush. My gloved fingers dug deeply into the soil, like claws hooked in meat. No one came upon me, and I hoped I hadn't made any noise. The cloth with Kurn's semen on it was hanging off a tiny branch, and it was mostly dry. My spiders had come out of my hair; they were on my bracers, agitated. They were looking for the danger but found no target to bite.

Shit.

I remembered so vividly that my spit tasted metallic. I sucked in a breath against the fading pain in my chest, blinking against the strengthening daylight. How much time had passed? I looked East.

The Sun was above the horizon.

Not much time was gone, but longer than I could account for. Slowly, I removed my stiff fingers from the earth and brushed off the dirt.

"It's okay, babies," I whispered. "Back in the pouch, the Sun rises."

I tucked them safe and arose to my feet. I meant to leave that male-essence on a stained scrap of cloth right where it was but, as I took a step, stopped again. Biting my lower lip, I plucked it up and almost tucked it in a pouch.

I froze. *What is wrong with me?*

"Elf!" I heard Rithal call from camp. "Leaving soon!"

I blinked, and the Surface world returned to me, vivid and real as it hadn't been a moment ago. All the scents and colors jumped upon me at once.

"Elf! Where are ya?!"

Damn it. He'd never had to call before.

I tossed down the semen-stained scrap and ground it under my boot heel, until it was buried beneath dirt and the roots of grass.

No. Just, no.

I circled so as not to come from the same direction as Kurn, but I had to hurry. The men had everything ready to go, and Kurn was mounted on his stallion as I jogged into the camp.

"Finished with your 'Red Sister things'?" he asked with a look that confirmed who he had thought about as he stroked off on that tree trunk.

I smiled. "Quite, Hellhound."

"Good," he sneered. "Let us go."

On mornings when there wasn't a convenient log or rock, Gavin had taken to offering me a reluctant arm so I could pull myself up onto the horse behind him. As I settled and shifted my rump to get straight, Gavin looked over his shoulder, lingering for long enough that I met the one dark eye I could see.

"What?"

"Your aura has shifted."

I didn't like that. "What do you mean, shifted?"

Gavin kicked his mare, following the others dead last, as usual, and keeping distance so we could talk.

"I have noticed a few times, Sirana. I don't know why it occurs. There are odd threads in your magical aura which could be natural to your race, but when they appear, your life aura warps as well."

I was silent. Holding to an oddly informal agreement, Gavin had been slowly teaching me about auras and those I had. He described exercises on a mind-body awareness that wasn't entirely new to me, but I found it difficult to "hold in" some nebulous energy he described being able to see when he focused on me.

I had kept practicing out of necessity, since he wasn't the only one able to see it, and the death mage was the only one interested in telling me the truth on whether it was working.

In addition, Gavin had a peculiar advantage over other mages such as Castis: he could see two distinct kinds of auras. According to him, he saw the life aura that came to him as a death mage, and the magical one I'd known about from growing up around mages. I was curious how Gavin might see Gaelan, a magic user, compared to Jael and me, who weren't.

"I might guess," he added, "that you were unsettled by something this morning. What happened?"

I pursed my lips in irritation. I couldn't explain it, and I couldn't tell him. I didn't want to remember and would not dwell on it. My change in pattern had already caused the others to look behind themselves at us. It was a vulnerability if any knew this happened.

I chuckled low and near his shoulder. "Spying on Kurn sword dancing. He was amusing and finished it off with a squishy pole-pull, muttering about *kus*."

I figured this would put him off; Gavin wasn't titillated by descriptions of such arousal, as the many jests from the Ma'ab and even Mathias about his former monkhood showed. I couldn't tell if the apprentice had ever tried it alone, much less with someone else.

He called my bluff. "I am guessing that's true but a diversion. You seemed afraid upon your return. And you were late. Did you see any danger we should know about?"

"No."

Honest enough, unless the danger was me.

"Mm. Very well."

He seemed willing to drop it, given how he blocked me about personal questions all the time, and I spent the quiet turning it over in my mind.

Afraid. This was something he could sense in my aura? That wasn't helpful to my situation.

"Can you see fear in all auras?" I asked. "Is it a quality of life, perhaps?"

Gavin glanced back so I could see his profile. I had amused him. "I have never heard that before, but what an interesting thought. Are you saying it *was* fear?"

I swallowed. "Yes, but nothing threatening to anyone in this moment."

"Hm. A haunt from the past?"

Internally, I sighed. "Yes. Dark Elves live a long time. Our memories are long."

Gavin turned forward as he guided his mare through a steeper and tighter path. "If my collection of nightmares can linger for decades, I hesitate to imagine those with centuries behind them."

I frowned. "Sometimes forgetting is the only way to move forward."

"Wise words. Until you stumble into the same haunts again."

Definitely too close to home.

"How does fear in a life aura work?" I asked.

He grunted and, surprising me, had a ready answer. "The Vitas and Vis, which are normally one, become separate, but in a chain response. It causes the warp I see."

I squinted, shaking my head. "The…what? Vitas?"

And Vis? Where had I heard that before?

The slouching death mage quieted again as he chose his words. "Vitas is the primal power that keeps a body alive. That unseen force to drive a heart beating and a body rebuilding."

Rebuilding?

"Manipulating this power," he continued, "especially in transition, is one aspect which makes death mages what we are."

Yes, Rausery had said something like this. She'd warned me about the potential value in a pregnant female for this "transition" power.

"Alright," I said. "What is Vis?"

"As intangible as Vitas. But can manifest as a persona or a collection of memories. Most call it a spirit, or a ghost."

"I was taught 'spirit' in Trade meant to describe all strange beings Humans do not recognize." I paused. "Also Dwarven drink, though I do not understand the connection."

"True enough for both," Gavin agreed. "I do not know why liquor is a spirit, either. Perhaps how it suffuses a feeling like mist through body and mind, like a possession."

I smiled at the morbid comparison, and he continued.

"But a ghost is unambiguous. A lingering Vis that hasn't transitioned."

Ghost.

A chill creeped up my spine as I thought about that thing which had been hovering above Gavin in the tower while he slept. Then I thought about Kain, and what the female Tragar, Lana, had said about his presence in my mind.

"Lingering. How do ghosts linger?"

Gavin heard my baffled tone. "You have never encountered this concept?"

"No. It doesn't exist among my own."

He sounded skeptical. "How could that be? You have a Vis, Sirana. You can bleed and die."

"I don't know how it is," I growled. "*You* are the death mage."

He grunted again. "Well. You shall hear it a lot for any townsfolk we encounter. Ghosts abound in their tales."

"I'll be sure to listen. But what would *you* say before then? What do you see and know?"

A shrug. "Sometimes they have the appearance of a body, resembling a point of mortal life or how they would rather have been. Other times, they are like wisps of fog, the only warning being the otherworldly chill around them. Other times, they take the forms of mankind's terrors."

"You've *seen* ghosts," I interjected, "like I see birds?"

"Since I was young. Haunting the old crypts of the monastery. As far as any would admit, I was the only one." Gavin paused. "I did not make the mistake to confess it more than once, though it caused such a stir, others never forgot."

"Why? What happens when a Human says they see ghosts?"

Gavin jerked his head around farther than usual to see my expression; his was incredulous. After a moment evaluating me, he said, "You don't jest."

I shook my head. "My leaders would be curious to study this claim, though you'd be sure to be kept in a locked space."

"A prison, yes. Can't say I'm surprised."

"But the other monks?"

His tone was removed, as if he no longer acknowledged it being connected to him. "They believed pain and hot iron upon the body would drive corruption from a child's soul, letting holy light in to cleanse it." He turned to face the front. "Which in truth only makes him stop speaking of it to avoid the pain, though sightings and seizures continue."

Sarilis said they tried to 'beat the Ma'ab' out of him.

I knew the wordless sign that Gavin was finished and wouldn't answer anything else; I had already obtained something quite personal.

Meanwhile, something else niggled at me for the rest of the day, but I was wary to drift too deep into my memories, given what just happened in the wood. It returned to me as soon as I relaxed and watched the passing scenery.

The Valsharess embracing me, trapping me as She spread her hand upon my flat belly, knowing somehow that I'd caught.

"He has not exposed his Vis to a cait in centuries," She said.

His Vis.

My heart pounded against Gavin's back, though he seemed neither to hear nor feel it. I swallowed and shivered. My Queen *knew* the word, the same one in both our languages, but what did it mean to Her? No one had ever spoken of seeing ghosts among the

Davrin, not as Gavin described. If the Valsharess did in some way, then what would he say, if he knew?

Is an Elf thousands of years old haunted by a ghost? The Vis of Her Son?

I resisted where my thoughts sought to flee next. I covered my womb with my hand and focused on the warmth. I knew Auslan was the sire, I *knew* this. The Queen thought it was Shyntre, but She was wrong.

Whether She sees ghosts or not, She is still insane.

Would being silent while assaulted by spirits drive one that direction? I could only speculate for the Valsharess, but it was worth noting for the death mage before me. As interesting as I found our conversations, I had yet to gauge Gavin's sanity under pressure; the prodding and teasing I'd done so far was nothing. He guarded areas I had yet to see.

Maybe, when threatened, a disgraced Manalari monk could be as volatile and vicious as any Queen or Priestess down below.

CHAPTER 11

"Not that way," Rithal grumbled as his pony caught up to the much younger Ma'ab who had been speeding along to this point.

Gavin and I had just caught up to where the group had paused at a split.

"There're clear markings."

"I see none," Kurn said.

"Y'aren't Dwarven."

I looked about with interest, wondering what markings the redbeard had spotted.

"This pass is treacherous," Rithal continued. "I'll lead."

Kurn appraised the rising, yellow cliffs and scoffed. "We've handled steeper."

"Not talkin' about the rocks but what's under them."

Mathias agreed. "I haven't seen any members of the clan that purportedly lives here, though."

"They don' wanna be bothered," the Dwarf answered with a shrug. "They leave traps fer the nosy but ask no toll when they could. Possible to come this way and shave a day or two off the route tah Troshin Bend."

Castis was tapping his chin. "Why did we not come this way on our way West to meet Sarilis?"

Rithal shrugged. "Still testin' each other at the time, remember? You two weren't always listening, an' I didn't want tah stumble into a Dwarven trap an' have you blame me."

The pale Ma'ab mage smiled, sharing a look with the Hellhound. "Fair. And now we *can* go this way."

"Yep. Make it through the canyon, and the land changes fast tah the Midway. We can pick up speed sooner. Just gotta watch the signs."

I thought I spotted one of those signs.

"Such as that stone, there?" I asked, indicating one that cast a curious shadow. It was possible it would maintain a straight edge that pointed down one ravine over the other, regardless of the position of the Sun.

Rithal blinked in surprise. "Yah. Bit of a labyrinth in here, but they cut the stone to point the way."

"Which way?" I asked.

"Sanctuary," he grunted. "But only if yer welcome. We won't be."

"Suggests we follow the same signs in the opposite way to get through," Gavin said quietly.

The stout male pushed his beard into his chest with his chin. "Exactly, monk."

"Then let's do this," Kurn interrupted, motioning for Rithal to take lead.

The Hellhound looked at the rest of us one at a time and nodded deliberately. "Listen to the Dwarf's instructions the moment he gives them. Avoid the traps."

As if you can see them.

I had to wonder if Rithal and Mathias were biting the inside of their cheek like I was.

"Heavens forbid we fart without his approval," Gavin muttered into his chest.

I pressed my forehead onto his damp robes and chortled.

The horses moved in single file over stony ground, again picking their way over rough terrain like the first two days, though we were much lower in elevation. We had finally left the trees behind; here began the string of days beneath the Sun I had not been eager to see.

The bare, yellow and brown stone radiating the heat it absorbed, the only vegetation scrubby spindles of brush and weed. I did my best to keep watch above and behind us; the high ledges above concerned me, seeing as this less-traveled path was claimed, unlike most of the forest we'd just left.

I overheard the exchanges at the next two splitting canyons. Rithal was sure we were far enough from the "stronghold" and only worth a glance from the sentries because we went in the opposite direction, but we had only his word to go on.

Meanwhile, the Sun reflected off the lighter colored stone, and I grew hot within my black covering well before midday. This was the highest temperature I'd been exposed to thus far on the Surface, and I had the added heat of Gavin's body and that of his mare to contend with. As I'd feared, there was no good way for me to cool down. Even removing my cloak was a harsh trade without the shade of my hood protecting my eyes, which were already in greater pain.

I could feel how strands of my hair stuck to my forehead, and my skin itched in places where moisture trickled down—my spine, my temples, beneath my breasts. The air was hot and dusty going into my lungs, and I felt drowsy despite my recent rest. I frequently sipped from my waterskin, wetting my lips as my body demanded more than I could give it until I knew where the next source would come from.

"You are quiet," Gavin murmured at one point. "Are you well?"

"Well," I responded. "The heat drains me."

"Don't fall off."

I breathed a laugh. "I will not."

An apt warning, though, as my balance *did* waver a few times; the apprentice was aware each time I suddenly tightened my hold on him. The weakness bothered me, but I did not know a remedy. While the horse's clopping steps remained consistent and danger was not imminent, I must fight the drowsiness.

After a time, I resorted to the worn sunblind I hadn't used since my acclimation, so I could drop my hood and expose my head to the open air. Much of my peripheral vision was blocked by the blind, but this did not matter while I could see little anyway. My ears opened up in response, and my mind formed the general shape of the space around me based on the way sound travelled in this canyon.

Gavin had glanced back during my shuffling. "Hm. Be careful of sunburned ears."

"I know, I know," I groused.

I alternated between hood up and hood down, but the distraction was as unwelcome as the sleepiness. In unguarded moments, I imagined a trap of collapsing stone for which the Dwarves were known.

Well…the Tragar, anyway.

Still, a Dwarf was a Dwarf when they handled stone.

In the end, it wasn't a trap that brought me alert but an opportunity. I was mostly blind as we continued on making that noise, but I became aware of a distant, welcome rush as we approached the mouth of another canyon. I closed my eyes fully, then.

"Water," I murmured to Gavin.

He paused inexplicably and sounded terse. "Have you run out?"

"Hm? No." I felt a bit bleary as I tried to catch up with him.

Ah. He thinks I'm demanding his.

"No, I hear water. A source."

"Where?" he asked, looking around.

"Left, I think. The sound bounces off the stone, but it is there. A waterfall."

"Odd," he commented, doubtful. "We'd have followed a river through the canyon if there had been one."

"Perhaps it emerges from beneath," I said. "If there is a Dwarf stronghold here, they *must* have water underground."

"Hm."

By the smell trailing back to me, no one was exempt from feeling the heat. I guessed we were all low on water, and that was why Gavin nudged his mare up to the front with Rithal and the Ma'ab to speak to them first.

"Sirana thinks she hears a waterfall."

"Oh?"

Rithal paused, probably looking at me although I couldn't see it with my eyes closed behind my blind. I was sightless but not in darkness, though the latter would have been preferable. The reddish glare of light remained with me even as I "saw" better with my ears.

Kurn snickered as the Dwarf asked me, "Snow mask?"

I smiled. "Works with Sun as well."

"Ah. Well…there ain't been a waterfall near here that I know of. No river until we get partway across the Midway."

"Unless one underground surfaced recently," I said, thinking it odd a Dwarf wouldn't think of such a thing.

"Yes, but not any that I know."

"In how long? Land changes every decade."

"Hm. True."

Castis cut in. "Trying to confuse our guide, Red Sister?"

I repeated it slowly for him. "I hear rushing water."

"We don't."

"Your senses are dulled by constant light."

Kurn snorted almost as loud as his stallion, but Rithal hushed them. "'Tis possible. Been forty years since I came through here."

"Worth checking, then," Gavin said.

"Yah, it is." The Dwarf turned to the Ma'ab. "Best check it out while we can. I warned yah good water was sparse for a while. Best we'll get is muddy spring melt in the hills ahead 'fore we reach the Flat River inna day or two."

The Hellhound grunted. "Very well. Lead the way, Dwarf."

"Eh," Rithal began, "we might be needin' to let the Davrin lead, Kurn. She's the one who hears it. I can't."

The pause was deafening. Then the Hellhound growled.

"You believe that? She hears a waterfall and you can't?"

"Aye. Just think about where she comes from."

"Only a demon's word."

"Don' be a fool," Rithal returned.

Kurn jerked on his horse's reins, and Gavin moved his mare as the horses began tossing their heads.

"I don't trust her *not* to lead us somewhere we don't want to be," he argued.

"I'm *thirsty*, Hellhound," I said. "I will get off here and walk, leaving the rest of you to wonder how to drink from your shriveled pricks instead."

Mathias guffawed, and Kurn snarled, "Quiet, *kus.*"

"*Yivi'gil,*" I retorted.

"What?!"

"Look at her, Ma'ab," Rithal barked. "The Sun is even harsher to her. She has motive not to mislead us."

"Unless it is to steal our water."

Of all the festering cum puddles I could ride with...

Rithal and Mathias sounded similar in their sighs.

"If fresh water is here," the skin hunter said, "we need it before crossing the Midway."

"Aye."

Kurn paused, and Castis spoke up as if prompted. "We will be wary. If it is too far, we will turn back."

The big Ma'ab cursed again in his own language, his horse's hooves crunching and scattering gravel as the stallion turned around; the beast champed and licked noisily at his bit.

"Get ahead, then, witch," he commanded. "Lead us to this silent waterfall."

I patted Gavin's shoulder. "Go on. I will say what I hear."

With a wary exhalation, the apprentice kicked his mare forward, and I felt the short hairs on my nape react to a stare I couldn't see. I pointed with my gloved hand to the South, at a sheer cliff face.

"Bit of a steep climb for horses," Kurn sneered.

"Forward and right," I said aloud.

"Jus' letter lead, Kurn," Rithal rumbled, and moved his stockier mount around. "Sooner tah drink for our horses and maybe we won' scare away any huntin' nearby."

The Ma'ab *finally* repressed further dissent, though I could well imagine his expression as the Dwarf got behind Gavin's mare, his pony between me and the Hound. I wondered whether the big Human considered that a flat challenge of his authority, or if he understood Rithal was just being practical? Either way, I doubted the Dwarf would care, and I knew Kurn's stallion suffered with the rest.

I gave Gavin a squeeze. "Forward."

Sighing quietly, he kept his mare out front while I concentrated on the dull roar as it shifted with our direction. It wasn't as easy as if I'd been in a tunnel or a cave; sometimes the wind would funnel past my ears in bursts, drowning out anything else. We also had to move away from it a fair distance, following the South wall as the only feasible path.

My ears chased the flowing liquid splashing onto rock; I imagined it dropped from a height that would kill any of us if we fell from the top. With the slow pace and my quiet instruction to Gavin, no one could be sure when I lost the source before I picked it up again. Kurn muttered his doubts and, aggravatingly, I wondered for one moment whether it could be rushing air playing tricks. What would I do if it turned out I was wrong?

I focused as the sound came stronger and pointed with certainty. "This way."

Now to hope it is potable.

Following a stretch, Rithal said behind me, "I hear it. She's tellin' the truth."

"Good for her," Kurn replied, the distinct sound of his boots kicking his stallion reaching me the moment before he passed on our right.

Something startled Gavin's mare, and she shied with an alarmed squeal, jerking several paces to the side. A gasp slipped out as I clung harder to the apprentice, managing not to slip. I heard two horses loping ahead of us and guessed it was Kurn and Castis.

"Worms rot his belly," Gavin hissed, low but venomous, as he brought his mare under control.

"What happened?" I asked.

"The stallion bit her."

"Any idea when she goes inta heat?" Rithal asked.

Gavin's back went quite stiff. "Not really. She's older."

I chuckled at that. "A pity. I think Kurn might burst a vessel to watch his stallion mounting Gavin's low caste mare."

Mathias laughed quietly as well, though the stout one sighed.

"Don' antagonize 'im with that, Elf," Rithal warned me.

"Oh? Why is it *I* am the one always required to care for his tender senses, Dwarf?" I asked. "His self-control is poor when challenged, he deserves it."

The redbeard paused. "Jus' don' wantcha tah get hurt. Reckon Gavin hasn't been repeating some o' the things Kurn's been sayin' about you when you're gone at night."

"I don't care to," the death mage confirmed with clear disgust.

"We've been trying to dissuade him," Mathias said to me, "but he's fixated on you."

"Then say nothing to him," I replied. "Do nothing. Let it be."

"Can't do that, Elf," Rithal said, sounding too firm to be real.

I turned toward him. "Yes, you can. Or you would have challenged and beaten him down already."

He was quiet. I smiled, showing my teeth. "Your concern comes from *your* past, Dwarf, not mine. I told you I choose my minds to watch. I also choose my time."

Mathias hummed curiously, but Rithal just grumbled, "Excuse the worry, then, Red Sister. Sorry I ever gave it, if yer fresh ever-ready."

I frowned at the bitter tone. "It's a waste for both of us if you won't trade that worry in full for what the Hellhound means to do against your Witch Hunters."

"Ain't 'my' anything."

I shrugged. "You chose before the woman slurs, Rithal, I've known it. I do not expect protection. I can fight. Kurn has never seen how."

"If yah say."

Gavin cleared his throat. "Meanwhile, the water?"

I licked my dry lips. "Indeed. Waiting on you, rein master."

He was exasperated, but we all moved forward at last.

The waterfall was soon confirmed with their eyes, and I could hear two horses slurping and sucking at the water as we approached. The two Ma'ab were in good humor as they spoke just beneath the drum of the falls. I opened my eyes to get some view of it through the slit of my blind.

It was a small waterfall; nothing like the one I'd found and sparred next to with Jael, and this water was indeed emerging from an underground source. About as wide as I was tall, and although the healthy stream continued down off the shale slopes and toward the rolling hills, it was slowing and would evaporate until it settled in a muddy pool somewhere beneath the baking Sun.

"It's new," Rithal muttered so I could hear, an acknowledgment of sorts.

He was right. The water splashing over jagged rocks had made little progress in wearing them smooth. A new discovery and valuable resource for the area's Dwarves and passers-by like us.

"We shall stay here the rest of this day and the night," Kurn announced as Gavin and I finally nudged out a spot to drink. "We'll hunt for food and prepare to cross the Midway."

Castis folded his arms with dignity, but the other three hunters were silent rather than point out that we'd be doing so regardless if Kurn stayed or not. However, I discovered quickly that neither Gavin nor I were expected or welcome on the hunt.

"Rithal, Mathias, come." The Hellhound smirked at me and Gavin refilling our skins. "You two will prepare what we catch, so you can pull your own weight for once."

"Are you sure she can cook?" Castis smirked.

"If not, I can think of something else she can do."

"Enough," Rithal rumbled. "Let's make tracks."

"You mean find tracks," Mathias quipped.

"Your skill is good, skin hunter," Kurn commanded. "Go first."

I almost waved them farewell. Indeed, that song was wearing out faster than others, though I didn't delay their departure, and neither did Gavin. I imagined we preferred the time alone to explore and replenish ourselves.

They will be the worse off when, or if, they come back.

The Sun was directly overhead, and I planned to wait a short while before I would crawl about, though I wanted to know this spot better than anyone for the coming night. Gavin was content to lie down in the shade of an outcrop of stone, as his "older" mare remained behind and enjoyed her time with her head down, standing where splashes of clean water would mist her face. I decided to join Gavin in the shade without lying down too close, and he seemed to appreciate that I did not try to make conversation.

In truth, I was overheating, and my headache was too great to be worth prodding him; I didn't have much appetite yet. I removed my cloak and rolled it up to place beneath my head with a sigh. I was warm in my armor but knew it would improve if I did not move and stayed out of the light. I rested, watching as the shadows of the high wall gradually lengthened, promising this crevasse would be filled with shade.

I spotted a few points that could be climbed, and there was more vegetation than I'd realized while riding mostly blind, new rustic scents I hadn't been sure were growing things amidst heat, dust, and rock. There were woody, green bushes growing out of tiny ledges and cracks in the stone, strands of yellow and green wild grasses cropping up in frequent bunches. I saw numerous places that might contain nests for birds or burrows of rodents and furry creatures, although I must also be wary of those snakes Rithal mentioned.

All this bounty didn't include the edible insects. Even unforested, the sources of food were greater than what I might find in a similar-sized territory in the Deepearth. I thought again how it would be nearly impossible to feed myself while pregnant if I was alone in the Deepearth wilderness.

Yet it might be possible up here.

It would, for certain, give me time before I might be forced to consider D'Shea's vial on my belt.

Later in the afternoon, when the Sunlight was a darker gold and there were plenty of shadows to keep to, I went out to hunt and explore the area. The first and easiest catch made its fair share of noise. I'd only planned to filch the eggs and leave, but the mother returned abruptly and started shrieking, diving at me. I barely avoided the wings and talons the first time, although I almost lost my grip.

Fucking knocker!

The spotted hawk circled around for another attack, crying loudly; I drew my hand crossbow, murmured the command word, and felt Callitro's ring warm on my finger. My perception tightened; my aim lined up despite the Sun, despite the speed of the bird. I struck the bird through the throat, and the feathered body fell to the rocky ground beneath me.

With the soft thud, I ignored my pounding heart, quickly scooped up the four eggs, and slipped them into the same pouch with my cloths. Swiftly, I climbed down to claim the body before another animal stole both it *and* my bolt!

By the time the Sun was two finger-widths above the horizon, I had similar success with a hare, three fat, ground rodents, and a healthy handful of live, leaping insects trapped in a spare pouch. There were several fragrant plants I plucked which I thought might help flavor the meat.

On my way back, and having eaten two of the eggs raw, I felt more comfortable. My headache had lessened as the shadows grew longer and deeper still. I set a few traps for the morning, memorized the layout and a possible place to sleep, and finally I made my way to Gavin. I was delighted to see he had a small fire going already.

His brows rose when I presented him with my fare. "You mean to share?"

"If you will help prepare it, there is enough for two."

Or three.

At first, Gavin seemed reluctant, maybe suspicious. This was the first time I'd hunted and brought him something, I realized. There was no need before; he had handled himself in the familiar mountain forests or partook of whatever the others brought in so long as he cooked it, making himself quite useful though Kurn and Castis only barely recognized it.

Had the others been here when I returned, it would have continued this way. But the others *weren't* back yet, and I felt inclined to feed the displaced apprentice and keep him in good health, especially after spurning Rithal's intangible worries on my behalf.

The apprentice wasn't familiar with toasting the leaping insects alive, so I took care of that while he plucked the bird and skinned the furry creatures. I used two of his pan-tins to create a shell trapping the insects, their little heads tapping the inside of the tin, and tied it closed with a length of thin, metal wire I kept, and baked it in the fire.

"Egg?" I offered.

He accepted, and I ate the last myself. When the insects were crunchy and ready, he watched me eat one.

"Uhm, no, thank you," he said.

I shrugged, letting the rest cool for a later snack and instead waited to enjoy the fresh meat mixed with the roots Gavin had dug up somewhere.

"You make a good meal," I said, wolfing it down.

He hummed to acknowledge me but spoke no words. The sky held light but twilight deepened, and the air grew cooler and pleasant. The others had not yet returned to camp; while I was not especially concerned, I wondered how their hunt went. Gavin and I had had our fill uninterrupted, and I dared think we were well rested. I was just about to ask Gavin something new about ghosts when I finally heard the heavy crunch of hooves break the drone of the waterfall.

"Someone coming?" Gavin asked.

"Four. On horseback."

"Our dear travel companions, I suspect."

Smirking, I concentrated past the constant rush of water, my eyes losing focus. I heard a voice at last, a boastful hoot. *Kurn.*

"It is," I answered. "And I think they caught something."

Gavin grunted. "I shall stop doubting your hearing at this point."

"Took long enough." I smiled at him. "Just enjoy the early warnings, hm?"

The noise of their return overwhelmed the flow of the water as they filled the rocky pocket of our camp. I watched the four ride in, dragging a large, hairy body along the ground between two of their horses. The hide would be ruined, but we weren't staying around here to preserve much of the carcass. There was an arrow hole in the throat, and it had bled profusely; there were also scorch marks covering the head of the cloven-hoofed, prong-horned beast.

Did Castis cast a fire burst on the animal?

That was a bit much.

The Hellhound leaped off his horse and proceeded to gut, skin, and butcher the beast. I noted that he could have done that out where they had caught it, leaving what they didn't want for the scavengers, and carried back much less weight. Mathias stood closer and watched, seeming antsy and critical of Kurn's technique.

The Hellhound didn't acknowledge this but glanced at me in the middle of his work, just once, and I concluded he wanted me to see this part. He would spend such extra effort on himself and his horse if it meant he could perform to make an impression, and yet I was curious how Mathias would have tended that same kill.

Ignoring all this, a frowning Rithal built up the fire to be brighter and hotter. He was close enough to note the bits of animal bones, feathers, and fur from our meal; he glanced at Gavin and me but said nothing.

"If you both contribute and cook this for us while we take a well-earned break," Kurn said, kneeling by the carcass, his gloves coated with gore and blood spattering his bracers, "you may have some. I've yet to see what our black witch can do with a hunk of meat."

Of course, Castis chuckled.

Sigh.

"I will pass," I said.

"As will I," Gavin seconded.

Kurn's prideful glow darkened, and he stood up, brandishing his blood-coated dagger. "*Maknuut*, get cooking, or I'll slaughter your old *sog* alongside the pronghorn."

"Don't threaten the horse 'less yah mean it," Rithal grumbled.

For the first time, I considered what I might do if Kurn indeed tried to harm our mare. Gavin glanced at me in silent question, unable to suppress an ugly downturn of his mouth.

"Kurn can't cook," I offered. "He learns by watching."

"*Kus*," Kurn hissed.

"*I'll* help cook th' damned thing," Rithal snarled. "An' frankly, Kurn, had I known yah were such a whelp about any woman bein' in sniffing distance, I'da left you both in Augran."

The Hellhound looked like he'd been slapped then promptly stomped up to the Dwarf. The man was almost double the height, though Rithal was practically as wide. Kurn gloated in the redbeard's face.

"Too late for that, is it not? Castis has the vial from Sarilis, and we have Mathias to get inside the Temple. We never needed the bleeder and the night-sweating catamite to join us, and *you* best branch North once we cross the Bozar, lest I forget your service to the Empire. You don't want the Witch Hunters and Bishops catching wind of you somehow, do you?"

"Fuckin' bluffin'," Rithal replied, his face reddening, eyes flickering as he was briefly distracted by Castis slipping up just behind his Ma'ab brother. "Yah can't network yer way to the next inn, bullboy."

"The 'next inn' houses the Ma'ab Daughter of a powerful sorcerer. He and Castis have an understanding."

Mathias had knelt by the skinned animal when I wasn't looking, but I noticed him despite the confrontation, or maybe because of it. With a sharp knife drawn, the man was slicing off thin strips of haunch and laying them on a piece of hide. When Mathias heard the brag, he rolled his eyes since neither Ma'ab was watching him as I was, but his voice was neutral and helpful as always.

"No one is favored by the innkeeper, Kurn, it can be dangerous to assume otherwise."

The Hellhound spun around then. "Are you doubting my leadership?"

Yes.

Mathias looked confused at the accusation. "No, but you *do* need Rithal. He knows it. So do I."

"But you agree we do not need the other two lazy tit-suckers unless they stay useful." Kurn tossed his chin in Gavin's and my direction.

Mathias glanced at us. "Um…"

Gavin rubbed his face and forehead like *all* of it ached; I sympathized. Hadn't this started with who was going to cook the pronghorn?

As if following my thought, and with a heavy sigh of derision, Gavin stood up and walked to Mathias, mutely offering to take the butchered portions from him. With Kurn watching, the skin hunter acquiesced and gave him the red meat, and Gavin returned to work, as he always did.

The apprentice had already swept clean a work surface on a boulder for his earlier meal; he had cleaned and put away his utensils. Now, he unrolled his kit again, heated his cooking pan with some fat from a jar, and began slicing the meat into smaller bits with little effort. The death mage kept his tools in fine shape.

Kurn grunted in satisfaction seeing this while Rithal stood stubbornly in place, scowling the deepest I'd ever seen, his burly arms crossed before him.

"What of you, Sirana?" rumbled the Hellhound, rolling my name off his tongue as a corner of his mouth crept up. "How will *you* earn your meal tonight?"

I smiled. "I have eaten. My hunting finished hours ago."

"Oh?" His nostril twitched. "You'll not have any of ours, then."

"Deal."

A grunt and a hesitant pause on his end.

"I know how you grow hungry, sudden like." He winked. "If you change your mind, just ask. I'll save some meat tonight. Just for you."

I winked back, beginning to wonder if he had any other innuendo in his language or if "meat" was all. It was low hanging as his balls.

Before too long, the men except Gavin were chewing greedily on the well-seasoned slices of seared meat. I stayed to watch, enjoying the smells for once, and rarely seeing them eat a hot meal. Mathias surprised me by asking the death mage a question like they were in a social conversation.

"So, you cooked a lot at that monastery, eh, Gavin? It's good."

"Hm. Not always, but plenty," he mumbled, placing a clean blade down alongside the rest upon his roll-kit. He picked up the whetstone and lubricated it with a bit of oil.

"Were you a monk or a servant?"

The apprentice glanced up from beneath a hooded brow and didn't answer, returning to the practiced, smooth draws across the whetstone. Gavin wouldn't be the only one sharpening their edges tonight, but I found him interesting to watch since he was neither a hunter nor warrior by trade. His motions were for precision: small cuts, fine-tuned motion, and the efficient reduction of raw flesh into their component parts. It showed when he tended his tools.

After a heavy pause, Kurn snorted in derision. "Answer, *maknu-ut*. How did you live among the castrates?"

"They weren't castrated," Gavin said.

"Does that mean *you* aren't, *wajatyan*?"

"Would you like to see?" I interjected, chuckling at the looks on both their faces. "What? *I* would like to see."

Kurn's thoughts hit a wall at the suggestion that we see Gavin unclothed. I enjoyed that *very* much. The former Manalari death mage, however, far less, from the threatening squint he darted at me.

"Well, Mathias," I added, "Gavin can read and write in more than one language. That is rarely the education of a servant."

"Ah, yes." Mathias eyed the apprentice with curiosity. "How many?"

"Just two," he answered. "Trade and Manalari."

Well, now I knew what Gavin sounded like when he was lying.

"You must learn Ma'ab next," Castis stated like it was a given, yet also given he wouldn't be the one to teach him.

Gavin muttered his response. "Perhaps."

"Why did you leave the cloister?" Mathias pondered aloud. "Did they ever know of your *other* talent?"

"No," he said flatly, sharpening his blades with intense focus, as if he would finish sooner and leave the light of the fire.

Mathias watched Gavin's working hands, evaluating them like he had been Kurn's with the pronghorn. I thought the skin hunter was favorable to the death mage's motions.

"Of course, they would not know," Kurn sneered, taking another hunk of meat and chewing noisily, a bit of grease making his lips glisten in the firelight. "He slinked away with his tail tucked, like a mutt does. Those sun-eaters are all better off with him gone if *this* food was their normal fare."

The Ma'ab plucked a half-chewed piece of gristle from between his teeth and flicked it away.

"That depends," Gavin said, sounding ominous, "if they found themselves beside Musanlo in the Beyond. I poisoned their food and water before I left."

All of them halted in their chewing as it struck each one that neither Gavin nor I had eaten their dinner tonight. Castis and Mathias looked a little green as they wondered what just happened. In truth, I was as shocked by the confession as the rest, yet I burst out laughing in delight.

"Silence, witch!" Kurn shouted, glad to take me as his distraction away from his fear.

"Your stomach froze like ice!" I howled. "Admit it! You want to vomit!"

"Shut your cunt mouth!"

He pitched his gnawed piece of meat at me, and I barely dodged, chortling as I looked at Gavin, who evidently regretted speaking. "I knew there was a reason I liked you, apprentice. You poisoned them all? You are a mage of my own ilk! We should discuss details."

He groaned.

"Indeed, poison is a *woman's* favorite weapon," Kurn said with a hack and spit in the dirt.

I grinned. "Among others."

"For underhanded cowards!"

Gavin had withdrawn as quickly as he'd engaged. Whether his small knife was to its preferred state or not, he put it away and rolled up his tools, preparing to leave the fireside.

"Hai, maknuut!" called the Hellhound. "If you fouled any part of our kill, I shall—"

"I did *nothing*," Gavin blurted, shaking either from anger or fear. "Your guts will suffer only from your own ignorance, Hound. Forget I said anything."

Indeed, the solitary monk *wouldn't* have spoken if he hadn't been provoked. But this was a good thing, in my opinion. We'd all just realized, even for a moment, that there was a line we could cross with this man, that this "mixed blood" did not let *every* insult or abuse go.

I still wasn't sure why the apprentice remained on this trek at all, having been shoved so abruptly out of the Ley Tower. For that reason alone, both Kurn and I should carry some wariness for him.

Gavin left to return to the rock overhang where he had slept earlier, and I did not follow him yet. I stayed listening to more remarks from the big man, waiting to see if there might be an opening to speak of demon stories among the Ma'ab. Sadly, Kurn only became agitated and intolerable. Good to Gavin's word, though, none of the men felt stomach cramps or intestinal woes from their meal and, because of this, they were content to leave the huddled monk alone for the night.

During this time, I made frequent trips to the pool, drinking as much water as I could hold and often leaving the firelight to pass it out again soon after, before drinking again. When we left this waterfall, we would not find another source of this quality until we reached the mountains waiting across the Midway. Better to be saturated tonight, even if it meant taking down my leathers twice as often and wetting the stone.

To my surprise, Kurn didn't try to interrupt me; in fact, he commanded the others to drink as well, as if it was his idea. Rithal might have had something to do with this, as I heard him speaking up to the big man more often, especially when I couldn't see them. Eventually, I spent the evening away and out of sight, so the men would lie down to rest without the Hellhound barking further and keeping everyone awake.

He just won't let go of the bone.

As I settled for my own rest, I chafed from this too-familiar illness whenever I thought seriously of killing Kurn. My hands were bound with an invisible rope because of my Queen. I hated it as much as I had with Jilrina though tried not to think on it too long. In another circumstance, I could have fucked the stupid beast into the ground like a Red Sister would, could have shut him up earlier, but...

I wouldn't risk my unborn that way.

I don't know what kind of fungal cheese that hairy man might have growing on his prick.

The sky was black, though the firelight had dimmed some of the brightness of the stars until it was banked. The wind came in gusts through the canyon, and the air was comfortably cool, the stones radiating lingering warmth from the day. Everyone knew their order of watch, and the routine once again fell into place when the day caught up with us.

My Reverie was a quiet, dreamless one. I woke in near-complete darkness, for the Moons were late in rising. I'd observed that their arrival and disappearance in the sky varied by a small bit of time each night, just as they each had their individual track and did not follow each other in sync. There would be those where the Moons could not be seen at all, as they shared the sky with the Sun, and the sky offered only stars for company.

We were close to one such night.

Regardless, I had no trouble navigating when it came my turn to relieve Gavin on watch. Per usual, I practiced suppressing my aura to see how close I could get before he might see me. This apprentice who was my teacher was difficult to approach at night if he was awake and focused on detecting life auras. Twenty paces was the closest distance I'd ever reached; enough to hit Gavin with a crossbow bolt if I wished but not to tap him on the shoulder and whisper in his ear to see him jump.

Tonight, as on previous nights, Gavin detected me by my life aura alone, not my Elven one.

"I did not hear or smell you, either," he murmured, knowing I could hear him. "I am sure Castis couldn't sense you unless you wanted him to. Well done."

I smiled, content with the evaluation.

The apprentice did not take long to bed down and return to sleep while I took over the watch, letting my spiders free to crawl into my hair. The damp scent and constant slap of water against stone forced me to depend on my night vision, which was unusual. Balancing the scents and sounds was both how I kept alert and entertained myself, so without the ear-teasing nuances of the insects and tiny creatures or the distant cry of some nocturnal pack, I became bored staring at the same rocky walls.

I sniffed my armpit. *Hm. I could use this time to wash my shirt. It needs it.*

I could also spot clean my leathers and bathe my body, ears to toes. I'd be watching this little gravel pit regardless and wouldn't hear well no matter if I sat here or stood calf-deep in the tiny pool. There was a bit of a contest in getting the deed done before Rithal awoke, which perked me up and banished my dangerous, drowsy boredom.

My last opportunity for a bath for a while.

I stepped away from the group and toward the pool, spotting a fold high in the rock, ideal for stashing my equipment. I must climb to reach it, but the others were either too bulky to squeeze into the same place—that would be Kurn, Rithal, and Mathias—or would have to display a bit of acrobatic skill I had not yet witnessed, which would be Castis and Gavin. My things may not remain hidden if either was trying to detect magic, they would find the cache, but I would take that worry as it came.

After scaling the wall to my hiding place, I braced myself and allowed my spiders out to crawl down my arms and into the crevice to wait for me. Next, I considered what items on my tool belt might be good to keep on me while naked, in case Kurn or another bothered me. Mainly, Kurn.

I was disinclined to use any powder; the water spray could turn it to paste, and the wind in this canyon was unpredictable to me; I was likely to have it stick to my fingers or blow back in my face. Likewise, blades and bolts, poison and infection were pointless, just slow methods of killing wastefully—assuming my geas would let me. I must use the spiders for anything lethal, since they could act on their own, revive their supply of venom, and couldn't be turned against me.

I possessed my small blow tube and tiny needles I dipped in a skin-numbing paste which could paralyze if it went deep enough. Not a kill, it might get around the restriction, but I used it for traps and hunting, not defense. I could prick myself with them in haste if I planned to be naked with no gloves or belt.

Too risky, too much preparation required.

I had a single web pellet left after those I'd used on Tamuril and Pilla, but I knew it had been exposed to a lot of heated traveling only in the day; I couldn't necessarily rely on its potency. At the same time, I considered a compressed paste formed into a shape like half of my pinky finger, a drug which dissolved in any orifice and entered the blood quickly.

The effected target lost focus as euphoria diffused through the body; it was intended as an interrogation tool. The one problem was that I needed to be close to use it, but it was my best non-lethal option coupled with the web pellet. I had three of the elongated capsules in a tiny, waterproof pouch.

Hmm. Better than the paralyzing needles. Any orifice will do.

Choosing at last, I added my last web pellet to the three capsules and closed the pouch tightly.

I'm ready for my bath.

A new, fun challenge followed: bracing myself in the narrow crack of rock to remove my pack, each weapon better not kept on my belt, placing them in their hiding spot with said belt and pouches. I placed my cloak, bracers, and boots there as well but kept my foot stockings, leathers, shirt, and the flexible armor bundled beneath my arm, with a gradually shrinking slice of scentless soap in my hand.

The weight and glimmer of a certain blue stone caught my attention, and I paused, shrugged, and left it on. It could use a wash, too; the platinum design was gritty, and the cord was soaked with sweat, oil, and dirt. I retrieved my spare pairs of stockings which needed a wash, coaxed back my guardians, and carried all of this to the ground.

Walking toward the waterfall, I kept my attention on those sleeping thirty paces away and on the area around us. I washed my shirt first, rinsed and wrung it out then spread it over a boulder. My stockings followed in quick order, and then the saphgar necklace, which I returned around my neck while I paid special detail to my leathers. Overall, my things were wearing well on the Surface; only a few small frays here or there after mending the holes poked in them by Tamuril's thorns.

I finished my washing in peace and collected everything to return to my cache, securing the leathers and soap before choosing a different, nearby crevasse to drape the shirt and black stockings to dry over woody branches sprouting well above a Human head.

Next, I had only my own bath to tend to. I sighed. All this work because several of these men might put their hands where they didn't belong.

At least there's plenty of time.

After my bare feet touched the gravel-strewn dirt for the second trip, I stopped to see I'd forgotten to remove Shyntre's pendant.

Augh, fuck.

I glanced up at my stash in annoyance, wishing I could toss it among my stockings, but it was too far.

Eh, whatever. I left it around my neck.

Both my spiders and the drugs were vulnerable to pounding water, so I tucked the pouch in a dry spot on the side of the pool opposite from the camp. I placed my black guardians there as well and, almost immediately, one of them darted out and snatched hold of a small insect also using the dry pocket near the falls. I smiled as she chomped down, the other two twitching about as if searching for more.

Good hunter. Always eat when possible.

I approached the rippling pool, unthreading my braid after looping the tie around my wrist, and admired the shimmer of stars making the surface glitter. The temperature as I stepped in was wonderful, that shocking chill to which I'd become accustomed in the mountains. I drew in a quiet breath and smiled—the strongest expression of pleasure I could afford—as the water crept up my calves.

Another check of my surroundings, and I squatted down hip-deep, scrubbed my hands and cupped them to drink again; finally, I dampened my skin. I did not use my limited soap on my body, which could be rubbed down with something as simple as a hand-ful of sand; I reserved it for my clothing.

Eventually, I moved closer to the falls, scanning again for distur-bances before placing myself directly beneath it.

Ah! Yes.

The cool water beat on my scalp, ran over my ears and down my breasts, belly, and legs to great sluicing effect. It was invigorating, and I wished I could laugh aloud. My nipples tightened from the cold and tiny bumps had risen from shoulders to haunches. When I cupped my breasts, I noticed how tender they were; a symptom of my pregnancy which didn't seem it would fade any time soon. Next, I rubbed the pads of my fingers through my snowy thatch and noticed the lips of my sex tightened and tingled in response.

How long had it been since I last pleasured myself? Not since that odd, rushed moment in the mountains after I'd watched Kurn jerk his rod. Not the sexiest male I could imagine; I had several in mind who were much better rub-fodder. Absently, I indulged in a few caressing strokes between my legs, but soon stopped.

Too foolish. Not here and now.

I certainly wished for a sweet thrill, but it might be a long time before I found another opportunity to grind alone, and less to imagine finding a Surfacer I would risk fucking. Perhaps I wouldn't have sex until I returned to the Deepearth.

A rather depressing thought.

The water's reflections brightened while I was in it, and I saw that the larger Moon finally hinted at showing herself. The waterfall faced West, so it had taken time for the Moon to climb high enough to offer any appreciable, silvery light. I could not see the celestial body itself, she was hidden behind the rocky walls, yet the change was clear to my eyes.

As was a dark hulk sneaking toward me from camp.

I jumped. *Fucking spinnerets!*

He was hunched over and moving relatively light on his feet; only the fact that water beat on my head kept me from hearing him. His height alone left no doubt who it was; I noted his dark shirt, trousers, boots, and he had a blade in his boot.

But no armor, bracers, or helm.

My heart had kicked up in a galloping rush of irritation that my sensual solitude was interrupted, but at least he approached from the direction I'd anticipated; I would keep the pool between us and stand near my guardians. His face came into clear focus a moment later, and the breeze swirled in the natural pit where I caught his scent.

He needs a bath.

"I see you, Hellhound," I said, stepping out of the falls, wringing out my hair in one stroke to begin a quick, tight braid, my arms raised and hands behind my head.

Kurn straightened up hearing my voice, his body language giving away his irritation at being made so quickly. However, he did not speak, which surprised me until I realized he stared hard at my chest, his gaze trailing down to my thighs then up again. His neck craned, as if he tried to make out greater detail than his Human eyes could see. I wagered he could tell I was nude under the rising Moon; my white hair, above and below, would be obvious to him.

"Posing for me, *wajil*?" he rumbled with a smile.

I finished tying off my braid and dropped it, where it slapped wetly against my back. "Posing? I was plaiting my hair."

He grinned. "Beginning the moment I could see? Lying *wajil,* you flirt."

I rolled my eyes. "So timed because I saw you sneaking up like a scavenger."

His smile faded only a little. "Hmph. You could cut your hair if you are so worried about someone *grabbing* it."

"Like you?"

He hummed, adjusting his crotch as he absorbed my body again. "Possibly."

I chuckled. "No, Ma'ab, I mean did *you* cut your hair so short *because* someone grabbed it?" My hum mimicked his. "Another Hellhound stuffing his cock in your mouth?"

Kurn jerked in unpleasant surprise then glowered at me; it grew uglier by the instant. *"Never."*

Oo, that's a tender spot.

I smirked, backing up out of the pool with an exaggerated sway of my hips. "Pity. I like *flexible* males."

"Hah," he said with derision, although low enough not to wake the others. "You mean the cuckold scum who perform for a chance to *sniff* at your prized gash, *heinya?* Not this Hellhound. I *take* what I want, and every arrogant mouth insulting me has gagged upon my rod by the time I was done."

He pulled something from underneath his shirt as though it was significant to his boast, and I recognized the dark red pendant I'd seen the other morning. Frowning, I refrained from dropping my eyes down between my breasts. I knew what value my blue gem had—nothing practical—but what use was his red one?

Nothing good for me, if it had anything to do with his threat. I touched my pendant with an equal air of significance, and he watched every motion.

"Intriguing, Ma'ab. Did you get this idea from us?"

"The Fourth *captured* it," he retorted like he was insulted. "As I will capture the next and bring you in." His large hand roughly repositioned his bulging crotch. "I will puff up your belly as my father has done for a hundred years."

I barely kept a straight face at that horrific idea. *As if I would keep it?*

The Ma'ab continued to display his pride and ignorance together. Conceiving was the easy part; delivering a child was a whole other game I knew much better, even still far from labor. At least, if his doubtful boast was possible, another bua had beaten him to it. I tossed the threat and focused on the interesting part.

Puffing up bellies for a century...

"Your father must be quite wrinkled," I taunted, "serving wombs in his deathbed."

"Do *not* speak of the Divigna line with your foul tongue, witch."

"What?" I laughed, confused. "*You* just did. I don't know who Divigna is."

"And thus, you know nothing."

I sighed. "So, tell me."

"Oh, I think I will *teach* you," the Hellhound growled.

He crossed thick arms to pull his shirt up and over his head, removing it in one smooth motion like I should be impressed. I took the break in his gaze to step out of the pool, palming my pouch as my spiders tickled the bare skin of my shoulder and neck before hiding in my hair. I fought an inconvenient flip of my stomach as they prepared to jump.

Not yet. Don't bite him until he's spilled what he knows.

I was closer than I'd ever been in getting him to talk. It seemed I only had to get naked in front of him. *Wish I'd known that at the Tower.*

Kurn tossed his shirt aside, blinking when he saw I'd left the pool, and I began to lead him along the water's edge. He stared hungrily at me as if preparing to leap across. Just as he started to charge, I turned and ran in the opposite direction, the stones sharp beneath my bare feet, though not as bad as the first time I'd run naked through the wilderness.

He chased me without his usual bawl of "coward." But, he didn't want the others awake. I would take it and make him regret it. How he believed to have any advantage in the dark was beyond me, but I wouldn't wake anyone either. I wanted this dance-and-taunt to end.

It must be decisive. I must do this without help.

Or the Ma'ab would never stop hounding me.

CHAPTER 12

THE LARGER MOON WAS HIGH ENOUGH TO SPILL SILVERY-BLUE light across our path as Kurn pursued me. His endurance was solid, but he was noisy; his boots slammed heavily on the ground behind me, and he puffed like his stallion. I was surprised he didn't neigh like one.

I kept an unflagging sprint for longer than I ever had to maintain my lead and draw him toward a ravine leading to a hillside cave I had scouted earlier. I wanted the big man in utter darkness, where Jaunda had had her mercenaries, where Kurn could not tell his direction, and those big, swinging fists worked against him. If I took away his eyes, I could wait, strike fast, and jam my capsule in whatever hole I pleased.

Then, we'll talk and, afterward, my hands will be free.

"Where will save you, witch?" he called behind me, a restrained rumble just good enough not to career off the high cliffs.

Where, indeed?

It was a good place and a good plan, except for the fact the Ma'ab could tell he was being led. I had no choice; with my shorter, quicker gait, I had to run in a direct track, lest he catch me before I reached the underground. No feinting, no earned confusion from losing sight of the prey.

We were fast approaching a bend in the steep rocks where I would turn left and scramble straight up a softer hill to my cave. Kurn hadn't closed the gap by a stride, but I hadn't lengthened it. I also couldn't go much farther at this pace, especially barefoot, while he was in boots.

I prepared to turn sharply at a full sprint; the Hellhound must have been watching for that signal.

Something cracked and burst upon the cliff wall on my left. Light blinded me from the left, stabbing my eyes, while a thunderous bang knocked my ears like a pair of clubs and set my head to ringing.

I stumbled, tried to catch my momentum, redirect it and pick a direction to run. Before I knew it, Kurn was coming right up on me. I couldn't see or hear him; my training shut off those senses the moment I lost them.

I smelled his sweat, felt the vibrations of his boots under my hot, bruised feet; he clumsily kicked gravel across them. He breathed in my face.

"*Nau!*" I shouted, my voice muted in my ears.

I didn't need my eyes to strike the gigantic, bony target on that thick neck with the blade of my hand. He withdrew while a high pitch shrilled through my blood. Then one sweaty hand tried to seize my arm; the other was protecting his throat. I slipped free before his meaty fingers dug in, and I ran.

I wasn't sure which direction I sprinted as the dry air clawed its way in and out of my chest. I tried to match the tilt of the canyon with my mental layout but could only rely upon that intangible sense of judging space around me. I didn't collide with any boulders by the time my vision turned spotty to hint its return. That was more than Kurn could claim with the same hobble.

I must have disappeared from his line of sight, as he shouted something angry and unintelligible behind me. A score of strides later, I drew down to a halt when the canyon I'd entered suddenly ended. I could see with my eyes, just enough in the moonlight, the right angles on both sides of me leading back toward Kurn.

Fuck!

I turned, preparing to sprint out, but the Hellhound's silhouette appeared at the other end, long legs bringing him into the box canyon without pausing. I had just enough time to leap for a handhold above my head and pull, seeking to climb out of his reach. Desperately, I pulled myself up, seizing handholds the instant I was sure. My ribs strained to contain both my sucking air and racing heart at once.

Halfway to a ledge where I might rest, my spiders finally moved to reassure me they were still with me. They had been stunned by whatever that was Kurn had thrown at us.

Be calm. We'll make it.

The Hellhound arrived at the end of the canyon as I neared that small ledge in my sights. It was several body lengths—Kurn's body—above the Ma'ab's head and out of easy reach, unless he had another of those light-burst things to use. Soon, Kurn skidded to a stop, stirring up a cloud of dust and sending pebbles skipping. He howled with glee, his voice bouncing off the stone.

I seized the ledge and pulled myself quickly onto it. Curled up, I wasn't easy to see from below where he stood but staying down longer than it took to catch my breath did no good. He knew I was here.

"Sirana!"

Ow. Shut up.

I sat up then got into a crouch, my waterproof pouch palmed in my left hand with ties looped around my fingers. I breathed slower, though I didn't like how this situation reminded me of Jilrina chasing me into the barn.

No. He's just as stupid as she was, not worth fearing. Use your wit, your will.

After a few shuffling moments below, he said, "Your hair makes you plain to see, Red Sister. You have no escape."

The Moon was directly overhead, and I thought his shirtless body was even paler to my eyes. I said nothing, however, licking my dry lips and trying to think what to do next. I wasn't in a cave where I had the choice of ambush; I was stuck on a bald cliffside with no cover out of moonlight.

I glanced above my head. All that, *and* a tough climb if I want to keep going to escape.

Which would end nothing. We'd be right where we started.

"Come down, Red Sister," Kurn challenged. "Show me again how you fight. Do you only take cheap shots and surprise attacks?"

"You talk?" I asked, arching my brow. "We fight to live, what rules are there except what works for my size?"

"Ha!" He laughed. "Hellhounds fight to win. To impress and make others submit to our strength!"

I sighed as my headache lessened, but his voice still rattled my eardrums.

Right. Win.

I counted a win as being the one that walked away. I'd won several of those, and I would win again.

Then the anger seeped out as nausea threatened the edges of my nerves.

Arrgh, the geas...

I rubbed my eyes only after checking that he didn't have something ready to throw. "Hellhound."

He adjusted the log in his crotch. "Yes, *kus?*"

"Tell me about the demon beast with my coloring," I said, my voice drifting calmly down to him. "You mentioned a 'fourth' captured it."

"*The* Fourth," he corrected without adding a reason.

Aggravating.

He regained my attention when he clasped the ruby pendant around his neck with reverence. Then he spat. "What's wrong, 'dark' Elf, did your race *lose* something? Did it venture too far from your suckling teat?"

The need to know gripped me despite my better judgment.

I prodded, "The Ma'ab have ventured quite far from the cold North in the last century."

Kurn sneered. "Farther than our enemies know. They do not know what comes soon to them, even now."

"Oh? You have a way to report to your superiors, like I do?"

My own bluff revealed the same on his face. *That's a relief.*

"Who have you told?" he demanded.

I smiled. "Would you like to trade, Hellhound?"

"Trade what?"

"Who I've told about this mission for the last story of the demon beast."

He scoffed, and I thought his bulge had shrunk a little as he reached for it again. "I cannot believe a word you say. I might trade for a spill into your hole."

"A base counteroffer when you were prepared to just 'take' it," I replied, reaching down to stroke my slit with the pads of two fingers, so he could watch. "Are Ma'ab Hounds so easy to satisfy bargaining their intelligence?"

Kurn thought that over like there might be a hidden meaning he didn't see, but then squinted at my busy fingers.

Well. There certainly is a double one.

I smiled, slipping a finger slow and deep into my sex. "Answer three questions up front. Answer three again after you spill in my hole. We finish before sunup and return to camp. You count your chase successful."

"Six questions?" he asked.

Three plus three, yes.

"That should be worth six holes." He smirked. "Twice each."

Or six bites. Three on each 'head.'

I sighed, gauging how well my eyes and ears were doing. My head hurt, and I pulled my finger out and gave it a lick for show. "If you can finish six times in one night, your nuts must be fruit-sized with pent-up cream."

He laughed, and it echoed off the stone. "Hellhounds are the virile elite of the Empire's army. If you are worn out after six cocks, Red Sister, then your training pales to mine."

Heh. Funny.

"Almost," I said, stroking my chin.

"Almost what?"

"Mmm. No." I shrugged. "I was almost insulted, Hound, but it fizzled like Castis's fire spells."

Amusing how Kurn took insult for the other man, and on something he knew I hadn't witnessed. *Wow, that expression.*

He seethed, "I pray to see you kneeling to a score of us, Davrin."

"Yet you stalk me alone when there could be two," I said. "Why not call Castis to come share my holes, Ma'ab? You said you build teams that way."

He frowned at the suggestion. "Castis is a noble, not a Hell-hound."

"Heh. He's too good to smear your cum on his cock?"

Kurn barked a syllable I couldn't make out. "Do not speak of him."

"I do not see why not. The scholar is better educated. Maybe I should bargain questions with him, not you."

His chest puffed up. "It would fail. He has no interest in you, but he agrees we should take you North."

Yes, you have a surplus in saying that.

"Castis has no interest in me?" I smiled. "He prefers your company, I imagine, but are you tired of hairy asshole on the road?"

"Hai!" he shouted. "Enough, witch, you'll speak *no more* of disgusting things."

I felt much better; my snickering lasted for a while before I brought myself under control and cleared my throat. "*Ahem*. So. You *will* bargain. Three questions, then maybe three holes? We bargain later. It will liven up boring travel across flatlands. The others get to watch you and know their place."

His face flushed a little in the moonlight, and he swallowed. "You'll not submit to that. I see your lie."

True, I wanted to see his face at the suggestion. I reached between my legs again, twisted my finger around inside my sex while the Ma'ab watched; I could wager he hadn't noticed there was something in my other hand.

"Is the Davrin demon, for certain, still in capture to the Ma'ab after one hundred years?" I asked, loud and deliberate.

Kurn ripped his stare up from my cunt and wavered on his big booted feet. Maybe he was coming down from the racer's high.

"Hm," he grunted, flexing his hand. "Yes. I have seen it myself."

Yes. Finally.

"But your *army* has not seen or captured a beautiful Elf like me before?"

"No. You are the first." He sneered, gripping his swollen rod through his pants. "That's your *kus* and your throat, Sirana. What question to stretch your tiny, black pucker tonight?"

It was purple, but I ignored that as I felt my own tremor inside. The Sathoet could be alive if he'd been shown before Hellhounds in the last ten or fifteen years. The Priestess may be long dead or imprisoned where no one had seen her in at least three decades, before Kurn was born.

What was that part about his father being fertile for a hundred years? That couldn't be related, could it? Would I use my third question on this? Not if my compulsion against harming this man wasn't lifted, but I wasn't sure. I didn't feel any different.

"What is the story of how the demon came to the Fourth?" I asked. "Tell me."

Kurn snorted; this one wasn't an easy negative or affirmative. "You'll have to come down first."

"Or you could climb up here."

"Your ledge is too thin to rut, it'll break under me. Come *down*, blue eyes. My memory clears after a swift suck-off and a successful hunt."

Now we were both lying.

I removed my finger from my cunt and stood up, slow and careful to hold my balance on the outcropping. My pouch was behind my back, and I worked it open with one hand while playing with my fur with the other. His gaze scoured me like pumice from toes to ears, and I wondered if I had ever stared at Auslan like that while he was running from me in his room?

"Come, Sirana," he chuckled, rubbing through his trousers. "Did I not answer your questions for the superior who holds your chain?"

I hated that we had two things in common.

For distraction, I peeled my netherlips apart, showing him a hint of pink in the moonlight. He bared his teeth in a bestial smile, his red pendant glinting as he shifted on his feet.

"What about the third?" I asked. "My demon story?"

"After I release my 'pent-up cream'." He tilted his head, one hand moving behind him like mine was. "What have you got behind you, Red Sister? Planning to *take* what you want, aren't you? No trade or respect to your word."

Don't even pretend.

We stood in the stinking muck borne of our words from this trip thus far. This wouldn't play through like either claimed. I also wasn't free yet because I hesitated to bring my guardians forward while they waited with supernatural patience to act. I wondered, if I refused to come down at all, waited him out, would the Hellhound climb after me? I discarded that the next moment when I glanced at his right hand, hidden like mine.

Either of us on the wall was a clear and open target.

Time to see if the web pellet is good or not.

I drew, and Kurn drew out his, already in the first swing. That was how he'd made such a good throw during a dead sprint earlier.

A sling with a stone.

He only needed the one swing before release; he wasn't aiming for my body.

Another burst of light and sound sent me over, my hand missing the ledge and leading to empty air.

I slipped.

~Jump now! JUMP!~

Nothing but spinning, swirling pain followed.

I blacked out before I landed on the rocks.

I heard grunting before I could see anything. I smelled a great deal; sweat and blood, magic and dust. I felt the heat and the fear. When I opened my eyes, there were only streaming tracers of light tearing the Moon to shreds.

A body, big and hot, was pressed close, pushing and shoving against me.

What the fuck...? Who—?

"Release me, spider-*kus!*"

I winced as my head rang with sound. *Ow.*

Kurn tried again to break the webbing, which stretched farther than I'd ever witnessed before. One frayed and snapped, which encouraged him. He doubled his efforts; he would get free eventually, but it would take raw strength out of him.

Meanwhile, my body felt numb.

What happened?

Straight above was the ledge from which I'd fallen, and I lay mixed up in the webbing with him on the ground. He must have rushed to catch me after knocking me off the wall, and the pellet was still potent enough to break and ensnare us both on impact.

I didn't know how long I'd been unconscious but imagining Kurn getting free of the web using pure muscle when I hadn't so much as a dagger to cut myself out kicked my heart into a gallop. My skin broke into a rushing, cold sweat while the large brute struggled constantly beside me. If I must wait until the webs naturally dissolved, the Hellhound would have a *lot* of fun, then!

I made no sound, nothing that would signal fear; I made myself breathe deep.

Calm. What are my options?

Where were my spiders? What about the capsules?

My questing fingers felt my pouch sticking to the edge of my palm, the web gunk fixing it there. Digging around with my pointer finger, I found at least one.

I hoped one was enough.

When another thick, magic-laden strand broken by the Hellhound loosened my hand as well, I focused on getting that one last tool between my fingers. Kurn rolled abruptly toward me, breathing in my face, spitting his demand.

"Dispel this spider trap!"

"I can't," I replied, smiling as I turned my head away for some fresh air. "You triggered it. I have no control over who it ensnares."

"How long does this last?"

"It could last until morning."

"What?!"

Or shorter, if you keep breaking them.

I turned my head to him with a closed-lipped smile, staring into dark eyes. His pale, snarling face was closer than I'd ever been, his black hair covered in strings of white webbing. The ruby around his neck was tangled up the same as my saphgar was against my chest. I couldn't see from where I was but would wager that his pants were on and stuck to his hips. It looked like we were both covered in a giant cum blob.

I smiled. "We have time, Kurn. Tell me that story about the Fourth's capture of a Davrin's demon."

He barked another laugh that made the edge of my ears vibrate. "I haven't unloaded in your cunt yet."

"You just said after you release. And you broke any deal, anyway."

"So did you," he sneered, jerking at the webbing but it failed to snap. "Sneaky bitch."

I tested my reach as well; I could touch his crotch. I rubbed at the softened log, and he jerked his hips away.

"*Hai!*"

I shrugged like it meant nothing, though my heart pounded. Lucky me, he couldn't hear it. "You said your mind would clear, and I know how to milk stallions."

He blinked then gritted his teeth again. "I will kill you if you touch me."

What the fuck. My head…

"For a hand jerk?" I sneered. "Picky beggar, aren't you?"

Kurn's muscles bulged again, his arm breaking strands which had kept it out from his torso. Once he had the leverage, he reached for his sticky, red jewel.

Uh-oh.

"*Urruk'rel!*" his voice boomed with utter command, staring into my eyes. "*Shithyn-kah!*"

Something… happened.

Something *hurt*. Piercing like a dart between my eyes. For the first time since I'd reached the Surface, Shyntre's pendant became hot and sparked an independent, blue glow. I cried out in denial.

Stop!

I tried to break eye contact with the Ma'ab, but he lunged half on top of me, squashing my aching breasts and crushing my breath and my shout. Both stones mashed painfully between our chests.

Nose-to-nose, he forced his way in, stared deep into me. It felt like my sister grabbing me, suffocating me between her legs. It felt like Kain's despair as he gave in, gave his will to Braqth's power. It felt like the blood puddle in which I lay as I was sacrificed to her.

You will obey Kurn Divigna from now on, Sirana.

Every exercise I'd performed to resist this kind of spell clacked into place, my thoughts retreating behind a barrier, entombing my mind like a stone egg.

You are my servant, and I am your master. Acknowledge me.

The oppressive command crashed against my mind.

Speak

Threatening to crack it.

Say it!

No! My spine arched and stiffened against the Hound clinging to me as my eyes widened. Motes of blue light escaped as Shyntre's pendant flared with heat. Never...

Never again!!

I pulled up my hand with fingers gripping the tacky capsule; I stretched the webbing until I was certain my arm would shatter from the rebound against the stone. I didn't care; I couldn't stop until I'd jammed the capsule up Kurn's left nostril and followed it with most of the length of my pinky.

"Augh!" he cried.

His head reared away, gagging and snorting as he rolled off me. The magical bond thinned and snapped before it grew too strong, and I could breathe again.

No. I could *laugh!*

"Hahaha!" I crowed. "It fizzes, doesn't it, Hellhound?"

Kurn coughed and tried to blow the fast-dissolving mass out of his nose like a glob of snot. Even if he was partly successful—*oh, that's delicious*—enough of the drug was already in his brain. I watched it happen, seeping in as he turned his head, trying to focus on me. His eyes glazed over, and he bared his large, square teeth.

"*F-furuzik ah-hasha…*"

He surged once more against the webs, elbowing me and smashing one shoulder instead of my ear as I threw my head out of the way. He bellowed once in frustration, and I wondered if this, too, had less effect on him as the sleep powder.

It's the most potent I have!

Indeed, it was. He didn't break the webs, and his struggles grew weaker until, eventually, they stopped. The warrior relaxed, slowly.

Quiet. At last.

"Hellhound?" I asked.

No response.

"Kurn?"

"…Mm?"

He sounded drunk.

I took a deep breath, licking dry lips. "Who is Divigna, other than your father?"

His mouth twitched, though his head lolled, and his eyes blinked up at the stars as if they were spinning many times their normal speed.

"The greatest. The eternal…"

"Eternal?"

He chuckled.

I frowned. "How old is this Ma'ab?"

"A century… still fighting and breeding. Proof of our gods' gifts."

"He was… 'gifted' to fight forever? How?"

Kurn's head flopped one way and then turned and sagged the other way. I realized that was him shaking his head; he didn't know. At least he was telling the truth now.

"What of the black demon with a white mane? You said you saw him?"

Kurn moaned. "Once. During my training…"

"Describe everything, from when he was visible until he wasn't."

"Visible… invisible…train against unseen enemies."

I swallowed. "Go on."

"Commander Vo'traj brought him to…arena."

"What did he look like?"

"Yellow eyes. Shadows and claws… good training…"

Those Ma'ab eyes were drooping.

"How is it said he came into the Empire's possession?"

"Captured by the Fourth."

Yes, you've said.

"Who is the Fourth?"

"As…Ascended. Can't… say her name. The Enslaver…"

"Enslaved him how?" I asked. "And was he alone when he was captured?"

The Hellhound's head flopped again. His eyes were empty of any recognition. My aching brain grasped for my next question.

"Does he have a name?"

"Only… his mistress knows the demon's name."

Shit.

A hard knot of fire had been growing in my chest and head ever since Kurn used that gem against me. Now, it petered out like a rainstorm had drenched it, although my head ached monstrously. I didn't know what it had been but dared to hope what I'd just learned had been enough to satisfy the Queen's Geas.

Kurn moaned, muttering about the sky spinning, and at the same time, one of my spiders crawled near my tangled pendant where I could see her.

"Oh, baby," I whispered, blinking rapidly as my vision blurred.

One guardian was alive and had crawled down from the wall! I watched the black, glossy body crawl around, unperturbed with the large Ma'ab so near yet so docile and unthreatening. Slowly, I understood that she wasn't just standing guard.

She was working.

Eating the web.

I tested where she'd just been, pulled at my other wrist, and a strand snapped. D'Shea was brilliant.

"Good. Yes."

"Mm?" Kurn asked me.

"Nothing. Be quiet."

Keep going, babies.

I lay still, eventually confirming all three spiders worked on the same task, snipping threads and consuming sticky parts with their mandibles. They weakened the strength of the webs around me much faster than it would take to wear out naturally. Soon, I tried sitting up, the substance giving with enough resistance that I had to try a second time before it worked.

I was free. *In more ways than one?*

I discovered either how hard we must have landed or how hard Kurn had been thrashing before I awoke by the number of bruises and scrapes on my body. I took a step and gasped at the flare of renewed burn coursing down and out to my arms.

Owwch... I reached and felt a tiny piece of gravel fall out; there was a touch of blood on my finger. *Great.*

Looking down at the subdued beast that walked like a man, I glared in blame that I needed another two or three days of Shyntre's medicine again. And for what?

I'm just trying to find my Sister. What did I ever do to you besides banter insults? Bah...

I could try killing him, having extracted what he knew about the Sathoet. He had that dagger in his boot. Yes, I should try.

With renewed determination, I crouched by his boot, plucking and breaking away strands with chewing help from my spiders. I found the handle and drew the weapon, testing the edge.

Sharp enough to slit his throat like I did Kain's.

I took to one knee beside him, looking into those dark, unfocused eyes.

I'm not afraid of you. I've already encountered much worse.

Yet, I *must* make sure I was not being held back. Placing the dagger's tip at the tacky hollow of the man's throat, I pushed until I spotted a well of blood arise. Then paused.

Nothing. No illness.

I smiled, withdrew the blade, and lined it up across the windpipe. *I can do this.*

It might cause some upset but, really, who but Castis cared? We didn't need the Ma'ab for this mission when they only wanted to capture me "for the Empire."

I can kill the mage, too. Then we can go to Manalar how we want.

A large rock broke loose from above and struck the ground nearby; I shot to my feet, all my senses seeking the source. Scanning the ridge above, I saw no one, heard nothing, but—

I *felt* something. *A warning.*

I looked around me, familiar dread gripping me. The opportunity to leave was becoming short, I believed it like I did outside the Tower, when Tamuril had run away and I had run straight into the path of Kurn's horse.

Fucking run.

I crouched and cut the ruby necklace from Kurn's neck, collected my babies and my web-sticky pouch, and left the canyon immediately.

I tried not to run so fast that I collided with a threat as big as a horse before seeing it.

My wits returned before I arrived at camp. My bare feet were too hot and dry and numbingly sore; the cuts and scrapes from my hard landing were dust-covered and full of grit. I was covered in webbing, able to rub only a little of it off so far. I needed to clean myself first before dressing, which would be difficult to reach in places without help.

The best I can do is stand under the waterfall again.

Rithal might be awake, and I practiced what I would say for abandoning watch and returning naked. Surely, he would have noticed Kurn was gone, too, and I had physical proof of our altercation. I just hoped all others were asleep; it would be easier to convince the Dwarf I hadn't started the fight.

I had nearly reached the camp when I saw a lanky, skulking figure watching over it. Not Rithal.

Gavin?

Stealth seemed prudent. Why was he awake again while the Dwarf slept despite the watch order?

I used any deeper shadows for as long as I could, but my riding partner was absolutely scanning for life signs; I could get no closer than I usually did by the time he spotted mine. His dark eyes pinned my location, his chin lifting up to study it. With an inward sigh, I entered the moonlight so he could be certain who approached the camp. Gavin looked over my body but not in the same way Kurn had. He knew I wore no clothes, but his gaze only paused twice: once at the ruby and pouch in my hand, and again at the blue gem which hung between my breasts. He ignored the stolen dagger; it didn't concern him.

"Why are you awake?" I whispered.

Gavin glanced over at the sleeping figures and back. He kept his low voice at a soft pitch, knowing how easily I could hear him, while he retrieved a rolled kit from one saddlebag. "Perhaps you would like to bathe as we talk."

Talk. He was suggesting we talk, first? *Uh-oh.*

The apprentice was correct that I wanted to get clean. Kurn might not have sprayed my skin and insides with semen like Kain, but I felt almost as dirty after the naked fight with a male involving mindbender magic. My lip curled in a silent snarl as I glanced at the ruby in my grip.

I should have put something deep in his ass before I left, so the stupid bull *remembered* who had won when the drug wore off. Fuck it, I should have killed him! He had been planning to drag me mentally chained wherever they'd taken the Sathoet! What had stopped me?

Fuck all this Drider shit!

I took a deep breath, and I didn't care that Gavin watched while I encouraged my spiders into their little, dry spot with my drug pouch, before I went into the water with Kurn's ruby and dagger. I stepped into the pool, my feet thanking me for the mercy.

The waterfall soon struck my head, seeming colder, flowing down my heated skin. I rinsed off the Ma'ab tools and placed them on a damp rock, then I focused on my skin and hair, making better progress on removing the webbing. In caring for my body, however, I noted that it made no difference to Gavin whether I was fully clothed or not. He was as disinterested as Castis, now I thought about it.

Is that a Ma'ab mage thing? Do they not have a mating instinct for having grand death magic in their lines?

"I sensed a powerful aura near the camp tonight, Sirana," said Gavin as I finally came out from underneath the falls. "It was not one of us."

My thoughts on impotent, dark-eyed mages flew from my head.

"Umm. What kind of aura?"

"Arcane, I think. Older than Sarilis, I am certain. Perhaps older than you."

I felt a cold trickle in the center of my chest. "Have you felt it before? Near the Tower?"

Gavin shook his head. "No. But either we narrowly missed crossing paths with something we'd rather not meet, or we are being followed."

I tried not to feel paranoid, tried to think of an alternative. "Something the Rock Dwarves might have in their land?"

"I wouldn't know." The apprentice sighed, seeming spooked despite his usual play at indifference. "It vanished before I received more than a vague impression. It may have become aware it was seen, or it may have simply moved on."

I paused, stepping out of the pool. "Do you need me to do anything?"

Gavin shook his head. "Nothing to be done. I suggest not to search for it tonight. I only thought you should know."

That sense of threat returned, when I had thought to cut Kurn's throat. Something had been there. Was it me it watched? Or was it Kurn and Castis, or even Rithal or Mathias, who had brought some kind of trouble with them?

Maybe Kurn won't return from the canyon where I left him.

"Forgive me, but I must ask the obvious," Gavin began, and I looked at him. "What happened? You returned naked, covered in something white and stringy, carrying Kurn's pendant and a blade. Your back is marked like you've fallen and rolled upon rocks."

I smiled in amusement. So he'd known about the ruby as well, probably saw it the first night with those mage's eyes of his. "What do you deduce from your evidence, apprentice?"

"A conflict we both knew was coming," he said, glancing where I'd set my guardians. "You had your most dangerous tool with you. Does Kurn live?"

My mouth twisted. "He was breathing when I left."

"Hm. I admit surprise."

Me, too.

"And a pity for both of us. He will be more dangerous now."

"We'll see," I said. "If he returns at all, I have options."

Gavin looked confused. "Options you didn't have before?"

"Correct."

That was the most I could say. I swallowed, smiling. "If you wish to sleep apart from them at night, that is understandable, and you are invited to be near me."

Gavin grunted, shifting awkwardly, and reached to tug the leather thong of his kit. I watched as he unrolled it along a dry spot on the rocks. They were his surgical tools, not his cooking ones.

"Shall I clean the wounds on your back?"

I arched a brow. "Another thing you learned at the monastery?"

"No. Self-taught after I left."

My mouth twisted. "Practicing on corpses?"

"Sometimes. Also upon some living footpads who needed a field surgeon for a time."

"Living what?"

Gavin grunted. "Scavenger men in a town or city, stealing by force. Sometimes they were injured trying."

I smiled to imagine that. The apprentice had said his journey from monastery to Ley Tower wasn't a direct one. "How many years aged were you?"

"About seventeen, I think," he said, straightening a couple tiny, fine scalpels on the clean cloth. "I can remove the debris from your skin and stitch any gashes that won't close on their own. Those wounds will fester if you leave them."

He didn't know about Shyntre's pellets, but I didn't enlighten him. I looked over his kit, noting needle, thread, and a similar pinching tool such as I had used to extract the glass out of Tamuril's buttock. He had the means for this, and I already knew how meticulously he tended his tools. They would be clean and sharp, of good quality.

This would require exposing my back, though. My unease showed, and I tested him. "I will accept but will also keep my spiders in my lap."

"Understandable." His dark eyes flicked toward the tiny cave in which I'd placed them. "Are they overprotective if you flinch? I *will* cause pain, but it is minor and necessary."

I considered how they hadn't attacked even as I was fighting blind, before trapping myself in that canyon. "My spiders seem to know when I believe I am under true threat and need aid. They will not jump on you if I merely wince from a stitch. I will not allow it."

The death mage was trying to hide his discomfort when he nodded agreement. At least we both had something to risk.

Then something else struck me. "One more condition."

"Yes?"

"I will trade you the cloth with my blood on it for one of my clean ones. I want to burn the one you use."

This did not baffle him for long. "Wiser than most I've met. Your race knows blood magic."

"Yes." *And it is terrifying.*

"You may have the bloody cloth after I finish, Sirana, in exchange for one of yours."

Good.

I collected my spiders in one hand and reached to drape my damp hair over one shoulder before turning around and sitting in front of him. My sore back complained a lot in doing so; something tore and I felt a trickle under my left shoulder blade—the first fresh blood the death mage saw. I focused on keeping my little companions calm, breathing to calm myself. *Shhh.*

"Ready," I said.

I was fascinated by the small knucklebone the death mage produced from his kit. With a word, it began to glow with a pale blue light so he could see what he was doing without something bright as a flame. It was magical light, heatless and familiar, which spread over my skin.

Where did you learn your craft?

And in less than a decade, from the sound of it.

Gavin was efficient with his work, figuring correctly that I could handle the discomfort without making any sound. He worked to scrape away dead and flayed skin; that stung. He removed the tiny pebbles and dirt with a combination of a rough cloth, a pungent, stinging solution, and that thin, pinching tool.

He was not particularly gentle, and it hurt a lot in places where the debris was deeper, but when he was finished with one spot, he covered the scrapes with a small, sticky bandage and moved on to the next. He only used the needle and thread in two spots; he was not excessive at all and did not complain about using his own supplies.

Despite all my restrained wincing and mental shushing of my spiders crawling around my arms, I was glad for his help. I hadn't realized the extent of the wounds and would not have been able to clean them so well on my own; this might have reduced the effect of any pellets I would take as well.

In time, Gavin drew breath to speak as he wiped off his tool with the cloth. "I've known grown men who make more noise being tended by a trained physician than you do by me without a numbing agent."

I warmed with pride at the compliment. I also thought of Tamuril and my tending her backside. She had squirmed and squeaked quite a bit.

Still, I said, "What would 'grown men' have to do with my training down below, apprentice?"

"Only an observation." He paused. "How were you injured?"

"Kurn has something that creates light and sound," I said. "He used it to knock me off a rock wall, and I fell."

"Ah. Yes, a thunderstone. Castis would have made it for him."

I frowned. "Can he make them any time?"

"With the right components. He will probably replenish them when we reach the inn at Troshin Bend."

Fuck me. And I was out of web pellets. What was I going to do? I couldn't keep traveling as if pretending I didn't know how they wanted to trap me, yet I couldn't go on alone at this point. I would be tracked and hunted, no doubt.

They need to die.

But how? And when?

"Is there anywhere else you are injured?" Gavin asked, breaking into my concerns. "I do not know as much about living female anatomy, but you fell an unknown distance."

"He caught me," I muttered.

"He did?"

"Yes. I didn't land straight upon the rocks, or my bones would be broken, too."

"Hm. So you struggled with him on the ground, and he is of... significant size. Have you noticed any internal aches that have not stopped?"

That was an indirect way to ask. As if I didn't already know what that felt like.

I shook my head. "He didn't fuck me. The webs held us both."

Thank Goddess.

Gavin made a noncommittal sound. "Fortunate. I can imagine Kurn's seed is caustic enough to wither a babe already in the womb, even an Elven one."

My blood ran like ice in my veins, and I waited, counting to five so my spiders wouldn't move. When he said nothing and began to clean and sort his kit, I spun around to stare at him, my guardians clinging to my forearms. Gavin wouldn't make eye contact at first, returning his needle to its slot with careful precision first, but when he finally did look up, I could see his certainty.

"How long have you known?" I hissed.

"For several days."

"*How* did you know?!"

One brow arched. "I sense life auras, Sirana, and I've studied yours quite thoroughly upon your request. You have two, and they are distinct from each other. The only obvious reason for that would be pregnancy."

I felt cold. *Damn it*. That was it; I saw the moment in my head where I would have to take D'Shea's expulsion potion: Kurn and Castis learning that I carried.

"If you tell any of the others—!" I threatened.

"I will not," he said. "There's no benefit in that and far more harm."

You have no idea. I blinked away moisture in my eyes.

The following quiet was an uncomfortable one, and Gavin tried shrugging it off. "I admit surprise that you were sent on such a long journey with this added factor. Though, it doesn't seem to slow you down yet but perhaps increases your appetite. Granted, we don't know what a typical amount of food is for your race and your size."

I sighed. *He's been thinking about this a lot.*

My mouth felt dry as I eyed the rippling pool; absently, I cradled one sore tit. I hadn't much to say; I certainly couldn't explain to him why I was sent.

Gavin glanced over at the camp; no one had moved, and the waterfall covered our conversation. "If I may ask, how long for a Davrin to gestate and give birth?"

So much for mystery.

I grumbled, "About twenty-four of your Surface months."

The apprentice could not cover his surprise, not on his face or in his tone. "I had no idea it could be so long. It's only nine months for Human women."

I smirked. "I'm envious, in a way."

Gavin's eyes shifted as he thought about this. "It makes some sense. Elves would be more numerous than Humans if they bred as quickly while living far longer. So, lengthy life but a greater gestation as well. Interesting."

Again, I didn't reply, having already pondered this. I also thought it must stretch out the skin of Human stomachs rather badly to grow so quickly.

"How far along are you?"

"Why?"

"Just being practical."

I grudgingly respected that. "Five months."

"Hm," he considered. "Then you do have time to complete this journey. I question your willingness to return to kill Sarilis at the end of it, though." He began rolling up his kit like he needed something to do with his hands. "I understand pregnant females get protective of their unborn the farther along they are."

I almost snorted a laugh. "This is a Queen's command, Gavin. The plan is flexible, but the goal remains until it's finished. If you want the tower as your new residence, you will help me find the best way to take *him* out of it."

The younger man tied off his roll and looked at my face as if to judge my truthfulness. He didn't find anything to argue, and this was the first time we had revisited that deal I'd suggested back in his room, when I'd told him I would return. Clearly, he turned this over in his mind again.

"The dreamer who sent you is your Queen," he repeated.

"Yes. Who is the dreamer who sent you? Who might have shown you those red dunes and fog on a sunny day?"

Gavin hesitated then looked away, grabbing his kit and climbing to his feet.

He was still afraid to say.

Rithal and Mathias both slept through their watches, and I wondered about that as Gavin remained awake. The death mage shrugged when I whispered the question to him.

"I did nothing. Their hunt must have worn them out. Why should we wake them?"

I squinted. "Why did you wake again?"

"A nightmare. They are frequent, and you aren't normally around."

He is a sharp one for always being fatigued.

"Then you sensed that 'old' aura while already awake."

"Indeed."

Well. The quiet was nice, I decided, and the peace wouldn't last once the Sun rose. First, I placed Shyntre's pellet beneath my tongue, letting it dissolve while I dressed and groomed myself for travel. For certain, I didn't wish to appear as though I been in a naked, web-bound wrestling match with a half-naked Hellhound.

I took up the usual habits alongside the apprentice to prepare for the day. Stars were fading into a purple canvas, and pink was swiftly turning to orange to the East. I had managed to collect food for another day or two crossing the Midway, and Gavin had fully rekindled the fire to boil some water in his pot. Smelling the smoke, the others finally shifted in their bedrolls. They all sensed the change in routine and woke up within moments of each other.

"Where is Kurn?" Castis rasped, noticing the empty bedroll.

Mathias was rubbing his stubbled, brown face and blinking sleep from his eyes. "Huh?"

"Why'dya not wake me, Elf?" Rithal asked, getting up quickly to dress.

"Gavin was restless," I said, "and I had little else to do. You could use the sleep."

"Where is Kurn?!" Castis broke in loudly. "What have you done with him, witch?"

I glared at the Ma'ab. "I take it you *knew* he planned to attack me last night? The Hellhound *failed.*"

"Whoa, whoa!" Mathias shook the final cobwebs out of his ears. "He's dead?"

"I did not say that. He was breathing when I left him."

"Hirat ghabiash!" Castis spewed, scrambling to don his robe and belt. "How dare you?!"

"Don' be foolish, mage!" Rithal shouted, mostly dressed and reaching for his hatchet. "If tha's true, she's every cause tah defend 'erself!"

Mathias was being smart and grabbing his things to get out of the way. I pulled my crossbow and dagger.

"She's lying!" Castis shouted, pointing at me. "She attacked him!"

Rithal tossed an arm out in disbelief. "C'mon, there's no sign o' struggle!"

"She drugged him!"

"Sure," I sneered, "*and* dragged the bull away under my own strength!"

I hadn't lifted to aim any attack when Castis's swelling surge of magic surprised everybody. The handsome man's face was twisted in rage, and he raised his hands, muttering.

Shit.

"Stop!" Rithal barked.

Too late!

I tumbled far to the side as the spell took effect; there was a spark of fire, and then—

Nothing.

No heat reached me; no gout of flame consumed me like the pronghorn he'd taken on the flats. The sound of aborted magic was unlike anything that existed while I was awake. Both a low, thunderous pop and an in-suck of some vaporous vortex in the same place and time. I watched from a crouch as the Ma'ab caster stumbled, his spell sputtering out before it could bloom, and the mage fell to his knees, drained.

"Maknuut!" Castis hissed.

I looked at Gavin. His hand was raised, fingers curled in an arcane gesture. His eyes were that eerie, solid black I had only seen a few times, the whites hinting to return as he lowered his arm. Cold air seeped out from around him a moment later, flowing to touch the rest of us.

The two mages glowered at each other from the distance. On Gavin, it looked like his normal face; on Castis's far prettier one, well, he looked to be choking on something fetid caught in his throat.

I stepped closer to my apprentice, and before Castis could try anything else, Rithal charged on hairy, bare feet, knocking the younger man out with the handle of his hatchet. Mathias was well far away from us, dressing in a hustle.

"Awright," the redbeard exhaled, looking around and seeing what I did. "Now. What, by Gerrit's Balls, just happened? Talk quick."

"I was bathing in the waterfall while you slept," I said. "Kurn tried to sneak up on me, and he chased me into the canyon." I indicated the direction and pulled out the ruby. "He tried to use *this* to force me to obey him, to come with him to his superiors. I had a counter spell. Yes, I *did* drug him to escape, but I left him there alive *despite* his attempt to enslave me!"

Rithal listened, his familiar, blue eyes focused on my words and the red pendant with the broken cord. He also noticed the dagger of Ma'ab make, missing its sheath and knotted to one of my own. "Yah didn't go back since?"

"Why should I? He failed, but I wasn't unhurt. I had wounds to tend. Gavin helped."

The Dwarf glanced at him, who confirmed in silence, and spoke no answer to that. Rithal picked up his pack to sling it on one bulky shoulder. "Aye... Hm. Awright. Will yah show me where you left 'im?"

Rage flashed through me. "Why do you care?"

"Rather not leave a humiliated Hellhound and his fire mage at our backs, if I can help it." The Dwarf frowned. "I didn't know what the ruby was for, Elf. Ida warned yah. An' that's exactly what I was afraid of with you comin' along."

"I can't leave," I pointed out.

"No," he agreed, indicating the pendant. "But yah have that. Hide it while we see what's what. Take me to where yah left him."

Very well. I had my spiders with me, and I would keep my distance.

"Mathias," Rithal said, "please stay an' watch Castis in case he wakes up."

The skin hunter was put together, standing at a good distance but coming closer. "Um. Alright?"

The Dwarf motioned for both me and Gavin to come. "Rather not leave the two mages in the same place, if that's well with yah."

Gavin shrugged wordlessly and came with us. I couldn't tell if the abrupt clash had winded him or not but was impressed, either way. Casting at speed and controlling the outcome was no easy task, as I understood it from mages below.

And he defended me.

Well, alright, it was possible Gavin just didn't want to get caught in Castis's fire as well, but he *could* have run like Mathias. Instead, the former monk had stood up to the Ma'ab nobleman when he attacked, just as I had his bull-dog.

I smiled at this "maknuut" while we walked toward the canyon, and he gave me an odd look in return. *Oh, come. Your actions have spoken. We are allies whether you claim it or not.*

In my mind, I firmly decided to watch his back to return the favor from now on, and this thought did not bother me. I had learned of its value through my Sisters.

Soon enough, we stood outside the box canyon where I had led Kurn under the larger Moon.

"In there," I lifted my chin to point. "We shall wait out here. You'd rather he not come alert as Castis did, yes?"

Rithal grunted wordless agreement, his mouth chewing enough hair to make his beard act like it had its own mind. I smothered a chuckle, and the Dwarf went in alone. I stood wondering which he'd find, a sleeping man or a corpse.

Something was here last night. I hope it ate him.

"You aren't certain he's alive," Gavin murmured.

"He was when I escaped," I whispered. "But he was without defense, an animal could have gotten to him."

"That, or whatever I sensed last night."

I smiled. "Or that."

Something powerful enough to make me afraid without showing itself. Gavin had felt it, too. Was it the same source as at Sarilis's tower? Were we being followed this whole way, or was this just a random encounter in the canyon alone?

I heard Kurn and Rithal talking, then, both male voices rumbling unintelligibly off the rock walls.

"So, the Hellhound is alive," Gavin said.

My gut tightened. "Unfortunately."

In addition, we might have some larger concern at our backs as we prepared to cross the Midway.

Kurn eventually staggered his way into view in the early dawn light, Rithal pacing him as if he'd try to catch the dog if he collapsed. The Ma'ab was shirtless still, his pants and boots in place, though missing his dagger and necklace. In stark contrast to his skin, the blood in the hollow of his throat had dried into a large, dark spot. I smirked.

The Ma'ab was covered in threadbare cobwebs which had lost their stickiness but marked where he'd been restrained. His eyes were red-rimmed, his nose swollen, and his face had poured sweat all night; he looked feverishly ill. This wasn't uncommon for the substance I'd shoved up his nostril, but after his shaking off most of the sleep powder at the Tower, I had expected a lesser effect here as well. Instead, the effect seemed enhanced to a degree my Elders would find alarming.

Ideally, a target didn't clearly remember what they'd said, and there were no obvious signs of the interrogation having taken place.

The big man somehow didn't notice me as Rithal steered him toward camp, and, although we shared a baffled glance, neither Gavin nor I made any sound to attract the attention. We trailed them back to the waterfall, and Kurn ignored everyone as he made straight for it and dunked himself into the pool.

Coming alert, he drank desperately and crawled beneath the falling water, washing himself as if he needed it as badly as I had. Rubbing his face and torso, his hands were brusque but uncoordinated. A few times, the Hellhound scratched his skin as if his entire body itched, leaving bright red lines and rashes on fog-white skin.

Castis wasn't awake yet, so we had some quiet moments, Rithal, Mathias, Gavin, and me, to wonder what to do next.

Abruptly, Kurn pushed himself up to his feet. "Let us leave this cursed place."

Mathias blinked, and Rithal asked, "Uh. Hey. Yah awake, Kurn?"

"Break camp," the Ma'ab growled hoarsely, his throat sounding raw. "Pack up. Now."

"Castis is passed out," Mathias said. "He can't ride yet."

With a dull roar leaking out, Kurn stomped over to the skin hunter. "So we'll tie him to his horse!"

True to his word, Kurn made ready to go like it was one of the same past mornings. He collected enough water for both him and Castis, tied it to each horse, and pointed at his Ma'ab brother. "I said, pick him up. We waste daylight."

The rest of us were ready regardless, but Rithal and Mathias hesitated between themselves, wondering which the Hellhound had just spoken to.

Kurn spun and shouted impatiently, "Come on! Mount up!"

He's insane. Yet I dared to think he didn't remember last night at all.

And we were going to follow him for ten days across the flats?

What in the Abyss happened after I left?

Gavin and I got onto his mare, and Mathias and Rithal both tied Castis to his horse before getting on theirs. Swifter than I could have imagined, we started out over the Midway where there was no shade to be had.

With the steady loping gait rolling in my ears, I realized Kurn had neither tried to search for his ruby nor looked to me for it. I wanted to take the credit for his broken behavior, but I didn't believe it had been so easy. Sooner or later, the shock and numbness would wear off, and the old Kurn would return full force. It was only a matter of time.

I had to talk to Rithal and Mathias. I must decide what to do about the Ma'ab.

Before the Sun grew so strong as to white-out the landscape for me, I looked behind us at the rocky, yellow-brown labyrinth gradually receding behind the horizon. I spotted nothing following us.

Nothing yet.

CHAPTER 13

SHYNTRE WAS GOING MAD.

He had been locked in his room in the Wizard's Tower for three cycles, visited by no one since Elder Rausery had left with the *Genethsa* pellets he'd pleaded she give to Sirana. It wasn't the length of time or the small space which agitated him beyond his ability to sleep; he had been locked in solitude as punishment for much longer stretches in the past.

It was knowing the Consort, the one they called Auslan and with whom Sirana had caught her first child after nearly dying, was imprisoned in the Red Sister's Cloister.

Alone.

It was knowing Elder Rausery was gone to the Surface again and couldn't protect him. It was having heard *nothing* from his Mother or his Headmaster, not from the Valsharess who had terrified him ever since he could remember.

Shyntre swore he would blast a hole in the Tower wall and climb down to go see for himself.

After he finished retching for the third time since his last meal.

His head swam as he gripped his work stool to remain upright. *So dizzy. Need to eat. Sleep. And I can't.*

He wouldn't be sneaking out of the Tower any time soon.

"Just... someone tell me what's happening out there!" he shouted, his voice bouncing off the smooth stone encasing him.

There was no answer to his plea.

The Elder Sorceress stood at attention in the Prime's favored planning room, calm and attentive while her superior grumbled over multiple dispatches and requests from the Palace usually handled by Rausery. The Sisterhood always noticed any time the Elder General was gone to the Surface, and no one left behind enjoyed the added work. Least of all, the First Sister.

"It begins again," the ancient Davrin muttered. "Fucking loathe Surface missions. There's nothing up there needing our noses poking in."

D'Shea said nothing, having heard these exact words before. She tended to agree with the Prime on this topic, however, which was why she was gifted with the private grousing. This time was different for the Sorceress, if only because it had so badly entangled Siranet's granddaughter and D'Shea's own son, all the while disrupting or destroying numerous plans and shredding careful webs of connections she'd been building for two hundred years.

But D'Shea wouldn't say this aloud.

The Prime sorted the priorities for Sivaraus and divided out the tasks between her and her remaining Elder in something close to reasonable balance. The Sorceress hid her surprise for the somber practicality of it, as if "Fadele" still remembered how to run a Sisterhood.

Fadele. I cannot believe I know this now.

Hearing the First Sister's given name from the Valsharess's mouth in that throne room, just before the Abyss had broken loose, had been surreal. Everyone had assumed it was forgotten long ago.

Even by the First.

"Delegate," the Prime growled, pushing a stack of parchment toward her. "In this order."

D'Shea stepped forward to accept her tasks. "Yes, Prime."

The older Davrin twiddled with a stylus in a way that didn't suit her presence. "Remind me why that Sanctuary slut is down in solitary. We don't need his testimony anymore with Wilsira's scheme found out, and he's no use as a House spy. He's been a big distraction to the caits."

The Sorceress prepared her thoughts, reminded herself how she was an expert at conveying serene confidence in her answers. Her words and tone frequently attained perfection to persuade.

Let it work its magic.

"Do you remember the young bua Rausery was searching for recently?" she asked the Prime. "Abducted from one House and held captive in another."

Fadele nodded. "The healer sent to the Sanctuary for training, yeah."

D'Shea smiled. "This Consort is another, but much older, his magic stronger. He is finished with his training, and the Priestesses believe he was purged with the rest."

Eyes like chipped red stone narrowed at her. "A healer."

"The most powerful one we know about. He mended Sirana so she could stand witness before the Queen about the Ornilleth escape."

The Prime sneered. "Don't need something like that in my Cloister. He touched Sirana, who was compromised by flayers, so *he* is."

D'Shea's lips tightened briefly. "Thralls can't ensnare more thralls for the Elder Mind, Prime. We know this, and the Queen stated it so. She had another use for Sirana regardless."

Her superior showed in her scowl how she still chafed at that outcome. She had wanted nothing more than to "cleanse" the Sisterhood of those touched by anything psionic.

"Maybe but look what the fuckin' breeder caused keeping her alive."

"He didn't cause this, Prime, but he *did* preserve our ability to speak against the Sanctuary under trial, and Sirana received her first leads from him about it. We also know the Valsharess prefers these heal-by-touch buas be preserved, they are so rarely born. We *cannot* execute him without a Queen's Writ."

An irritable shrug. "So, hand him over to Her. Let Her decide what to do with him."

"She may give him to the Priestesses, who are desperate to recover from their loss by any means."

"I don't care what they scratch at. That is Her decision, D'Shea."

"Of course, Prime. Yet I have it on good authority that the Priestesses do *not* know that this Consort was so skilled. Wilsira kept it a secret, and it died with her while never benefitting the Queen." D'Shea paused to let that treachery sink in. "The Sisterhood has both the healer *and* the secret from the Priestesses."

The Prime squinted then smirked. "What the fuck are you plotting, Varessa?"

The Sorceress smiled and tilted her head in a self-assured way the First still found attractive, whether she admitted it or not. "Lead Jaunda has been given a difficult mission by the Valsharess, and we do not have as many resources to support her the deeper she must go in hostile territory."

"She'll have all the potions she needs."

"Yes, she will. But a mage like the one in our possession should be retained at our order for when Jaunda reports back, to revive and cleanse her of any ill. This Consort can provide a faster recovery and mission turnaround as she learns of what is out there."

"Weakness," the Prime muttered. "I know what's out there. Jaunda can handle it."

"Our Queen provides the goal but gives us leave to discover the best way," the Elder said for what seemed the hundredth time. "We only have so much time to prepare before we discover what the

Elder Mind knows and plots against us. Our Lead *must* find what she seeks for our Queen and as soon as possible. We *must* use all our resources, and this Consort has fallen to us from Braqth's own cradle."

She paused, waiting for the inevitable eye contact. "Allow me to *use* him, my Prime, as I would any other tool, for the good of the Sisterhood and our service to the Throne of Sivaraus. This healer will serve us well under the strict hand of another mage."

The First Sister broke her stylus, whether on purpose or not, her annoyance and acceptance simultaneously scrawled on her face. "So be it."

Elder D'Shea lifted her chin, waiting at attention until the Prime had come to terms with it.

Fadele glanced up again. "What?"

"May I remove him from solitary, Prime?"

"And put him where?"

"Somewhere he won't distract the Sisters."

The First Sister grunted, pleased with that much. She flipped her red-gloved hand. "Do it. Keep me informed."

The Sorceress left the planning room for solitary confinement immediately, at last having what she sought. She had an incredible amount of work ahead of her and needed to stay collected. Focused.

Delegate.

She had twice as many Red Sisters to keep in line without Rausery here, and those accustomed to being directly under the General would test the boundaries with the Sorceress every damned moment she was gone. The Elder Sorceress was prepared to cause pain for the insubordination.

D'Shea opened the door and slipped down the lighted steps, her red cloak brushing the stone behind her. The caits didn't hear her coming because their ears were stuffed with taunting grunts, the slapping of flesh, and someone gagging.

She smirked. *Last time, slits. Hope you enjoyed the opportunity.*

The Sorceress breathed, clearing her mind and reviving her spell before she filled the smelly, tiny prison cell with her voice.

"Sisters! At attention!"

Three were leaning against the opposite wall, catching their breath and waiting for another turn; they straightened up immediately. D'Shea expected the others to be slower to respond, given one sat on the cot, feet planted on the floor and the Consort in her lap, her Feldeu buried between his buttocks. Another Sister balanced on her booted feet atop the cot, facing the wall and lunging her own cock into his mouth, often too deep as he heaved, spittle dripping down his chin and neck. Meanwhile, a third Sister kneeled between his legs, willingly and generously throating him, sucking his hard staff like she couldn't get enough.

It must be enough.

It had taken three cycles to work through the Prime, to get her to even discuss the Consort in any way and convince her that he had other value. This would stop.

"Sisters!! Fresla jarfik!"

The magic-laced command forced the group on the cot to cease all movement, while the three stared with their mouths closed, standing at attention with Feldeus sticking out.

"Release the prisoner," D'Shea ordered.

"*Ergh,* let us finish," Corpora Thena panted, "…Elder."

Her hips thrust up, lifting her ass off the cot despite the magical suggestion, and made Auslan gasp; Suna took advantage and leaned in, blocking his windpipe again. He struggled to breathe, tears draining out of his eyes. Meanwhile, the Sister kneeling and doing a fair amount of cock worship—Moria, she thought—didn't acknowledge the order at all.

"You *will* stop," D'Shea commanded, caressing the rune upon a ring that helped maintain her swelling presence in the cell. "Remove your Feldeus and stand to your Elder, *now.*"

The three standing Sisters muttered soft curses and bowed at the waist, fumbling to take their cocks off. Reluctantly, Suna backed up and stumbled off the cot to her feet, beginning to do the same.

Neither Moria nor Thena moved nearly quick enough to obey, and D'Shea took the two strides forward to seize the kneeling Sister's hair and yank her face out of Auslan's lap. The bua made a fearful sound like she might use teeth to hold on to him, but the Sorceress knew that particular slurping sound; he was fine.

"*Nooo,*" Moria moaned like she was twenty and received a slap across her face.

"What the fuck is wrong with you," D'Shea snarled, tossing her to one side. "Get up! Remember your reds!"

Suna and Moria scrambled together, working on putting themselves in order with shaking hands. D'Shea met the Corpora's eyes while she hid behind the Consort in her lap. Thena's fingers dug hard into his bruised sides in an attempt to hold on; she tried to force him to bounce his ass on her.

Goddess damn it.

The Elder's coolest contempt flowed out as she raised her hand elegantly to cast a spell. "I had no idea you were this stupid without the General breathing down your neck, Corpora Thena. *Hiysha'tren.*"

"Eld—*hck!*"

Thena's eyes flew wide; her hands left the bua as she grappled for her neck, searching for a noose which had no form. D'Shea "squeezed" harder, and within a few moments, the Corpora passed out in the cot from the lack of blood to her head.

Empty, though it is. Certainly wasn't my choice.

D'Shea released the mediocre Sister once the normal red in her purple lips was replaced with blue. Thena's eyes remained closed but her chest rose and fell a moment later. Auslan held still, seeming too scared to roll off her lap and pull his body off the phallus without being told.

Scared or disciplined, given he's alive at his age.

He was also someone both Sirana and Shyntre wanted to *keep* alive.

We'll see how long.

"Consort," D'Shea ordered. "Get off her, gather your things and kneel by me."

Inwardly, she sighed as he obeyed her the first time and without hesitation; she darted a look at those who should know and do better. At least they were paying attention. The Sorceress waited until the healer had gathered his discarded clothing, his body trembling with exhaustion, and kneeled beside her, close to the open door. He didn't try to dress, only clutched the fabric to his front and kept his eyes on the floor.

Good.

She walked forward, holding out her hand and beckoning to Panagan to give her the key to the lock. She did.

"You know what, caits?" D'Shea said. "That wasn't acceptable. Very poor response. You'd already be buried under a Tragar trap."

"Apologies, Elder," the archer mumbled, glancing at Moria and Suna standing against the far wall while D'Shea looked over the rest.

She wanted to do something painful. To help them remember, but...

They all look like they're floating on the ceiling.

"Did you take anything before coming down here?" she asked.

Several shook their heads, murmuring, "No, Elder, nothing..."

Moria almost lost her balance and caught herself on all fours as D'Shea watched. She scrambled to her feet. "S-Sorry, Elder..."

What in the Abyss?

At the same time, the Sorceress finally sensed something else in the small space, something beyond the thick scents of sweat and sex fluids. There was a mage presence *not* her own, and not any Sister she knew.

She glanced at the Consort; he hadn't moved, despite the door being wide open. *Ah-ha.*

"Sister Moria," she asked, "thoughts on this prisoner?"

The cait showed her a dumb smile. "He tastes…wonderful. Wanted more."

D'Shea looked around. "Anyone else swallow the Consort's seed?"

Panagan cautiously indicated Thena passed out on the cot.

"What about his seed in your cunts?"

The ones awake glanced down at their Feldeus in their grips.

Hmm.

"Very well, Sisters," said the Sorceress thoughtfully as she passed the healer in three strides, stepping out of the cell. "I think you need to sleep it off. I'll check on all of you upon the waking."

"Elder, wait!" one Sister cried.

D'Shea gestured for her prisoner to follow, and Auslan scrambled out of the cell with the Elder slamming it shut behind him, locking all six brother-fuckers inside and ignoring their bellowing protests.

She'd deal with this later.

"Sweet Reverie, Sisters."

Auslan wore only the cloak, stockings, and waist-wrap he'd been given when D'Shea first brought him here, but at least he was fully covered. She reflected that she had tossed him into that first interrogation room along with her newly pregnant novice barely over a span ago, yet so much had happened.

So much has changed.

After over three hundred years, the Royal Consorts were no more, except for this last one, a healer walking unsteadily beside her. Once valued and sought by Matron Nobles to raise the state of their Houses, the Valsharess had just ordered them all purged due to proof of demonic taint.

The Priestesses were *quite* busy sorting through the prisoners in the Palace dungeon, brutally taken by the Sisterhood if they had not been killed outright: pregnant matas and the Noble offspring possibly unmarked by a fouled bloodline. The Sanctuary must determine who was "pure" and present their methods and choices to the Queen, who had the final say in whether any of these Nobles would ever return to their home.

This will take quad-spans to settle out.

And, once again, the Valsharess showed to all of them that turning the Davrin into a Sathoet City was not Her desire, despite the power given them by Braqth with these creatures, despite the worship of the Abyss in Sivaraus, to keep the rest of the dangers of the Deepearth at bay.

Wilsira crossed the line.

And the Conceiver was dead; the Elder Sister's compulsion to silence was broken. Another massive change in the Sorceress's personal life, before contemplating the public one. The control which Wilsira had held over D'Shea and many other powerful females was gone over-eve. D'Shea grappled with how she had survived the long, long game, beginning prior to conceiving her child.

Survived, although the memory of fighting for them both, herself and her son, in that hidden Forming Pit would always remain. Phaelous and Tarra had been the two assigned to deal with *that* mess, and the Sorceress was glad. She had heard there was still a commoner imprisoned down there, her mind gone, her belly swollen with an unborn Consort awaiting delivery.

I will not go down there again.

"Eyes forward, Sister," she rumbled to a passing cait in uniform who had stopped to gawk at the bua in the Cloister.

"Yes, Elder."

The Elder swiftly led Auslan to her own quarters where she would catch her breath and make him presentable for what came next. He had not been bothered in solitary—indeed, he had not been discovered in the Cloister—until the Prime had said something loose to ears below D'Shea, Jaunda, or Qivni, only a cycle after Rausery had left, and word had spread.

Then, ironically, he was never alone in solitary.

The pretty male had kept himself reasonably clean until then, despite everything. Unfortunately, he looked like he had been serving raucous barracks-dwellers for the last two cycles with few breaks for grooming; he and his clothes were beginning to smell.

It could have been much worse.

Safe inside her spacious suite, D'Shea first hung her cloak and removed her belt while Auslan stood unmoving, his eyes blank and staring into space.

"Strip down," she ordered. "Leave your clothes on the floor."

Expressionless, he did as she said. Watching his lackluster yet careful motions, D'Shea stepped over to her tub and began the hot water running. Auslan perked up, looking yearningly at the tub.

"Yes, it's for you," she confirmed.

He paused as if waiting for some added condition; she couldn't blame him, but he'd figure out there were none. She ignored him while she removed her boots and sorted her parchments on her desk, glancing at the order the Prime had proposed. D'Shea would have to give some to Lead Qivni, if the Prime didn't load her down with most of those tasks which she had supposedly taken for herself.

If not her, then Lunents Agalia and Nyllel.

Her long ears twitched, hearing the water at a certain level, and she looked at the tub. Auslan hadn't moved from the far end of the room to approach it. She got up to stop the flow with a huff of annoyance.

"Much more, and it will overflow once you get in," she snapped, pointing at it. "Scrub ears to toes and wash your hair. I want you clean enough to please your most difficult Matron, understand?"

"Thank you, Elder," he whispered, sounding hoarse.

D'Shea returned to her desk.

She was distracted when Auslan complained, thoughtless and wordless, as he lowered himself into the tub. The Elder turned in her chair, but he was facing the other way.

"Are you injured?" she asked.

The Consort had not looked so in the cell, and he could walk, but she had not thought to check him for internal bleeding, leastwise smelling so ripe from the sweat of numerous Sisters.

At last, he picked up the washcloth and the soap. "No, Elder. Just sore."

"I imagine a healer can be sure of wounds not on the surface?"

His hands paused in their work, tremoring a moment but then resumed as he nodded. His hair was tangled and matted with fluids. "Yes, Elder. I am sure."

D'Shea was satisfied. "Curious, are you able to heal yourself in similar fashion to how you healed my novice?"

Now, he scrubbed a little harder.

"No, Elder," he said. "Not alone. If I am... bleeding how she was, I will die like any other without the help they need to live."

"Not alone," she repeated, confused but unwilling to sound it. "You are truly unable to use your healing magic on yourself?"

He held on to both sides of the tub for a moment like he was dizzy, his hand squeezing the cloth against the edge. D'Shea watched water dribble down the outside and onto her clean floor.

He's struggling to answer correctly.

"A discussion for another cycle," she said, turning to her mass of plans to organize. "Finish your bath, Auslan. Take the time needed."

In her periphery, she noted his shoulders lowered somewhat as she spoke softly Sirana's chosen name for him. He continued washing, and although he stayed under a long time when he dunked his sudsy head, the Consort with the gold streak in his hair *did* surface eventually, taking a deep breath.

The corner of the Sorceress's mouth tightened as she made another note. *Yes, healer, any of us can stay under only so long before drowning.*

Some for longer than others.

Two riding lizards travelled along the road, their riders guiding them well outside the center of Sivaraus, where canals, corrals, and lines of dung boxes aided in harvesting the meatiest mushrooms. Jaunda sighed, long and a bit too loud for anyone trying to claim stealth.

"Weren't we just here, Elder, you and me?"

D'Shea turned her head and smiled. "What do you mean, Lead?"

"I'm getting heavy been-here-done-this vibrations."

"It's been almost twenty turns."

"Already?"

"And I am certain you weren't cuddling a side-sitting companion on the way back then, either."

Jaunda grinned, looking down at her slender "cuddler." The last Consort had his wrists bound together in front, always visible, but otherwise was cradled comfortably across her lap and wrapped up in her red cloak while they rode away from the Cloister. On impulse, she lowered her nose to smell his fresh-washed hair. He slouched lower, kept his face buried in her uniform and avoided eye contact.

Cute, but not much of a challenge.

"Smells nice," she said aloud with a chuckle. "Better than me right now. You going to tell me why you waylaid me at the door? I didn't even take a sluice before smuggling this one out."

"You can guess, Jaunda. They wouldn't let him rest, and the Prime can always change her mind. Unlike a recruit, I don't see an end to it if we keep him in there."

"Aw, damn, so I missed my turn?" she laughed, noting that the bua kept his cool pretty well at that; he took a deeper breath but otherwise ignored her. Eyes hidden. "So, we taking him where I think we are?"

"Hmm. Where do you think, Lead?"

"Last time you and me headed out fast like this, Elder, wanting to make it before the Prime changed her mind."

"Remind me which time."

Jaunda snickered. "Let's see. How about 'First Daughter at House Thalluen died falling in a barn'."

"Oh, *that* time." D'Shea looked her way again, her wink barely visible by Dark Sight. "Yes, I'll need to speak with the Matron again in private. Like last time, you keep the one in the fire-seat under control. Don't let him panic."

"Gotcha, Elder. Hear that, Auslan? Don't panic. We got this."

The Consort gave no sign whether he believed them or not.

Rohenvi clutched her fist against her flat gut and tried to breathe slow and deep. One hand lightly resting atop the front of her desk, the Matron kept her back turned to the Elder Red Sister to allow the nausea and anger to pass.

The Red Sister waited patiently, having spoken her mind.

Why? Why me?

A stupid question, really, reflecting only the sense of her own impotence. This was the one Davrin in all of Sivaraus whom the

Matron didn't care whether she could see her or not. Elder D'Shea was always watching in some way; she knew so much about House Thalluen, more than Rohenvi herself, that the Matron had long ago accepted and resigned to the reality that this Elder Sorceress possessed all the power between them.

Many of her peers still deluded themselves, while Rohenvi had freed herself from any cautious Court-dance in D'Shea's presence. She would expose her back to D'Shea and feel nothing—no fear, no worry—having accepted that the blade or poison may come or may not, and it made no difference when she turned away.

Perhaps it was a sign of supplication for the Sorceress, who never abused it with physical harassment. The Elder was clearly the strongest investigating mind behind the Sisterhood, free of her own Courtly trappings as well.

"I swore never to have another Consort in this House," the Matron murmured, to speak this protest even as she knew the other would not change her mind. "I knew their offspring was tainted *long* before the Purge. My first two Daughters were proof enough."

"Not all the Consorts were tainted," D'Shea said. "And I believe there was something else to your first two Daughters in how they behaved."

Rohenvi turned to face her. "You are familiar with the Abyssal rituals they go through?"

"Intimately. I do not saddle you with a Priestess's misborn servant, Rohenvi. I would not have come here if I was not sure."

The Matron was silent for a moment. Then, "Rumor will spread, Elder. I can't keep *all* my servants and guards from mentioning him forever."

"You do better than most."

"Yes, but what happens to my lands, then? My House, which depends on me, when a Priestess hears we are keeping one Consort despite the Valsharess's Command?"

"I will prepare for that," said the Sorceress. "The truth that he *is* a hand-healer supersedes that he *was* a Consort. My advice would be to only mention the former to your subordinates. Auslan won't contradict you, he is both intelligent and terrified. He knows his position."

The Matron shook her head in denial. "He is too beautiful to be anything else! My House has *eyes*, Elder, like any other."

D'Shea lifted her chin. "Then this shall be another test of loyalty, will it not? I have heard how you've been 'cleaning House' since Kaltra's execution and Vekika's birth. The most ruthless you have ever been, Matron Thalluen."

Rohenvi blinked, a lump in her throat. "It is necessary."

"I agree. A Fourth Daughter is rarely born an Heir."

"Tell me, Elder… why you need to hide him from the Priestesses," she said. "I do not believe it is only that he is a healer."

"You are correct, Rohenvi, but for your own protection, I dare not." D'Shea smirked. "Rumor spreads."

Rohenvi tried to consider the other, obvious difficulties in having this Davrin under her roof. "I take it he is fertile."

"Very. But also well disciplined. He will not rut without your command regardless."

The Matron couldn't prevent a skeptical sound from escaping; she shook her head in reflex.

D'Shea arched one eyebrow in response. "Comment?"

"My other two Consorts were the same, but they never understood the nuances and let their vanity and flirting cause all sorts of trouble among my own."

"They were young, for one. Consider this one's age."

"His age, Elder?"

"Yes, Auslan is two and a half centuries. From the second generation, just after yours. All from the first are dead, are they not?"

Rohenvi nodded.

"Time has worn down his vanity and flirting. I think he has had enough of being used as an object and would welcome a period of celibacy. I say again, Matron, he is intelligent *and* experienced. He will follow your lead if you protect him, and I recommend against underestimating his ability to understand your nuances."

Matron Thalluen stood by her desk, frowning with her arms crossed beneath her breasts still swollen from nursing. "I have never heard you speak highly of any male. This comes close."

D'Shea smirked. "I have seen him under pressure lately. I know what it looks like when a bua breaks. He did not, though he may take time to recover."

"What do you mean?"

"You will accept guardianship of this Consort, Matron?"

"I do not have a choice, Elder."

"I would hear you speak it."

The Matron exhaled. "I will accept him and delay as I can his presence being known here."

"Good. Then you should know he was only recently pulled out of a cell where he had many... visitors. He has not slept a full eve nor eaten well for many cycles, and it seems he is not able to heal himself. He still recovers from this trial."

Rohenvi blanched to imagine, nodding. "I... see, Elder. You have no other place where you are sure he will be *allowed* to recover."

"Correct, Matron."

"Hm. Please, let me see him."

Auslan was curled on his side facing the door and the Red Sister sitting in a chair next to him; he stayed utterly silent lest he draw her attention. The bed within the quiet room was of the quality he had long been used to since leaving the Sanctuary for the Noble Houses, yet the contrast to his recent time on a cot or a stone floor astonished him, holding him in hazy wonder.

The Consort was dressed in a clean shirt and bottoms of solid black, the sleeves too long and half-covering his hands and the pant legs the same, falling to the floor. The scanty waist-wrap, stockings, and cloak had been destroyed, blackened without light upon some firestones D'Shea had led them to on their way here.

Elder D'Shea had kept him barefoot so he wouldn't get far if he ran away, and his wrists were tied together.

Auslan looked up at the short-haired warrior a couple times. He remembered the Lead Sister who had brought Sirana to him in the first place, demanding he heal her.

"I know you can!" she growled. "Shyntre told me you could save her. Do it! Whatever it costs."

And so he had. It had cost quite a lot.

Shyntre had outed the healer in a way where everything that followed was unavoidable. Auslan had been afraid but unsurprised when the Lead had put a bag over his head and dragged him out of House Itlaun along with the shaken and pregnant, but breathing, survivor.

Now Lead Jaunda had helped drag him out of the Cloister to bring him here. His body might wish for a time that it had been sooner, but Auslan wouldn't complain aloud. The soreness would recede.

He wasn't sure if he believed what she had said about "missing her turn," whether she would have mounted him along with the rest if she'd discovered him in solitary. Regardless, his heart sped up, and he broke into a sweat again. The Red Sister noticed.

"Easy," she murmured, sounding like she wasn't thinking of fucking him. "You're safe."

He swallowed. "May I speak?"

She shrugged. "If you want."

He hesitated, never having heard that before.

He whispered, "Wh-where are we?"

Jaunda looked at him. "I told you, House Thalluen."

Auslan shook his head against the pillow. "Why here?"

She made a face like she thought he was pranking her but then blinked. "Oh, wait. You never knew Sirana's full name, did you?"

He stared. *It can't be.*

Jaunda bared her teeth. "Sirana Thalluensareci."

He was in Sirana's *Mother's* House? His heart kept pounding.

Jaunda shrugged again. "You might as well know before she gets here. Watch your expression. They look alike."

Oh, Goddess...

"D-does the Matron *know* what happened to her Daughter?"

"Probably not yet, if I know my Elder. Don't make the connection *for* her, bua, she doesn't like Consorts. You're here because Elder D'Shea and Matron Thalluen make private deals, and have for a long time, not because you impregnated Rohenvi's Daughter, as if she should give a single fuck about you on that account. Got it?"

He nodded earnestly. "Understood, Lead."

Jaunda had been watching the door but glanced down at his wide, sober eyes with a smirk. "You say that well as any recruit, Consort."

He winced. "Please... do not call me that anymore, Lead? I am Auslan."

She grunted. "Fine. Auslan."

They had resumed silence until the two elder females joined them—and not through the hallway door he had been listening toward.

D'Shea and Sirana's Mother entered through a corner panel.

Auslan sat up in alarm, his hands bound, and he nearly fell backward again. Jaunda planted a heavy, gloved hand on his shoulder to hold him upright and in place. He trembled, unable to bring his body's responses under control; it was unnerving. One corner of the Elder's mouth rose and tightened to see him, and the Lead stood up to acknowledge the two, taking her hand away. Auslan winced to feel how uncomfortable it was to sit like upright like this.

I should be on my knees regardless.

He got in position, watching them secure the room. Jaunda was correct; Sirana looked like her Mother. However, he did not miss that this mature female was not pleased to be here.

She doesn't like Consorts.

There were no pleasantries. D'Shea began speaking.

"Auslan, meet your Matron and protector for the time being, Rohenvi Thalluen. This is temporary, but I expect exemplary obedience, as your presence here puts her House at risk."

He bowed, distressed that he couldn't seem to stop his random shaking. "Matron Thalluen. I-I will obey you in all you say."

His eyes were down, but he heard the Matron say, as if resigned, "You may remove the ropes, Elder Sister."

"You do the honors," D'Shea suggested. "A formal transference."

"Without witnesses," Rohenvi remarked.

"Jaunda's testimony always counts, you know this."

With a sigh, the Matron accepted a dagger from the Sorceress and approached the bed. Auslan could smell her soap and cleanliness as she leaned above him, reaching for his bound wrists. He lifted them up for her, his eyes drawn to the dark cleavage of her breasts. How full they were, filling out a regular, every-cycle gown to straining. There was a subtle stain over one nipple, once damp but now dry. He knew the signs.

She's nursing.

There was an infant in the House.

And I am putting this at risk as well.

Colliding with this thought was the single, sharp cut which released his hands and made him gasp; his member began to swell in relief. He dragged the pillow to him and hugged it, willing to look the fragile fool over insulting the Matron with an ill-timed erection.

"Thank you, Matron."

She didn't reply but took hold of his chin instead, lifting his eyes. Hundreds of tiny bumps arose on his skin underneath his dark clothing.

"Look up," she demanded.

He did, but he never remembered any Matron doing this at the first touch. His cock had little chance of shrinking quickly, studying the Matron's face as she touched him, looking her in the eyes. Now he knew where Sirana got her impulses, although Rohenvi's gaze was distinct, her eyes a similar scarlet color to his own.

"You will not leave this room until I say," she ordered. "I must consider this disruption carefully."

"Yes, Matron."

"Are you ready to hear your code of conduct?"

"I am, Matron."

"You will not use your Consort charms on anyone here, cait or bua. You will not show your naked body at all in view of others, including me. You will be modest at all times unless you are alone in this room."

"Yes, Matron."

"You will neither suggest nor accept touches or propositions from caits or buas, either of my House or any visitor. You will inform me if they happen, and without delay. No teasing or mutual climaxes allowed, whether or not it is for breeding. Is every word I've said clear as crystal, Auslan?"

He was further relieved at these restrictions, how thorough they were without any room for doubt how to interpret them. Under the pillow, his prick grew harder. "Clear as crystal, Matron. I will obey and follow this conduct in your House."

Rohenvi's face drew down in concern, like she was having doubts. She released his chin and straightened up. "I am told you are a mage healer, by touch. Is this true?"

All three females could hear his heart again.

"Yes, Matron," he whispered.

Sirana's Mother wetted her lips and considered. "Are you willing to tend illness or injury while you are here, should I request it?"

Auslan blinked, quite confused. "As you wish, Matron. I obey you in all things."

Rohenvi shook her head. "No. Healing like this is fouled when it is coerced. This inborn talent, that alone is yours, Auslan. You may refuse this one task without retaliation from me. I will only request."

Auslan stared at her in disbelief, and a glance at D'Shea and Jaunda reflected a similar, if minor, bafflement. He didn't see the harm in such a promise, though he had never, and would never, refuse the task.

"Very well, Matron. I will consider healing for you, if you ask."

This satisfied her; Rohenvi confirmed her acceptance of his presence with Elder D'Shea, who smiled her own satisfaction. Before too long, the Red Sisters moved on to the next problem needing a solution, and Auslan sat in the quiet room which felt unreal, like in a dreamscape.

No longer Consort or companion. Neither prisoner, nor servant, nor free body. Without an assigned place in Sivaraus.

Hidden away, lingering unseen, he was a ghost in the Deepearth.

"Vanry, you're back so soon?" Natia cried as soon as the old male slipped into the nursery.

"Shhh, the heir sleeps," he shushed with a smile, which creased his eyes like no one else. "And I haven't informed the Matron yet."

The Davrin child ran to him as he kneeled, muttering her apologies into his coat as she clung to him for a lengthy hug. He squeezed and held on, both of them quiet.

Only my sire would hug me this long before.

The governor had shown up shortly after her sire died. He was hired to help with the baby just after birth, and he had also really liked the young cait attending her Matron. Natia liked him, too, and wished he would stay.

Just live here to be a tutor in the nursery.

She had already suggested it. Vanry had told her he couldn't but not why. *She* didn't see why not, if he was a commoner for hire anyway.

A commoner like me.

Matron Rohenvi was teaching Natia how to help with the baby, with the cleaning, with attending her, serving her around guests… while her Mother would have been making potions in a shop.

Miss her… and Treyl… now Vanry says he can't stay, either! Mata!

Her visiting governor leaned to look at her face. "Natia? Are you well?"

"Fine! I'm not crying." She rubbed her eyes. "They itch."

He smiled. "I know. Want to show me Vekika?"

"You know where she is."

"I got lost last time without you."

"Did not!" She struggled *not* to smile. *Braqth damn it.*

Still, she clasped and held his hand on the way to the quiet heir's cradle. They would take turns holding and cleaning her while they waited for the Matron to return from whatever had been so important to interrupt feeding time.

Rohenvi's mind was full of D'Shea's plans—real and imagined— when she returned to her Daughter's nursery. Inside, a rugged, male commoner was chatting with Natia and holding Vekika. She was so startled that she nearly blurted his name.

"Oh!" she gasped. "Um. Vanry. Did you forget something?"

The mature male stood, smiled, and bowed formally while holding her Daughter carefully in both arms. "No, Matron. I was passing through the area and came upon news you may consider important. Whenever you wish."

"Ah, I see. Well, let me feed the baby, and we'll talk in private."

Rohenvi had allowed Vekika to suckle around anyone in the House since she was born, even in front of the Conceiver—of all guests—and her third Daughter, a Red Sister. This simple thing was a change for everyone except Natia, who found nothing unusual in the ritual, and had not noticed the way this common male watched the Matron in her nursery.

Rohenvi felt her cheeks become warm, however, as she kept a placid face and did not rush her child's feeding.

In time, all duties delegated, tended, or balanced, and the Matron Thalluen saw the hired male alone in her office where she had recently been with the Elder Sorceress. She allowed him to check for himself that D'Shea had not left anything behind to spy in this space.

"I have another room as needed," she suggested serenely, yet his mouth twitched as if she had made innuendo.

★No, here,★ he signed. ★I cannot stay long.★

The Matron nodded. *Always the case, it seems.*

★The General Rausery will be gone from Sivaraus for some time. Several quad-spans, at least.★

Rohenvi's eyes widened. *Now?! So soon after the purge when the Houses are still in chaos?* She said nothing, keeping her hands folded in front of her, alert to his every hand move.

★Something happened to Sirana on mission—★

The Matron gasped.

★—which triggered the purge. She is alive, as is Gaelan, but they have both been sent away with Rausery. I don't know when or if they will be coming back.★

She stood there, body stiff and throat tight, and waited for what else he could share. He always knew more than he said.

Lead Jaunda is preparing for a mission in the deep-trader territory, he continued, his expression firm, red eyes unblinking. *She is the Red Sister who came here with Elder D'Shea.*

Rohenvi signed confirmation of whom they spoke.

I must know what the Elder asked of you.

She hesitated.

Please, Matron. His bright, intelligent eyes gazed into hers. *I must know, or I can't help this House *and* help hold Sivaraus together during this.*

Is it that bad?

He could read her expression; his was grave. *The cracks are showing, Matron. Something *will* get through them. It's just a matter of when and what.*

Matron Thalluen had heard claims like this from many others in the past; others who always wanted something from her. Rohenvi had reason to believe none of them; she had reason to believe *him*.

She took one slow breath and raised her hands, preparing to speak in the silent tongue of the Davrin. Her shadowy guest read them carefully without interruption. When she finished, putting her hands before her again, she could see he was confused as she was why this last Royal Consort was alive, why he was banished here after being tormented by the Sisterhood.

Not enlightening, but helpful to know if he needs a healer.

Regardless, she would do what she had agreed with D'Shea.

I will come around for updates, he promised.

As you wish.

When he was about to take his leave, Rohenvi reached out and grasped the older male's hand as tightly as Natia had. She didn't want him to go just yet; he saw it in her gaze.

Will you...? she signed, her mouth twitching. *Please. Even quickly.*

His face warmed in the dim of her office; he swallowed then smirked, playfully. *So hungry this soon after giving life, Matron?*

Rohenvi leaned against her desk and beckoned him. *I starve. Come here, forgettable one.*

Forgotten by all but you.

Once his arms were around her, she pressed her mouth to his, bringing him close. She lifted her gown, her legs rose to clasp around his waist, and they broke a kiss to work on opening his trousers. Rohenvi wanted to *free* him.

With his hot erection pressed to her thigh, they each paused again, tilting their sharp ears to listen. Then the Matron encircled her fingers around his shaft; she pressed the head into her slit. Her sex pulsed once in welcome, and he pushed his hips forward.

She gasped. "Ruk!"

His cock halfway in, the mature Davrin pulled back and lunged inside her again.

"Yes!"

She nipped his ear, and he seized her full hips for leverage, preparing for more. Rohenvi gripped his shoulders in anticipation.

"Yes, Ruk... *Oh!* Fuck me..."

Grinding against him, pleasure roaring through her, the Matron muffled her moan against his unwashed neck, breathing his musky scent. Then things became truly slick between her and this common-blood traveler between her legs.

"Ruk, don't dare pull out of me until you've come..."

"As you wish, Matron," he gasped, breathing to control his stamina.

She moaned, her clenching sex preparing to come on his cock. She would take what she could have right now.

Perhaps some turn, he would choose to stay with her, always.

CHAPTER 14

"My Queen, you summoned?"

"Yes, Taneous."

"Phaelous, your Majesty," said the Headmaster with tranquil patience. "Taneous was my Grandsire."

The Valsharess was silent for a time, staring at Her ornate mirror, tawny eyes tracing the curves and complexities of the frame, only glancing at the reflective surface.

"I was thinking of House Ja'Prohn. Of Taneous, and Captain Xala."

This time, Phaelous did not correct Her. General Xala had died before he was born; he'd never known her. *'Captain' must be long before my time.*

"Yes, my Queen."

"He was quite brilliant, your Grandsire," She continued. "He found so many solutions to help our survival at its darkest. If only he and Y'shir hadn't…"

Phaelous listened. Who was Y'shir?

The Valsharess paused, frowned into the mirror and shook her head, turning around to face him. She stepped closer, Her slippers purely silent upon plush carpet, as if the Queen glided above the stone toward him. She lifted Her bejeweled hand.

Phaelous didn't resist as She took hold of his jaw, lifting and turning it so the candlelight in Her chambers would catch the gold flecks inside the red irises of his eyes. He knew from previous lessons to keep his eyes open and look directly at Her. He was one of the few of whom this was expected.

Satisfied with whatever She saw, the Valsharess released him with no further comment.

"What have you found among Wilsira's possessions, Phaelous?" She asked, Her voice clear and strong once again. She was fully present with him.

"Notes of bloodlines, I believe," he answered. "But it will take some time to decipher her code."

The Valsharess smiled a little, the fine lines in Her skin more apparent than his. "You taught her how. You can undo it."

"Yes, my Queen, but she used a demonic phonetic which is unfamiliar to me, and I don't suggest giving Tarra unfettered access. I may need *your* eyes to further guide me, your Majesty."

She nodded without resistance. "Collect them at your leisure, Headmaster, and bring them to Us. We shall look, though this pursuit is not a priority."

"Yes, my Queen."

"What else remains of the Conceiver's work?"

"Three commoners are gestating new would-be Consorts in three cells. Two are early enough to abort the tainted growth and rehabilitate the matas. One is viable, and the auras are entwined enough, it may kill her if we try."

"She is common, Phaelous, that is your answer."

"The purge left us with many voids seeking to be filled, my Queen," he protested carefully, "and when the Elder Mind attacks, we will need our whole population to survive it, every servant and crafter and slave." Phaelous paused. "I would recommend suspending all Sanctuary rituals for the time being, should any Priestess ask to use it as a shortcut. We cannot afford to keep killing young caits and buas when they are healthy and untainted, and we shall need every pair of hands soon, even male ones."

The Valsharess *was* listening to him, but Her eyes had drifted far away again. "War... Once again. Always war."

"Your Majesty has Seen it," the Headmaster bowed. "Like my sire and grandsire before me, I seek solutions to safeguard the foundation of Sivaraus entwined with what my Queen grants me to know of our people's future."

She was contemplative. Her eyes sought some place beyond the stone walls.

"Come with Us to the Forming Pit," She commanded, stepping toward the chamber doors without checking that he followed. "We wish to See something."

Of course, the Headmaster followed his Queen, hoping the Drider Mistress didn't appear to obstruct them.

This hope was short-lived.

"Valsharesss," greeted the fanged, wild-haired Davrin as they turned a corner.

"Auranka," acknowledged the Queen.

Wearing a sleeveless, purple gown she would shed at an instant, Auranka bowed low, her body controlled with a predator's smooth grace, despite the unusually large size of her always-lactating breasts.

"Where do you go without proper essscort?"

"Nowhere," replied the Queen, snapping Her fingers. "Come."

The dark spots on Auranka's temples mimicked pairs of spider eyes winking as she simpered toward Phaelous. "Yesss, my Queen."

The Headmaster continued on without visible reaction, though he was not eager to be in this particular space once again with the former Priestess. No doubt she would draw upon the memories needed to make it as disruptive and unproductive as possible. Phaelous would go and stay focused, nonetheless.

He must do this if Bathila and the others were ever to be released.

This was only the beginning of his penance.

"You must eat, you stupid thing!" Tarra hissed while she kneeled outside the cell bars.

The comatose commoner stared at her blankly, barely chewing the mash spooned between her lips and forgetting to swallow before some oozed back out with her spittle. The Priestess tossed the utensil into the mush with a *thup* and set the bowl on the dank floor.

A servant should be doing this.

But, for now, all except her and Phaelous were forbidden from entering the Forming Pit. No exceptions.

Frustrated and disgusted, the Priestess Lelinahdara stood up, smoothing her plain black robe made special for this task; her others were too fine and elegant to tolerate collecting unknowable stains down here.

The divine mage walked away from the cell and to the end of the short hallway for the fifth or sixth time. She needed to see the exclusive altar long ago hidden away from the rest of the Priestesses by the Conceiver. Tarra could taste the power upon her tongue, soaking up the gossamer layers for centuries. She could almost see which runes lit up and linked with others engraved into the ceiling and walls and floor into an intricate pattern in three dimensions.

That would have been D'Shea's doing when she was held here, as laden with Shyntre as Bathila is with her tainted unborn.

Tarra had been a young novice at the time, not yet conceived of her Sathoet, when she had tended the pregnant Red Sister. Like many, she had known this place had existed but didn't know where it was or how to reach it. She had only ever drawn the scantest description from a delirious Sorceress of what lay down here, though she had long kept seeking despite the effective compulsion laid upon D'Shea.

What could Tarra offer the Queen to improve the use of such a potent fertility focus?

Surely, She won't have it destroyed. It's too valuable.

Tarra felt eyes on her and looked behind her at the cages she had just passed. There were two other prisoners who hadn't yet gone deaf, blind, and mute with the swelling of their bellies. The young caits were hopeful and terrified at once to learn their original Priestess was dead; they hadn't been here as long as Bathila and watched Lelinahdara's every move.

A pity they can't remember how they arrived here or what happened after they did.

Yet given Sirana's strange response to the special breed of buas once living on the Fourth floor of the Sanctuary, and given the hints during the throne room trial of what occurred between Wilsira and the novice Red Sister, with Kerse in the middle…

Mere commoners stand not a chance of controlling their will under such geas.

Just as Tarra convinced herself that her time would be better spent studying the altar up close, three Davrin arrived inside the jump circle and gave her a start. Sheer age and power flooded the small space, and a rushing chain response among the runes numbed her sense and blinded her mage's eyes for a lingering instant. The commoners mewled. The Priestess choked on her greeting.

"My Queen!"

Tarra bowed and, though her jangled nerves had not yet begun to settle, made out Headmaster Phaelous with the Drider Mistress directly behind him.

Why were they here? What had he told them?

Tagging the heels of these concerns was the stark remembrance of her youth. The former Liaison believed herself a peer with Elder D'Shea even being two centuries younger; Tarra's swift rise in the Sanctuary reflected it, and caits such as the unfaithful Sirana were mere children to her, barely learning how to fuck in her red uniform.

Yet, before these three, the Priestess was an infant learning to crawl.

"Confessor," acknowledged the Valsharess, stepping out of the circle and upon the dank floor with little hesitation compared to Tarra's first time. "Tell Us what you have learned thus far."

A vague and abrupt command that must be obeyed. Nonetheless, the Priestess was distracted by the Drider Mistress breaking from the three and slinking along the walls, studying the runes while giggling under her breath. The small hairs on Tarra's forearms stood up as the transformed Priestess winked at her and slipped past and into the hallway.

"Confessor."

Tarra blinked and bowed again, speaking the correct apology while Phaelous remained near. She glanced again at the two conscious prisoners, who were curled into balls and covering their ears with their dark hands, trembling as Auranka came near, hissing something softly to them.

"Uhm, three matas, your Highness. Two just started, one nearly to birth."

"Yes, We know. You will flush out the two in early state without ritual."

Without ritual? How?

"Place them in the dungeon and make certain they remember nothing before being released."

Tarra shivered in shock. She had never—*never!*—heard of such a command. "M-My Queen, I…"

"Phaelous will provide the potion. You are to see it complete."

Tarra's mouth nearly twisted, but she watched herself as she flicked a look at him. *Of course, him. How could I forget?*

She had never liked a male having this arcane knowledge. It was time to learn it herself.

Tarra bowed. "Yes, Majesty. And the one close to her time?"

She motioned behind her to indicate the commoner Bathila, and the Valsharess nodded though She could not see the prisoner.

"Keep her healthy and see through to the birthing. Inform Us, for We shall attend it. If she may be transferred to the dungeon with the others to recover afterward, We shall do this."

And the tainted infant? When that was not forthcoming, Tarra knew she must wait to know. "Yes, my Queen."

Phaelous had his head turned, closely watching Auranka, who had returned from teasing the prisoners and followed the wall away from Tarra. The Drider Mistress lightly brushed hooked fingertips along some of the runes, and one flared a bright red-gold. The former Priestess quietly hissed, taking her hand away. The Headmaster had no change in expression but studied her every move. Tarra wondered what in the Deepearth was going on.

"Confessor."

She snapped her eyes forward. "Yes, Valsharess."

The Queen's tawny eyes were resting upon the altar in the center of the open space, and the Confessor's gaze followed. The risen, dark basalt possessed runes of its own while sitting in the center of an extending web of them, the chiseled carvings crawling over most surfaces. There were only a few unmarked paths where it was safe to walk, though the Drider Mistress had no trouble prancing over and around them, seeming to set off no ill effect.

Yet.

Perhaps that was why Phaelous was watching her.

"Do not change anything of that altar," the Queen commanded. "Keep it secret and protected for now."

Tarra wanted to exhale with relief. "Yes, your Highness."

"Do not use it."

Those semi-translucent eyes like topaz turned slowly and captured Tarra's directly. The young Priestess was unexpectedly required to resist emptying her bladder in her dark robes.

"On pain of sacrifice," She said. "Do not experiment."

Tarra was dismayed. "Yes, your Majesty. I will not use it."

The waiting royal nodded slowly, expecting it done.

"My Queen?"

"Yes, Confessor?"

"What of the... bloodlines?" Tarra asked. "I had thought to use these runes to help decipher Wilsira's code."

The Valsharess looked at Phaelous, whose attention was immediately given to Her, nearly such that one would think he had never been distracted. "We will give you both a place to start. Work on it as you are able but do not ignore your other tasks on account."

Well enough. Tarra bowed. "Thank you, my Queen."

Soon after, the Confessor was alone in the Forming Pit, after having watched a creeping, feral Drider Mistress disengage from teasing prisoners or prodding runes. She had almost snuggled up to Phaelous's side behind the Queen's back, moments before they vanished elsewhere with a pulse of power. If Auranka had done it to unnerve him, well—

I might guess all the Headmaster's nerves are dead at this point, for how much satisfaction he gives any female anymore.

The only time Tarra had witnessed any loss of control whatsoever in the old male had been on account of D'Shea. But given what history the Confessor knew about the Sorceress's extinct House and the Headmaster's House—faded behind the scenes and out of public memory—that did not surprise her.

The arcane mages of D'Shea and Ja'Prohn always sparked fires with their friction.

When someone finally did come to Shyntre's room in the Wizard's Tower, it was one of the last Davrin he would have wanted to see again.

"Get cleaned up, trull," said the Prime, clearly furious having been saddled with this task. "You're coming with me."

His Headmaster remained nearby, watching in silence every moment the First Sister was there crowding his doorway. She was too disgusted to step inside.

Shyntre *had* slept, he believed, but he didn't know how much time had passed since those first cycles of relentless worry and debilitating turmoil. Eventually, the drowning sense of horror had receded from his inability to bear it any longer, and he had lain in a stupor ever since. Without solid food, only liquid had passed into his chamber's waste disposal.

This seemed unlike him. Since when did he go catatonic from something imagined? Or something *real*, for that matter?

"Move!" roared the Prime.

Shyntre moved, dizzy and shaking from weakness and lack of food. His Headmaster entered the room to help.

"D-Don't touch me," he muttered, jerking his arm out of its sleeve.

"Shyntre," Phaelous said, "rein it in. You are being taken to see the Queen."

No, not again, so soon.

Shyntre tolerated the help; he knew he needed it. The Headmaster himself gave his student-son a quick wipe down to remove the layers of dried sweat and helped him into fresh robes from his wardrobe. Finally, Phaelous uncorked a vial from his deep pocket and lifted it close to the bua's lips.

"Wh-what is it?" asked the younger.

"It will keep you calm," the Headmaster answered, "and allow you to eat."

"Drink it, shit smear," growled the Prime. "I'm busy, don't have time for your attitude."

If she had ever been allowed to try to beat the attitude out of him, she'd have done it.

His trepidation remained, but Shyntre quaffed the oddly fragrant liquid and swallowed without tasting it much. Phaelous placed an arm around his shoulders, guiding him out of the room and to a jump circle on the top floor. It took them directly to a locked room within the Palace; he recognized the scent. Stepping out into the hallway, the illustrious entry to Queen's Chambers was on the right.

"Go back to the Tower, Phaelous," snarled the oldest Sister. "I'll take it from here."

Shyntre would have reacted with loud, verbal alarm without that potion, but his head felt wrapped in guarro's wool. He met his sire's eyes, gold-flecked like his, who nodded his encouragement and returned to the jump circle. With the disappearance of the only male and the only Davrin who held any care for him at all, Shyntre had the brief thought to run.

To find a window and jump out.

The young wizard stood trembling, resisting all action upon that disturbing, livid impulse. *That isn't me. I'm not... I'm not that weak.*

Yet, why did it seem he had tried before?

I've never tried to escape that way.

Yes, he had. He thought the Prime had been there to stop him.

Shyntre shook his head. *Argh! Stop! What in the Abyss was in that vial?*

The Prime placed her hand on the panel, her silent announcement of arrival. One heavy, ornate door opened on its own, and they crossed the threshold. There were multiple rooms and a small hallway inside; Shyntre could see no private resting space from where he stood upon thick carpet. With just the couple of lounges and tables and all those tapestries and statues, this was a reception area.

Still, he knew where this first room would lead him, if he walked farther in.

The Valsharess emerged from Her hallway, wearing a beautiful but simple purple robe, showing a hint of cleavage, the material a bit too thin to keep nipples from showing when turgid. The Queen's pure blonde hair was down and hanging over one shoulder, plaited in the simplest way. *Too* simple for one in the peak august role in Sivaraus.

The next panicked instant, Shyntre's focus was pinned to the intricate colors and patterns of the carpet. Next to him, the Prime bowed.

"Here he is, my Queen."

"Thank you, Fadele. Leave us and return to your tasks."

"How will he get back to the Tower, your Majesty?"

"We will see to it. You may go."

With a pause and rumbling acknowledgement, the First Sister bowed and saw herself out, securing the door behind her. Shyntre wondered why, if he felt so dizzy as to pass out from not having eaten in cycles, it hadn't happened yet?

He waited in silence.

"Tell Us who you are," She commanded.

He swallowed. "Shyntre, son of Elder D'Shea and Headmaster Phaelous."

The Queen was quiet. Was She displeased? He dared not look at Her face to check.

"Now tell Us what you have done."

He stood frozen. What had he done? Which time? What did She want to hear? Shyntre selected something. "I... left the Wizard's Tower to tell the Sisterhood of a rogue Sathoet having escaped with a hostage."

"Sirana," the Queen said, cutting to the quick. "She was tainted by rogue ritual, then cleansed in a healing We find ...curious. Her fertility was at its peak, and you *laid* with her. Your auras entwined *many* times. We could *taste* you upon her. Everywhere."

Shyntre's face flushed deeply. The memories of Sirana's body, wet and hot around him, her cries of pleasure, her laughter and playful bites as she encouraged him, all turned his blood to lava. He had never felt equal and admired while rutting with a female. Except with her.

The following shame and sweeping sense of exposure surprised him.

"We know what you've done, Son, and why."

He couldn't speak. His thoughts grew hazier since taking the vial his Headmaster offered.

"She was pregnant with your child. You *tested* Us. We… could not kill her by Our Hand." The Valsharess came closer, until he could smell Her fragrance. "So. We have sent her to serve Us instead, and perhaps she will help Us save Our people. Let the Visions play forward, beautiful bua. We shall See what comes, one day at a time."

Her warm, dry fingers touched his chin, and the wizard's cheeks were wet with tears the moment he blinked. Her manicured thumb touched his lower lip, feeling it quiver. She smiled a little.

What's wrong with me?

"We imagine you will dream of her," said the Queen, Her voice sounding distant. "And We shall be there. We *must* know where she goes. What she sees. Who she finds to aid her. This is the *only* way We have a chance to avoid consumption by the Broken One's children. Do you understand?"

Nothing. He understood not one word She said.

"Mazdel. Listen."

Shyntre blinked. *That's not my name.*

"You will not resist. You will yield your dreams of Sirana to your Mother."

*She is **mad**.*

"We have made a room for you here to sleep."

No…

"You will stay close to Us, and the dreams will come."

Finally, blessedly, Shyntre passed out from the strain and lack of food, collapsing unhurt onto the thick carpet in his Queen's private chambers.

His dreams slowly changed as time inevitably passed in the quiet room which he was not allowed to leave unbidden. From dark and filled with shadows and sheer, blade-sharp threads binding him, to a golden light slowly grew. The barren, damp stone beneath his feet changed to warm, dry sand. A blurry wave of red and blue illuminated to sweeping dunes and clear weather above.

And an ancient marketplace formed, complete with a familiar, colorful tent and Master Toushek hawking his wares.

Oh, no. Him. Lead her away, don't let him see her. Not yet, it's too soon.

Her sapphire-blue eyes were stunning in daylight, as he had always known they would be. The cait in uniform allowed him to take her gloved hand and urge her away, and in the alley where they rested in shade, he tasted the grey mist flowing in from Koorul, drifting from leagues and leagues away. He felt a tiny burst of hope.

That's a start, if they can forgive. May she ask for me at the crossroads.

Once she had escaped Reverie and all unfriendly eyes, he stood there alone, not yet ready to return. Turning in place, he read the sands and their sign. The canyons of Koorul lay directly behind him, a nexus twisting and wending in every direction. V'Gedra was to his right, and the prison and the pillar were not far South of the ancient capital city. He stood outside of all of it.

Why had he begun here? Why this small, desert town, whose only note of worth was a military presence, a natural spring, and robust trade for the area?

"Avel!" someone long-dead cried, and he turned to greet her.

"...Zorsha?"

The young Elf was deeply tanned, her hair blonde-white. She wore loose, army garb that blended in with the desert, and by the smell of her sweat as she hugged him, she had just finished her grunt work. She leaned back, light green eyes twinkling as she held up a clinking coin pouch. He could smell the metal inside.

"I just got paid, pretty bua," she said. "Lookin' for some no-binds fun. Unless you *want* the binds, of course."

He grinned, lifting his smoke-black hand and caressing her breast through the rough fabric. "Looking for fun? You've come to the right side of town, my quivering cait."

"Not yet, I'm not." She seized an excited kiss. "And it's definitely the *wrong* side. That's why I'm here."

He had always been a whore for as long as he could remember, yet he didn't mind that in this dream. He knew what he wanted, and what she wanted; it was his choice to offer, and her choice to accept. He was a free will and body. Like any trader here, he kept every gold coin he earned.

Much later that night, Zorsha had left his pleasure room sighing in satisfaction and, with that adorable smirk, playfully arranged her coins one-by-one upon his bare, black chest. After she was gone, as he swept the money into his small chest of treasure, Avel remembered.

His heart stopped midbeat.

He remembered.

The noise, the rising voices. His sire, Szoroan, tried to bar the entrance. The door broke outward, letting in the Moonless night.

"Run, Avel!"

The Blade Singer had turned his swords and cast a concussive sphere, which was returned upon at him in a blink. The deep shudder as it struck Szoroan could be felt throughout the dwelling, and as he collapsed, blood spontaneously flowed from the Davrin's ears and mouth.

"No!"

Avel froze as the fearsome, tawny-eyed sorceress strode into the room with black cloak flowing. She approached his sire, leaned down to grip him by his throat. She didn't look muscular enough to pull him to his feet with one arm, though his feet were dangling when she had him pressed to the wall.

"You'd dare attack me, Szoroan?"

"I-I...."

"Think harder, Blade Singer. Remember me?"

"I-Ishuna...?"

"Yes, old lover. I am here. I have found you at last."

Avel jerked in shock as black and purple flames erupted around the sorceress's free fist, and she jammed it beneath his rib cage to seize his heart. Red blood poured down onto the stone floor, and the room filled with someone screaming.

Someone grabbed him, kept him on his feet. An older female's voice spoke in his ear. "Stop it. Stop it, Mazdel!"

His eyes rolled up as his vision swam, and she pinched a nerve. The fire climbing his back and into his head kept him awake.

"Now is not the time to faint. This is your Mother. Show some respect."

The sorceress dropped the corpse of his sire and turned around to look at him with yellow eyes sparking, her forearm caked in red and gore.

"I-I'm not who y-you think I am!" Avel pleaded as she came closer, filling his vision. "Y-you've made a mistake! I'm a soldier's son! I'm just a whore!"

The sorceress was smirking at him, and after a beat she flicked a few spatters of Szoroan's blood onto his face and whispered a command word. It felt for a moment like something had been ripped off the bottom of his brainpan and turned over so she could examine what was underneath.

Avel screamed harshly as his voice broke on a sob.

She had his chin gripped in her clean hand and forced him to look her in the eyes. Her face changed so completely, it stunned him. A beautiful, soft smile that clashed with all the violence and horror in the room.

"Mazdel. It *is* you."

"I-I don't know who you are…" he whispered, pleading.

His soft voice sank like water into sand. While the older female held him trapped, the sorceress commanded another in the room.

"You, hand me that mirror."

Once she had it in her bloody grip, the sorceress held it up in front of him.

"Look! Do you see it now? Do you?"

Avel blinked through his tears, seeing how terrified he looked. But he could also see that the familiar gold flecks in his red eyes weren't just flecks anymore. The yellow sheen had filled in and overtaken all the dark red of his irises.

His eyes were metallic, like pure gold coins.

He looked away, only to see the corpse of the Davrin who had raised him.

"I've uncovered the mask they put you in," she said with triumph. "I am glad to see you well, Mazdel."

"I am Avel!" he shouted, and she slapped him.

"Quiet. You know better."

The powerful sorceress took him by both sides of his face then, stroking as if to soothe the strike she delivered and not seeming to realize she was smearing Szoroan's blood over half his face. He trembled in the officer's grip, wanting to run.

To disappear. To hide from this bad dream.

"This humiliation ceases now," she promised. "No selling your body for coin. You are *far* more than a whore, my son. I will protect you. You don't have to worry anymore."

Avel lifted his head slowly, gold eyes locking onto ones like smoke-tinted topaz. Who was this? Who was this insane murderer who ripped out hearts and tore open minds?

"You are *not* my Mother," he whispered. "You'll never be."

The words hit harder for not having been a shout. The sorceress recoiled; he'd never forget the look on her face.

"Ishuna," the warrior behind him pleaded softly, desperation in her voice. "Give him time. He's in shock. He'll come around."

The sorceress did not acknowledge her; this stranger only glared at him as if to set him aflame.

Finally she commanded, "Captain. Bind him. And bring him."

Something tickled his arm like spider's legs, and he jolted upright on the bed, scrambling the opposite way.

Only for his forehead to be stopped by the wall.

He pressed to it, shivering, his head aching. He tried to get the smell of blood and acrid magic out of his nose.

"S-sorry," said a young voice. "You were in bad Reverie, making noise."

Auslan blinked once, and again, blinking until he could see something with his own eyes. *Anything.* He made out the shape of a young cait kneeling on the floor by his bed, looking at him with large, concerned eyes.

"Where am I?" he asked in the barest whisper.

She lowered her voice, too. "House Thalluen. Red Sisters brought you here."

He reentered the Deepearth clasping to that anchor. *Red Sisters. Sirana.*

"Apologies, young mistress," he murmured, "that I was noisy."

She shrugged, rolling the hem of her nice shirt. "Not a mistress. Just a servant. Don't want others to hear you." She craned her neck. "You act like you've been hurt."

Auslan stared at her, dismayed to see recognition in the child's face, that she already knew the essence of its cause. He swallowed. "It will fade. Thank you for waking me. What is your name?"

"Natia. Yours?"

"Auslan." He smiled as he said it, reflecting this was the first time he had introduced himself as such.

Natia responded to his smile, giving a tiny one of her own. "You're pretty."

"Uhm?"

His stomach growled, and the cait perked up. "And you're hungry?"

"...Yes."

"I'll get something."

She was gone before he could stop her, and it seemed she was a stealthy one; she returned alone. He was grateful for whatever she brought, beginning to chew and swallow before she lit the dim candle and he could see he was eating padcakes. Next, he guzzled the large cup of cold sweet-taze. He was finished before he realized it could be poisoned, and he considered retching it back out.

No. Lead Jaunda said I was safe.

Either way, he would find out in time how much Matron Thalluen "didn't like" Consorts. Meanwhile, Natia watched every motion with eyes like sparkling garnet, clearly curious about him. He let her get her fill of his face; he could never stop females looking at him anyway, even if they were too young to think much of him besides that he was "pretty."

"What point of the cycle is it?" he asked when the food and drink had settled peacefully.

"Middle of Matron's Reverie." Natia yawned as she said it.

"Ah. Shouldn't you be resting as well? Or are you on a different work pattern?"

"Should be sleeping," she muttered guiltily. "Tired of sharing with the baby."

"Your bed is in the nursery?"

Natia nodded.

Not just a servant, then.

"Can I sleep here?" she asked abruptly. "I can wake you if you make noise again."

Auslan stared while an uncomfortable chill creeped over his covered shoulders. He wondered how Matron Thalluen would react to that but then forced a smile. "How is my disturbing your rest with noise preferable to a baby doing the same?"

"You're hurt," she replied. "She's just cranky, or hungry. Or soiled. She's fine."

In any other House of his past, he would have shuffled this child out of the bedroom door immediately, lest he be accused of something loathsome and unforgiveable. Goddess, he would have kept the door locked and warded so she couldn't sneak in in the first place!

But all that was under the old expectations and boundaries which were shattered. As weakness and exhaustion dragged at him, begging him to lie down again and rest, he *felt* how alone he'd been. How solitary, even with the Red Sisters present.

Especially with them present.

It seems he is not able to heal himself, D'Shea had told the Matron.

Not alone, he had told her while sitting in her bathtub.

She hadn't understood.

"You may sleep here, Natia," Auslan accepted. "Wake me if I make noise, please. I would welcome that."

She smiled, slipped off her sandals, and climbed onto the mattress covered in her sleep gown. She dragged a folded blanket up from the foot of the bed and snuggled down, clearly tired as her lids began to droop. The former Consort followed her lead after extinguishing the light.

Listening to Natia breathe, to the regular beat of her heart, Auslan relaxed faster than he expected. He closed his eyes to the darkness.

He continued the eve in quiet Reverie.

Something tickled his arm like spider's legs, and he jolted upright on the bed, scrambling away.

"Wha—?!"

Auranka snickered, folding her arms beneath her heavy breasts. "Oopss. Did I disturb your dreamsss?"

Shyntre came aware pressed to the smooth stone coated in gilded paint; pure revulsion made him feel sick. "Get away from me."

She exhaled through venomous fangs, licking one and touching the tip with her tongue. "You were not dreaming, anyway. Nothing to feed on this eve."

The wild female stood up from her knees, placing her palms upon the sheets. His eyes darted from her lactating teats staining her sleeveless gown to the stiff, dark hairs which sprouted backwards along her arms and extended off her elbows. The bed began to creak under her weight.

"I said get away from me!" he bellowed, releasing his aura's strength without heed.

The Drider Mistress paused, blinking as she shivered. She looked at her hands as if checking that they were whole. Her breasts leaked, and the wet stains grew. She squealed a laugh, "Oo, you singed! We've not seen this before! What is your name, again, wizard?"

"Auranka."

The creature turned around, stepping off the bed as if knowing she was caught. An ancient, blonde Davrin stood in Her own doorway, arms crossed and focused sternly on the other female. The Valsharess was fully present with them, Her far-seeing eyes sharp as a sacrificial dagger. Shyntre and Auranka shifted beneath the weight and pressure of Her powerful aura.

"He does not remember," She intoned. "You can do nothing."

Auranka cooed, twisting her body in a curvaceous flaunt before Shyntre's eyes. "He has chosen again. His recollection beginsss, and you have no young mata of your own."

"We do. We have options."

"So you say. Soon, my Queen, sssoon you shall need usss again. I smell it." Her black eyes lifted to the ceiling. "The familiar heat drifts in from above through their link."

The ruler tilted Her head before lifting Her chin with pride. "Soon, but not yet. Leave Our chambers this eve, Drider Priestess. Return to your Pit until We call."

Auranka bowed deeply, on the blade's edge of mockery. "But of course, my Queen. Sssend me another bua, and I shall remain there for some time. Entertaining myself."

"We shall consider it. Leave."

Auranka curtsied and moved with swaying hips to the door, where the elder female had stepped inside his room, making space for her while being closer to the mage upon the bed. When the Drider Mistress glanced at him, as he knew she would, the many, void-black spots around her eyes glittered in a dozen winks.

"I look forward to the day he remembersss," said Auranka to the Queen. "We shall play the Game again, and it shall be interesting, as alwaysss."

Her sibilant tongue dripped down Shyntre's back like blood, and she laughed at his ignorant expression.

At his utter lack of understanding.

You have the wrong Davrin. I am not your son.

CHAPTER 15

GAELAN TRAVELED SOLELY AT NIGHT DESPITE THE INTENSE, two-month Sun-training with her Sisters and Elder Rausery. The dim light and shadow-filled forests suited her mood, and she was not required to endure the Sun's battering light and heat; she conserved strength which was drained by regular weeping. These bouts happened whether she intended to or not; she couldn't hold them back, no matter her effort, and would have to stop and curl up until it passed.

How did I get here?

From her Mother making that first, damned compulsion potion for Sirana's elder sister. Polynia had roped her own daughter into feeding the First's selfish and nauseating indulgences, until that critical point when a too-young Sirana had nearly died. Gaelan had run out of choices then.

I wouldn't be here on the Surface if she had died.

Which wasn't to say she would be well if the cait bled out. No, the potion maker may have been dead within a span from crossing and failing Jilrina. Or, if she'd known she was pregnant then and confessed, Gaelan could be locked with Polynia this moment in the dungeon. The Queen never ordered an execution of an expecting mata.

And I'd have never known my daughter at all. They would have taken her from me still wet from the womb.

Instead, Sirana had survived from Gaelan's help, and Jilrina was dead not long after Natia's birth. There was that investigation Gaelan had heard of through gossip; she worried, but no one ever came for them. She'd dared hope their small, potion-making family was forgotten in their forbidden dealing of tonics that formed a permanent geas in the mind of an Elf.

Her Mother had been so stupid, and Gaelan wept for all that had tumbled down around them.

My Natia…I hope you are well, and Matron Thalluen is taking care of you.

Those first twelve turns raising her first child in the potion shop had been Gaelan's life-joy alongside her Mother and siblings. They had bonded closer, like some matas did with their infants and those around them, and she wished Treyl could see his child. The poor, merchant females had been forbidden from visiting the House Guard of Thalluen, however. Gaelan had to recall his face through Natia, as the two had the same beautiful, garnet-red eyes.

Then Gaelan's Mother broke her promise, and someone confessed to someone in Sivaraus, and compulsion contraband had been found in the shop. This time, someone came for them. Elder D'Shea had arrived to take Natia away from her Mother.

It only got worse after that.

As Kaltra grieved and tried to emulate the late Jilrina, Sirana's second sister had *hurt* Natia. Gaelan knew she had, and Treyl had done something to challenge her. That was why he was dead, and Gaelan never saw him again before he was gone. Natia lost both her parents; her Mother was alive on the Surface but that wouldn't last. Neither Mother nor Daughter was never given a chance to say farewell.

Gaelan would never come back. The Valsharess had Seen this in Her Vision. She had *shown* it in that mind rape before pronouncing their sentence to be served above. Tears streamed down her cheeks every day, not just from bright light.

Fuck D'Shea! Fuck the Queen! How could you do all that to my little cait? How could you do this to me? Why?!

On sustained anger and thoughtless obedience to a compulsion of her own—the second in her life—Gaelan made fast progress during a fortunate stretch of fair weather, taking the paths of least resistance, those created by non-Human animals at the most comfortable times of the Surface. Food was not difficult to come by up here; as the Sun's warmth lingered further into each evening, so did the bounty seem to grow.

For all the talk of Humans and Dwarves upon the Surface, for all the practice in the Trade tongue, Gaelan hadn't seen any of these inhabitants nor needed their words, their knowledge, or their help. She traveled in the dark; she could feed herself; she followed not one road, cart trail, or imprint from a horse's shoe leading to so much as a single farm. She had no reason to steal or to spy on them; her mission did not require stirring up trouble, and she had no taste for it, regardless.

The Red Sister possessed no curiosity for this cursed place to which she had been sent to die. There was no point in being curious when she spent most of her time slapping insects and scratching their bites

Don't drag this out. Hurry! The festering warp rot grows larger by the day!

Yet it was so, so far away.

Gaelan skirted a spread of dry, rocky canyon that she had spied from a higher elevation, moving North within the forested West mountains. Eventually, she met a thick mountain stream gushing down toward the flatlands she had viewed from afar for three days and decided to follow it down to the shade-less grasslands.

The smaller stream joined with a massive river flowing North to South, so wide that she stared at a loss. Its banks were full to this season's grassy growth, swollen from snowmelt, its current no doubt as deceptively swift like many underground rivers. Spending long periods in cold rushing water was to be avoided, and she wasn't sure how to protect her gear that long, and she had not trained for this.

The Red Sister pondered how to cross until the sky was pink and Sun was nearly up. There were only two landmarks Gaelan had to navigate by: the flatlands themselves, which were too large to miss, and a Human town on the Eastern side. A place that cut down trees for trade and was the largest center of commerce on the far side of the flatlands. Not that Gaelan imagined strolling in to chat with fellow merchants.

I can't imagine getting across this damned river without losing everything!

She couldn't go back, so Gaelan settled down for the day, giving herself time to think than she had thus far.

The warp rot was North of that Human commerce center; she had been told to cross the flatlands and turn left at that large settlement. But first, she had to cross the river. Fortunately, she was struck by an idea later in the afternoon as she awoke sweating from the day.

Build a raft of branches for my gear to float upon. Swim tethered to the raft.

She'd have a mild healing potion ready should the cold water prove too much to endure. It was better than nothing.

Gaelan was delayed another night and day before successfully fording the river with her pouches and potions reasonably dry. To dry her clothes, she took a risk on a tiny fire in the evening time, which nearly spread beyond her camp, thanks to the strong winds. Panicked and paranoid, Gaelan smothered the flames and traveled for another cold and miserable night, staying up late into the morning to dry and warm in the Sun.

After over two weeks on the Midway, traveling part of the day as well as all night and drinking muddy water that took all her purifying pellets to cleanse, at last, she saw signs of a Human center of trade. Deep cart ruts, frequent dung plops and road apples from grazing livestock, the distant barking of dogs and that odd clucking noise of flightless birds that nested only to be eaten.

Turn North now. Don't go near them.

The weather helped with that, soon turning gray and rainy and discouraging all but the most determined to travel. Those like herself—collecting as much fresh water as she could—and like the one group of riders from whom she hid from after pushing far again into the daytime.

She had heard them coming from far off, their horses clanking with gear and metal, the men themselves talkative and boastful, with an odd fervor to their tones. Though entirely without magic, these men enjoyed holding up metal symbols and shouting at the sky with histrionic expressions of face and hand gesture. It reminded her somewhat of Priestesses at an altar.

As if... what? As if that flailing and shouting will stop the rain from falling?

Gaelan couldn't know all that caused the weather up here, but any potion maker understood a complex system held many factors, most unseen, with a few only revealed through long study and testing. Practice, writing, and teaching. Trusting her gut, the dark-skinned Elf remained out of their view until they were long gone, heading South. They were probably headed to that Human center.

I need nothing from them.

She only needed to keep going.

One black, cloudy night, Gaelan failed to notice the precise moment when the trees had changed shape, when they had begun to twist upon their roots, bending over as if in agony. The shadows were too dark, and she had grown complacent with the lonely but relatively easy travel.

But something had changed. *Stop.*

Gaelan waited patiently for the morning.

At dawn, her eyes widened with horror. The drift of illness was all around her, as far as she could see. Somehow, in the daytime but *not* the night, her mage's eyes detected a strange, sickly green aura around every living thing in the forest.

It was as if the Sun itself made the sickness visible.

The Dark Elf lifted her hands and arms. She breathed and focused on her own aura, which was harder to see for its familiarity, searching for that color.

It was faint, but it was there.

Something I ate?

She bit her trembling bottom lip. She wanted to leave, to run away and cleanse herself. She tried to move her leg, one step in retreat.

I c-can't. I'm here. I know it.

How long had it been since she ran from the cave without saying goodbye to Sirana or Jael? Six weeks of the hardest hiking she had ever done. *But I made it.*

In the distance, within the forest infected with warp rot, something screamed.

Or... laughed?

The shrill call came again, lingering and fouling the air.

Perhaps it was crying.

Gaelan checked her potions, guarded so jealously this whole time, and tried to reassure that these and her spells were all she needed to take care of this problem for the Valsharess. Rausery's stories said they had done it at the Ley Tower with two mages, but that was because of the intersection. Whatever injured the network of life here was newer, not as long entrenched; it would take just one mage to cleanse it.

Then she could get away soon enough to purge herself of the taint already taking hold.

Then what? Go home?

Gaelan stalked the screams with care, feeling the entropy rising in every, stiff-barked body she touched, shimmers of festering green and black rising like dissolving flames under the Sun.

She thought of Sirana, remembering the moment when she realized her young Sister was pregnant. The Third Daughter of Thalluen had caught down below, either from Auslan or Shyntre, and the Valsharess had seen fit to set the novice free up here. How filled with envy and drowning despair Gaelan had been, thinking of her own daughter. The Queen *must* have known Sirana carried; there was no way She wouldn't.

That was why Gaelan had left so quickly; she couldn't ask, and it hurt so much not to.

Faint wailing arose from the horizon of contorted trees as the Red Sister walked deeper into the distorting forest to fulfill her mission, her vision tinted a festering green.

I should have said farewell.

ACKNOWLEDGEMENTS

Many thanks to my team who always makes sure my efforts pass muster:

Eris Adderly, Leonard, Gerrit, Ile Depak, Dark Pulse, NecrosisBob, & Axelotl.

Much love to my Hubs, for his everlasting support.

Deepest gratitude to *Doc Kangey*, for his support, guidance, and expertise in giving me www.Etaski.com

My recognition and sincere appreciation go to these generous patrons, who believe in what I set out to do:

Sir Cumference, Baelus, Lesley P.L.A.Y., Johnathon Roswell, Does, John K., Roy & Stacy Meyer, Julie S., Jay Aeskelin, Josanna, Briana R., RainbowNight, Lexanii, Elizapad, Zeroharas, and Elan.

Special honor to patron *Carla H.*, one of our country's brave healthcare workers facing the pandemic on the ground.

ABOUT THE AUTHOR

Etaski has entertained herself with fantasy stories since the first day she sat on a school bus looking out the window. When hand-written letters were disappearing, she scribbled no less than five pages to be worth the postage. Her early stories were written by hand, and she had a writer's callus and three embarrassing novels before graduating high school.

She studied science, archaeology and history, and theater. Frank discussion of sexuality was rare growing up, so she wrote fantasies, theories, and observations within stories to contemplate deeper or just be entertained.

History rarely speaks on sexuality, yet biology demonstrates how it sways basic choices. Drama reveals our strongest bonds but may still fade to black at its most intimate. In the Sister Seekers, the sex and the story are inseparable, and their discoveries will change the story of Miurag without cutting away.

Please consider leaving a review of this book. It truly helps!

smarturl.it/etaskiamazon

www.goodreads.com/etaski

www.bookbub.com/authors/a-s-etaski

Sign up to Etaski's newsletter for Sister Seekers releases at:

www.etaski.com